PRAISE FOR GINNY AIKEN'S BOOKS

"Captivating. I became a part of the story as it was unfolding."
—***Jean Klusmeier, Pennsylvania***

"Couldn't put it down! Ginny Aiken can tell a good story."
—***Carole McAllaster, California***

"Terrific. I laughed and I cried. But mostly, I just fell in love."
—***Kay Allen, Oklahoma***

"Wonderful. A novel with heart and soul involved."
—***Shirene Broadwater***

"Helped me through a bad time. I needed your wit and fun to help bring me out of it."
—*KG*

"Great book—thoroughly enjoyed each page! Easy to read, never slow, great plot."
—***Cyndy Roggeman, Michigan***

"Loved your characters. So much heart and emotion, not to mention an engaging story line."
—*M*

romance the way it's meant to be

HeartQuest brings you romantic fiction with a foundation of biblical truth. Adventure, mystery, intrigue, and suspense mingle in these heartwarming stories of men and women of faith striving to build a love that will last a lifetime.

May HeartQuest books sweep you into the arms of God, who longs for you and pursues you always.

Camellia

GINNY AIKEN

Romance fiction from
Tyndale House Publishers, Inc., Wheaton, Illinois
www.heartquest.com

Visit Tyndale's exciting Web site at www.tyndale.com

Check out the latest about HeartQuest Books at www.heartquest.com

Edited by Ramona Cramer Tucker

Designed by Melinda Schumacher

Library of Congress Cataloging-in-Publication Data

Aiken, Ginny.
Camellia / Ginny Aiken.
p. cm. — (HeartQuest) (Bellamy's Blossoms series ; bk. 3)
ISBN 0-8423-3561-7
1. Pregnant women—Fiction. 2. Physicians—Fiction. 3. Women—Fiction. I. Title. II. Series.

PS3551.I339 C3 2001
813′.54—dc21 2001027219

Printed in the United States of America

07 06 05 04 03 02 01
9 8 7 6 5 4 3 2 1

To my sister,
Lou Schmitz, with whom, by the grace of God,
I have a wonderful relationship.

Be silent, and know that I am God!
Psalm 46:10

Acknowledgments

GRATITUDE AND THANKS TO:

My Savior Jesus — *my hiding place*

Claudia Cross — *the best agent and a pro at keeping me from leaping to conclusions*

Tyndale's HeartQuest team — *You're a blessing to this writer*

Ramona Cramer Tucker — *for making the Blossoms and me look so good*

The 'Questers — *You ladies are great—I'm honored to be one of you.*

Karl Fieldhouse and Elizabeth Darrach — *for awesome critiquing and friendship. Add Ruth's friendship to that, too.*

George Ivan, Gregory, Geoffrey, and Grant — *my four heroes-in-the-making*

And, of course, to George — *twenty-four years, and counting!*

ONE

Bellamy, Loudon County, Virginia; Present Day

THAT WAS BELLAMY'S NEW FAMILY DOCTOR?

Camellia Bellamy Sprague stared in dismay and disbelief at the too-young, too-handsome man at her dear, elderly friend Sophie Hardesty's side.

Oh, my. Was she ever in trouble. Big trouble. No way could she go to that man as frequently as necessary with all the personal and private matters relating to her pregnancy.

Nuh-uh.

Doc Calloway approached Sophie and the newcomer, and Cammie experienced a pang of anger. Why had Doc chosen this particular time to retire? Didn't he know she needed him to see her through this pregnancy? She was alone, newly widowed, and with no family she could count on. True, she had two older sisters, but they wanted to run her life rather than support the choices she made.

She needed a doctor who knew her, one who had years of wisdom and experience behind him, a father figure, a physician she could trust. She trusted the man who'd delivered her sisters and her—not to mention the greater half of Bellamy's residents. Not that there were that many of them altogether, Bellamy being the small town she loved, but that made Doc even more desirable as a doctor. She knew him to be up to the task.

How could she trust someone who looked like Tom Selleck, mustache and all, ready to take on crooks, Magnum, P.I.–style, to deliver her baby?

She couldn't. She simply couldn't.

She wouldn't. Since she had to accept the reality of a new doctor monitoring her pregnancy, despite the occasional twinges of illogical anger, she might as well find one in Leesburg—one with more experience and less appeal than this one.

Mind made up, Cammie headed toward the refreshment table. The ladies of the Bellamy Garden Club had outdone themselves tonight. The arrival of autumn's shorter days and September's cool weather always inspired great bursts of culinary expression in Bellamy's kitchens. This party had afforded those gifted ladies the opportunity to show off their talents. On the long, linen-draped table, they'd displayed every imaginable pastry and baked goody to its best advantage. By doing so, the ladies were treating the guests at Doc Calloway's bon voyage/retirement party and the new physician's welcome-to-town gathering to a luscious rainbow of scents. Vanilla faded into almond, while cinnamon and chocolate blended sinfully.

Right then, however, Cammie's throat felt parched. She needed something cool and wet before she could tackle any of the dreamy confections.

"Camellia, sugar. Now don't *you* look the very picture of womanly health?" called Louella Ashworth, president of the Bellamy Garden Club and social maven.

Cammie smiled and patted her rounded middle. "Thanks, Miss Louella. I feel better than I ever have. Pregnancy does agree with me—except for the raging thirst. Could you please pour me a cup of plain ginger ale? I don't think I'd care for all the sticky sweetness in the punch right now."

"Why, sure, honey." The meticulously maintained, chestnut-haired matron reached under the linen-garbed table and brought up a bottle of soda. As she poured, she stole a glance at the new doctor. "Do tell, Camellia, dear, what do *you* think of Sophie's grandnephew?"

"Think of him?" Cammie asked, startled. "Why, Miss Louella, I couldn't possibly think anything of the man. I haven't even met him."

Thrusting the drink at Cammie, the older woman bustled out from behind her serving post. "Well, then, darlin', it's fine time we remedied that."

Miss Louella grasped Cammie's elbow, and despite Cammie's gentle demurring, marched her up to the man in question. "Here, Sophie. You do the introductions. I'm mannin'—er . . . womanin'—the punch bowl."

With that, Miss Louella trotted back the punch table, leaving Cammie tongue-tied and embarrassed to a flush.

Miss Sophie, on the other hand, was in fine form. "I'm plumb thrilled to do the honors, Camellia, honey." Turning to her grandnephew, she said, "Stephen, this lovely young woman here is Camellia Bellamy Sprague, granddaughter of one of my dearest, most-lamented friends. Don't you know, Cammie? I still miss your Granny Iris every solitary day. I loved that woman like a sister, and I'll never stop wishin' the dear Lord had seen fit to leave her with us a mite longer."

Cammie smiled. "I know, Miss Sophie. I feel the same way. Granny Iris was . . . oh, I don't know . . . a true original."

Miss Sophie's snow-white Gibson girl do bobbed in agreement. "And wasn't *she* pure proof the good Lord makes each and every one of us individually and in his own image?"

"Oh, I'd have to say you're one of a kind yourself, Aunt Sophie," said the new doctor. Cammie turned to him, surprised she'd managed to forget his presence while chatting with Miss Sophie.

"I'll be takin' that as a compliment, my dear Stephen," his great-aunt said with another bob of her cloud-soft topknot. "Anyway, son, as I was saying, this is my very dear Cammie Sprague, and this, Cammie, is my nephew, Stephen."

"Pleasure," she murmured, extending her hand.

"It's all mine, Mrs. Sprague," he responded, wrapping warm, sturdy fingers around hers.

Cammie felt the heat swim straight to her middle. His smile flew right up to her head. The rich, deep voice tumbled down into her lonely heart. *Oh, my.* Time to make a discreet escape.

But it wasn't to be.

"Your due date's in . . . about four or five months, right?" the young physician asked after perusing Cammie's midsection.

His scrutiny made her even more self-conscious, and Cammie wished she'd made her getaway a second earlier. "No. I'm seven months along."

One of his dark eyebrows rose. "Small baby, or not enough weight gain? You're not trying to diet, are you?"

A pinch of pique pierced Cammie. What right did this perfect stranger have to ask her such questions? At a public gathering, no less. With dignity, she met his gaze. "According to my doctor, my baby and I are doing just fine. Now, if you'll excuse me—"

"Of course," he cut in with a nod. "I'll see you in the office on . . . ?"

Cammie's cheeks went from hot to scalding. "Actually, you won't. I'm . . . ah . . . going to see another . . . doctor. In Leesburg, that is." It *wasn't* technically a lie. After all, she *had* decided no more than ten minutes ago she'd do just that.

But Dr. Stephen Hardesty's skeptically arched brow made

Cammie squirm inside. "I see," he murmured. "Well, I won't keep you any longer."

"Ah . . . thank you. There's someone I should . . . speak to," she responded, knowing how lame she sounded.

As she hurried off, Cammie berated herself. That had *not* been one of her finer moments. Stealing a guilty glance over her shoulder, she caught Sophie's bewildered expression and Dr. Hardesty's ironic smile. Speeding up her pace, she kept her gaze on the tips of her shoes as they made their way toward the kitchen. That way she could avoid anyone she might meet on the way out.

"There you are," said Magnolia Bellamy Marlowe, one of her sisters. "We've been searchin' every last haystack of folks we come up to, but kept on findin' neither hide nor hair of you."

Terrific. After her awful performance before the town's newest resident, the last thing Cammie wanted was a run-in with either of her sisters. Both older than she—Maggie by two years and Lark by four—they felt honor-bound to tell Cammie how to live—if not how to breathe and walk and talk.

Dear Lord, please give me an extra measure of your grace. I sure seem to have used up all I had to start with. "How can I help you, Maggie?" she said.

"Oh no, Cammie," inserted Lark, Cammie's other sister, appearing at her shoulder. "You don't need to help us. We're the ones who want to help *you.*"

Cammie sighed. "I'm fine, Lark. I can't think of a thing I need."

Maggie *tsk-tsk*ed. "Why, sugar, I simply can't believe that a'tall. You're pregnant out to here." Her arms drew a mammoth circle in front of her slim, diminutive frame. "You have a house full of—" her voice dropped—*"strangers,* and you've never had a head for business."

Lark nodded sagely. "Why don't you let us come over and help? I just sent the latest issue of my *Critic's Choice* magazine to the printers, so I have plenty of time to put things to rights for you. You want to have your life in order by the time the baby comes, don't you?"

Cammie drew a deep breath. "Lark, Maggie, what gives either of you the notion that my life is out of order? I'm doing exactly what the Lord's called me to do: I'm making a home. I don't have money troubles—praise God—and everything is under his control. I'm content with my life as it is."

"Yes, but, sugar," Maggie objected, her Southern drawl thickening even to Cammie's decidedly Southern ear, "you're all alone over there with no one of your very own—"

"How can I be alone when Willie Johnson, Suze McEntire, Stu Richards, and Ray Ling are in and out of the house all day long? And Sophie stops by for a visit every day after she and Rich close up the Country Store?"

At the mention of her fiancé's name, Lark smiled. "Speaking of Rich, is there anything he could special order for you? I mean, you need nutrition for two, you know. Sea veggies would do you good, not to mention soy milk instead of the cow stuff—to avoid allergies in the baby, you understand—and of course, tofu every day would boost your protein intake."

Cammie wrinkled her nose. "Thanks, Lark. I know you mean well, but I doubt I could stomach any of those things."

"Amen!" chimed Maggie.

Lark frowned, then went on. "But you're still at the mercy of a bunch of strangers. What do you know about them? Are they really who they say they are? Do any of them have police records? How about their personal finances—what *do* you know? Are any of them likely to pull a swindle—"

"Stop!" Cammie cried. "That's enough. Those 'strangers' are like family to me. They're my friends. I don't appreciate your big-city-reporter questions, Lark, any more than I appreciate your wrongheaded notions. You *don't* have to tell me how to lead my life." She squared her shoulders and took another step toward the kitchen. "If this is what I have to look forward to in your efforts to 'help' me, I'm glad I'm as alone as you two like to think I am."

Maggie's china blue eyes popped wide open while Lark's emerald green ones narrowed. To forestall any further upsetting comments from either of them, Cammie forged ahead. "I came and welcomed the new doctor, said farewell to Doc and Mrs. Calloway, and now I'll say the same to you. Good night, Lark, Maggie. I'm heading home."

Leaving her stunned-silent sisters behind, Cammie entered the vast kitchen of the Bellamy Community Church's fellowship hall at a hearty clip. She crossed the delectably fragranced expanse and strode out to the cool autumn-evening peace.

The last thing she needed was two older sisters, to whom she'd never been close, suddenly hovering over her like . . . well, like a younger, less-numerous version of the Bellamy Garden Club. With God's help she could handle her pregnancy without the intrusion of the flower-loving busybodies who stuck their noses into everything in Bellamy with appalling regularity.

She certainly didn't need Lark and Maggie.

And since she'd recently decided it was time to stand up for herself as they always had, she'd felt the need to set them straight about her feelings. Even though she wished things were different among the three of them, the last three living Bellamys.

Then a stray thought crossed her mind. Was her decision to become more assertive Christlike? Although it had felt great to finally tell her sisters where she stood, she wasn't sure how God would view her actions.

Still, both Maggie and Lark had recently professed faith in Christ. Maybe there *was* hope for them yet.

And for sisterhood.

"Well, I'll be hog-tied," said Maggie.

"I'll say," answered Lark.

"I can't believe baby Cammie's out-stubbornin' any ol' mule."

"Me neither."

The two sisters remained silent for a moment, their gazes on the still swinging kitchen door. Then Lark turned to Maggie. "She's headed for trouble."

"Amen. Makin' a beeline right to it. And she's lonely, too. I still remember how bad it was before I got Buford. And met Clay, of course."

Lark gave a self-effacing shrug. "I have to confess I was, too. I mean, lonely. Before you gave me Mycroft, of course."

Maggie winked a blue eye. "And before you *finally* got together with your childhood sweetheart, Rich Desmond, I reckon."

Lark's cheeks turned a becoming shade of coral. "Oh, yes. He's a gift from God. Well, an occasionally obstinate, ornery, obstreperous gift, I'll grant you, but a gift nonetheless."

Maggie chuckled. "Do you all talk to each other in those five-dollar words all day?" At Lark's nod, she continued. "Then you're as well matched as a peck of peas in a pod—"

"Yes, but we weren't talkin' about Rich and me, remember? What should we do about Cammie?"

"She won't let us near."

"Then we'll have to find someone else to get near her."

"Miss Sophie's not the right one, though. The two of them

already get on like gangbusters in a house afire, so she's more likely to agree with Cammie than with us."

"You're right."

Maggie reached a hand out to Lark. "We need some real help here—heavenly help, that is."

Lark squeezed back. Then she prayed, "Father God, you know we haven't had the kind of relationship we should with Cammie. But we want to help her. Open our eyes, Lord. Show us how best to bring her out of her loneliness—and to show her how much trouble she's headed for."

"Amen."

"What are you two up to?" asked Clay Marlowe, slipping an arm around his wife's slim waist.

"Trouble, no doubt, Clay," answered Rich Desmond, dropping a kiss on top of his fiancée's short red curls. "These Bellamy women are nothing but trouble."

"But they're so lovable, aren't they?" Clay queried as he dodged Maggie's elbow jab.

"Oh my, yes," Rich answered, mischief dancing in his eyes as he soft-shoed his toes away from Lark's stomping heel.

Clay wrapped one of Maggie's long blond locks around his finger. "They're always such delightful, agreeable, wonderful company—"

"Delightful . . . ," drawled Lark, weighing the concept.

"Agreeable . . . ," murmured Maggie, the word honey-sweet and molasses-slow.

"Wonderful company," the sisters chorused.

"That's it, Lark!"

"Of course, Mags!"

They trotted off, chattering quietly if with lively animation, and leaving their respective escorts staring after them. Long moments later, the men faced each other.

"Trouble," they said as one.

Halfway home, Cammie applied the brakes to her rapid-fire pace. She couldn't go home just yet. She'd volunteered for cleanup after the party. But she couldn't go back and face her sisters again.

Nor could she imagine coming face-to-face with Stephen Hardesty another time. At the mere thought of the handsome new doctor, a flutter of the same heat she'd felt when he'd clasped her hand riffled through her. What an incredible, unsettling impression he'd made.

Was it her guilty conscience over "fudging" a bit that had her steaming up at the thought of him? Was it embarrassment? Or was it more a matter of his intense eyes, dark wavy hair, and tall, solid frame?

More than likely, in spite of her being pregnant and widowed, it was a matter of his robust masculinity wreaking havoc on her common sense. Which meant she had to remember who she was: Camellia Bellamy Sprague—settled, commonsense Cammie. The dependable Blossom, as the town referred to the three florally monikered Bellamy sisters. The one who everyone said knew her lot in life and, as Scripture taught, had learned to be content in whatever situation befell her. Even while she'd been trapped for five years, working to turn around a loveless marriage. Even when her husband's car had crashed, leaving her a widow.

She reckoned that God had allowed everything that had happened to her—including her husband's death. So she'd asked God to help her accept what came her way, and he had.

"And right now, Camellia Sprague," she told herself out loud, stiffening her spine, "a pile of messy dishes and a mile of dirty tables are headed your way."

Reluctance weighing down every step, Cammie went back to fulfill her responsibility. For a while the good-natured chatter of the other women on kitchen duty kept her mind off less pleasant matters.

As she slid the last drippy plate into the yawning maw of the commercial dishwasher, the door to the fellowship hall swung ajar. Cammie glanced that way, and what she saw had her biting her bottom lip. "Oh, dear."

Miss Louella, known far and abroad as Bellamy's most devoted matchmaker, had cornered Cammie's elderly, debonair boarder, Willie Johnson—all of seventy-five, if a day—and Miss Sophie. The dear, sweet widow, alone for decades, hadn't a clue what had hit her—if one could go by her starry-eyed look.

What was Miss Louella thinking? Miss Sophie wasn't some pining spinster, desperate to find a mate. No, sirree, she was happily single and secure in her present life. So why would a content widow—especially one of Miss Sophie's vintage—need a man? After all, yet another abandonment seemed likely, since Willie was no spring chicken either.

Someone had to protect Miss Sophie from Miss Louella's matchmaking, before it was too late. Marching up to her dazzled friend's side, Cammie donned her most polite expression. "If you all will excuse me, I need Miss Sophie for a moment."

Miss Louella gave Cammie a reproving look while Willie's smile melted into drooping dejection. "But you'll bring her back, won't you?" he asked.

Not hardly. "I don't rightly know, Willie," Cammie answered, cupping Miss Sophie's elbow. "I'll leave that up to Miss Sophie herself. But right now I do need to speak to her."

With a series of determined tugs, Cammie led her friend to a quiet corner in the emptying room. "Miss Sophie!" she cried in an alarmed whisper. "What were you thinking?"

"Excuse me, dear," said Miss Sophie, shaking herself.

"What do you mean, what was I thinkin'? I plumb don't know if I've been rightly thinkin' a'tall."

"That's just what I mean. Miss Louella's up to no good, and she's up to it with you and Willie Johnson."

"Oh, pshaw." Miss Sophie's cheeks bloomed with roses. "Don't be silly, sugar. There's no mystery for her to sniff out here."

Cammie closed her eyes and shook her head. "That's not what I meant—"

"Well, that's good, dear, because for a second, I thought *your* mind had begun to wander. I'd hate for you to wind up like Euphonia Hickerstrop's granddaughter, with all that vague talk of little green men and outlandish travels. Still, she was decades older'n you, goin' through—" Miss Sophie cast a surreptitious look around—"the *change.* Although, of course, you're far from that kind of trouble."

"So are you," countered Cammie. "Well, not for the change, of course, but you're *not* senile. Besides, it wasn't your mind that went a-roving. It looked to me as if your eyes were taking some kind of tour of Mr. Johnson's dapper self."

Miss Sophie's flush reached her hairline. "Oh, nonsense, honey. I was merely bein' polite, is all. You must know how he is, with him living at your house and all. Why, he's so handsome and interestin', and he's always tellin' the best stories."

Things did not look good. "But, Miss Sophie, Miss Louella's up to her usual matchmaking."

If Miss Sophie got any redder, Cammie feared she'd have to call on Stephen Hardesty to treat his great-aunt for apoplexy or something.

With a dismissive wave of her plump hand, Miss Sophie said, "Pshaw. Lou knows I'm a happy woman right enough. I'm not in the market for a romance. I've got my job at Desmond's Country Store, the Garden Club, my Bible study, prayer group, and you. What—" her voice faltered—"what more could a woman want?"

Cammie's relief broke through in a smile. "That's more like it. As you and I have often remarked, life for us is calm, routines are simple, and days are full. Besides, nothing happens to God's children unless it goes through his personal filter first."

"There you are, Aunt Sophie," interrupted the new doctor as he leaned down and gave his elderly relative a hug. "I was wondering if you were ready to head home."

"Oh no!" cried Willie Johnson, stepping out from behind Stephen. "It's far too early in this lovely eve for a star of Miss Sophie's magnitudinous shine to be put to bed. Come, dear lady. Let us enjoy the quiet hours. The night is still young."

"That's exactly right, Willie," chirped a beaming Miss Louella from Cammie's right. "The night is truly young, as are dear Camellia and Stephen."

Matters were indeed becoming dire. Trouble was a-brewing, all right. If the gleam in Miss Louella's gray eyes meant what Cammie feared it did, Sophie wasn't the matchmaker's only target.

It was time to make her escape, before things got any worse.

TWO

"WELL, MISS CAMMIE," SAID HORACE HOBEY, THE FINEST masonry contractor in three counties, as he crawled out from the belly of the fireplace in her living room the next morning, "I figger this here beaut—" he patted the old redbrick structure—"will be lastin' you another century or so."

Cammie chuckled. "I won't be around then to see it, Hobey, but my little one might."

"I don't doubt it one bit," the large bald man answered. He scraped a glob of mortar from his metal spatula into the open container from which he'd worked. "You know, Miss Cammie, time is an amazin' thing. Just look at yourself. Who woulda thought no more'n six or so months ago you'd be doin' so well? Not after that accident what took David's life."

Cammie sighed and looked away. The days—weeks—after her husband's death in late February had been difficult ones. And she knew that, although many friends like Hobey had stuck by her, no one except God really knew how many tears she'd quietly shed. How she'd grieved not only her husband's death but the death of her dreams of a loving marriage.

"It was hard to get through that time," Cammie admitted. "And I couldn't have done it without your prayers and visits, Hobey—not to mention God's constant strength. I sure had none left after the police call that wintry night that turned my world upside down."

"You had yourself a load of stuff to work through," Hobey empathized. "I'm thankful God put me here in Bellamy so's you could have an ear an' a big wide shoulder to cry on. Especially with your mama an' papa being with the good Lord in heaven."

"Guilt's bad stuff, all right."

Hobey wrapped a gentle, massive arm around Cammie's shoulders. "More'n more when it's uncalled for, missy. I don't reckon there was anything else you coulda done to make things right all by yourself. Takes two to make a marriage. An' one of you wasn't workin' on it."

The inevitable tears stung Cammie's eyes. "A part of me always knew that, even when I was sure some failing in me pushed David away and made him stay all those hours at his office. So I kept trying to make the marriage better, our home more inviting. Day after day, year after year, I worked to become the best wife ever—more loving, understanding, always putting him and his needs first. I hoped my actions would bring him back to me. But nothing I did ever seemed to be enough."

"That's because David wasn't puttin' in his nickel's worth, Miss Cammie. He chose that there work of his over you an' your marriage—a sin before the Lord, you know. That boy promised to love an' cherish you the way Jesus loved his church, if I recollect 'em vows the two of you took at that weddin' of yours. Jesus has never abandoned his bride, but David Sprague abandoned you pert near from the get-go."

Cammie shrugged, wishing the knot in her throat would go away. "Our marriage was a failure, wasn't it?"

"I hate sayin' that," Hobey answered, clapping his cap over his shiny pate and picking up his paraphernalia. "But from where I stand, I have to be agreein' with you."

"As long as he was alive, though," Cammie said, revealing her deepest regret to the man she trusted like a father, "I had hope that if I tried just a little harder, learned some new . . . I don't know, some marriage-enriching method or something, I could reach David. I really wanted to save our marriage—to reach out to him."

"You couldn't've reached 'im, missy. Only the good Lord coulda done that, the way that boy closed his eyes to his blessings. An' from where I'm lookin', it sure looks to me like David even closed himself to God. I reckon he was driven crazy by the need that ruins a lot of folks—to make the kinda money they never had growin' up. He was scared of bein' so poor again."

"Somewhere inside I know that, but—"

"But nothin', child. You been mournin' that marriage since just about the time the ink dried on your signatures. True, him dyin' on you that way was a terrible thing, an' we all have grieved that loss with you. But I know you haven't been doin' the mournin' only over a man who couldn't love you the way God meant a husband to love his wife. You also been grievin' all them hopes an' commitments you took wid you to that there altar when you said your 'I do's.' But look at yourself now, Miss Cammie. Look how far you've come."

"God knew I'd have to face the future when he gave me this baby." She placed both hands over her belly. "I couldn't just close myself up and think of my pain and regrets. I couldn't just mourn all that might have been but now can never be. I have to take care of myself for this little one's sake."

Hobey slipped on a buffalo-checked, padded flannel shirt while Cammie held his tool bucket and the now-covered pail of mortar. "Speaks a lot to your faith in him, missy. 'Stead of wallowin' in the hurt, or gettin' good an' angry an' actin' out somethin' crazy, you took Jesus' hand. You trusted him to see you through."

"I had some prodding in the right direction, if I recollect rightly," Cammie said with a wry smile. "You sure listened to a lot of sobbing and gave me good, solid counsel."

Hobey reddened. "That's what a good pa—" He stopped abruptly, turned nearly puce, and shook his head. *"Ahem!* That's what brothers and sisters in Christ are called to do, you know. 'Tweren't nothin' what I did. Just wish your own pa would've been here to do it."

Cammie followed him into the foyer. When he paused at the door, she followed her impulse, rose to her toes, and planted a kiss on his cheek. "It was a wonderful, kind, and loving thing you did—stopping by to see me so many times over the past difficult months. You helped me bear my pain and keep my eyes on Jesus. I love you for it, Horace Hobey. You're one fine, godly man."

"Ah . . . er . . . well, thanks, missy. I'll be seein' you round town, then." Mist in his mud-colored eyes, Hobey yanked open the door and grabbed his belongings from her. "You let me know if that there mortar round them bricks starts to crumble on you again, you hear? It don't do you much good if you keep callin' in that chimney sweep guy if he don't bother to look for cracks in what holds the thing together, you know." The three-hundred-pound man hurried down the front walk in a rush as great as that of the words pouring from his mouth. "Bricks is bricks, but it's what you put between 'em what makes a chimney last."

Cammie chuckled. "You're a true saint, Hobey," she called out. "Even if my telling you makes you so uncomfortable you wind up running for safety. The Lord bless you, now."

The memory of Hobey's sweet, fatherly visits and the way

he held her tightly against his chest as she'd cried out her pain, her grief, her disappointment, returned to her mind. Cammie remembered gratefully the many prayers they'd uttered together. She also remembered the phrase he'd offered each time she sank into guilt or self-pity during those first few awful months.

"With God," Hobey had repeated, "all things are possible. Even livin' through this, Miss Cammie."

God had proven the mason right. With the Father's strength, comfort, and grace, it had been possible to live through the pain of sudden widowhood . . . the grief . . . the *if onlys* . . . the shock of discovering she was pregnant . . . and that David had never even known.

God was at last helping her heal.

Later, Cammie still blushed at the memory of her actions at the disastrous bon voyage/welcome-to-town event. In the privacy of her parlor, seated at her quilting frame, with the ripe, fall-morning sunlight brightening her spot by the window, her face flushed warm.

As she rocked the tip of her needle five or six times through the muslin, batting, and pieced top of the latest quilt in progress, she again sought the heavenly Father's comfort.

Oh, Lord, I really wasn't at my best last night, was I? How could I have let that man's arrival affect me so much? And then the way I treated Lark and Maggie. I should be used to them by now.

Cammie thought back on the many occasions when her sisters had barged in on her life. She'd been a full eighteen before she'd managed to choose her own wardrobe—and only then because Lark was off at college and Maggie had been busy scrabbling her way up the echelons of the Bellamy Fiduciary Trust. Those clothes she'd chosen had made up her trousseau.

A few weeks later, after she'd turned nineteen, she'd become Mrs. David Allen Sprague. And within several days after her honeymoon she'd had no one butting into her decisions, sharing her choices, or offering a sometimes welcome, sometimes not welcome, opinion.

David's career had consumed him from the very beginning. It had felt as if once he'd completed the "marriage job," he could again focus on his career.

As she reached the end of her quilting thread, Cammie tied a knot in the length, then tugged it through the top layer of the quilt "sandwich."

The memory of those disappointing, early days of marriage returned full force, sharp and hurting. The intimate dinners she had planned and prepared had often gone cold, victims of David's late meetings. Her dreams of quiet evenings of shared thoughts by the fire had rarely materialized, sacrificed at the altar of the fat briefcase that had commanded David's attention.

Disillusioned, Cammie soon wondered if David had wanted a wife—a soul mate—or merely a housekeeper. At least she'd done that job well. He'd provided a lovely home. True, it had needed updating, and the woodwork had required stripping in order to restore it to its former glory. But Cammie had loved investing the energy and creativity that had made the old house shine with beauty.

It was too bad that David had spent so little time at home. By the time the accident claimed his life six and a half months ago—

The knock at the front door mercifully broke into her sad thoughts. Cammie stood, placed her fists in the hollow of her back, and stretched, the baby wriggling inside her at the change in posture.

She smiled. Impending maternity was pure, God-given joy. Every time her child gave proof of its burgeoning life, she felt a surge of happiness. This gift from the Lord had helped to overshadow the wounds inflicted by her unsuccessful marriage and her subsequent widowhood.

She went to the door, wondering who'd be visiting at ten in the morning. Everyone she knew was working or at school. "Yes?" she said, drawing open the heavy oak door.

Then she groaned—inwardly, of course.

"Hi, Cam," said Lark in her brisk voice.

"Mornin', Cammie, honey," oozed Maggie in her sweet drawl.

As Cammie braced for what might come next, she prayed for grace in dealing with her sisters—never an easy-to-attain goal. "How can I help you?"

Maggie waved a slender, well-manicured hand and shook her head. "Now, there's your problem, sugar. You don't have to help us one tiny little ol' bit. We're here to help you."

Cammie struggled to keep the dismay from her features. "But I've told you both, I'm fine. I don't need any help. I do have some fresh tea with mint, though. How about we go to the kitchen and I'll serve us all a tall glass?"

"Herbal?" asked Lark, suspicion in her green eyes.

"Why, no," Cammie said, knowing that even her innocent invitation would now be dissected and scrutinized. "It's regular Lipton's—but it's great. I make a mean pitcher of iced tea, if I do say so myself."

"I'm sure you do, Cam. But don't you think you should lay off the caffeine for a while? For the baby's sake, you understand."

"Doc said I should pay no mind to the little caffeine I drink," Cammie answered, holding her head high. "It's a simple pleasure that won't hurt my child at all."

Lark looked unconvinced, but she shrugged. "Anyway,

that's not why we're here. Remember the other night at Doc's bon voyage party when we talked about you being so lonely?"

A grim little smile tugged Cammie's lips sideways. "How could I forget?"

"Well, honey," offered Maggie, a sunny smile beaming from her lovely china-doll face, "we prayed for God to show us how to help you overcome that loneliness, and sure as shootin', he answered our prayers."

"That's right," concurred Lark. "We have your answer."

Cammie shut her eyes tight. *Lord, why couldn't you have given me to some well-deserving childless couple? And left Maggie and Lark with Mama and Daddy?*

After a breath for courage, she replied, "I'm afraid to ask what you two think the answer to my imagined loneliness might be." Then Cammie's natural good humor beat out her conflicted emotions about her sibling relationships. She grinned. "You have piqued my curiosity, though."

"Stay right there, sugar," Maggie said, dancing down the front steps toward Lark's less-than-immaculate red Ford Escort at the curb, "and we'll bring it straight to you."

"Don't move an inch," ordered Lark, vaulting down the same steps and following Maggie in her athletic lope.

Cammie closed her eyes and prayed aloud. "Lord, I have a funny feeling about this. Help me handle it in a way that will please you, one that won't make matters worse among the three of us."

"Well, sugar, here he is."

"Open your eyes, Cam."

When she did, Cammie fell in love. Totally, deeply, irrevocably. Between her two sisters and attached to a forest green nylon leash stood the most adorable puppy she had ever seen. An obvious mishmash mixed breed, the little guy boasted Doberman eyebrows over shepherd-shaped, golden eyes, chocolate Labrador muzzle and coat, hound ears, and the crooning voice and curling white-feathered tail of a malamute.

Cammie dropped to cuddle the comical critter. "What's his name?" she asked, rubbing the round, warm belly the sweet pup offered up for her attention.

"Why, it's the cutest thing," Maggie chirped. "Lark and I figured we needed a dog. So when my darlin' Clay found him abandoned at Marlowe Historical Restorations's latest work site, he called me right over. I plumb lost my heart to the poor baby. Just think, some monster dumped him—in a cardboard box, for goodness' sake. As if he'd been no more'n a day's haul after strippin' a century's worth of wallpaper."

"Animal cruelty," Lark said in summation. "Nothing more, nothing less."

"I don't get it," Cammie murmured, rubbing his velvety ears. "Why are you here? I'm not much of an activist, so I can't see where you two would think fighting for this little guy's rights would be any kind of answer to my supposed—and, I repeat, supposed only by you two—loneliness."

To her amazement, her older siblings laughed.

"Would you let me in on the joke?" she said, straightening. The puppy squirmed upright and scooted over to her feet. He plopped his chin onto her bare toes with a contented snuffle.

"See?" Maggie said. "Even little Heinz knows."

Lark nodded sagely.

"Heinz?" Cammie asked. "Is he German or something?"

Lark rolled her green eyes. "No, silly. He's Heinz—of the 57 varieties."

Just then, two of Cammie's boarders, Ray Ling and Stu Richards, dashed up the walk, backpacks bulging with books.

"Hey, Miss Cammie. Izzat your dog?" Ray asked.

"No—"

"Yes," sang Maggie and Lark.

Cammie's eyebrows shot up under her bangs. "What?"

"Why, sugar, it's just like we said. You're lonely, so God sent Heinz."

Cammie stared at Maggie, who stood smiling as if her odd proclamation explained everything. How . . . Maggie of her. She turned to Lark. "Am I missing something here?"

"Of course. You're missin' companionship."

"I'm supposed to find companionship by joining some crusade for the rights of abandoned puppies?"

"Is that what I'm goin' to be like the day I get pregnant?" Maggie asked, her nose wrinkled in distaste. "Makin' no sense?"

Lark and Cammie exchanged telling looks, both fighting mischievous grins.

"We can only hope not, Mags," Lark answered with more aplomb than Cammie felt she'd ever have.

"Well then, Cammie, sugar," Maggie exclaimed, "why can't you figure this teeny-tiny thing out?"

In helpless surrender, Cammie again turned to Lark. "Help me, here, please."

Lark gave her short mahogany curls a shake. "He's why we're here. You're lonely, and Heinz is homeless. Since you've been taking in strays forever and a day, we brought you an innocuous one this time."

"But I've already got Sheba," Cammie said, pointing to the large feline reclining on the flowered chintz front window seat.

Maggie and Lark exchanged exasperated looks. "There's no comparison, sugar. Why, no ol' cat can be the friend and companion a dog is. And you're all lonesome an' all these days."

"Hey, Mrs. Marlowe! What are we?" asked Stu. "Roadkill?"

"Thank you," Cammie told her boarder, then turned back to her sisters. "That's what I tried to tell you at the party. I'm not alone. My house is full of guests. I'm much too busy to even think of being lonely."

Again her sisters exchanged odd looks—the kind that brought the unease back to Cammie's middle.

Stu came to her rescue once again. "Did you really call him Heinz, Miss Bellamy?" he asked Lark.

"Sure. It fits. He's a mix of just about every breed of dog. You know, Heinz 57 varieties."

The youths looked at each other, then at the pup, who cocked an ear, slurped his big pink tongue around his lips, and snuffled at them. "Mrs. Sprague?" asked Ray, his almond-shaped eyes asking forgiveness ahead of time.

"Yes?"

"Well, just look at him. He's too funny, too friendly, and too little to be a serious—" he took a mincing step, tipped his nose skyward, then gave an exaggerated bow—"elegantly Germanic Heinz."

Stu, his best friend, nodded.

Cammie glanced at the little dog, who bowwowed out a question of his own. Her heart melted again. "I don't know. He's a hodgepodge of types. Heinz does make sense."

"No, ma'am," countered Stu. "I think something more . . . um . . . casual would be better."

"Oh, yeah!" his buddy chimed in.

"Hey, I've got it! Muttley. Muttley works best."

At Stu's exuberant cry, the pup's turbo-tail went into enthusiastic concurring action.

"You may have something there," Cammie said, smiling broadly.

"Oh, dear me, no," Maggie argued. "The darlin' unfortunate needs some dignity. He's a foundlin', you know. We need to bolster his self-esteem. Muttley just won't do a'tall. It'll surely lead to a poor self-image."

Just then, the "darlin' unfortunate" collapsed onto his belly with a deep, deflating *whoosh.* His front paws splayed to the sides of his sausagelike body, which led to frogged-out legs at his nether end.

Cammie laughed. "Dignity, Maggie? I don't think so. Muttley it is."

"But—"

"Didn't you say he is mine?"

"Well, yes, sugar—"

"Of course, Cam," Lark interrupted. "That's why we brought him here. To keep you company."

Cammie's young boarders snorted, rolled their eyes, and headed to the kitchen, asking loudly what was wrong with Miss Cammie's older sisters.

"See?" Cammie asked. "Even they think you two are nuts. I'm *not* lonely, but if you're serious about my keeping this little sweetie, I'm happy to oblige. He's adorable."

With a glance at her new pet, Cammie noticed the expression in his gold-colored eyes. *Don't I know it?* they seemed to say.

After she finally shooed her sisters on their way, Cammie picked up her new baby and, propping him on her upcoming baby, hugged him as she carried him to the brick-floored kitchen. "I guess it's time for me to invest in a couple of baby gates, don't you think?"

Muttley gave her a damp, warm kiss. Cammie chuckled. "You're just a darling, aren't you?"

The puppy repeated his caress.

As a feeling of rightness settled in Cammie's heart, she rummaged through her cupboards and dug out an old dented metal mixing bowl. "This'll do until we buy you a proper water bowl."

The small dog wriggled in her arms. She set him and his drink on the floor simultaneously. With noisy, sloppy verve, he focused on slaking his thirst.

Cammie glanced at the clock. Hmm . . . only ten-thirty. She had time to run to the pet store and pick up a few necessities for Muttley. Like a crate, puppy kibble, toys, Odo-Rid.

As soon as her new companion turned away from the empty bowl, she hurried him out the door to avoid an "accident."

Maybe her sisters were right this time. There was something inherently companionable about the brown critter dancing at the end of the rope. Maybe they *had* known best.

This time.

But *only* this time.

Two days later, Cammie bent to her task with a bowl of Odo-Rid solution and a scrub brush. "Muttley, baby," she said to the mournful pup in the gray plastic crate, "we have to figure out a way to teach you to ask to go outside. My braided rug can't take much more of your toileting."

Unhappy about his current situation, the dog hunkered lower on the pillow-covered bottom of his prison and groaned.

With a towel Cammie began to soak up the excess cleaning and deodorizing solution. Then the doorbell rang.

"Yes?" she said, opening the door. She was still holding her puppy survival supplies.

Stephen Hardesty's eyes widened. "Did I catch you at a bad time?"

Envisioning the picture she presented—brush and bowl in hand, damp towel over a shoulder, bangs ruffled, and hair pulled back into a ponytail—Cammie chuckled. "No, not me. My new puppy. I was just cleaning up after him."

"Breaking in the baby's pet before the birth. Great idea."

Her smile broadened. "Well, it didn't exactly happen like that, but now that you put it that way, it *is* a good idea."

The handsome doctor arched an eyebrow. "You didn't get the puppy for your soon-to-arrive child?"

Cammie's laughter burst out. "No. I didn't even get him for myself. It's a long story, but suffice it to say that my misguided sisters did something very right this time when they gave me little Muttley."

"Muttley?" Stephen asked, his mustache lifting with his smile.

She laughed. "That's an aside to the long story. One of my boarders didn't like the name my sisters had picked. He felt Muttley fit better."

Curiosity danced in her visitor's eyes. "Could I meet the intriguing Muttley?"

"Of course." She stepped aside, and Stephen came inside. "But he's in the pokey right now."

He nodded toward her hands. "For infringement of housebreaking rules, no doubt."

Once in the kitchen she waved him toward the box in the corner. "No doubt whatsoever. If you'll excuse me, I'll take this to the laundry sink."

"While I take the opportunity to make a new friend."

Cammie rushed to dispose of her weapons in the war against kennel smell, then stole a peek at herself in the small vintage mirror hanging in the hall between the kitchen and laundry. "Oh my."

She really did look a sight. She pulled out the scrunchy that had failed to hold her stick-straight, light brown hair in place and ran her fingers through the silky, shoulder-length strands. She then patted down the bristling bangs and reminded herself it was time for a trim.

Why couldn't she have noticed how ragged her long bob had grown before Stephen Hardesty came to town? On the heels of that thought, she chastised herself inwardly. *You're just being silly. What does the new doctor care how you look? He's probably here only to talk you into going to his practice.*

But that wasn't going to happen. If his mere catching her in disheveled shape affected her so much, she couldn't imagine what having Dr. Hardesty as her doctor would do to her.

Why, she might do something foolish and let attraction bloom.

After all, she had spent years dealing with the disappointment of her marriage and then the last six-plus months looking for shreds of contentment in widowhood. There was no need for silly romantic notions to creep in and disrupt her now. The one man in her life had proven to her that the rush of romance turned to the misery of neglect in the face of a fascinating career.

And no career was as seductive as medicine. Or so she'd heard. Cammie had no intention of finding out firsthand.

Squaring her shoulders, she returned to the kitchen. There she found Muttley and the good doctor playing tug-of-war with a multicolored knotted rope. "I see you're getting along well," she said, smiling.

"I love animals. Generally, they like me too."

I'll bet those of the Homo sapiens *female kind fight for position in line.*

As the thought flitted through her misbehaving mind, Cammie shook herself. This just wouldn't do. "Since you didn't know I had a dog, I'm sure your visit isn't for a play date with Muttley. How can I help you?"

Her tone must have been sharper than she'd intended, because Stephen gave her a piercing look. He stood and continued to gaze at her. For long moments he said nothing; he just watched her, with no discernible expression on his face.

Finally he answered. "I was taking my usual after-work

walk, and I remembered Willie Johnson lives here. When we met the other night, we discovered a shared passion for chess. I was hoping to interest him in supper with Aunt Sophie, followed by a challenging match."

All of Cammie's alarm systems pealed their warnings. It couldn't be. Stephen couldn't possibly be of the same mind as Miss Louella.

"Mr. Johnson isn't home right now, but I can give him the message." She hoped her boarder didn't return until it was too late for him to take Stephen up on his offer.

The doctor nodded. "I liked the man, and it seemed to me that he and Aunt Sophie struck sparks off each other. She's been lonely far too long."

What was wrong with everyone? What was it with this loneliness thing? Why did everyone assume widows had to be lonely? Had Noah's two-by-two virus suddenly stormed Bellamy?

"I beg to differ with you," she said in her most polite, gentle tone. "Your aunt seems most satisfied with her life as it is. She's told me so quite a number of times. We're very close friends, you see. We spend a great deal of time together, share a lot of interests, so neither one of us is particularly lonely. We—er . . . she doesn't need any of this absurd matchmaking everyone seems bent on of late."

Again those penetrating eyes studied her. The stillness of the man made Cammie uncomfortable, restless. His breathing soughed out smooth and measured, raising his wide shoulders, drawing her attention to his taut, muscular build.

How did he do it? Stay so still, so focused? Had he fully attained that peace Christ had come to give his own? Goodness knows she hadn't, no matter how hard she'd worked to achieve the contentment Paul spoke of in his letter to the Romans.

In some ways she was content. She no longer mulled over

her inadequacies and failings like she used to while waiting for her husband to come home from the office during the wee hours of the night. And soon she would become a mother—something she had longed for, hoped for, for years.

But peace? No, she hadn't attained that yet. Had Stephen?

Before she could stop herself, she blurted out, "Are you a Christian?"

He blinked, obviously caught off guard. "No," he replied. "I'm . . ." A strange expression settled over his features. "Let's just say I'm sort of a Buddhist—for now."

Cammie's jaw dropped. A Buddhist in Bellamy. "My goodness."

What would the Garden Club make of that?

THREE

"I'M TELLIN' YOU, SUGAR," EXPOUNDED LOUELLA Ashworth as she sat across from Maggie Bellamy Marlowe's organized office desk, "that boy of Sophie's is nothin' less than the dear Lord's gift to your baby sister."

Maggie lifted a skeptical brow. "He doesn't look like he'd fall for a down-home girl like Cammie. He seems as slick and pretty as a trout in a stream and . . . oh, I don't know . . . New Yorkified."

"Nonsense, Magnolia. Why, he's *Sophie's* grandnephew. Can't be much wrong with him." Bellamy's social doyenne tapped her impeccable nails on Maggie's desktop. "I have to tell you, though. I feel called to make sure that little girl is all set before that baby pops out. And what could be better for the both of them than a doctor? I'm tellin' you, Maggie, I've made it my mission to make sure that match is made."

"Sure, Cammie needs someone like a pod needs two peas—even Lark agrees. But Miss Louella, how can you be so sure Stephen Hardesty's the one?"

A superior smile widened Miss Louella's bittersweetlipsticked mouth. "I'd say—as you should right well know—my track record's a mighty fine one so far. There's you and your Clay, Lark and her Rich, and if you're bein' perfectly accurate, why, you have to count even your late mama and papa as one of my greatest successes."

"You don't say? I hadn't heard that."

Miss Louella patted her rigorously maintained chestnut hair. "Why, sure, sugar. I had a hand in bringin' those two lovebirds together. Your Granny Iris and I were great friends, you know, and she well knew how mightily the Lord had blessed me in this matchmakin' field—"

The ringing phone cut off the tale before it got started. Maggie answered, then donned a quizzical expression. *"Myrna Stafford?"* After an instant of silence, her cheeks colored. "Why, no, ma'am, I'm not being disrespectful a'tall. I'm just more surprised'n a deer in a trucker's headlights you'd be calling *me."*

Maggie pursed her lips. "Oh. I see. Yes, ma'am. She's right here." Tipping her chin skyward, Maggie extended the phone to Miss Louella. "She wants you."

"Really now. A body has to wonder what kind of bee the woman's got in her bonnet. I tell you, Myrna Stafford never calls unless she has a bone to pick." A gleam lit her eyes. "Or a story to tell. You know how nosy she can be." Into the receiver she said, "What's wrong this time, Myrna?"

Silence.

Then Miss Louella blanched. Her breath came in sharp, shallow gasps. Her free hand waved ineffectually, then fluttered to rest in the vicinity of her heart. "It can't be."

"What?" Maggie asked.

Ignoring the younger woman, Miss Louella said, "Are you sure?" Without warning, she let out a sharp, keening yowl. The phone dropped from her limp hand.

Maggie lunged across her desk in an effort to catch it. "What *is* it?"

Miss Louella shook herself, blinked furiously, and struggled to regain control. "I can barely believe it."

Maggie lost the reins on her patience. "What? What? Tell me, please. I'm fair busting to know. How bad can it be?"

Miss Louella's gray eyes opened saucer-wide. "Oh, it's bad. It's awful bad."

Maggie ran around the desk, dropped to her knees before Miss Louella, and placed her hands on her elderly friend's shoulders. "You know you can tell me *any*thing. No matter how terrible it may be."

Miss Louella patted her evidently affected heart. "Oh, Maggie, honey, it's bad, all right. Bellamy's been invaded."

"Say what?"

Miss Louella drew herself up. "You heard me, girl. And I must get a-movin'. I have to marshal my troops to do battle for the Lord. We're right smack-dab in the middle of a Buddhist invasion."

Stephen walked home after another unique day at the office. He'd had to wrestle with Doc Calloway's unorthodox filing system again. It was alphabetical, but not necessarily by the patient's last name. No, that would have been too simple. Especially in this town. It seemed everyone had a nickname around here. And *that's* what Doc used to set up his files.

Had Stephen made a mistake coming to Bellamy?

No matter how hard he tried, Stephen couldn't forget the look on Cammie Sprague's guileless face when he'd told her he was currently trying Buddhism on for size. At first it had struck him as funny. But later, as he'd thought over the encounter, he'd begun to feel there was more to her reaction than simple surprise.

True, she'd tried to cover up her response. The tea and cookies she'd offered him had been delicious. But he hadn't missed the shock in her eyes nor the odd glances she'd kept sending his way.

He didn't often reveal such personal details, but the words had slipped from his mouth before he'd had a chance to smother them.

And now the office mess. How was he ever going to figure out who was who? Would he have to rely on Doc's—er . . . *his*—secretary/receptionist for years? He hadn't missed the look of muted humor on Laura's face.

And that, after his dad's call last night had left him tense. Not only had the man not forgiven Stephen for *not* specializing in the lucrative field of plastic surgery—like he himself had—but the elder Dr. Hardesty simply couldn't fathom his son's flight from the Virginia suburbs near D.C. for "old Sophie's hick hometown," as Dad called it.

Stephen's father couldn't conceive of life away from a cosmopolitan area, nor could he accept Stephen's rejection of the potential fortune to be made from nipping and tucking the wealthy's flaws.

Mother had been just as bad. She'd pointed out that his wardrobe would soon be out of date, and there wasn't a Saks anywhere near Bellamy. She couldn't imagine living more than a few miles from the closest one. It was uncivilized, at best.

No wonder his mind had buzzed with static all day.

It irritated Stephen to think that after so many years of faithful seeking, he still hadn't reached true enlightenment, that plane of peace offered by the different faith paths he'd checked out thus far.

Inside his condo, he dropped his white coat and navy tie on

the cinnabar-lacquered Chinese chest near the door. From the small kitchen, he heard the sound of chimes and was glad he'd left the window open so he could hear the fall breeze playing the metal pipes against each other. The faint scent of incense that permeated the apartment spoke of the hours he'd spent trying out Zen meditation.

After changing into a special robe, he went into the second bedroom. He spared a glare for the bookshelf full of texts on such esoteric subjects as Yoga, transcendental meditation, Scientology, and a few of the other philosophies and faiths with which he'd experimented. He had to get around to ridding himself of most of them, since none of the paths the books touted had led him to what they promised—what he sought. Besides, Zen held pride of place in his search right now, and the stack of books on that subject piled at his bedside threatened his life when he rose to answer a patient's call in the middle of the night.

Heading toward the small table against the back wall, he withdrew a matchbook from the pocket of his robe. On the table sat a covered bowl of water, a candle ready to flame, incense to make the air visible, and a perfect chrysanthemum he'd begged from Aunt Sophie's garden after dinner last night. These were meant to remind him of the four earthly elements.

Stephen lit the candle and the incense. He stepped backward, and when he reached the thin mat in the middle of the room, he sat on a small, pumpkin-shaped cushion. Then he began to count his breaths. One, in . . . out; two, in . . . out; three, in . . .

What could possibly have shocked Cammie Sprague about Buddhism? It wasn't as if Buddhists were mass murderers or anything.

Well, he *had* moved to a small Southern town, and he was used to the anything-goes atmosphere of a large city. But this was the new millennium, after all. People knew there were other paths than theirs.

Obviously Cammie wasn't into Zen.

Stephen realized his mind had strayed from his breathing, so he roped it back in. One, in . . . out; two, in . . . out; three, in . . .

She *had* been seeing Doc Calloway for her pregnancy in spite of what she'd said. He'd found her file. So she'd lied. Or at the very least, fudged.

Why?

As he again recognized that his mind had lost its focus, Stephen knew Cammie had done whatever she'd done because of him. What was it about him that had made her run?

Where had she run to? Had she found competent medical care? Stephen would never be able to live with himself if she risked her well-being, and that of her unborn child, because of him.

Three days after his least successful meditation attempt so far, Stephen took his regular walk after work. He liked to mull over his cases as he soaked up the brilliant coloring of the late fall flowers and the muted tones of early dusk. The spicy scent of approaching winter always gave him a thrill.

He'd gone only a few blocks when the dapper Willie Johnson joined him. "How're you doing there, my boy?"

Stephen smiled ruefully. "Struggling to get my bearings in this town."

Willie laughed. "Took me a while."

"Then you're not from around here?"

"Goodness, no. One day I stumbled upon Cammie's—the Widow Sprague, you understand—boardinghouse and decided to stay. But I'll tell you, boy, these folks are hard to keep straight in your head."

"I'm learning all about their nicknames."

"Mm-hmm." Willie picked up his pace. "So tell me, how is that exquisite, charming aunt of yours today?"

Stephen gave his companion a knowing look. "Kept an eye out for me, did you?"

Willie stumbled, blushed, and sputtered like a defective radiator. "Why, no, of course not. I was just . . . er . . . taking my daily constitutional, you see. Yes! In fact, Doc Calloway insisted that I needed more regular exercise, so I'm following your illustrious colleague's orders. I merely asked after your lady-aunt for . . . for the sake of well-mannered politeness."

Stephen clapped a hand on Willie's erect back. "Protesting too much, I think. I'll put you out of your misery. Aunt Sophie was fine last night when I drove her to her missionary society meeting, but I haven't spoken with her today."

"Ah, the incomparable joys of family life."

Stephen felt more than heard the man's wistfulness. "You have no family?"

"No. My dearest departed Maida and I had no children. She passed on long ago. Besides, fortune decreed me an only child, so there are no more Johnsons left. Of my immediate family, you understand—the country is otherwise teeming with branches of them. Of course, I *could* delve into our vast genealogy and see what relational shoots I come up with."

The gleam of interest lit Willie's faded blue eyes. Stephen felt a swell of compassion—a quality much respected and developed by Zen followers, as he'd read just last night—for the old man. "Tell me, Willie. Are you busy tonight?"

He shook his silver head. "After Cammie's delightful meals I usually sit around her charming abode and chat with her and the kids. Then I read a bit and retire at a sensible time.

Not a very exciting routine, although wholly pleasurable and generally satisfying. But, no, I'm not busy tonight."

"Do you have to dine with Mrs. Sprague?"

"No . . . , I guess I don't. I just usually do. Unless there's some kind of to-do at the Bellamy Community Church. Those women can cook!"

Remembering his welcome to town, Stephen nodded in agreement. "I'll say. Tell you what. How about if you come over to my place? We can see what I have in the fridge and play a game of chess."

"Why, son, that's just jim-dandy! All I'll have to do is call Camellia when we get there and tell her I won't be coming—"

"Oh-ho!" Stephen broke in. "This looks to be your lucky day, Willie. Not only will you not have to wait until we get to my place to call Mrs. Sprague, but you're about to have the opportunity to ask my great-aunt in person how she's faring. Here they come."

The two women had indeed turned the corner a block away and were heading in their direction. Muttley led the small parade down the sidewalk, prancing, sniffing every which way, his tail resembling more an overactive propeller than the usual canine appendage.

Something about that dog made Stephen smile. Or so he told himself. It couldn't have anything to do with catching a glimpse of the pretty, pregnant widow.

Besides, he had no idea how she would respond to him after that awkward impromptu tea party they'd shared. After he'd revealed his current spiritual explorations.

While Willie picked up his pace even more, Stephen slowed his. He studied Cammie's face for some hint of her response, but she was too busy chatting with Aunt Sophie and hanging on to her pet. When he could no longer avoid the two women without appearing rude, he called out a greeting.

"Hi, Aunt Sophie, Mrs. Sprague. Nice to see you two share my love of fall evening walks."

Cammie looked up from her dog, met Stephen's gaze, then turned her eyes to the setting sun. "It's my favorite season. My baking smells just that much better, and there's nothin' like curlin' up with a craft project before the fire."

"You're a real homebody," Stephen observed.

Aunt Sophie beamed. "Oh, Stephen, dearest, this girl's nothin' if not a wonder! You should taste her cookin'—"

"Amen!" echoed Willie.

Stephen's great-aunt pinkened as she nodded at Willie Johnson. "And her sewin'?" she said. "Why, there's nothin' quite like it. She does true art—nothing more, nothing less."

"I don't know a thing about art," Willie commented, "but I recognize beauty when I see it. And our dear Camellia, stitching away by the fire, is an *étude* in magnificent splendor."

A sweet, beckoning picture formed in Stephen's mind. He could almost hear the crackle of the flames in the hearth, smell the spice of burning wood mingled with the perfume of an earlier baking spree, see the glow of the blaze bring a hint of red to Cammie's silky, honey brown hair. The needle in her hand caught a glimmer of the light and sparkled as she wove it through the fabric.

Stephen shook himself. What was he doing, fantasizing over a pregnant woman while standing in the middle of the sidewalk? He'd never done anything like that before. And he'd better put an end to it right away.

"Didn't you have something to tell Mrs. Sprague?" he asked Willie.

Willie shot him a surprised look. "Oh, well, yes. But we're in no hurry now, are we?"

Stephen shrugged. "It's been a while since lunchtime, and my stomach's reminding me of that."

Cammie smiled. "Oh, you poor man. I have a kettle full of

Irish stew simmerin' away at home, and my fresh bread should be about ready to slice. Please join us for supper. I always make more than enough."

Taken aback by her direct and apparently sincere offer, Stephen faltered. He wasn't sure it was wise to spend any more time with a woman who—who what? She didn't irritate him exactly. Nor did she rouse in him a wild rush of desire. She just made him smile . . . and wonder why she wouldn't trust him with her medical care.

Aunt Sophie placed a soft hand on Stephen's arm. "You don't want to miss tonight's supper at Cammie's, you know. She's baked an apple pie—"

"Oh, I'm in rapture," cried Willie, his eyes rolling comically. "This girl's pies are incomparable. Sorry, Stephen. I'm not missing this banquet in honor of whatever your fridge might have to offer. I'll be eating at the Widow Sprague's. If you're still interested in a chess game, why, by all means, I'll come to your place afterward."

"You don't have to leave to play chess," Cammie said. "I have my great-granddaddy's set. The boys and Willie have had some mighty fierce matches over those pieces, and I'm sure you can enjoy a quiet evenin' without havin' to fuss about cookin' or whatnot."

Stephen raised his hands in defeat. "You win. It's Irish stew at the Sprague home for me."

Cammie smiled again. "I think you'll enjoy the evenin'. At least, I sure hope so."

As he watched her, that desire to smile flooded him again. Stephen found himself anticipating the time to come. What would it be like? He knew what dinners at his parents' home were like: stuffy, formal, filled with discussions about the latest fashions by his mother and sister, and underscored by his father's gripes over the latest dips and swells of the stock market.

Obviously, there'd be none of that at Cammie's place. But what exactly would he find there?

Before he could think of a possible answer to his question, Aunt Sophie's housemate, Louella Ashworth, joined them. "Well, hello, there," the well-turned-out lady said, her gaze fixed on Stephen's face. "Fancy meetin' you all here at one time."

"Miss Sophie and I came out to walk Muttley before supper," Cammie said after a one-armed hug, her other arm stretched out by the lively pup on his leash.

Willie doffed his fedora and took Miss Louella's hand. He kissed it in continental fashion. "Dear lady, it's a rare pleasure to chance upon you during the good doctor's and my evening constitutional."

Miss Louella narrowed her eyes, still pinned on Stephen, and said, "Well, why don't we all head on home then? It's growin' a mite chilly out here, and we sure wouldn't want Camellia and the baby to catch consumption. Good night, Dr. Hardesty."

That was odd, Stephen thought. The other night, Miss Louella couldn't be budged from his and Willie's side, and now she'd clearly sent him packing. What had happened?

She went on. "I'm sure you have another mighty busy day ahead of you tomorrow, and you'll be wantin' to catch up on your rest to be ready for it. Mr. Johnson and I'll see your aunt and Mrs. Sprague home."

Bemused, Stephen looked at Cammie. "I'm getting confused. Should I—"

Cammie's cheeks turned a soft rose shade. "Oh, Miss Louella, Dr. Hardesty's comin' over for supper tonight. We'll be just fine on our walk. Would you care to join us—"

"Cammie!" screamed a panicked female voice.

The group turned in the direction of the cry, and Stephen

caught sight of Magnolia Bellamy Marlowe running toward them as fast as her short legs could carry her.

Cammie hurried to her sibling's side. Concerned by the pinched, white look to the lovely blonde's features, Stephen followed.

"What is it, Maggie?" asked Cammie in her soft voice.

The petite woman panted in great heaves. Tears poured down her cheeks. Her disheveled curls rioted over her shoulders, and her blue eyes held pain and anguish in their depths.

"He's gone!" she blurted out on a ragged gasp.

"Harrumph!" snorted a rapidly approaching woman of a certain age.

A strange-looking one, at that. Rail thin and avian-featured, she sported the most unlikely hued mass of sausagelike hair rolls all over her head. Purple? Stephen had never seen anything like it before.

"I warned you, didn't I, Magnolia?" asked the stranger, an avid gleam in her black eyes. "I told you that Yankee scoundrel you married was not to be trusted. Now he's up and left you, ain't he?"

Maggie fought to catch her breath, then glared at the condemning woman. "My Clay's right where he should be. It's my . . . *Buford!"* she wailed. "He's gone. And from the looks of things, someone's—" she hiccuped—"stolen him!"

"What?"

"When?"

"Who would do such a thing?"

"Why?"

The cluster on the sidewalk spat their questions all at once, not giving Maggie the chance to respond. To Stephen's right, a whimper became a cry that turned into a banshee shriek.

He turned and saw Miss Louella clutch her chest, her eyes wide, her face ashen. "Somebody *do* something!" she begged.

"Straightaway. Rotten miscreants can't get away with it. My grandpuppy's been dognapped!"

As she started to fall, Stephen leaped to automatic action. He caught Miss Louella before she hit the sidewalk and held her head upright. The others gathered around him, offering assistance, jabbering at each other.

Stephen looked at the elderly woman in his arms. He studied the faces ranged before him. He heard the anxious howl of the pup.

What had he gotten himself into?

FOUR

To Stephen's immense relief, Miss Louella's eyelids began fluttering even as he lowered her to the ground. The onlookers, however, didn't recover quite as quickly. Worse yet, their ranks swelled as others came to see what had happened. All proved curious.

"Why, Louella Ashworth, what *are* you doin' in that young man's arms?" asked a well-constructed matron.

"Hmph!" offered the curmudgeon with the purple curls. "I'd say she's forgettin' her advanced age again, Savannah Hollings."

A slender, pewter-haired lady, her tiny body dwarfed by voluminous layer upon layer of clothing, waggled a thin finger in front of the crusty one's beakish nose. "Now, Myrna Stafford, you hush your mouth," she susurrated. "Poor Louella's had herself a shock. Can't you be showin' a mite of Christian compassion?"

Tipping her sharp chin and narrowing her eyes laden with bright turquoise makeup, Myrna answered, "When compassion's called for, I'm first in line to offer it."

"Now, Myrna, how can you say such a thing?" chided a slight, white-haired woman with a spark in her faded blue eyes.

Myrna spun and glared. "Are you questionin' my compassion, Florinda Sumner? Why, I never—"

"Good to see you acceptin' facts, Myrna," cut in Miss Louella, pulling herself together. "Haven't seen any of your compassion a-showin' for a mighty long while."

"Louella Ashworth!" cried Aunt Sophie, clearly distressed. "Now what kind of a thing is that for a godly woman to say?"

Miss Louella stood with Stephen's help, shook herself, then held her head to a haughty height. "A true thing, Sophie, and you well know it." Turning to Maggie Marlowe, she went on. "Now, Magnolia, darlin', please tell me what's happened to my dear grandpuppy."

Attention shifted from the fallen maven to the bearer of bad news. "Oh, Miss Louella, it's plumb worse'n a bushel full of hornets' nests. I let my darlin' boy outside a little while ago—as I always do this time of day, you know—then, when I went to call him in again, why, he wasn't there. Or anywhere."

Miss Louella pursed her lips, then said, "Where have you looked? Have you gone down to Langhorn Creek? over to the elementary school playground? across to the butcher shop?"

Maggie blushed. "Well, no. I looked all around our yard, then up and down the street. That's what I was doin' when I noticed you all standin' here."

"For goodness' sake, girl, didn't you call the police?"

"Clay said he'd do that for me. I simply couldn't just sit around and *do* nothin' but wait. Why, Buford's my *baby!*"

Maggie's words melted and blended into a taffy-thick drawl, difficult for Stephen to understand. Obviously the woman's Southern accent worsened when she grew stressed.

To Stephen's way of thinking, Maggie could gain a lot from Zen meditation.

With no hesitation, Miss Louella took charge. "Well, he's my grandpuppy, and goodness knows I'm not about to stand around just jawin' while he's missin'. There's plenty of us here to start a search."

In seconds she dispersed the crowd with instructions as to where to search. The only ones left standing on the sidewalk were Cammie, Aunt Sophie, Willie Johnson, Maggie, and Stephen himself.

Although he would have expected the directed action to help Maggie's agitation, she still seemed distraught. Then Aunt Sophie stepped up to bat. "Well, girls," she said, "this would seem to me a fine time to call for *extra* help." She reached out to each sister. The women clasped hands and bent their heads.

"Heavenly Father," Aunt Sophie intoned, "we have us a fine mess here. You know how much Maggie loves her Buford, and his disappearance is mighty troublin' to her. I pray for your protection for the dear boy and your peace for her. We know you love her and don't want her to fret or be anxious for nothin'. Let her cast this trouble at the foot of your Son's cross, as you work your will. We expect your answer to our prayer, knowin' you said that where two or more of your own are gathered, why, there you are. In Jesus' precious and holy name I pray these things. Amen."

The younger women nodded along to Sophie's words, uttering occasional heartfelt murmurs. At the evidence of such devotion, Stephen felt uneasy. He glanced at Willie and found the older gent's rapt attention on the supplicants.

"Thank you, Miss Sophie," said Maggie, a smile on her face. "I know I shouldn't fret; I should just turn to the Lord. But when I couldn't find my precious, why, I just plain ol' lost it. You have reminded me I'm not alone. It's so good to have Christian friends who bring me right back to where I need to be."

Cammie calmly placed a hand on Maggie's shoulder. "It's so good to see you trustin' the Lord. I prayed years for this."

Maggie covered her sister's hand with hers. "I'm so glad you had the patience of Job and the perseverance of Wile E. Coyote. Your prayers went straight from your lips to God's ears then, and I'm countin' on them goin' there now again. I don't know what I'll do if we can't find my baby."

Although it seemed to have brought a measure of peace to Cammie's sister, the entire faith-and-prayer scene had become too disturbing to Stephen. "Tell you what, Maggie," he suggested. "Why don't you go home? If your husband called the police, they probably want to talk to you."

She nodded. "You're right, Dr. Hardesty. I belong back home."

"You'll let us know what they say, won't you?" asked Cammie.

Maggie smiled. "If you'd like. I'm sorry I behaved like a nanny goat of a ninny—"

"Hush, Maggie," Cammie said. "It's normal to be upset. And I do want to know. Now go on home. Maybe Buford's already there before you."

Nodding, Maggie turned and walked away. Then she paused, turned around again, and with what appeared to be unusual shyness, addressed her sister. "The Lord bless you."

A soft gasp escaped Cammie's lips. "And you, Maggie. You, too."

To Stephen's amazement, a tear rolled down Cammie's cheek as her sister strode away. What was that all about? What had gone on here? A prayer . . . a tear . . . that shyness from Maggie?

Before he could give the event much thought, Willie Johnson cleared his throat. "Well, now. I feel there should be *something* we can do to help. Don't you, son?"

Put on the spot, Stephen scrambled for an adequate answer.

Cammie came to his rescue with her gentle smile. "I think it'd be best if we went on home and had some supper. I'm sure Maggie will call us with whatever news she gets from the police."

After a short walk, the foursome arrived at Cammie's boardinghouse. Stephen took the time to study the home as they approached. Large, and with a gable in the front center of the roof, the house looked inviting, cheerful, and comfortable. Its sprightly yellow siding was set off by white trim around the windows and the Italianate-style supports under the eaves. A wraparound porch, furnished in Victorian white wicker, suggested peaceful repose.

What a contrast between Cammie's house and his parents' stately Georgian brick estate.

"Er . . . son?" asked Willie.

To Stephen's embarrassment, he realized the women had already gone inside and Willie stood holding the front door open for him. "Sorry," he murmured, taking the front steps two at a time. "It's a great house, and I was just admiring it."

Willie shook his head. "No, I daresay it's not a house but rather a *home.* There's quite a difference between the two."

"I wouldn't know from personal experience, I'm afraid," Stephen said a bit sadly.

Willie's sharp blue eyes studied Stephen.

Uncomfortable with the scrutiny, Stephen shrugged and tried to explain. "My family isn't into homey stuff. They entertain too much."

Willie's piercing gaze narrowed as he obviously weighed Stephen's statement. Stephen would have done better keeping his mouth shut.

"You can entertain in a home, and do a fine job of it," Willie said, gesturing toward Cammie's front parlor. "But you can't make a home in a place designed for entertainment."

Stephen let his gaze follow Willie's gesture. What he saw tugged at something deep within him, something unfamiliar or perhaps long forgotten.

A caramel-colored sofa faced the brick-fronted open hearth, where a fire crackled briskly. To the right, a matching love seat looked head-on over a pine coffee table at two navy-and-cream-striped armchairs. Colorful pillows and coordinating throws nestled in the upholstered pieces while a spectacular and obviously antique pitcher and bowl, replete with autumn's russet and gold chrysanthemums, reigned on the table.

On the oak mantel Cammie had displayed a collection of delicate blue-and-white porcelain plates, echoing their color with attractive groupings of paintings and pictures on the walls. Among the china displays hung a kaleidoscopic assortment of small quilts. To the right of the hearth, by the northern-exposure window, a large quilting frame held an intricate piece in the making, its navy, cobalt, gold, and white fabrics melding well with the warm tones of the room.

Stephen stepped into the well-appointed, embracing room and approached the sofa, eager to sink into its apparent comfort. As he did, he caught the scent of food in the air. He stopped and breathed deeply.

Willie chuckled. "You can almost taste it already, can't you?"

Stephen tipped his head. "If supper tastes half as good as it smells, then we're in for a treat."

Sophie bustled in. "What are you two doing lollygaggin' out here still? Why, everyone's headin' for the table and the food's goin' to get cold. You wouldn't want that to happen, now, would you? You a doctor and all, Stephen."

"I guess not," he said, following his great-aunt but not her logic.

She nodded her snowy Gibson girl head emphatically. "Of course not. It's a known fact that cold food causes the worst kind of dyspepsia. And you don't have your black bag, and I don't have my digestive powders, either. Come on, come on. Time to eat Camellia's lovely meal."

The dining room sparkled with light from the overhead chandelier, its brass and flower-etched glass glowing with care and polish. More blue-and-white patterned china adorned the table, which was covered with a soft, butter yellow cloth. Tall, clear glasses awaited what looked like iced tea in the crystal pitcher at the center of the table. Stephen's eyes and nose, however, zeroed in on the tureen next to the pitcher. *The stew.*

"Please take a seat," Cammie said, entering the room through a swinging door. "Any one will do."

Choosing the nearest chair, Stephen complied. His hostess set down a napkin-covered basket that, he suspected, held the just-baked bread she'd mentioned earlier. His stomach growled in eager anticipation.

As if that intestinal noise had been a secret cue, people flooded the room. Two young men came in from the front of the house, their banter and laughter rowdy. A sweet-faced teen girl slipped in behind Aunt Sophie, who'd followed Cammie from what Stephen assumed was the kitchen. Willie, who'd been at Stephen's side, took a chair across from him. When all the bodies sorted themselves out, he found himself seated between the Asian youth to his left and his hostess at the head of the table. The eight-person table had only one empty chair.

"It's a pleasure to have you all here tonight," Cammie said with a smile. "I'll just give a brief thank-you for our meal, since I know you all must be famished by now."

She extended her slender hands, one to him and one to Willie. As everyone seated clasped his or her neighbor's hand, Stephen had no alternative but to do the same. Cammie's slender fingers slid over his—soft, warm, and to his surprise, very welcome. In automatic response, he wrapped his own over hers, relishing the contact between them. There was something . . . special, private, and somehow unsettling about their touch. Something . . . that *definitely* wasn't there in the cool, matter-of-fact clasp of the youth on his left. Stephen shook his head to dispel the disturbing thoughts, then listened to what Cammie was saying.

"Thank you, Father, for bringin' Stephen to us tonight. I ask your blessin' on each one gathered here. I thank you for the bounty with which you've graced us and pray that you'll use it to strengthen us as we do your will. Oh, and Father God, please help Maggie find Buford. Soon. Amen."

As the other diners voiced quiet amens, Stephen's earlier discomfort at Cammie's ease with prayer returned to a greater degree, even though he'd felt a stir of . . . comfort, maybe . . . when she'd thanked God for his presence in her home. Not that God had anything to do with it. She was the one who'd offered the invitation, Aunt Sophie and Willie had sung the praises of her cooking, and Stephen himself had accepted. Nothing particularly God-requiring about that.

Willie thrust the bread basket at Stephen, breaking into his thoughts. "Make sure you help yourself to as much as you're likely to want from the start, because I can gleefully eat the entire loaf."

The youth at Stephen's left hooted. "No way, Willie. It's coming my way and I'm starved. There won't be any left by the time I'm done with it." Facing Stephen, he held out his hand. "By the way, I'm Ray Ling. Are you a new boarder?"

Stephen juggled the bread basket, then took Ray's hand.

"Good to meet you. I'm Stephen Hardesty, and I'm only visiting for supper."

"Oh," said the African-American young man at Ray's left, "you're the new doc the ladies are all talkin' about. You oughta hear them, man."

Stephen blushed. "Trust me, I'd rather not. But, yes, I'm the new doctor in town."

"Oh, hey, I'm Stu Richards. You're gonna love Miss Cammie's stew." He preened, winked, and gave a cocky grin.

Ray hooted again, jabbed an elbow into Stu's side, and heckled him for the lousy pun. That set the mood for the most enjoyable meal Stephen had consumed in ages. The conversation consisted of retelling the day's events, individual highs and lows, no-nonsense advice from Aunt Sophie, Southern hospitality from Cammie, and jokes shared all around.

Stephen joined the easy flow, recounting his difficulty in matching patients with Doc Calloway's files. After generous wedges of pie—as scrumptious as Aunt Sophie had said—Cammie invited everyone to the parlor for another cup of coffee.

"Willie," she added, as she headed toward the kitchen, "remember the chessboard. You all can start playing while I brew this fresh pot."

The teenaged girl excused herself, saying she had too much homework, but Stu and Ray commandeered the sofa, declaring themselves judges in the upcoming match between Willie and Stephen. Aunt Sophie plopped her knitting bag at her side on the love seat, and soon her needles clacked a rhythmic beat.

Willie, with impressive agility, sat on the well-used Oriental rug, legs beneath the pine table. "Raymond, boy," he said, nodding toward the pitcher and bowl, "would you be so kind as to please remove Miss Cammie's pride and joy from harm's way?"

Without a trace of his prior ebullience, Ray carefully picked up the beautiful porcelain pieces and left the room.

"Miss Cammie'd have our heads if we broke her great-grand-something-or-other's washstand stuff," Stu said. "She loves those things, but I can't figure out why. The picture on them is all blurred even. And they're *old,* man. You know, the stuff's got these skinny little crackles all over the place."

Cammie came in carrying a steaming blue-and-white porcelain pot, sugar bowl, and creamer on a large silver tray. Matching cups and saucers nestled around the serving pieces. "Help yourselves," she said, placing the tray carefully on the floor next to Willie, then going to her quilting frame. "And I won't bore you all again with the virtues of antique English porcelains."

The returning Ray turned an exaggerated glance heavenward and gave thanks.

Chuckling, Stephen poured himself a cup of the rich brew, then sipped, savoring the excellent flavor. Cammie did have a way with food and drink. And her home. Her boarders and guest had eaten their fill in an atmosphere of friendship, and now, in the parlor, that sense of pleasure and ease continued. Stephen noticed the soft smile on Aunt Sophie's lips as she worked on her latest project. The two young men he'd expected to take off the moment the food was gone hung around the house, joining in the after-dinner fellowship. Willie was in his element, and Stephen felt right—just right—as if something had fallen into place and clicked.

It wasn't quite nirvana, but it came close.

Stephen looked at the woman responsible for the wonderful ambiance in her small domain and felt a stirring deep inside. Cammie looked happy and lovely, serene and diligent, fresh and beautiful. Even with her pregnancy, he could tell she had a strong, healthy, well-exercised figure. With her all-American-girl-next-door looks and maternal ways, she'd turned her house into a home for the lonely and seemed to thrive on it.

That sweet smile of hers again played over her lips as she sent a tiny silver needle dancing through the fabric stretched out over the wooden frame. The light from the fire painted glints of rust on her brown hair, apricot on her cheeks, gilt on her slim hands.

Peace.

He was at peace. And it startled him.

Aunt Sophie had often talked of the joy of living in Bellamy. The folks, she'd said, were genuine and caring. In Stephen's prior experience, there'd never been much of that floating around.

He settled on the rug, leaning back against the sofa. City living had been exciting—in an automatic, vibrant way. Something was always happening that kept everyone moving at a rapid pace. He couldn't remember ever seeing even a hint of peace on either of his parents' faces. They were too busy.

Looking at Aunt Sophie, an involuntary smile curved his mouth. Her soft white topknot bobbed with each knit or purl she made in the jade green froth floating off her needles. Just as it took a great deal of time and patience to produce such intricate treasures, it also had taken a great deal of her love to win over a city youth like himself, who'd initially considered her home and life boring and backward—as his father had termed it.

But Stephen had soon learned how wrong his father had been. When he had come to stay with Aunt Sophie that first summer, he'd felt wanted and valued. Loved, for the first time in his life. It was no wonder Aunt Sophie became his confidante and favorite family member during his early teen summer vacations. Then during the years filled with summer jobs, their relationship had grown through letters and frequent phone calls.

So when he'd discovered that her trusted physician was preparing to retire, he'd jumped on the opportunity to ensure the excellence of her medical care. Even before that, Stephen had been ready to leave behind the assembly-line style of the medical practice he'd joined in the city. He'd also known that with his up-to-date knowledge he could benefit Aunt Sophie and her fellow Bellamy citizens.

The thought of losing her sooner rather than later because of antiquated methods or second-rate care was intolerable. He had to keep the one person who'd always loved him without reservation hearty for as long as possible. He needed Aunt Sophie's comforting motherly presence in his life. She was the only person he truly loved, the only one he trusted with his love. He'd do anything for Aunt Sophie, give her anything she wanted or needed.

The doorbell chimed and Stephen blinked, startled out of his thoughts. Stu scrambled to his feet. "I'll get it, Miss Cammie. No need for you to get up."

A murmured greeting rolled back into the parlor, followed by heavy footsteps. A minute later, a tall string bean in uniform filled the doorway. "Howdy, folks. Cammie, how're you doin' tonight?" the officer asked.

"Wiggon!" she exclaimed, catching her needle in the fabric and standing. "Come on in. I'm doin' fine, and you? How about some coffee? I just brewed it fresh."

Officer Wiggon removed his hat and made a beeline to the offered drink. "For your coffee, Cammie, I'd walk a few extra miles. Thanks."

Cammie poured; he added sugar and cream. As Wiggon took a long, appreciative drink, Cammie said, "I reckon you're here about Maggie's Buford, right?"

Wiggon nodded. "It's like this. She was too much beside

herself to come over, so she asked if I'd do it for her. So here I am."

"And . . . ?" Cammie said.

A pause ensued as Wiggon drank again. "And . . . well . . . it's like this, Cammie. I guess I got to agree with your sister. Someone's made off with that dog."

"Oh, dear," Cammie murmured. "I'd hoped he'd only gone off for a frisky run or something like that."

"What I found just a while back sure don't point to no doggy clownin' or nothin'. I'd have to say, it's clear as day: it's a dognappin' we got us on our hands here."

"Wiggon, honey," Aunt Sophie said, "why don't you take a seat with us and tell us what you've found. We haven't a clue, you know."

The officer hesitated. "Well . . . ah . . . um . . . I'm not so sure I should be discussin' these matters. It's a ongoin' investigation into a crime, you know."

"Cecil Wiggon, you get off that high horse right this minute," Aunt Sophie ordered in her most serious tone. "I'm fixin' to call your mama and tell her how uppity you've become. Why, I recollect when I helped her change your diapers, young man. We're near expirin' to know what's happened to Maggie's Buford, and you're busy pretendin' you're some Tee-Vee cop. My goodness, boy. Just wait'll I tell your mama."

The threat was apparently a dire one.

"No need to go botherin' Mama, Miss Sophie," the officer said with alacrity. "I'll tell you all what I found. Why, I have the evidence right here with me. I can even show it to you, if you'd like."

"Why, honey," Aunt Sophie responded in her normal cheery voice. "Of *course* we want to see what you have."

Wiggon set down his coffee cup—reluctantly, at that—and reached into his shirt pocket. He withdrew what to Stephen looked like a zip-closure plastic bag, and with great ceremony displayed it for all to see. "There it is, folks. The evidence."

Stephen looked, blinked, and looked again. He glanced around the room, only to find puzzled expressions on those gathered round—expressions that mirrored his own bewilderment.

When no one seemed willing to comment, Stephen took a deep breath. "A soggy, crumpled fast-food wrapper?" he asked.

Wiggon nodded, his chest swelling with pride. "Sure looks that way, don't it?"

"That's what you have there, all right," Stephen answered, still not following the connection. "But what does it have to do with Buford's disappearance?"

Wiggon rolled his eyes in obvious disgust at Stephen's lack of deductive ability. "Why, it's plain as pie. We found the wrapper under Buford's favorite shrub in the Marlowes' backyard. Looks to me like the poor guy was lured away to his fateful destiny when he fell victim to a Big Mac attack."

FIVE

"YOO-HOO!" CALLED LOUELLA ASHWORTH, SMACKING THE podium with her gavel the next Monday evening. "Ladies, ladies. Silence, please. I'm set to call this meetin' of the Bellamy Garden Club to order. And we've got us a hefty agenda tonight."

Myrna Stafford huffed into the basement meeting room at the Bellamy Public Library. "Hold your horses, Louella Ashworth. A body's got a right to stop by the ladies' room when she needs to. And at your age, I'm sure you know what I'm talkin' about."

Louella narrowed her eyes. "I'm sure I don't have a clue what you're referrin' to, Myrna. If I recollect rightly, you're a considerable bit older than me."

With a harrumph and a shake of her purple curls, Myrna took a seat. "Of course, Louella, of course. All of two days and seven whole hours older. You and I heard our mamas say so many, many times."

Ruffling the sheaf of papers in her hand and thumbing up her half-moon glasses, Louella made a point of reading her agenda. "Let's be gettin' back to business now, shall we?"

A titter ran around the room.

"First order of business for tonight is a report from the maintenance committee. Chairwoman Roberta Ann Waggleman, could you please inform us as to the condition of the fall plantings?"

The short, squat Roberta dragged herself to her feet. "We replaced eighteen mums down to Langhorn Park. Somethin's been eatin' at them somethin' fierce. But ever'thing else's doin' just fine. Just fine, I tell you."

"Thank you, Bobby Ann," Louella said. "We're much obliged to you and your group for keepin' things spruced up. You all are doin' a mighty fine job."

Setting down her papers, Louella peered at the gathered gardeners over her glasses. "Let's get down to what's really important, ladies. This matter of a Buddhist in our midst."

Sharp intakes of breath, reminiscent of wheezing bellows, echoed through the crowd.

"Oh, dear . . ."

"Then it's true!"

"How dreadful."

"Indeed . . ."

"Harrumph!"

"Now, now," Louella said, seeking to calm her minions. "I must agree it's a sad situation, especially for Sophie, who's prayed so long for that boy. But it's certainly not one we cannot conquer. Right?"

A chorus of assent chimed in.

"So are we all agreed we're in this for the long haul?"

"Yes!" cried the cultivators.

"Then may we all remember we're doin' battle for the Lord Jesus."

"Amen!" chorused the congregation.

"I knew I could count on you all," Louella said with satisfaction. "I have a plan—"

"Don't she always?" cut in Myrna, her voice acid as rain.

"Hush, now, Myrna," Philadelphia Philpott said in her whispery voice from within her cocoon of turtleneck under cardigan sweater, plaid wool skirt, hand-knit shawl, rabbit-fur earmuffs, black wool stockings, and orthopedic shoes. "This is mighty important. We're true Christian soldiers, and as president, Louella's our commandin' officer."

Myrna sniffed again. "Well, I want it on record that I ain't so sure 'bout whatever cockamamie scheme *Commander* Louella's cooked up this time."

"Duly noted," Mariah Desmond said from her front-and-center seat as recording secretary. "Now let's let our dear Lou, here, tell us what she wants us all to do."

"Thank you, Mariah," Louella said with a gracious nod. "Now, ladies. He's a doctor, right?"

Heads nodded.

"And a body gets sick *some*time, right?"

More nods.

"Well, then, here's what we're goin' to do . . ."

"Miss Philadelphia Philpott's here to see you, Dr. Hardesty," said Laura Bigler, his assistant, on Tuesday morning. "Bunions."

"Ah," answered Stephen with a grin. "Serious stuff."

Laura smiled. "To her it is."

"Show her in. I'll see what I can do."

As Laura held the door open, in scurried the tiny, elderly sprite he'd noticed on the sidewalk the day Maggie's dog was stolen, the one who indulged in the multitudinous wardrobe. "Make yourself comfortable," he said.

"Thank you, dear," she said in a soft, papery voice. "One

tries, but at my age . . ." She waved a blue-veined, age-spotted hand.

"What's this Miss Bigler tells me about your bunions?"

The pewter-toned knot at her nape bounced once. "That's right. They've been actin' up somethin' fierce lately. I figured I'd best get myself on down here and see if there isn't somethin' you can do to put them to rights again."

"Tell you what, Miss Philpott. I'm going to step outside while you remove your shoes and stockings. I'll be right back to take a look at those bunions."

Stephen took the woman's slim chart out of the room and scanned Doc Calloway's few notes. Influenza with no complications seven years ago, a simple broken tibia last year after she'd climbed her roof to clean out gutters; beyond that, Miss Philpott seemed to be the picture of elderly health.

No mention of foot troubles ever.

Several minutes later, he knocked on the door, then went back inside. On the floor at the side of the examining table, Miss Philpott had placed her clunky orthopedic shoes in perfect alignment with the grout between the tiles. On the chair where she'd sat, her thick black stockings made a tidy little square next to her boxy handbag. The lady herself perched on the very edge of the table, ankles crossed demurely, hands folded in her lap.

Stephen dropped the file on his desk. "Let's see those feet, please."

The lady complied. He examined first one, then the other fragile-skinned foot, noting how well kept that skin was, how neatly trimmed the nails. Neither big toe showed the slightest hint of inflammation at the first joint, no bunion anywhere.

"You're sure you've been having trouble with your *bunions?*" he asked.

The pert chin tipped up. "Of course I'm sure. Why, they've

been so bad I . . . I . . . couldn't hardly finish mowin' my lawn day before yesterday."

"Hmm . . ." So she'd mowed her lawn just two days ago. "Could you point with your finger to the place that hurts the most?"

She grasped the edges of her cardigan and crossed them over her thin chest. Her chin jutted a tad more. "Well, son, it's a bunion, I tell you. You're the doctor, so just look where bunions grow."

"Which foot?"

A frown. "Ah . . . both. That's right, both."

Something wasn't right about these particular bunions. "Tell you what, Miss Philpott," Stephen said to test the waters. "We're going to make sure you stay off your feet for the next three weeks—to give those bunions a chance to heal." He shook a finger at her. "No more lawn mowing for you. You have to hire someone to do that kind of hard work from now on."

Her delicate features took on a mulish set. "We'll see how long it takes me to get back on my feet—so to speak, you understand." With impressive agility, Miss Philpott bounced off the examining table, bent to snag her shoes, and went for her stockings. "Oh, and before you take off, son, I have somethin' here for you. Just friendly-like, and all, you know."

Miss Philpott rummaged in her black-patent-leather, circa-1950 handbag and withdrew a folded sheet of paper covered in black type and a colored picture. She handed it to him and gave him a gentle push toward the examining-room door. "Now, go on with you, boy. A body needs her privacy to put herself back to rights, you know. Oh, and God bless you."

Bemused, Stephen left the room as asked, his odd patient's file in one hand, her gift in the other. Closing the door behind him, he looked down at what Miss Philpott had given him.

Jesus loves you, it said in big, bold, black print.

With a rueful smile, he headed for Laura's file-laden desk.

"How bad are her toes?" his assistant asked.

He held out the tract and shook his head. "Good enough to bring her here to give me this. Miss Philadelphia Philpott is healthy as a horse. It's me she thinks is ailing. Spiritually, at that."

The next Saturday afternoon, Cammie picked up her two canvas shopping bags and turned toward the door of Desmond's Country Store. "Thanks so much for preparing my order ahead of time, Miss Sophie."

"Pshaw! It wasn't anythin' a'tall, dear. And you have so much to do already."

As she reached the end of the detergent aisle, the door opened, ringing the cowbell her future brother-in-law, Rich Desmond, used to announce the arrival of customers.

"Yoo-hoo!" called Miss Louella. "Sophie, sugar, are you plannin' on workin' late this afternoon?"

Cammie pressed back against the display of fabric softener to let Louella Ashworth truck on in toward the storage room where Miss Sophie stood. "Morning, Miss Louella," she murmured.

"Well, the dear Lord bless you, darlin' girl. I didn't even see you there." Miss Louella's gray eyes appraised Cammie. "Dear, should you be carryin' those heavy bags in your advanced condition?"

Cammie smiled and shook her head. "Honestly, everyone's so concerned about my pregnancy, and everything's going just fine. I can handle two bags of food. I'm only taking them to my van."

Miss Louella gave the sacks a final, skeptical look. "If you insist on sayin' so . . ." Turning, she resumed her trek to the back. "Now, Sophie, as I was sayin', we need your help. It's that time of year again."

"What time of year, Lou?"

"Why, it's fall, and the weather's gettin' cooler. Soon's you know it, we'll be neck deep in the white stuff. I for one won't be doin' any gardenin' in those circumstances."

"Neither will I," answered Miss Sophie. "I guess you all want me to head on over to Leesburg and pick us up a load of yarns again."

Miss Louella slapped the countertop in front of Miss Sophie. "Exactly. You do have a way with choosin' wool, since you knit round the year—don't ask me how, in the hot summer months and all. Anyway, the prices you charm those folks into givin' you . . . why, no one else can even come close. Besides, some of our ladies are on restricted incomes, I'll have you know. I'm one of 'em."

"I know all about your money troubles, Lou. That's one of the reasons Mariah and I agreed to share a house with you. Well, besides the fun, you know."

"And I'm much obliged to you both," Miss Louella answered. "So are you workin' this afternoon?"

"I wasn't plannin' on it. Rich called to say he was stuck on a tricky part of this book he's writin', and he wanted to get out of the house, so he's comin' in any minute now for a spell. But you know my problem's the car . . ."

Cammie stepped right up. "Miss Sophie, I'd be happy to take you—"

Miss Louella waved dismissively. "No need to put yourself out, Camellia. I have a splendid volunteer for the chauffeurin' duty." She turned around, hurried to the door, and yanked it open, setting the cowbell to clanging again. Then she gave one of her trademark *yoo-hoos.*

Seconds later, Willie Johnson strode into the store, followed by Stephen Hardesty.

Cammie gasped. Surely Miss Louella wouldn't be that blatant?

With an atypical giggle, the president of the Garden Club and Bellamy's matchmaker *par excellence* made a small bow. "Your chariot is ready, madam, and your charioteer awaits."

Cammie groaned inwardly. But before she could utter an objection, Stephen piped up.

"Aunt Sophie," he said, awe in his voice, "have you seen Willie's car?"

Miss Sophie gave her grandnephew a blank stare. "Can't say I'm one to notice cars much, Stephen."

"Oh, but you'd have to pay special attention to *this* one," he countered enthusiastically. "She's a powder blue 1965 Caddy, fins and all. Aunt Sophie, she's in perfect—I mean absolute mint—condition. Willie, here, has taken unbelievable care of her."

Willie-here preened. "My much-esteemed-and-admired Lady Sophie, it would do me the greatest honor and endow me with enormous pleasure to escort you on your mission to Leesburg. My humble sedan can only be enhanced by your radiant beauty."

Cammie choked a chuckle at the overflorid chatter, then caught a glimpse of Miss Sophie's flushed cheeks. *Oh, dear.*

"No need to trouble yourself, Willie," Cammie hurried to say. "I . . . I have to see my doctor sometime anyway." She sure hoped she could get an instant appointment at this last minute—on a Saturday, no less. "I'll take Miss Sophie to the wholesaler's outlet. I've taken her before, so I know the way."

Stephen arched an eyebrow and smoothed his mustache. "Problems, Cammie?"

"No, no. Not at all. It's just . . . umm . . . time for my next checkup, you see."

"I see," he said, his expression belying his words.

"So it makes sense," she continued, "for me to take your great-aunt to Leesburg with me."

"Hmm . . . ," the doctor murmured.

But at Willie's crestfallen expression, Cammie's resolve weakened. She hated disappointing anyone. Still, this was for her dear friend's own good, even if that friend now wore the same disenchanted look as her wanna-be beau. Cammie would hate for Miss Sophie to fall for Willie, then be left alone and heartbroken, as she'd been when David died.

Miss Louella trotted over to Cammie. "Now, Camellia, there's no call for you to put yourself out. You go on home now, and make your supper for tonight. I'm sure with a gentleman escortin' her, Sophie will be fine. Besides, you shouldn't be pickin' up heavy things, you know."

Cammie laughed. "Yarn? Yarn's not heavy, Miss Louella, and the wholesaler packages it in same-color lots. None of the bundles weigh more than ten pounds, if that. I can handle ten pounds. I'll take care of my dearest friend's driving needs."

Miss Louella pursed her glossed lips and jerked her head. She repeated the action, and Cammie suspected the woman hoped to recruit Cammie into the matchmaking scheme. But Cammie was having none of it.

"What's wrong, Miss Louella?" she asked, her voice sugared. "Have you developed a tic? I'm sure Dr. Hardesty wouldn't mind giving you his professional opinion on that problem. Why don't you ask him, while I take off with Miss Sophie?"

An exasperated huff burst from Miss Louella. "I don't have a tic, child. I'm just tellin' you to head on home, and let us adults take care of ourselves this afternoon."

Stephen stepped forward, a suspicious glint in his eyes. "Tell you what, Mrs. Sprague. I'll go along with Aunt Sophie and Willie. To help with all that yarn, you understand."

Having suddenly gone from Cammie to Mrs. Sprague, she feared he knew what she was up to and didn't agree with her one bit. She could play that game too.

"But don't you have all those patients to see?" she asked. "Starting with Miss Louella's tic, of course. I'm sure it must be bothering her a great deal."

"I said," Miss Louella started, "I *don't* have any tics—nervous or dog-type either. Why, I can't imagine what could ever make you say such a thing, Camellia. Anyway, I'd say it's settled. Mr. Johnson and Dr. Hardesty will take Sophie to Leesburg this afternoon while you go home and . . . and . . . *be* pregnant."

Uh-oh. Miss Louella's determination wasn't flagging. "But—but, what about my doctor's appointment?" *The one you haven't made yet,* piped up Cammie's conscience. *I will. I will,* she argued back. *As soon as I prevent this disaster.*

Miss Louella waved. "Oh, well, you can take yourself to that, then come back to your supper preparations. We wouldn't want those boys of yours to go hungry now, would we?"

"They won't," Cammie assured the obstinate Cupid. "But it's silly for us to take two cars. Just think of the wasted gas. I . . ." *Gulp!* "I'll just hitch a ride with them."

To Cammie's surprise, Miss Louella's eyes popped wide open. A look of distinct horror crossed her face. She darted glances between Cammie and Stephen and shook her head. "No, no, dear girl. It's best if you stay home—"

"I guess it's decided," cut in Dr. Hardesty. "We'll make a foursome of it. How long do you need to store your groceries, Mrs. Sprague?"

"Ah . . . oh, about fifteen minutes." Well, the groceries would take only five to put away, but the call to the OB's office to negotiate a precious Saturday appointment might take lots longer.

"Great," Stephen said with a canary-feathered grin. "We'll swing by your place and pick you up then. Come on, Willie; I can't wait to get behind the wheel of your beaut!"

Cammie stood frozen as the two men went out to the car. Rich Desmond entered the store and called a greeting. She nodded and took a step after the other two men. As she took another, Miss Louella sailed right past her.

"You'd better be on your best behavior, Camellia Bellamy Sprague," Louella muttered under her breath. "I can't believe I just saw what I did. I might have expected such contrariness from Magnolia or Lark, but you? I never . . . and after all our careful preparation."

Well, Miss Louella wasn't making any secret of her latest machinations. And evidently Stephen Hardesty was ready to hand Cupid her arrows. With a final look at Miss Sophie, Cammie took note of her friend's dreamy smile.

Oh, yes. Trouble was a-brewing.

The new Cammie, the one who'd decided to stand up for herself and for what was right, knew what she had to do. As Miss Sophie's dearest friend, Cammie knew she had to look out for the elderly lady's best interests. A cooked-up romance couldn't possibly be for the best—especially when it could lead to such sadness down the road.

Cammie would make sure things stayed as they were.

To Cammie's immense relief, the large obstetrics practice she'd decided to go to had a cancellation for that afternoon. "Thank you so much for your willingness to squeeze me in."

"Well, honey, at this late date in your pregnancy, if you're bent on changin' doctors, I'd say you should have been in here yesterday," said the appointment secretary at the other end of the line. "And on a Saturday . . . you don't know how lucky you are."

"Well, yes, I do. Thank you so much once again."

"We'll see you at one-fifteen."

She hung up and let out a sigh of relief. Muttley slurped at her knee, and she bent to scratch his neck. "You can't be hungry again, can you?"

The pup nosed his food bowl as if he'd understood her words.

"I guess you can. Hang on there, boy. I'll feed you." She measured out Muttley's midday dose of premium puppy kibble and thought about the trip ahead.

True, a lot could happen during the time she was with the obstetrician, but at least she'd be right next to Miss Sophie on the way into town and on the way back. She could nip any further trouble in the bud.

Muttley let out a loud belch and collapsed right next to his empty food bowl. His eyelids grew heavy.

Cammie smiled at her oldest baby, patting his rounded head. "I'm afraid I'm going to have to lock you back in your crate, honey bunch. Come on. I'll be leaving as soon as those *men* get here with Miss Sophie."

She dragged the uncooperative pooch to his airline-approved plastic kennel and ignored his tearful pleas. As she offered him a puppy cookie, a car horn honked outside. It sounded just like the luxury-liner-sized vehicle Willie drove around. She peeked out her front bay window, ruffling the fur behind Sheba's right ear.

"Mrrreow . . . !"

"It's good-bye, dearie. I have to do my duty by Miss Sophie."

Running out the door, Cammie donned her sunglasses and spotted her first batch of trouble. Stephen was driving. In the backseat Miss Sophie and Willie wore sappy grins, eyes on each other.

Cammie had to do something about that state of affairs. "Oh, dear," she said softly into the open rear window. "I do hate to bother you, Willie, but would you be so kind as to move to the front seat?"

Stephen gave her another piercing look. She fought to keep from squirming.

"Is something wrong?" asked Willie, obviously reluctant to relinquish his plum spot.

Stephen's eyes slanted. "Yes, Mrs. Sprague, are you and the baby all right?"

"We're fine, Dr. Hardesty. It's just having itself a very active day today. When the baby kicks so much, I find I need to stretch out to give my poor ribs a break."

Again the doctor arched his very skeptical brow. "I see."

Oooooh . . . She'd really come to hate the way he said that. He put such innuendo into those simple two words.

Willie sighed. "Well, never let it be said that Willard Johnson ever stood between a fair lady and her ease." He slid into the passenger front seat as Cammie took his place in the rear behind Stephen.

The engine roared to life and they were on their way to Leesburg.

"Buckle up," said Stephen.

"A car this old has seat belts?" Cammie asked, removing her sunglasses.

"I had her retrofitted," Willie answered, pleased to talk about his pride and joy. "Not just that, but her engine . . . well, she's souped-up, too."

Terrific. She'd insisted on sitting in the rear of a tweaked tank—she, with her pregnancy-acquired tendency toward car sickness. But when she glanced at Miss Sophie and caught her admiring the back of Willie's head, Cammie's resolve returned. Anything to help her friend.

She looked up and, to her dismay, caught Stephen's gaze in the rearview mirror. An odd light burned in his dark eyes, a question and something more. Worse yet, a warm current zipped through her at the meeting of their eyes, leaving an uncommon awareness of the man in its wake.

Stephen was like no other man she had ever met. With just one glance he could throw her equanimity out the window and replace it with . . . okay, fine, she'd admit it . . . a certain form of excitement she'd never before experienced.

It irritated her. It baffled her. It scared her.

This was not the right seat for her.

But she had only herself to blame, since she'd insisted on coming along and prying Willie from Miss Sophie's side. As she forced her eyes to focus elsewhere, Cammie doubted she'd done the smart thing. After all, the distracting new doctor seemed able to see right through her and her motives. That didn't sit well with her.

Not one bit.

SIX

A FEW HOURS LATER, AS FAR AS CAMMIE COULD TELL, SHE had accomplished only one thing by accompanying Miss Sophie, Willie, and Stephen Hardesty to Leesburg. She'd convinced her new obstetrician—Dr. Warfield—that she was nuts. He'd known Doc Calloway for years and couldn't understand why Cammie wouldn't trust Doc's replacement.

She couldn't tell Dr. Warfield—or *anyone*—that Stephen Hardesty was too attractive, too distracting, too . . . *too* for her own good.

Or, evidently, for her sanity.

Dr. Warfield performed a brief examination, had his nurse take the necessary samples, and sent Cammie on her way with a refill for her prenatal vitamin prescription. Now, as she stood on the sidewalk waiting for the others to return and pick her up, her cheeks still burned.

She had the drive back to Bellamy to survive.

Maybe this business of standing up for herself and protecting Miss Sophie wasn't all it was cracked up to be. After all, if she'd stayed home, she could have tried that new recipe for zucchini bread, worked some more on the Mariner's Compass patchwork quilt she was finishing, played with Muttley, and done all her normal routine things.

When she'd just begun to reach some measure of contentment in her life after David's death, was she crazy to fight the fire of do-gooder busybodies with the fire of her newfound assertiveness? And was that what God wanted her to do?

"We're here," called Miss Sophie as the car pulled up to a stop in front of Cammie.

Here we go again. Willie and Sophie occupied the backseat, and Stephen, leaning to open the front passenger door for Cammie, wore a steely stare. No kicking baby was going to get her wedged between the two would-be lovebirds in the rear if the good doctor had anything to do with it.

Without a comment, Cammie slipped in and buckled her seat belt.

"So," said Stephen, "what did *my colleague* have to say?"

"Very little," Cammie answered, again blushing. "Everything's going just fine. The baby's heartbeat is strong, and my blood pressure's perfect. No need to worry about us."

"What a blessing, dear," said Miss Sophie from Willie's side.

"Yes, it is," Cammie answered. On pretext of shading her eyes from the setting sun, she lowered the visor to which Willie had clipped a slip-on mirror. Although Miss Sophie had spoken to Cammie, she only had eyes for her beau.

It was all Cammie could do to keep from groaning.

Reminding herself that discretion is often the better part of valor, she kept quiet, leaning her head back against the seat. Why would Miss Sophie be willing to give the rest of her life to a man now and risk losing her contentment? At this late date?

The misery Cammie had experienced in her own marriage flashed vividly in her mind. It did something terrible to a woman to learn that her new husband loved his job a great deal more than he did her. Day by day, missed dinner by lonely weekend, she'd felt more and more diminished as a wife. As a person.

After five years of watching her dreams of family, love, and home wither, Cammie had come up with an idea. She'd prayed—oh, my, how she'd prayed. After all those prayers, she'd put her idea into motion on Valentine's Day. She'd "kidnapped" David and dragged him—yes, kicking and screaming—on a second honeymoon as a last-ditch effort to renew a sense of romance, of closeness, of marriage.

While in Barbados, her plan had seemed to work. But by the time they'd been back in Bellamy for less than a week, Cammie realized it had all been for naught. David's focus was again on his work.

Then the accident, just a couple of weeks later. He hadn't known she was pregnant—neither had she—when he died. Every time she thought of her little one growing up without a daddy, her heart nearly broke in two. *Dear Lord, will I be good enough? Can I take the place of a father?*

Although Cammie's own father had died when she was six, she held tightly to a few, crystal-clear memories of him. She remembered riding on his shoulders at the county fair one fall. He hadn't minded the dirty smudges her sneakers had drawn on his clean blue shirt.

There hadn't been anything her daddy couldn't do—not in Cammie's eyes. When a toy would break, he'd fix it or replace it with a better one. There'd been no one as good as her dad at reading stories. Every night, he'd read a chapter of a book—her favorite had been *A Little Princess*—then he'd tuck her in and, holding her hand, pray with her.

Her father had been everything a little girl could have wanted in a dad. But he'd died too early. Now her own child would have no father, no memories.

Could she do a fair job? Her sisters didn't think so. Neither did the dear, dotty ladies of the Garden Club, for they were always trying to "help" her.

Did God?

She sure hoped so, since she had very little time left before her bundle of joy would need everything she could give him or her. She rubbed her belly with her hands, and her child kicked as if to reassure her. Renewed joy at David's legacy filled her. Of course she could do it. With God's help she could do *anything.*

Even keep Miss Sophie from making the greatest mistake ever—falling for a man again. That risky maneuver could only bring heartache to a woman when the man was older, or when he found himself drawn to his other priorities once the honeymoon was over.

Cammie sat up straight. She realized the others had been having a grand old time while she'd been mulling over her past. Now they were laughing at something Willie had said.

"My goodness," said Miss Sophie, "would you just look at the time? I don't reckon an afternoon has ever gone by quite so fast."

"Dearest lady," Willie answered, launching into his troubadour voice, "might I remind you of that old chestnut: Time flies when one's having fun."

Cammie rolled her eyes, then caught her friend's rosy cheeks and smile in the rearview mirror. Time to do something here before things got any more out of hand. "We don't have much longer to go now, Miss Sophie," she said. "Ten minutes or so, I reckon. Would you be willing to come over and keep me company while I make supper?"

Her elderly friend leaned forward and patted Cammie's shoulder. "Why, of course, dear. I'd be delighted—*if* these gentlemen would be so kind as to deliver the yarn to Louella.

I'd hate to keep her waitin' for it until I return home later this evenin'."

"That'll be fine, Aunt Sophie," Stephen said, his gaze boring into Cammie. "I'll drop you, Willie, and Mrs. Sprague at her home, then take the wool to Miss Louella. I'll come back, park the car in the garage, then head on over to my place."

"Nonsense, dear boy," Willie said. "By all means deliver the string to Louella, but come back to the house for supper." Cammie's elderly boarder turned to her. "You'll have plenty to feed another, won't you?"

What could she say? "I always do." Although Cammie had to force it, she smiled. "But why don't you go with Dr. Hardesty, Willie? I'm sure he'd like the company and the chance to chat about your car some more. Miss Sophie and I can indulge ourselves with some good old girl talk."

Yech! If that had sounded as silly to the others as she'd felt saying it, she'd soon be on the receiving end of another one of those perceptive and amused looks from good old Dr. Hardesty.

Yes. There it was.

"I think I can handle the wool by myself," he said. "And I've already talked Willie's ear off about the car all the way back from Leesburg. You must have fallen asleep." Stephen's rascally grin made it clear he didn't think anything of the sort.

"Oh, I didn't sleep," Cammie answered, wishing the ride over. "I was just . . . thinking through my meal preparation. I like to be ready."

"Why, dear," said Miss Sophie, "are you tryin' out a new dish? You always work so smoothly and with hardly any thought to what you're doin', knowin' your recipes as well as you do."

Good grief. Were they all onto her?

"No," she hurried to say, "I'm not trying out anything new.

I'm just making sure I have all the ingredients I need, and that I remember where I put everything the last time I used them. I'm a little later than usual starting the meal tonight, you know."

"Well, aren't you glad we're finally home?" asked Stephen, the twitching of his mustache revealing his struggle with laughter, at her expense.

"Indeed," Cammie said, scrambling out of the car despite her rounded middle. "Come on, Miss Sophie. I can't wait to brew up a pot of tea and get that meat loaf cooking."

"Ah, yes," Stephen commented archly, "a most tricky dish, that meat loaf. Go on, Willie. I bet they'll soon be glad for your slicing and dicing help in the kitchen. I'll be back once I complete my errand for Miss Louella and the ladies of the Garden Club. Have fun!"

This time he failed to squash his chuckle. Cammie caught her bottom lip between her teeth. That man. Why did he have to be as sharp as he was good-looking? Evidently quick to laugh, too.

At her.

No. This entire situation didn't sit right with her at all. And she had to endure another supper with him in her hair.

Dear Jesus, she prayed as she climbed her front stairs, the pair of chattering senior citizens behind her, *why did you have to bring this particular man to this particular town at this particular time? Couldn't you have taken him elsewhere? Help me, Father. Help me handle this intriguing would-be Buddhist of Miss Sophie's.*

As soon as she finished her prayer, words rang in the deepest center of her heart. *He's not Miss Sophie's, Camellia. He's my child—lost, but he's mine. Just as you are mine.*

She faltered, nearly falling over her own two feet. Or had she suddenly grown a third one for the express purpose of tripping her up? As if Stephen needed any help doing that all on his own.

"Oh, Cammie, darlin'," Miss Sophie cried, reaching for her. "Are you all right?"

Pulling herself together, Cammie answered, "I hope so. I sure do hope so."

That night, Cammie proved to be all thumbs. She dropped nearly everything she picked up, breaking two glasses and a saucer. Miss Sophie had to warn her as she went to pour vanilla instead of Worcestershire sauce into the meat loaf mixture. She scorched the milk for the scalloped potatoes, scooped the pecan-butterscotch cookies off the baking sheet before they'd cooled enough not to turn into mush, and cut herself as she sliced mushrooms for a salad.

All because of the man who'd taken it upon himself to keep Muttley entertained since he'd returned from his errand for Miss Louella. From the sounds of the playful growling and masculine chuckles wafting back from the parlor, Cammie deduced that the two had become best of friends. One could see that puppy didn't have a hair of discernment on his furry body. Couldn't he tell that Stephen was doing everything in his power to keep Willie in Miss Sophie's pocket?

Who would have thought a big-city doctor would wind up being as much trouble as Miss Louella and the rest of the Garden Club? And who would have thought that same big-city doctor could rattle calm, small-town Camellia Bellamy Sprague to the point where she practically ruined a meal?

Not her, not ever.

She ate her supper in virtual silence. Those around the table cast frequent questioning looks her way, but she wasn't about to say a word. What could she say? That she was afraid of voicing anything that might make Stephen or Willie any more determined to lull Miss Sophie into the deceptive euphoria of romance?

Nuh-uh. Not her.

So she kept her peace, even though she felt none of that special commodity deep inside. Although she prayed for God to bless her with an extra measure of it, and brewed the after-dinner coffee in expectation of that godly gift, it never got to her. Even if it had, all semblance of peace would have vanished the moment Willie led Miss Sophie to her favorite spot on the love seat and parked himself right by her ever-present knitting bag.

"Here we are," Cammie said, setting down the tray. "Please help yourselves."

While Willie and Stephen did as she'd suggested, she looked around the room in desperation. What could she do to keep that long-in-the-tooth lothario from plying any more of his wiles on her dear friend? Not that there was anything wrong with Willie himself. After all, she loved the old scamp. What Cammie so opposed was the threat he represented to her friend's settled life—and to Miss Sophie's innocent, romantic heart.

But Cammie saw nothing to inspire her. The parlor looked as it always did: her English porcelain gleamed, her quilts softened, the gourds in the basket on the fireplace apron cheered, and the fire in the hearth sparked and crackled.

As Willie went back to take his seat next to Miss Sophie, an idea struck Cammie. "I think this would be a lovely time to rearrange the accessories in here," she said, beaming a bright smile to all. "Yes, of course. Stephen's height will be a boon, and Willie's eye for detail will serve me well. You'll tell me what works and what doesn't, won't you, Miss Sophie?"

Thankfully the junior residents of the home weren't around at the moment, the three of them busy with their studies.

Cammie didn't think she could have survived any more looks of the sort aimed at her right then.

Stephen stared at her as if she'd sprouted seven heads and wings, not to mention spouted a new language. Willie's befuddlement showed in his wrinkly frown and his total quiet.

Miss Sophie was the worst, however. Cammie's efforts on her behalf had only managed to frighten the older woman. "Camellia, I purely think you've overdone it today, sugar. It's time you called it a day. I'm goin' to brew you a nice cup of chamomile, bring it up to your room, and tuck you into bed."

Heading out of the parlor, Miss Sophie continued, her words interspersed with maternal clucks. "I don't know what gets into these girls these days."

As if Miss Sophie's take-charge actions had jolted the two men back to their senses, both grew overly solicitous. Willie she could handle, but Stephen? He was another matter altogether.

In his most doctorly voice, he said, "I think it'd be best if you did as Aunt Sophie suggested. As soon as you're in bed I'll come up and check on you and the baby. We wouldn't want a stressful day to cause any trouble at this late date. Fortunately, my new ultrasound machine is up and running, so we can take advantage of it and do a sonogram sometime tomorrow. You don't have to go to Leesburg for one anymore, you know. I'm stocking my clinic with the most up-to-date equipment available. I'm committed to providing every bit as good of care for Bellamy as that which is available in larger cities—"

"Oh, for goodness' sake!" Cammie burst out in frustration. "There's not a single thing wrong with me but that I want to rearrange some things in this room. What's wrong? Can't a woman change the looks of her house these days?"

"At seven-thirty at night?" Willie asked, again wearing that look of extreme puzzlement.

Cammie couldn't believe the can of worms she'd just opened. "What does the time of day have to do with anything—"

Mercifully, the doorbell rang. With a brief prayer of thanksgiving, she hurried to open the door.

"Where's Muttley?" demanded Lark as she stormed into the house, her curly red hair rioting, green eyes blazing. She wore an expression that Cammie considered pugnaciously journalistic.

A muffled *whoof* came from the oval braided rug on the fireplace apron, the pup's favorite place at night.

Cammie reached out to halt her sister's wild pacing. "What's wrong, Lark? Muttley's right where he should be. Lying over there. What are *you* doing here?"

Lark tugged on her short curls, a distinct sign of trouble. "You're not going to believe this. I can hardly believe it, and I'm the one who found the evidence."

"Did you learn something about Buford's disappearance?" Cammie asked.

Lark wriggled out of Cammie's clasp and started marching back and forth all over again, this time clenching her fists at her hips. "Hardly. This is too much—just too, too much."

"Lark, please," Cammie said, frightened.

Stephen stepped in front of Cammie's distraught sister and clasped her shoulder in a firm grip. "Take a deep breath, Lark. You've suffered a shock of some kind. Breathe deeply, evenly. In . . . out; in . . . out . . ."

Stephen's masterful tone and actions calmed Lark's jerky, nervous movements. Unfortunately, they also brought about an uncharacteristic reaction: she started to cry. Great big, racking sobs ripped from Lark as tears flowed down her cheeks.

Cammie went to her sister's side and wiped the tears with a tissue she had taken from the dispenser by her quilting frame.

Running footsteps came from the front porch. Assessing the situation before him, Willie sprang into action. He opened the door, and Rich Desmond, Lark's soon-to-be husband, ran in.

"Is she here—oh, thank you, Jesus," he said reverently. "Why didn't you wait for Wiggon?" he asked his fiancée. "I'm sure he's waiting for you at your house, and, instead, you're here."

Lark shuddered. "I had to make sure Cammie's Muttley was okay. I couldn't let the same thing happen to that poor puppy as happened to . . . to Mycroft."

Cammie's heart pounded harder. "Oh, Lark, honey. What happened to *your* puppy?"

Before Lark could answer, yet more footsteps, these heavy, came up the front steps. "Figgered I'd find you all here," said Wiggon, huffing. "I got me a call sayin' somethin' was wrong with your dog, Lark. What happened?"

Anger flared in Lark's eyes. "Nothing better have happened to that poor, innocent pooch."

Wiggon doffed his hat and scratched his head. "So then why'd you call me?"

"This is why," Lark cried, holding something out.

Cammie looked, blinked, then squinted to get a better view of what her sister had pulled out of her loose carpenter-jeans pocket. At first Cammie thought her eyes had betrayed her, but upon further examination, she ascertained that they hadn't. "Lark," she asked, "why are you holding a crushed-up box of Twinkies?"

"Can't you figure it out?"

"I'm not the ace reporter, you are."

"Well, it doesn't take a Pulitzer prizewinner to know what happened."

At that moment, Rich stepped up and, removing his future wife from Stephen Hardesty's clasp, wrapped both arms around Lark. "I'll tell them, sweetheart."

Facing the others, he said, "Mycroft's missing, and Lark found that box of Twinkies next to the doghouse in her backyard. She's sure someone used the cakes to lure him away."

"Aha!" cried Wiggon. "I'll be a two-headed skunk. Why, it's the same *mow-deuce oh-pear-ann-dye!* We got us someone in town who's got it in for the Bellamy sisters. Yessir, this investigation's heatin' up right nice, I'd say."

"So what are you doin' about it?" asked Lark. "Have you found any trace of Buford's thief? Have you interrogated Maggie's neighbors? Have you put out a bulletin with the dog's description? And what about that fast-food wrapper you found in Maggie's yard? Have you had it analyzed—"

Rich gently covered Lark's lips with a firm finger. "I'm sure the police are doing their best to find Buford, honey. Let's get you back to your house, give Wiggon a chance to check over the scene of the crime, ask us any questions he wants, and let your *pregnant* sister catch some sleep."

"Fine," Lark answered. "But, Cammie? You make sure you keep a close eye on Muttley. Who knows what's goin' on here? I sure don't want him snatched away, too."

Cammie turned to Muttley, who sat watching the action, his funny little head turning from one human to the next as the conversation poured out. He looked so sweet that she just had to go to his side and rub between his ears.

"Don't you worry yourself about Muttley," she said. "I'll be happy to take good care of him. You just let Rich see you home and let Wiggon carry out his investigation. I'm sure this is all just some kind of misunderstanding that will soon be straightened out."

She hoped. Because from where she stood, it smelled

awfully foul. Two sisters, two stolen dogs—in less than a week.

As the trio left the house, Cammie found herself face-to-face with Stephen. At that instant, he looked less like a troublesome cupid than the hero of the moment. "Thanks for helping my sister," she said. "Lark is very intense. It's what makes her such an outstanding reporter and businesswoman. I don't think I could have kept her from chasing off after whoever took her dog."

"Part of the job, ma'am," Stephen answered, obviously trying to lighten the moment. "As a doctor, I've learned that even, directed breathing is the best thing to restore a person's sense of balance. And according to the Zen masters I've been reading recently, even breathing can also lead to peace through regular *zazen* practice."

Cammie tried the word on for size. "Zah-zenn?"

"*Zazen.* Meditation. Zen teaches that when one focuses on one's breath, one recognizes that everything is nothing but an illusion. That's when troubles and stress fall away as the practitioner recognizes them for the absurdity they truly are. This leaves one's mind empty, ready to be filled with true enlightenment."

"Ah," Cammie murmured. "So that's what Buddhists believe."

"Yes, well," said Miss Sophie from where she'd stood during Lark's disturbing visit. "I don't cotton to any of that Zenny Boodhy stuff, Stephen. I'm sure your parents raised you differently. And I *know* I've taught you differently. If that Eastern stuff is supposed to leave your mind empty . . ." She let her words die off, her eyebrow arched meaningfully. Before Stephen had a chance to speak on his own behalf, his great-aunt continued. "Almighty God is the one and awesome God who gave his only begotten Son to die for our sins," she said, bustling back to her knitting. "Jesus gave his all for you back on that cross at Calvary, and all this illusion and sass-ssen nonsense and empty-headedness is just interferin' with your relationship with him. I've told you this a million times if I've told you once."

She stuffed her jade green project into her bag, then turned to her beau. "You can take me home now, Willard, if you please. I've had just about all I can push past my craw of Stephen's philosophy stuff."

Cammie stared at her friend in disbelief. Miss Sophie? She'd never known the sweet, gentle older lady to have a sharp edge to her tongue. But, boy, she'd sure found it tonight.

True, Stephen had been speaking of things that to Cammie sounded pretty strange. But Miss Sophie had sure laid into him hard.

A prickling of sympathy tickled her heart. As Miss Sophie made her grand exit, accompanied by the beaming Willie, Cammie reached toward Stephen's arm. Although her fingers felt the strength of muscle and sinew she viewed each time he moved, she recognized that, in his heart, he was weak and needy. "I'm sorry. I don't know what got into her. I've never seen Miss Sophie like that before."

Stephen covered the hand she'd placed on his forearm with one of his own. Warmth tingled through her.

"Don't worry about it," he said. "I'm used to her. We've been having this kind of flare-up for the past several years. She's never understood my search for spiritual fulfillment."

Cammie didn't think she'd ever get used to anyone she cared about turning his or her back on God and following such a bizarre set of beliefs, but she didn't think it prudent to say so. Or that she'd be praying for him to realize that spiritual fulfillment separate from Jesus just didn't exist.

Instead, she qualified her apology. "I'm sorry it happened in my house. I try to keep an atmosphere of peace and joy here, but tonight . . . I don't know. I-I guess I wasn't rightly myself either."

Stephen gave her fingers a gentle squeeze, then let go. The warmth she'd experienced cranked up a notch, and Cammie felt her cheeks catch on fire.

To her relief, Stephen didn't seem to notice. "A good reason for me to go home then," he said. "You're sure you and the baby will be okay?"

Now her cheeks blazed. Oh, dear. "I'm certain. Don't be worrying about us. We'll be just fine."

Muttley chose that moment to mouth one of his loud, yowly yawns.

Human gazes met, and they both laughed. The laughter slowly died as a sense of ease flowed between them. Each had developed a great affection for the funny little dog, and that yawn had brought them another measure of closeness.

"Good night," Stephen said.

"Good night," Cammie answered.

They walked toward the door together. As he made his way down the porch steps, she added, "May the Lord Jesus go with you and bless you."

Stephen paused, glanced over his shoulder, then walked on.

Cammie watched him go, remembering the pleasure she'd felt as they'd both laughed at her dog. And the warmth that had flooded her at his gentle touch. She caught her breath.

Stephen was nice. Very, very nice.

That was scary.

SEVEN

"DEAR ME, DR. HARDESTY," SAID MRS. FLORINDA SUMNER when he walked into the examining room. "Did you hear what happened night before last?"

Stephen arched his eyebrow. "About . . . ?"

"Why, about dear Lark's doggie!"

"I'm afraid I did."

As soon as the door to his office had opened that morning, every patient he'd seen had regaled him with varying versions of the tale of Lark's stolen Mycroft. Even Laura, his assistant, was up on the details—what few details there seemed to be.

"Well, isn't that just the awfulest thing you ever heard?" Mrs. Sumner continued.

"With all due respect, ma'am, there are many worse things. To be honest, the condition of your eyes strikes me as more troubling than a missing dog."

At the elderly woman's shocked look, Stephen felt he had to explain himself. "Don't get me wrong. I love animals and can't stomach the thought of harm coming to any of them. But a woman's vision is of much more importance to me than a dog who might have run off for a rambunctious romp."

"You don't rightly believe that now, do you?"

"I'm afraid I don't know enough about the situation to be sure what to believe. Besides, for all we know, the dog's back home by now."

Mrs. Sumner shook her head so hard her eyeglasses bounced down to the tip of her nose. "No, I heard it straight from Savannah Hollings, who got it right from Sarah Langhorn, who called LaDonna Morgan, who talked with Myrna Stafford this mornin'. And if anyone wants to know *anythin'* what goes on in Bellamy, why, they know to call Myrna for every last little detail."

Stephen stifled a smile. So the purple-curled curmudgeon spent her days sniffing out local gossip. "And where would Myrna get her facts?"

His patient shrugged. "You know, I never thought to ask. She likely called one of the Bellamy girls or else had herself a chat with Louella Ashworth first thing."

"I see. Now, about your eyes . . . ?"

"Well, I didn't come see you about my eyes. They're not troublin' me overmuch these days."

"Okay. What *did* you need me for?"

"It's like this, son. It sure looks like I got myself an ingrown toenail."

"Ah, yes. Those can be very painful, even though they're not especially serious."

Mrs. Sumner smiled and nodded.

He cast a look at her feet, clad in thick, pinky beige support hose and the latest offering from Nike. "I'm afraid I can't see through your stockings and shoes."

The lady twittered and flushed. "Oh, silly me. Well, I will have to have my privacy while I . . . well, you know—" she lowered her voice—"disrobe my legs and feet."

Stephen forced his features into their normal, neutral cast

and stepped outside. When he closed the door, the chuckles burst out.

"What's so funny, boss?" asked Laura from her desk a couple of yards away.

He shook his head. "Trust me, you had to be there."

"Who're you seein' now?" Laura checked the computer screen in front of her. "Oh, Florinda. She's sweet."

"I'm not about to argue that."

"But you know," Laura said skeptically, "she's one of them Garden Club ladies. They're a caution sometimes."

"I'm beginning to learn that." He chuckled again. "I'd better get back in there and see about that ingrown toenail of hers."

"Toenail? I thought she came to see you about heart palpitations." With a glance at the notebook to the right side of her desk, Laura added, "There it is. The note I made this morning when she called to make the appointment."

"She didn't say a thing to me about her heart. I'd better take a listen just in case."

"Don't forget her toenail."

"As if I could," Stephen countered, wondering what was really bothering the old woman.

Inside the examining room, Mrs. Sumner sat on the table. "I'm ready," she chirped as he came close.

"My assistant says you mentioned heart palpitations this morning. Let me take your pulse and listen to your heart before I look at that nail."

"Why . . . I . . . mercy! What's come over that dear girl? I'm sure I didn't say a thing about my heart. It's my toenail, son, what's gone bad. Maybe you should take a look at your assistant. Maybe she's goin'—" Florinda darted looks around the room—"through the *change.*"

Stephen was certain that at twenty-nine Laura had years

ahead of her before menopause. "I'll look into it, Mrs. Sumner, *after* we listen to your heart and look at your toe."

A chastened expression came over her face. "Very well."

The lady's heart rang steady and sure, no sign of palpitations, extra beats, or irregularities. Stephen turned to the toe. "Let's see your nail."

A soft pink foot landed on his palm, the nails tinted a pale shade of peach. None looked as though its edge had grown into the adjoining tissue.

"Now which one's the one you say is hurting?"

"The big one."

Stephen stared at the indicated, well-maintained toe and pressed all around the nail. The skin looked clear, the nail growing straight. Florinda's occasional "Ouch" coincided with none of his prods.

There was nothing wrong with that toe. "Let me see the other one, please."

He was happy to note the identical condition of the other foot. "Well, Mrs. Sumner, I can assure you your toenails are not ingrowing. In fact, your feet are perfectly healthy—as are your legs. I see no reason for you to wear such thick, tight hose. Maybe the heavy weave is pressing against your toes and causing your discomfort."

"Oh. Well, I never thought of that. I've been wearin' these kind of hose since I was—" again that theatrical whisper—"in the family way. I'm sure you have a point there and have solved my problem. Now, if you'll let me set myself to rights again, I'll be on my way to not troublin' you anymore today."

"No, trouble, ma'am. I'm here to help."

"Well, dear boy, there is the chance *I* can help *you.*"

"Oh?"

"Hold on to your britches now, and I'll get it for you."

Mrs. Sumner gingerly stepped off the table, wriggled her manicured toes when they touched the cold tile, and went to her large straw bag. "Now where is it? I know I put it in here this mornin'—aha! There you are."

Turning, she jabbed Stephen's middle with a slim blue paperback. "Here. Put it to good use now, you hear?"

Bemused, Stephen took the book. "Take care of yourself. And make sure Laura gives you the order for a stress test I want you to have. Just to make sure your heart's in as good a shape as I think, you understand."

She pursed her lips as though to hold in an objection.

Outside the room, Stephen confirmed his suspicion. *The Holy Gospel according to St. John.* Hmm . . . could it be a coincidence? Highly unlikely, in view of his great-aunt's displeasure a couple of nights before.

He sighed. At least the ladies meant well, even though he couldn't buy all that about a personal relationship with God through his Son, no matter how staunchly they—and Aunt Sophie—believed. In his experience, relationships didn't add up to much. One look at his distant, disappointing, shallow family was all the proof he needed.

That was why he'd recently begun looking into Zen Buddhism, his latest dabbling in a long list of possible paths to spirituality. Seeking personal enlightenment by understanding one's own self didn't require establishing troublesome, unsatisfactory, potentially pain-causing relationships. After all, few people were as unconditionally loving, forgiving, faithfully trustworthy, and open as Aunt Sophie. That was why Stephen loved the old dear so much—despite his negative opinion of relationships. Besides, the detachment of Zen promised peace, the commodity he most avidly sought.

Tossing the book on his desk, Stephen headed toward the other examining room, where he hoped his next patient would need real, modern, state-of-the-art medical help. *That* he had mastered and could provide. Spiritual truth? He'd sought it for so long . . . what could lead him there?

Five days after Lark's Mycroft was stolen, Cammie met Miss Sophie for their usual Thursday lunch date.

"How've you been, honey?" Miss Sophie asked as they hugged.

"Perfectly fine," Cammie answered, still feeling pangs of guilt over the concern she'd caused her friend last Saturday night.

Miss Sophie released a deep breath. "I'm so glad to hear that. I've been prayin' up a storm for you and that baby-child."

"Don't quit now." Cammie took her usual spot at the booth they always used. "I'm not so sure what to expect with labor and delivery."

Miss Sophie sat across from her. "I can't help you there, sugar. You know my deepest regret is never bein' blessed with a child."

"Now you know that's not totally true," Cammie countered, patting the soft white hand. "You have me, and you're practically a mother to me. I'm counting on you being my little one's granny, you know."

"Dear child . . . ," Miss Sophie whispered, her eyes welling with tears.

"Now, girls," said Ellamae, Hobey's wife and owner of Ellamae's Dinner Diner, "what's this tearin' up I see today? What's wrong?"

Dabbing her eyes with a napkin, Miss Sophie shook her head. "Nothin's wrong, Ellamae. This sweet girl here just made me the happiest old woman in this town—no, in the whole wide world."

Ellamae stuck her pencil in her gray beehive and scooted in the booth right next to Miss Sophie. "You go on and tell me all 'bout it, honey. I just love good news."

Cammie chuckled. "It's not that big a thing, Ellamae. I just told Miss Sophie I'm counting on her to be my baby's granny."

The sassy diner proprietress slapped Cammie's hand. "Is so a great big thing. It ain't every day a woman gets herself a grandbaby." Turning to Sophie, she added, "I'm right jealous of you. Neither of my two boys is doin' much of anythin' 'bout makin' me a granny. I tell you, it's all that livin' out there in them heathen big cities. Why'd they have to go and move themselves to New York and L.A.?"

"I know what you're sayin', Ellamae," answered Miss Sophie. "I'm just plumb tickled the good Lord kept my precious Camellia here in town. Oh, and no matter what that Zenny Boodhy nephew of mine says, God's brought him here now for a reason. A good one, I'm sure."

"So it's true what we been hearin' then, Sophie," boomed Horace Hobey, who'd just stepped in from his wife's diner's kitchen. "That boy o' Dale's went an' got hisself hooked up wid 'em Eastern folks, huh?"

"True enough," Miss Sophie said, then dove into the menu.

Since they both always ordered the same meal and never bothered with menus, Cammie realized the subject must distress her friend. "What are you working on these days, Hobey?" she asked, hoping to change the topic. "Did you finish the police department walls?"

"While back." Dismissing that vein of talk, Hobey turned back to Miss Sophie. "Tell me, now. Did Dale ever teach that boy o' his 'bout Jesus? Or did he just let 'im run wild? That might could explain why he's wound up turnin' to fahrrin' faiths an' such."

Miss Sophie gave a tight shake of her head. "I can't speak for Dale and Regina." Dropping her menu on the tabletop, she added, "How's this chicken 'n dumplings of yours, Ellamae?"

The diner's owner gaped. "What *are* you talkin' 'bout, Sophie Hardesty? You know you always eat the pot roast sandwich on toasted potato bread."

Slamming the laminated folder shut, Miss Sophie tipped her chin. "Well, I decided to change my mind today. I'll have the chicken."

Ellamae pulled the pencil from its spot in her hair and scribbled on her order pad. She turned to Cammie. "Are you gonna choose somethin' new, too?"

Cammie nibbled on her bottom lip. "No. I'll have my usual chicken salad sandwich. And sweet tea, please."

Ellamae sighed. "That's better." To Miss Sophie she said, "I s'pose you're not gonna want your regular birch beer soda now, are you?"

Miss Sophie stared at her utensils. "No, I'll have the soda just the same."

Ellamae tromped off, muttering beneath her breath.

Hobey dropped his massive body to a squatting position at Miss Sophie's side. "Listen here, sister. Don't give up prayin' for that Stephen o' yours. The Lord answers fervent prayers, you know. An' you're one mighty fine prayer warrior. I'll be doin' some talkin' with the Father 'bout the boy, too. Don't you go frettin', though. 'Cast all your worries . . .' an' all that." He patted Miss Sophie's shoulder, then followed his wife back to the kitchen.

Cammie reached for her friend's hand. "Would it help to know I've begun praying for Stephen, too?"

Miss Sophie met Cammie's gaze. Tears pooled in her eyes, but these were very different from the earlier ones. "It helps a great deal, sugar. And I'm sorry to have ruined our lunch like this."

"Hush, now. You haven't ruined a thing. Why, we haven't even begun to catch up with each other yet."

Asking silently for the Lord's help, Cammie did her level best to keep the lunch conversation heading in a cheerful direction.

At about ten minutes before twelve on Thursday, Stephen got a personal phone call. He only managed a few "yeses," some "I sees," a couple of "hmms . . ." and a "well, yes, I can, but—"

In the end, he wound up agreeing with his caller and leaving the office to do something he would never have imagined himself doing. Some things just boggled the mind when one thought about them too much, so he concentrated on the vibrant colors of the season as he walked toward his destination. A lover of nature in all its gorgeous forms, Stephen had always enjoyed the arrival of fall.

Focusing on the beauty surrounding him and knowing what he'd face all too soon, he decided he needed all the distance and detachment he could get from any thought, opinion, or preconceived notion. He needed to try to experience his oneness with the universe in order to regard himself and his mission within Zen's context of absolute absurdity.

"Why, Camellia, dear. Look behind you and see who's come into the diner," Miss Sophie said as they were finishing their respective meals.

From the look on her lunch companion's face, Cammie knew only too well. "Looks like Willie got hungry."

Miss Sophie pursed her lips. "He's not the only one, it would seem."

Cammie turned. Heading straight for their table were both Willie and Stephen, who seemed joined at the hip of late.

"Hello, ladies," said Stephen.

Cammie murmured a greeting.

Miss Sophie simpered—in Cammie's opinion—and scooted over to let Willie slide in at her side.

Here we go again.

"May I?" asked Stephen.

What could she say? "Of course." Then, noting how tightly the two across from her were wedged in the booth, an idea struck her. "Tell you what. You're so tall, and I'm so pregnant that we each take up more than our fair share of the sitting space on this bench. It makes more sense if I sit next to Miss Sophie. She and I will take up a lot less room together, and you two gentlemen will be more comfy that way."

Stephen's stare got to her again.

"Then again, maybe not," she acquiesced, returning to the final crumbs of her chicken salad sandwich.

"Heard anything about your sisters' missing dogs lately?" Stephen asked after he and Willie had ordered their meals.

"Nothing new. Wiggon's certain the two dogs were stolen—both are purebred and relatively valuable—and by the same person."

He neatened his smile-quirked mustache. "The junk food *modus operandi,* I presume."

Cammie couldn't hold back a chuckle. "It's his favorite theory. He insists the same person took both dogs. He's certain it's someone who's too fond of junk food."

"How about Lark? Is she still as upset as the other night?"

"Well, she's calmed down some, but she's as determined as ever to sniff out whoever took the dogs. In fact, she talked Wiggon into sending that grubby McDonald's wrapper and that soggy Twinkies box off to the state police lab for testing."

"That's not a bad idea," Stephen said, leaning back to let

Ellamae slide before him a mountainous salad topped with grilled chicken. "Maybe the 'evidence' does have something to tell us."

"We have something to tell *you,*" said Willie. "Just as soon as I'm done with my soup and sandwich, my dearest Sophie has consented to accompany me on a stroll down to Langhorn Park. We intend to partake of the banquet of leaf colors creation has set out before us mere mortals. Care to come along?"

Oh no! Stephen Hardesty was a wily one, all right. He'd kept Cammie so involved in his discussion of her sisters' missing dogs that she'd failed to pay any attention to what was going on under her very nose.

"Yoo-hoo!"

Terrific. He had even called out the major artillery as backup. "Hi, there, Miss Louella," Cammie said.

"I'm so glad to find you here, honey," the president of the Garden Club said.

"Me?"

"Yes, you. You're the chairwoman of the Bellamy Community Church's Baskets for Babies ministry, aren't you?"

"Well, yes. But we just had our meeting last night, and there was nothing left to do before November and Thanksgiving."

"There is now," Miss Louella said, satisfaction in her eyes. "The reverend asked me to fetch you to him straightaway."

Cammie looked at Miss Sophie and Willie. She glared—politely, of course—at Stephen. She frowned at Miss Louella. In the end, however, she knew when she'd been beat. "Fine." Turning to Stephen, she said, "If you'll excuse me?"

He stood and extended his hand to help her out. Cammie looked at it, remembering the previous times they'd touched. That hand was dangerous. It did . . . interesting things to her middle. Not to mention rattling her brain.

No way was she taking hold of it again.

Nuh-uh.

Then again, she couldn't bring herself to insult the man that way. It wouldn't be a Christlike thing to do. Swallowing her nervousness, she slipped her fingers over Stephen's. Again, that intriguing tingle ran up her arm, turned into rich warmth in her belly, then fizzed up toward her brain. She couldn't even think about what it did to her breathing.

Why did this man have to be the new doctor in town? Why did he have to be so attractive? Why did he have to be a spiritual seeker—instead of a Christian?

Forcing those thoughts to the farthest corner of her mind, Cammie let go of Stephen's hand. To her amazement, he didn't move away as she'd expected. Instead, he seemed reluctant to release her hand. When he looked up, his eyes appeared darker, and to her mind, mirrored her own surprise, her own bewilderment.

What was happening here?

Maybe it *was* for the best if she hurried over to the church.

"You'll call me later and let me know what's wrong, won't you, Camellia?" asked Miss Sophie.

Oh no! Who was going to watch out for Miss Sophie? "Of course I will."

"Why, Hobey, what are you doin' here for lunch?" Miss Louella asked as Hobey emerged from the kitchen, cutting off Cammie's worries. "I thought you were always much too busy to come and enjoy your wife's good cookin'."

To Cammie's amazement, Hobey turned dark red all over, even across his nearly bald head.

"Well, Louella," he answered, "I had me some bidness to look after this mornin' over to Leesburg. By the time I was done, I figgered it'd be a good idea to come an' give Ellamae a hug an' steal myself one of her sandwiches. I'm headin' back to the site right now, though."

A light went on in Cammie's head. "Where are you working these days?"

"Over to Daltree's, down by Langhorn Crick."

Perfect! "I'm on my way over to the BCC myself," Cammie said, "but I'd like to have a private minute of your valuable time."

"Of course, Miss Cammie."

Hobey led her to two empty stools at the counter. "Will this do?"

Cammie glanced over her shoulder. None of the others were paying them any mind. That she could tell, anyway. "I think so."

"Wanna tell ol' Hobey what's troublin' you? It ain't the past again, now izzit?"

She took a paper napkin from the chrome holder and began to wad it up. "It's a mite embarrassing, actually. But please bear with me until I've told you the whole story."

Hobey's eyebrows shot up toward the top of his bare pate. "I thought you said y'only wanted a minute o' my time?"

"Oh, I won't be long. It's pretty simple."

In minutes, Cammie had laid out the whole scenario for Hobey. She took a deep breath. "Now comes the hard part," she admitted. "I have a favor to ask."

"An' that would be . . . ?"

The napkin in her hands tore, the soft rip striking her ears as loudly as the Bellamy High School's marching band. "Please go with Miss Sophie and Willie down to the park and keep him from sweeping her off her feet," she blurted out in a rush.

Hobey pulled a billed cap out of his back pocket, turned it around a few times, tugged it on his head, and tapped the countertop. "Let me get this straight here. You want ol' Hobey to play party pooper to Miss Louella's cupid?"

"Oh, and Dr. Hardesty's just as bad as she is."

"Mm-hmm." He nudged the bill of his cap so it didn't block his view and studied her. "Can I ask you a question, Miss Cammie?"

"Why, sure."

"When did the heavenly Father anoint you Miss Sophie's keeper?"

Cammie gasped. "Why, Hobey, I'm not any such thing. I'm just being a friend. I'm trying to look out for her best interests."

"Are you, now?"

His scrutiny made her mighty uncomfortable. "Of course."

"Tell me, here. If that was you over yonder, would you be wantin' your friend to come buttin' in on your romance? If it is a romance goin' on 'stead of just another friendship, that is."

"Trust me. Willie's got romance on the mind, all right."

"That weren't my question, Miss Cammie. How 'bout you look at things this way. How'd you like it if them sisters o' yours was to come in an' decide who you could take yourself a private walk with?"

Hobey's question stole Cammie's breath away. She'd hate it. No doubt about it. Was that what she was doing to Miss Sophie? Butting in where she shouldn't? Where she wasn't welcome? Where she had no right to go?

No. Of course not.

She couldn't be.

It wouldn't be a particularly Christian thing to do, and Cammie always strove to be the best Christian she could be. She only wanted to help—and to keep her friend from facing disappointment in the future. As she always did. With everyone she knew.

Didn't she?

EIGHT

CAMMIE STUMBLED OUT OF THE DINER, STOMACH churning, head throbbing from the thoughts tumbling in it. Hobey's comments had hit her hard, right at the core of her heart.

She'd never considered her actions in the light he'd cast them. Should she have? She didn't believe so . . . but what did Jesus think?

As she pondered that, she ran right into Sarah Langhorn—literally. "Oh, dear. I'm so dreadfully sorry. I was . . . well, I was busy thinking and I guess I didn't watch where I was going."

Mrs. Langhorn, Bellamy's bookstore entrepreneur and a tidy, organized woman, stared at Cammie as if she couldn't trust her eyes. "Camellia, honey. Is there somethin' I can do for you? I've never seen you so agitated. Not even after your dear David's passin'. This isn't one bit like you."

Cammie caught her bottom lip between her teeth. "I'm fine, Mrs. Langhorn. Don't trouble yourself about me." She cast around for something to excuse her behavior. "Miss

Louella just came to fetch me to the BCC. It seems the reverend needs to see me. Something to do with the Baskets for Babies ministry."

Mariah Desmond, Lark's future mother-in-law, came up and laid a comforting arm around Cammie's shoulders. "You do seem a mite pale to me." With her other hand, she felt Cammie's forehead. "I don't think you're runnin' a temperature—praise God—but you've got a peaked look to you. As I've been tellin' my own daughter, Reenie, you girls have to take special care of yourselves for your babies' sakes, now that you're both of you expectin'."

"I'm fine, Miss Mariah."

Cammie figured that if she repeated the simple statement often enough, she'd soon convince herself it was true. Still, the churning in her stomach hadn't abated much.

Florinda Sumner popped up out of nowhere. "Surely you know you can count on us all to help you wherever you need, don't you, now?"

"I'll be happy to rake your leaves for you, honey child," whispered Philadelphia Philpott from behind Cammie.

Before she could formulate a polite refusal, seeing as how Stu and Ray shared those responsibilities in exchange for part of their room and board, she realized the bulk of the membership of the Bellamy Garden Club had surrounded her. What were they all doing outside Ellamae's Dinner Diner at noon?

Especially Miss Mariah. Her thriving girdle empire in Leesburg took nearly every ounce of her attention, now that the recent outlandish charges of fraud and racketeering leveled against her had been dropped.

Miss Louella stepped out of the diner.

"Well?" asked Miss Mariah, looking at her one housemate—Miss Sophie being the last leg of the formidable trio who lived together.

Miss Louella's eyes widened. "Hush, now," she answered,

then came to Cammie's side. "We need to make sure the chairwoman of the Baskets for Babies gets to church right away."

To Cammie's amazement, Miss Mariah sighed in obvious relief. "Well, ladies," said the girdle maven in her take-charge way, "it's clear what the good Lord wants from us all now. Let's get our Camellia to where she belongs and, as always, things will work for the good of those who love him and are called to his purpose."

En masse, the group turned toward the center of town, where the BCC was located. As Cammie fell into step, she heard Miss Louella whisper loudly, "Mission accomplished."

"Which one?" asked Miss Mariah at the same low decibel level.

"Why, Mariah, dear," said Miss Louella, her voice now triumphant, "both of them. Did you doubt I could do it?"

"No, and praise God."

"Amen!"

Cammie's curiosity had already sparked to life and, by now, burned bright. "What kind of mischief are the two of you up to now—"

"Miss Cammie!" called Stu as he ran down the street.

"Hey, there!" echoed Ray, a step behind his buddy. "Hold on a minute, Mrs. Sprague. Something awful's happened back home."

Cammie's feet turned leaden, a vision of her house in leaping flames in her head. "Oh, dear. Did I forget to turn off the coffeepot? Or was it the iron I left on?"

The young men screeched to a halt. Stu bent over, clasping his knees as he panted. Ray leaned against a light post on the sidewalk.

Ray caught his breath first. He waved at her. "The house's fine," he said on a heavy exhale. "You're always careful with your things."

"So what's wrong?" Cammie asked, confused.

Stu gulped air. "Muttley."

A fist of fear clutched at Cammie's chest. "Muttley? What do you mean, Muttley? I locked him in his crate before I came for lunch with Miss Sophie. Did he get that door unlatched? It's supposed to be dogproof—"

"He couldn't have opened it," piped in Miss Sophie as she approached, having just exited the diner with Willie and Stephen. "I was with Camellia when she bought the thing. Why, I'd have to say it locks tighter'n that Alcatraz place in California is s'posed to."

Both Stu and Ray shook their heads. Again, Ray regained his composure first. "I don't think Muttley had anything to do with it, but one thing's for sure. He's gone."

The bottom of Cammie's stomach dropped right down to her toes. "It can't be . . ."

"But it is, ma'am," countered Stu. "You know how we always like to take him down to the park for a run about now? Neither Ray nor I have classes again until two-thirty today, and we needed to work out the desk kinks, so we went to get him. He wasn't there."

Ray nodded. "He wasn't anywhere. We checked all over your house—I'm sorry, Willie, we had to go into your room. Oh, and yours, too, Miss Cammie—but we couldn't find him. Then we looked outside, and nothing."

Stu held something out to Cammie. "I did find this in the kitchen, though. I don't think you eat 'em, do you?"

Cammie looked at his offering. Dread filled her. In his hand her youthful boarder held a ripped and mangled Butterfinger wrapper.

"Dear Jesus, help me . . . ," she said, feeling her knees give way.

"Look out!" yelled Stephen.

That was the last thing Cammie heard.

When Cammie blanched, Stephen began to run, but as soon as her eyes fluttered closed, he yelled. When her knees buckled, he could have sworn he flew. His heart squeezed.

Somehow, against all logical odds, he reached her before she hit the hard cement sidewalk. It seemed almost . . . miraculous, but every rational person knew miracles didn't really happen.

"Move away," he said, glancing at the shocked women around him. "She needs air, and I need to take her pulse. Willie, run to my office and get my bag, please."

With a sharp nod, Willie took off.

"Ah, man, we really did it this time," muttered Stu.

"I told you we shouldn't tell her until we had no other choice," argued his friend.

"Yeah, right. As if we had a choice even now."

"Well, you didn't have to run like a crazy—"

"Hey!" Stephen had no time for bickering kids with an unconscious Cammie on his hands. He had to take care of her. "Go squabble somewhere else, guys. We have an emergency here."

"Oh, Stephen," chided Aunt Sophie, "that's not hardly constructive for the boys to do." Turning to Stu and Ray, she added, "I suggest you two get yourselves straight down to the police station and tell Wiggon what's happened now."

The love and respect he'd always felt for his aunt returned full strength. "That's a great idea, Aunt Sophie. Go on, guys, and hurry. Something strange *is* going on around here, and this time, it's affected a pregnant woman."

While his geriatric audience jockeyed for position, quieter than he'd ever known them to be, Stephen took Cammie's pulse. It pumped somewhat weak and thready, consistent with a faint. Unlike his heart, which pounded with . . . was it fear? He wasn't sure, but he did know he couldn't let anything happen to Cammie. Her well-being was essential.

After all, he'd come to Bellamy to improve the medical care its residents received. Cammie, as Aunt Sophie's closest friend, mattered greatly to his establishing himself. Her defection to a Leesburg physician could be perceived as lack of confidence in him. Here was Stephen's opportunity to make sure everyone saw him in a positive light.

Of course, his concern had nothing to do with her personally—other than as someone he'd come to know. She was just Aunt Sophie's friend. And his too. A potential patient. Not anyone specifically special to him.

Of course not.

Cammie's breathing was shallow but steady. He suspected the shock, combined with her fluctuating hormone levels, had caused her to lose consciousness. A hand to her smooth, round middle reassured him. The baby kicked with gusto.

To his relief, Cammie blinked. He again checked her pulse and felt it strengthening.

"Louella!"

Everyone turned in the direction of the breathless bray.

"What's happened?" asked the colorfully garbed Myrna Stafford. "Am I too late? I had some chores to finish earlier, like I told you when we talked before, but I'm here now. Did I miss everythin'?"

Miss Louella made a show of hushing up the newcomer, but Myrna wasn't about to be denied. She pushed her way between Miss Sophie and Philadelphia Philpott, craning her head, which she'd topped with an orange knit hat, to peer inside the circle.

She rolled her turquoise-rimmed eyes. "Harrumph! It's one of 'em Bellamy girls again. I tell you, they're nothin' if not trouble. An' her expectin' an' all. Why, when I was carryin' little Bernie, I didn't do no gallivantin' around like this one's been doin'—"

Stephen had heard all he was willing to take. "Mrs. Stafford, I'm going to ask you to keep your thoughts to yourself. We have an emergency here, and we don't need your negativity complicating matters."

Myrna drew her gray-and-blue zebra-striped coat tighter around her. "Why, I never—"

"We know, Myrna," cut in Miss Louella. "And it's best if you don't now, either." She dropped down to her knees at Cammie's side. "Sugar, Mariah has her new car just around the corner. We can take you home straightaway."

Cammie smiled . . . weakly . . . in Stephen's professional opinion.

"Thanks, Miss Louella," Cammie said, sitting up, leaving Stephen's hands with a distinctly and unexpectedly empty feeling. "I hate to put you two out, but I think it's a good idea if I get back home and—"

"Not before I give you a complete checkup," cut in Stephen, his tone brooking no objection.

But object this stubborn woman did. "I'm fine, Stephen. I just grew a bit faint when I heard about . . ." She sobbed a small hiccup. "When I heard my Muttley's gone missin'. I need to go home, call my sisters, start lookin' for my pup—"

"Absolutely not. I will not let you endanger yourself or your child in such an irresponsible way."

Cammie's rounded chin tipped up. "Would you please tell me—in your learned opinion, of course—what about goin' home and gettin' in bed with my telephone could cause me or my child any harm?"

He'd been right about that stubborn streak, even if she kept it hidden most of the time. "Nothing. That's an excellent plan—*after* a physician makes sure nothing has gone wrong."

Her stubborn chin rose higher. "Is there any reason for you to suspect somethin's wrong?"

"You fainted."

"I'm fine now."

"But I'm the doctor. It's my duty—and my place—to determine how fine you really are."

"But it's *my* child. And it's *my* right to tell you I don't need your medical expertise. I just saw my own doctor but a few days ago, and he said we were doin' great."

"Anything can and often does go wrong at any time during a pregnancy. Wouldn't a wise mother want to have everything checked out?"

"Truce, children," said Miss Sophie, her forehead pleated into a ferocious frown. "Stephen, your pesterin' is likely to do this dear girl more harm than any little ol' swoon. Most every woman does that at least once in her lifetime."

"Harrumph! I never—"

"Shush, Myrna!" hissed the gathered gardeners in unison.

"Well, if that's how you all're gonna be 'bout it, I'm headin' on home." Myrna spun on the heel of her olive army surplus rubber boot, and stalked away, complaining stridently. "An' you can count me out of this latest scheme o' yours, Louella Ashworth. Why, a body'd think you ain't got yourself nothin' better to do than stick your nose in people's business an' sass 'em around. . . ."

Cammie chuckled.

Aunt Sophie giggled.

Willie, who'd just returned with the doctor's bag, barked a laugh.

The rest of the crowd roared, drawing Stephen in with their mirth. Was it him, or was this entire town crazy?

Did it matter?

For right then he realized he felt at home. He cared what happened to Cammie Sprague and her baby. He loved helping Miss Louella and her cronies nudge Aunt Sophie's romance along. He wanted to make sure Florinda's heart was solid, and that Philadelphia Philpott stayed as sprightly as she clearly was. He'd never felt this way before. Not even at his parents' house.

Then it hit him. He, of all people, *shouldn't* feel this way. He was looking into becoming a Buddhist. He was learning to rid himself of these kind of troublesome attachments. He shouldn't feel connected to these people. He shouldn't care so deeply about them. He'd cared for his parents, and all that had brought him was a feeling of failure—he'd never measured up to their expectations. He couldn't afford to get close to the people of Bellamy.

Instead he needed to retreat and meditate, which was eventually supposed to help him become unstuck from these emotional and mental bogs. He needed to find that reputed Zen awareness of peace.

Resolve established, Stephen stood and looked around. Where'd they all gone?

About ten yards away, he saw Aunt Sophie, Miss Louella, and the woman he'd heard them call Miss Mariah help Cammie into a forest green Lexus. At least they'd get her home in comfort.

But would she be all right?

His conscience wouldn't let him drop the matter so easily. Call it professional ethics, nothing more. Not that pang he'd experienced in his chest when he'd seen her faint, not the panic that had hovered in his thoughts as he'd counted her pulse, not the need he'd felt to see her smile again.

He was a doctor. And no matter what Cammie had to say about it, she was his patient. He was responsible for the medical care of those who lived in Bellamy. Right then, he decided to run back to the office, let Laura know where he'd be in case of emergency, then head over to the Widow Sprague's.

For his own—professional, naturally—peace of mind he had to make sure Cammie was going to be okay.

Zen or no Zen.

By the time Stephen had made sure Laura could reschedule the rest of his appointments for that afternoon, a considerable amount of time—or so it felt to him—had gone by. Although he usually preferred to walk around Bellamy, today he regretted not having his car. He would rather drive to Cammie's just to check on her that much sooner.

Since that couldn't be changed, he jogged over, arriving as Aunt Sophie stepped out the front door. "Stephen! Why aren't you at the office?"

He shrugged. "I couldn't stop thinking about Cammie's fainting spell. I just want to make sure everything's all right with her and the child."

Aunt Sophie came to the top step on the porch and, since Stephen stood on the bottom one, looked him eye to eye. Patting his cheek, she said, "You've a core of Christian goodness in you, son, that no amount of that Zenny Boodhy business can touch. You're a good man, Stephen Hardesty."

He didn't know whether to object to her indirect slam or thank her for the compliment. Before he could say anything, his aunt went on.

"I can tell you Cammie's lyin' on the parlor sofa with her phone in her hand. I fetched her favorite quilt down from her bed and tucked it around her. Louella and Mariah took charge of the ladies, sendin' them off to search for any clue to Muttley's whereabouts. And I decided the boys, Suze, and Willie can come over to supper at our house. I'm on my way to cook up a meal for us all."

Stephen smiled. "I can see you ladies are a force to reckon

with. I'm glad you did all that. Cammie doesn't need to worry about feeding anyone but herself, and I'm sure she can find something to tide her over until tomorrow—"

"Stephen, Stephen, Stephen. I don't know what's come over you lately. Do you honestly think I'd be leavin' Cammie without a meal in her condition? With her still all pale and teary over that pup? Shame on you, boy."

He laughed. "What was I thinking?" He surprised himself by reaching out and giving his elderly relative a bear hug. "Just to show you how terrific you are, Aunt Sophie. But maybe you should go home now. I've seen those two boys eat."

Aunt Sophie gave him a shrewd look. "And you don't?"

"Hey! A man's gotta keep up his strength if he's going to battle the evil forces of illness all day long."

"A likely story, son." She batted his hand in mock reproof. "But you're right. I'm on my way. Oh, and if you need help finding things around the house, Suze is up in her room. Those seniors got let out of school early today for some newfangled reason. She'll be happy to show you around."

"Thanks, Auntie. I'm sure I can find my way. And I'll take good care of your friend."

"I know, dear. I have faith in you. And in the Lord Jesus."

With that, she leaned over and gave him a kiss on the cheek. She then descended the porch steps and bustled off, her white Gibson girl knot swaying atop her head.

Smiling crookedly, Stephen opened the door to Cammie's home. Without much noise he crossed the wide foyer and went to the parlor archway. Again the room reached out to him with its coziness, its inviting nature, its flavor of . . . well, he guessed it had to be Cammie, since he couldn't quite otherwise put his finger on what it was he sensed.

He noticed she hadn't moved her "accessories," as she'd called her lovely decorations the other night. He was glad; he liked the room just as it was. The delicate blue-and-white porcelain spoke of its owner's femininity, while the magnificently crafted quilts revealed the depth of her imagination and creativity. As always the fireplace sparked with a warm fire, and Stephen came closer to its luring light.

Then he saw Cammie on the couch.

She'd fallen asleep quite possibly as soon as Aunt Sophie had tucked the rose-and-blue-and-white quilt snugly around her. A dried tear track marred the smoothness of her cheek, and her Bible lay open over her hip. One hand still covered it as if to reassure her it remained where she'd left it, while the other cradled her cheek. The cordless phone lay on the floor, forgotten.

The sweetness of the picture she made was more than Stephen had ever experienced. Something in his heart urged him closer, around the sofa, right to her side. He sat down next to her on the antique Persian rug and watched her sleep.

She sighed, a sob ruffling the sound.

That foreign something in his heart made him reach out and run a finger down her tearstained cheek. Its softness pleased him. Cammie was all woman, soft and gentle . . . well, she had that stubborn streak to her, true, but now it seemed far, far away.

While he was here. Right by her.

She whimpered.

He made a shushing sound, then placed a hand on her silky brown hair. "It's okay," he said, hoping to comfort her. "I'm here with you."

She seemed to settle down, her breathing again deep and even. He sighed in relief and let his fingers sift through her hair. Cool and smooth to the touch, Cammie's tresses tied delicate knots around his hand, as if she didn't want to lose the tenuous contact.

Neither did he.

But that shouldn't be.

Reluctant to do so, he nevertheless took his fingers from her hair. Working quietly, he removed the priceless porcelain pitcher and bowl from their usual spot on the coffee table, then pushed the table out of his way. As he carefully placed one of the striped armchairs next to the sofa, he was glad he'd developed the habit of working out. Too many doctors he knew let themselves get out of shape. He didn't think that presented patients with a good example, but today his efforts paid off in a more tangible way. He didn't disturb Cammie's slumber.

Nudging the chair close enough so he could reassure her should she cry out again, he sat and closed his eyes.

For a while he counted his breaths. Then he tried meditating. It didn't work. Finally, he just let his mind replay all that had happened since his move to Bellamy. Objectively, and with his usual logic, he concluded that he'd been as crazy to move here as his parents had said.

He opened one eye, noted the even rise and fall of the intricate quilt Cammie had made. He studied her fresh, pretty features, her cheeks rosy from sleep.

He wasn't leaving any time soon.

No matter how much sense doing so made.

NINE

BANG, BANG, BANG, BANG!

For good measure, Louella Ashworth crashed her gavel against the podium one more time, then said, "I'd like to call this emergency meetin' of the Bellamy Garden Club to order, if you please, ladies."

The buzz in the room went down to a dull roar. Speculation ran rampant among the membership. Why Louella had called the meeting was the question of the hour.

After Madame President tried again—unsuccessfully—to quiet down her minions, Reenie Desmond Ainsley stood, stuck two fingers into each corner of her mouth, and let out a piercing whistle.

Stunned silence reigned supreme.

"Why, thank you, dear," Mariah Desmond told her daughter. "Lou, the floor's all yours now."

With a benevolent nod, Louella doffed her reading glasses and jabbed the air before her with one of their gold-toned stems. "Sister gardeners," she intoned, "we have us two mighty serious problems in our fair Bellamy these days."

"Oh my, yes," wheezed Florinda as she ran in and collapsed into the last available chair.

"We're glad you could join us, Flo," said Louella. Seamlessly, she continued. "In the first place, it sure looks to me like our darlin' Camellia is fallin' into the wily clutches of that newly arrived misguided doctor."

A rumble of dismay rolled across the room.

"Indeedy, yes," Louella went on. "And it sure does look to me like we have to do somethin' to keep her from makin' a mess of her life. For her and her baby's sake, you understand."

Waves of assent wafted toward the front.

Louella raised reverent eyes ceiling-ward. "Praise be to the Lord, it appears neither one of them has taken any notice of how perfectly good the other one of them really looks."

"Hallelujah . . ."

"Glory be . . ."

"Thank you, Jesus . . ."

"Hmph! Are you fixin' to tell us those two've gone deaf an' blind all of a sudden, Louella?" brayed Myrna Stafford. "I don't know . . . I saw me plenty on that sidewalk earlier today. That there Bellamy girl looked mighty comfy in that Boodhist feller's arms. Ain't nohow you're gonna be persuadin' me they ain't noticed nothin' 'bout each other." Crossing her arms over her thin chest, Myrna beamed her overly made-up eyes on Louella, seemingly challenging her to disagree.

Which Louella did. "Let *me* tell *you,* Myrna, what with all the time those two have been spendin' together in their tug-o'-war over Sophie and Willie—"

"Louella!" wailed Sophie. "How could you? And here I always thought you were my friend."

"Oh, shush, Sophie. I've done nothin' wrong."

Mariah cleared her throat delicately. "Well . . ."

Louella's face crumpled in chagrin. "Oh, dear. Yes, well. I have made one minor mistake. One I'm sure all of us together can put to rights."

"*Only* one mistake?" challenged Myrna, bouncing her crossed right leg faster than a run-amok pendulum in a grandfather clock.

The president of the group donned her glasses and held her head higher. "Yes, Myrna, only one. And I'm fixin' to make amends."

"This should be good." Turning to face the other gardeners, Myrna said, "Look out, you all. She's cooked up another one of 'em crazy schemes of hers."

With a wave, Louella dismissed her challenger's claim. "I haven't even finished statin' our objective."

Mariah stood, cutting off the unproductive and unpleasant byplay. "Why don't you do just that, dear Lou? I'm fair dyin' to hear what you have to say."

A chorus of encouragement rang out.

Louella beamed. "Well, ladies, what we all have to do is mighty simple. We just have to make sure those two don't get around to noticin' how good the other looks—and I'm not hardly talkin' about pretty eyes or big, broad shoulders here."

Myrna leaped to her feet. "Oh, I see what you're fixin' to do," she said in a mocking voice. "You're wantin' to blindfold 'em an' plug up their ears. I'm havin' none of your nonsense, Louella. I'm shut of this so-called Garden Club what does less gardenin' than gettin' into trouble with the law."

With that she stormed out—as she had in the past every time the group had forged plans she hadn't liked. A few disgusted looks followed her exit.

Someone in the farthest corner of the room said, "Oh, don't be worryin' none about that Myrna Stafford. She'll be back soon's we take care of things."

"Who's that back there?" Louella asked, squinting against

the fluorescent-light glare on her glasses. "Sarah Langhorn? Is that you?"

"Yes, dear. And what I want to know is what's the other problem you said we have here in Bellamy?"

Louella grasped the edges of the podium and leaned forward. "Why, Sarah, it's plain as that gaudy mess on Myrna's eyelids—oh, dear. That *was* an awful thing to say, wasn't it? Hardly somethin' a Christian lady should even be thinkin'. I'm gonna be havin' myself quite a confession time tonight with the Father in heaven."

"Louella," chided Mariah, "I haven't a clue what's got into you tonight. Are you feelin' punk? You don't ever ramble, but you haven't done any little thing but ramble since you started."

"You're right, Mariah. I'm right troubled tonight. After all, my grandpuppy's gone missin' for ten days now. And Larkspur's Mycroft got taken, too. Then just today Camellia's Muttley vanished as well."

Hand shaking, she picked up the tumbler of water she always placed on the podium before starting her meetings. Taking a sip, she looked around the room. "I tell you all, somethin's got to be done about this state of affairs."

Philadelphia raised a hand. "What do you mean, Lou?"

"Why, Philly, we gardeners know what's what. And we're the best ones to be doin' somethin' about it. Remember, we're experienced investigators now."

Savannah Hollings, wife of the president of the Bellamy Fiduciary Trust and immediate past president of the Garden Club herself, stood. "Cut to the chase, dearie. We're fit to be tied here, wantin' to know what you're talkin' about."

True distress added years to Louella's attractive face. "Vannie, I'm afraid to even put it into words, but it sure does look like none of us is safe anymore. Bellamy's fallen into the evil clutches of a dastardly serial dognapper."

The next Sunday after church, Cammie waited in line to shake Reverend Melbourne's hand and comment on his sermon. To her mind, it had been especially uninspired, even if she couldn't tell him that.

Then again her opinion might have been colored by the little attention she'd given the godly man's words. Ever since the morning after Muttley was stolen, she'd done little but think about the unusual dream she'd had.

That awful afternoon, Miss Sophie had watched as Cammie drank enough chamomile tea to sink the *Titanic;* then she'd tucked Cammie's favorite Wedding Ring quilt up under her chin before going home to cook a meal for Cammie and her boarders.

Cammie had stared at the fire in the fireplace. But this time the crackling flames and the rich scent of apple wood had failed to cheer her.

Tears had flowed. Tears for herself, her missing dog, and her sisters, too. After a while, she reached for the drawer in the coffee table and took out her Bible. She went straight for the book of Psalms, her refuge in times of trouble. After some comforting reading, every vestige of energy drained from her, leaving her exhausted and weak. What a year it had been. . . .

She had propped the open Word on her hip and had begun to pray. Before long she dozed off. When she awoke in the middle of the night, she remembered only fragments of her dream. In it, she'd wept, heartsore and lonely, until a gentle finger stroked her cheek.

But the comfort hadn't lasted, and her misery had returned that much stronger. She'd cried again, and again that hand had responded. This time it had slid into her hair, the fingers strong and sure, smoothing and combing, leaving a pleasant tingle in their wake.

A soft crooning had accompanied the caresses—a rich, deep sound full of caring and warmth. Cammie recalled that even while sleeping, she had wanted that tender sensation never to end.

Once fully awake, she'd identified her deep yearning for more of that attention, and she'd wondered if by any chance the Lord had comforted her even in her dreams. But somehow she had the sensation that God hadn't been the one who'd tended to her that night.

There'd been an earthiness, a certain substance and solidity to the one who'd helped her sleep. At no time, though, had she caught even a glimpse of her benefactor.

Dreams made unsatisfying companions.

Even now, days later, the longing in her heart grew nearly unbearable at times. She'd so hungered for human love and companionship in her marriage. . . . Cammie could still envision a relationship where both partners cared for each other like her dream caretaker had done for her.

But she'd had her chance. Although she knew she hadn't been solely responsible for the disaster her marriage had become, she felt deep within the well of pain in her heart that she couldn't put herself through that again.

So she intended to focus on her child, her quilting, her boarders, her friends. . . .

And she was going to get her dog back. One way or another she was going to make sure the Bellamy Police Department kept on the case until all three Bellamy pets were back home where they belonged.

Her thoughts jumbling in her head, Cammie marched—straight into Reverend Melbourne.

"Oh no," she said on a groan. "I've done it again. I can't believe how careless I've become of late." Patting the frail gentleman's shoulder, she gave him a thorough once-over. "Did I hurt you? Please come over into the narthex. Take a seat, and let me fetch you a cup of water. Should I call the doctor for you?"

The elderly soul chuckled. "Camellia, it would seem to me you're in need of mothering more than I am. I'm fine. You certainly did me no harm when you bumped into me, child. How are you?"

"Oh, fine, fine. Absolutely fine and dandy." Was he going to buy her assertion?

Wisdom shone from his brown eyes. "I'd say you aren't hurt, but fine?" He shook his silvery head. "I think you have some praying to do. Something's troubling you, and you haven't come to your pastor with it yet."

Cammie blushed. "Oh, it's nothing. Well, it is, but not something spiritual. You know about my dog, don't you?"

Again, those warm-toned eyes suggested they saw more than she wanted them to see. "Everyone knows about the three missing Bellamy dogs. Are you sure, now, that's all that's troubling you?"

She simply couldn't talk about her dream. Not to her pastor. Not yet. "Of course, of course. I'm really and truly fine, but you know, I'm running a mite late for Sunday dinner. And I'm sure you can imagine how my boys do eat. I'd best be on my way."

The reverend nodded and smiled. "Go on, then, feed those young men. But remember, Camellia. I'm here. More importantly, the Lord is always here. Seek him when the day-to-day doing gets too hard on you. You're bearing a heavy load, what with David's death, the baby's coming, and now your missing dog."

Cammie couldn't find a thing to say.

It didn't matter; the pastor had plenty to add. "Jesus said he would never leave us nor forsake us, and you and I can always take that to the bank."

Trying to smile, Cammie descended the steps and made

her way down to the sidewalk. "Oh!" she said. "I almost forgot. Fine sermon this morning."

The reverend laughed.

She hurried home.

What was wrong with her these days? All that calm she'd always cultivated in the spirit of Christlikeness seemed to have deserted her. She'd begun to stand up for herself, and suddenly things seemed to have flipped upside down around her.

Then that disturbing dream . . . her erstwhile contentment seemed to have vanished right along with her dog. Now a gaping hole had taken residence right in the middle of her heart.

And she had to make things right again before the baby came. So she'd have to try twice as hard to do God's will, to seek him, to find that peace his Son had promised.

"Thank goodness for the genius of timed ovens," Cammie said when she checked the roast. While she'd been in church, the meat had cooked to perfection, its seasoned crust golden and the pan in which it sat filled with juices.

The root-vegetable medley had simmered in the Crock-Pot on the counter all morning, and now she only had to throw together a pan of biscuits and a salad to round out the meal. She'd baked the applesauce cake the night before.

Giving its usual squeaky complaint, the door to her back porch opened. In marched Miss Sophie, a truculent look on her face. "Now you listen here, Camellia. I don't rightly know what's come over you of late, but I'm not likely to stand for your stompin' right past me without so much as a howdy."

"Why, Miss Sophie," Cammie said, taken aback, "I never stomp. That's Lark you're thinking about."

"Not at all. I know red hair when I see it, and there's not one single solitary red curl growin' on your noggin." With brisk movements, Miss Sophie removed her gray felt hat and clapped it on the table. Finger by finger, she dragged off matching gray gloves, then pulled out a chair, sat, clasped her hands before her, and stared straight at Cammie. "Would you be willin' to start the mornin' over right? Give me a decent greetin', *then* tell me what kind of bee's got into your bonnet? Why, you're beginnin' to remind me of Magnolia, too."

"No, no, Miss Sophie. We're nothing alike at all." Cammie turned back to her flour and measuring cup. "Besides, there's nothing wrong at all. I just . . . oh, had Muttley on my mind."

"Oh, dear," Miss Sophie said, dismay in her voice. "I'm so sorry to have brought the sad subject back up. Silly me. I should have thought."

Once again, guilt swamped Cammie. Hoping to divert the discussion from a subject she didn't want to broach, she'd unwittingly distressed her dearest friend. "I'm sorry, Miss Sophie. There's no need for you to feel badly. I'm just missing my pup and, in fact, wondering if the Bellamy PD has come up with any results on those tests they were having done on Wiggon's evidence."

"You know, it'd be a good thing to ask about." Bending, Miss Sophie rummaged through her vast tapestry handbag and withdrew a shiny black leather notebook. "What will they think of next?"

"I beg your pardon?" asked Cammie, not following.

"Take a look at this cunning little thing." Cammie turned and saw Miss Sophie withdraw a short slender pen from inside the spine of the notebook.

"How convenient," Cammie said quietly, then began cutting the soft biscuit dough into generous circles.

"Indeed. And especially for me these days."

"Oh?"

"Why yes, Cammie, dear. That's why I was so intent on talkin' to you this mornin'. I wanted to tell you not to fret another minute about your puppy. His return home is in experienced, competent hands—if I do say so myself."

An unsettled feeling lodged in Cammie's stomach. As advanced as her pregnancy was, she knew it wasn't due to morning sickness. "What do you mean?"

"Honey, it's all set up. The Bellamy Garden Club is on the job, and as you can imagine, it won't be but a lick of time before we've cracked this case wider'n a pothole on the road to Leesburg."

Cammie didn't know whether to laugh or to cry. Or to run and hug every last one of the dear, misguided, elderly women. Plus one or two younger ones, too. Yes, the Garden Club had recently done a series of investigations but, in her opinion, had only managed to divert attention from what really had been going on. Each time they'd wound up tottering on the brink of trouble with the law.

If she and her sisters had to count on the Garden Club for the safe return of their pets, then the three Bellamy Blossoms were in deep, dark trouble indeed.

"Ah . . . that's awfully nice of you ladies," she said, fighting to keep a straight face. "But shouldn't you be planting your bulbs? Isn't it that time of year?"

"It's true—it is indeed that time of year. But, sugar, we can't just let the three of you girls pine away for your darlin's and not lift a finger to come to your aid. For your sake, and in honor to your dear departed Granny Iris. She was one of us, if you'll recollect."

"How could I forget Granny and her flowers? But I'm sure Wiggon and the rest of the PD are on top of things."

Miss Sophie turned her nose up. "And what have you heard from them lately?"

Cammie bit her bottom lip.

Scraping back her chair, Miss Sophie stood. "Precisely, Camellia. Nothing. Not one puny little thing. We aim to fix that. I'm afraid I can't be stayin' today to enjoy your Sunday dinner—much though I'd love to, you know. Louella's called a strategy meetin', and I'm not about to miss even one minute of it. It's too important to our cause."

She stuffed her hat back on her twisted knot of hair, then jabbed it with a lethal, pearl-topped hatpin. Bustling to Cammie's side, she added, "Give me my hug now, honey. I must be headin' back home for the meetin' with Louella and Mariah and the others."

Cammie pressed close, holding her doughy hands out to the sides, then whispered, "I love you, you know."

"I do know that, darlin' girl. And I love you right back. I'll call you later, once we've designed a master plan of attack—that's undercover lingo, you know."

Cammie again fought to keep from laughing. "I'll be looking forward to that call."

As her friend left, Cammie didn't know if she felt more discouraged or frustrated. She had no faith in the Garden Club's sleuthing abilities, but she'd reached the point that she wasn't rightly sure she trusted Wiggon's acumen either.

While Lark did have sterling investigative credentials, Cammie wasn't sure she wanted to give her oldest sister an inch. She was afraid that Lark, in typical Lark fashion, would storm her little corner of the kingdom and usurp all power. Cammie wasn't about to surrender her will and her life to her sister.

She only gave that to Jesus, her Lord and Savior.

What was she going to do?

"It might help if you did as Miss Sophie suggested," she told herself and went to wash her hands. After drying them on a blue-and-white checked kitchen towel, she picked up the phone.

Seconds later she had Wiggon on the line. "Afternoon, Wiggon. It's Camellia Sprague calling. I know you're not on duty now, but I was wondering if you'd heard anything new about my missing puppy—and the other two as well, of course."

She fell silent as the tall thin cop went through his waffling routine. Wiggon had always dithered in his speech, especially when he knew what he had to say would either upset or disappoint his listener.

It was no different this time. Cammie called on every ounce of patience God had ever given her, and eventually it paid off.

Sort of.

Wiggon got to the point, but his point was sadly lacking. "I'm afraid, Cammie, I ain't got much to tell you. The results from the lab ain't in quite yet, so nothin' much's changed since I last talked to you."

She sighed. "That's okay, Wiggon. No need to apologize. It's not your fault if you don't have any news. You'll make sure to call me when you hear anything, right?"

"Of course. I'd never not do my duty by you, you bein' a longtime friend of Jill's an' all."

Cammie smiled, thinking of her sassy, dark-haired former classmate. "Tell me, how is that sweet wife of yours these days?"

"Runnin' plumb crazy after them twins of ours. Bright little crumb-crushers, they are, you know."

Cammie chuckled, even though her heart hung heavy with disappointment. "I'll bet they're a handful. Tell you what; I can give Jill a hand with the boys one day. Maybe she wants to go get her hair cut without them clinging to her, or maybe she wants to read a magazine all by herself. Have her bring them over or let me know if she'd rather I come to your place. I'd love to spend some time with your little ones."

"Now, Cammie, you're all busy an' pregnant an' all. You sure you're wantin' to truck with my crazies?"

"I wouldn't have offered to help if I hadn't wanted to. I know Jill must need a break. Just have her call me—better yet, I'll call her. Talk to you soon—soon's you hear about my dog, right?"

"Right. An' thanks, Cammie. You're a saint."

As Cammie hung up, she chuckled at Wiggon's parting comment. She was no saint; she had no doubt about that. But she did try to honor God's call to servanthood. Wherever she saw a need she tried to fill it, and if she wasn't much mistaken, Jill needed time off.

She scribbled a message to herself on the calendar to make sure she rang Jill sometime midweek. That done, she returned to her dinner preparations. With vigor, she tore into the greens for the salad, taking her irritation out on the large romaine leaves.

Then it hit her. Maggie was always spouting off clichés and hackneyed phrases—all twisted in her own inimitable way, of course. But over the years Cammie had learned that those clichés of her sister's had become part of the language because they carried a wealth of truth in them.

It could be no different this time.

She nodded, her mind made up. If a woman wanted something done right, why it sure looked to her as if she'd have to do it herself.

TEN

AROUND FIVE ON MONDAY EVENING, STEPHEN SPOTTED the oddest sight he'd ever beheld. Yes, even stranger than Myrna Stafford at her best . . . er . . . worst, and that was saying plenty.

Initially he tried to tell himself he was seeing things, to go on with his late-afternoon walk, to focus on the glorious colors garbing the trees, the spicy scent of autumn, the unexpected balm of Indian-summer warmth. But the more Stephen argued with himself, the more certain he grew of what he'd seen.

What he wished he hadn't seen.

Stephen had approached the busy local Sunoco. Outside the structure stood a massive junk-food vending machine—one of those things he wished he could abolish due to the havoc their contents wreaked on human nutrition.

But it wasn't the machine that had captured his interest. Well, in a way it was, but then again, it wasn't. Not really.

"Oh, for crying out loud!" Stephen couldn't believe this was happening to him. He was beginning to think and talk in ways similar to those along which the Garden Club ladies did.

It was time to put a stop to the constant chatter of thought bubbling in his mind. Time to regain the full awareness of himself, of his life, of who he was in the greater scheme of things.

But since his curiosity wouldn't let up, he had to have a closer look. He approached and took visual inventory of the person in front of the candy machine. On the being's head sat a hat that had seen better days. Made of felt, in a shade somewhere between olive and lime green, it had lost its war against exhaustion. The brim now drooped down over the wearer's head, shadowing all features. If Stephen wasn't much mistaken—again—a hand-tied fishing lure clung to the crown by a hook.

Clad in a trench coat, the person's body appeared nondescript, especially since it had taken an awkward squatting position at eye level with the machine's dispensing jaws. The coat had once been gray but by now had faded to a dingy, indistinct shade of blah. Although the coat's shoulders fit, the middle appeared to strain, as if the owner had put on considerable weight since purchasing the garment.

Over this individual's shoulder hung a mammoth canvas tote bag, the kind preferred by environmentally savvy grocery shoppers. Its dimensions dwarfed its bearer.

As Stephen drew closer, he realized that other patrons of the gas station had also taken note of this character. He'd decided to confront the person, when a familiar voice emerged from beneath the awful hat.

"How disgustin'!" Cammie said. She wrestled her way upright, hampered by the protrusion of her unborn child, dropped something shiny into the gaping sack, then opened the door to the small store, where the attendant manned the computerized gas pumps.

Unless Stephen was very much mistaken, Cammie Bellamy Sprague had taken leave of her senses . . . whatever senses she had, nutty woman that she was. He'd heard Aunt Sophie describe her friend as calm, levelheaded, compassionate, and contented. While he'd seen Cammie's compassion, he hadn't seen much calm, levelheadedness, or contentment since he'd met her.

And now this.

What was she up to? And what could have disgusted her about an ordinary vending machine? Not to mention, why would she dress herself up like that, go into the store, and . . . ?

Stephen craned his neck to see what she would do next. Chat with the attendant? He saw nothing in her hands that might indicate an imminent purchase.

Squelching the urge to follow her inside and get answers to his questions—answers he feared she wouldn't give him anyway—he took up a post across the street where he could see which way she went after she concluded her business inside.

No more than ten minutes later, she came out. He verified without a doubt her identity—as if he'd needed to. He'd had firsthand experience of the softness of the hair that swung at chin level with every step she took. And the coat? Well, it strained to the bursting point over her firm, rounded belly.

As Cammie headed down Main Street, Stephen maintained a judicious distance between them. Until she darted into—

No way! She wouldn't have.

But she had. And if she made any purchases in *that* establishment, Stephen would happily throttle her. She was pregnant. And she'd walked into a tobacco store.

He fumed.

He paced.

He fought the urge to run inside and yank her out by the scruff of her pretty neck—

Cheeks bearing a faint pea green tint, Cammie stumbled

out, coughing and gagging from the smoke inside the shop. Stephen smiled.

Aha! Poetic justice, he thought.

She sat on the tobacconist's top step and hauled her luggage off her shoulder. Sticking her head in her sack and knocking the green abomination off her hair in the process, she scrabbled around and finally withdrew a shiny black notebook from the bowels of the bag.

The little book looked familiar; Stephen thought he'd seen Aunt Sophie jotting something in it the day before. Had Cammie taken his aunt's book? Or had she simply bought one like it? Right now he couldn't begin to guess—Cammie's behavior struck him as so bizarre.

After she'd scribbled something, she popped the thing back in her bag, crammed the hideous hat back on her beautiful brown hair, and sailed off, heading north again. This time she entered the large chain drugstore next to Four Paws Pet Supply. Stephen darted in behind her, grateful he could wander around while keeping a close eye on the pregnant crazy.

By now he'd grown concerned. Was Cammie suffering from some form of personality disorder? Sudden derangement? Was she likely to endanger herself or her child as she trotted around town doing who knew what?

He couldn't run the risk of finding out after the fact. Not when he was trying so hard to establish his progressive medical practice. Stephen believed in preventive medicine. In his opinion, that was just what the doctor ordered for that precise moment.

Approaching his prey, Stephen came close enough to listen in on her conversation with the cashier.

". . . and you can't remember if you sold someone a Butterfinger bar last Thursday afternoon, Lucille?"

The teenager tried hard not to gape. "Miss Cammie, I prob'ly sold dozens of them that afternoon. Just like I do every day. There's just no way I could recollect everyone who bought a candy bar that day."

"But it's very, very important, Lucille."

"But it's very, very impossible, Miss Cammie."

"Of course!" Stephen exclaimed, then glanced at Cammie and ducked, hoping she hadn't heard him. Thanks to the women's back-and-forth yet futile exchange, everything had just clicked into place for him. Cammie had taken it upon herself to investigate Muttley's disappearance.

On one hand, he felt relieved that matters weren't quite as dire as he'd imagined. On the other hand, they were bad enough. "Little fool doesn't know what she could be getting herself into," he muttered.

"Well, then," said the little fool, "what *do* you remember about the sales of boxes of Twinkies on the Saturday before that?"

With what Stephen recognized as great forbearance on the part of the teenager, Lucille answered. "Miss Cammie? D'you see that tower back there? Well, it ain't the leanin' one of Pizza nor the I-fell one from Paris. Take a good look at it. We been runnin' us a special promotion on Twinkies all month long. Three boxes for the price o' two. I reckon everybody in Bellamy's picked up more'n a coupla' them boxes by now. I cain't tell you who bought them when."

From an aisle away, Stephen heard Cammie's defeated sigh. "I understand, dear," she said. "I'm so dreadfully sorry for makin' such a pest of myself. I'm just worried sick about my Muttley since he went missin', and I thought . . . well, it doesn't matter what I thought, does it, now? What matters is that I took up your work time. You won't get into any trouble for chattin' with me, will you?"

Lucille gasped. "I-I don't rightly know. Mr. Cowpers is awf'ly strict about personal conversations during work hours'n such."

"Tell you what, Lucille. What else are you runnin' a promo on? I'll buy somethin' from you so we can tell him you were seein' to my needs as a customer."

"You'd do that, Miss Cammie? For me?"

"Why, sure, honey. I bothered you, and I don't want anythin' I do to endanger your job. Come on. What else can you sell me?"

"Well, we have us a special on our Marvelous Me line of cosmetics an' fragrances. . . ."

A short while later, Cammie left the drugstore enveloped in a cloud of scent capable of repelling the most ravenous bug ever evolved from the primordial ooze. Stephen's eyes watered when she walked past his hiding spot behind the magazine display by the exit. Before the heavy glass door to the drugstore closed behind her, he heard her stifle a sneeze.

Giving her some lead time, he followed at a discreet distance. This time, however, he ran no risk whatsoever of losing his quarry. The pungent miasma that clung to her also stuck to the air like cobwebs on an unsuspecting face. Every time he came too close, his eyes overflowed.

Every few steps she sneezed.

To his relief, she headed straight for Ellamae's Dinner Diner. If nothing else, she'd be taking a break, which meant he could too. A glass of ice water might help clear the burning sensation the so-called perfume she'd bought left at the back of his throat.

It couldn't be good for her or the baby.

Despite the urge to charge right in, Stephen shuffled around outside the diner, waiting until a reasonable amount of time had elapsed. When he couldn't take the waiting a second longer, he went in.

Although he'd planned on taking a seat at the counter, Cammie's dejected posture and weepy eyes changed his mind. He slid into the booth across from her. "May I?"

She blinked a number of times, sneezed, wiped her nose with a napkin, and said, "Of course. How are you?"

Her stench enveloped him, and his eyes resumed their flow. "Better than you. Do you care to share with me what's bothering you?"

Shrugging, she made another attempt to blot her watering nose. "Muttley's gone. I can't believe that after havin' him for such a short time I miss him so much."

"Have you heard anything from the police?"

"No. We're waitin' on the state police lab to get the results to some tests they're doin' on the evidence, you know."

"I heard Wiggon say something to that effect. But why are you crying?"

Surprise widened her eyes. "Me? I'm not cryin'; *you* are—" She clapped her hand over her mouth. "Dear me, Stephen. Here I'm blatherin' on and you're the one in need of unburdenin' yourself. What's wrong?" She reached out and patted his hand. "What can I do to help? It must be awful, whatever it is."

"It's awful, all right—"

Her sneeze cut him off.

His eyes watered more profusely. "What *is* that horrible stuff you bathed yourself in, Cammie? It's killing my eyes, and your nose doesn't look as though it's going to make it through the next hour's worth of wiping."

Her cheeks turned rosy. "It's a mite strong, isn't it?"

Stephen rolled his drippy eyes. "Strong? I'd say it's strong. It could fell a herd of stampeding buffalo with only one whiff. What possessed you to get that stuff?"

"Well, I . . . it's like this. I bothered someone and could have gotten her in trouble. But since I didn't want that to happen, it was easiest if I bought somethin' from her, since she's a saleswoman, you see."

If Stephen hadn't been spying on the entire transaction in

the first place, he would never have followed that deficient explanation. "It must have been big trouble that person was risking to make you drench yourself in that stuff, much less buy it."

Cammie shrugged. "She gets a commission from every sale of this Marvelous Me line. I wanted to help, since I know her little sister's bein' treated for leukemia and her family needs all the money they can get."

"That was very kind and generous of you," Stephen replied, "but couldn't you just have given them a check? Did you have to go and buy the pollutant?"

"Why, Stephen, you should know better'n that. They're proud folks, and I'd likely offend them if I outright handed them the money."

"Ah, yes. Southern sensibilities."

"Of course, and you should know all about them, since you're a Southerner yourself."

"Peee-yewwwww!" cried Ellamae, backing away the instant she reached their table. "What *is* that stink?"

Although Cammie's cheeks darkened some more, when her gaze met Stephen's, she chuckled. As did he. Ellamae tapped the toe of her cowboy boot, her nose wrinkling at the assault.

Cammie and Stephen laughed louder.

"Come on now, you two. You'd best be orderin' yourselves somethin'. I can't have you comin' in here an' smellin' up my place without you at least buyin' somethin' from me."

Jabbing the tip of her pencil into her beehive, she scratched her head. "Well?"

Cammie recovered first. Swiping her running eyes and nose with yet another napkin, she smiled at the diner's owner. "I apologize, Ellamae. It's a long silly story. Take my word, I'll hightail it out of here soon's I have some sweet tea to wash the burnin' out of the back of my throat."

Ellamae's snapping black eyes narrowed. "Are you two set on poisonin' my establishment?"

Again Cammie laughed, shaking her head in helpless hilarity.

Stephen took pity on his companion and forced himself to speak. "I'm sorry, Ellamae. As a doctor, I can tell you it's probably not poisonous, but it is awful. I was only going to have some water to wash the terrible taste from my mouth, but Cammie's sweet tea sounds much better."

"So which one of you should I thank for the smell?"

Cammie raised her hand sheepishly.

"You know?" Ellamae said. "I guess I don't rightly wanna know any details, after all. I'll get you those teas right quick, then hustle the two of you straight outta here. A woman's gotta think of her customers, you know. I love you dearly, Camellia Bellamy Sprague, but I cain't risk the food in here gettin' tainted with . . . with whatever that is."

Ellamae marched off to take the order at another table.

Stephen used a couple more napkins to sop up his most recent teary flood, still chuckling sporadically. "We've made *her* day, haven't we?"

"I'm afraid so." Cammie's smile again did that warming thing to Stephen's heart. He didn't know whether to be glad or run like mad—in the opposite direction, of course.

He quieted the urge to escape by remembering her recent actions. "I have to confess. I followed you this afternoon."

Her smile vanished. "Why would you do such a thing?"

"When a doctor takes the Hippocratic oath, he takes it seriously. I'm sworn to protect and help preserve human life—even when the person has become someone else's patient. I'm worried about you. And when I saw you hunkering in front of a gas station vending machine, I didn't know what to think. Then I watched you nearly knock yourself unconscious again by going into a tobacconist . . ."

He let his words die off when Cammie's eyes crackled with outrage. Her voice, however, came out as soft as ever. "So you knew all along what had happened at the drugstore, didn't you?"

"No, not all of it. Although I did know the smell began when you left there."

She held her head high. "Fine. So now you know. I'm tryin' to track down my pet's thief. There's not a single thing you can find wrong with me doin' that."

"I'm afraid there is." He ticked off a finger at each of her infractions. "You inhaled gasoline fumes, heavy tobacco smoke, and are even now polluting your lungs—not to mention your child's bloodstream—with who knows what kind of chemicals from that so-called perfume you bought." Stephen waved at the mountain of napkins they'd used to try and stem the reek-induced deluge. "Might I point out we're *both* suffering allergic reactions?"

"I can be reasonable," Cammie answered in her soft voice. "I won't use this fragrance again."

Stephen arched a brow. "What about skulking around with those outrageous sunglasses, that horrible hat, and that grocery sack hanging off your shoulder? Who do you think you are? The female Columbo?"

"My goodness, Stephen," she said icily, "I certainly hope I don't look half *that* ratty."

He tapped his fingers on the table between them. "That's not what I meant, and you know it."

"I'm afraid I have no idea what you're talkin' about—oh, good." She turned to the approaching Ellamae. "Thank you for the tea. And give my love to your mama next time you stop out to the nursin' home, you hear?"

Ellamae grinned. "Honey, you can count on me tellin' her all about your smelly day. Mama's gonna have herself a time laughin' it up."

Cammie's smile turned wry. "At least someone'll benefit from it, right?"

"Maybe you can stop out and tell her yourself—*after* a good long scrub with soap an' water, now. She said she ain't seen you in a coon's age, anyways."

"I'm afraid I've had to cut down on my visits to the home lately. I'm real busy gettin' ready for the baby and with my boarders and all. But I'll try real hard to get in to see her soon. She loves me readin' the Scriptures to her."

"I'll tell her that, honey. I sure will. Drink up, now. You know—the smell an' all."

Obediently, Cammie took a long swallow.

Stephen followed suit. He remained dissatisfied. "Well?" he asked, once Ellamae had left.

"Well, what?"

"Are you going to refrain from putting yourself and your baby in the way of trouble again?"

"Trouble will find a way to come across me if it wants to. You know that's true, Stephen."

"But you can leave this investigation to the police. They're the experts."

She gave him a suspicious look. "Are you suggestin' I'm incapable of findin' my own dog? Because I'm not, you know. I can find my Muttley." Her chin flew up nearly sky-high. "And I'm goin' to do it."

"I guess a guy knows when he's trounced, even if the trouncer is a pregnant woman who should be taking it somewhat easy as she approaches delivery," he conceded. Then he came to a desperate decision. A doctor had to do what a doctor had to do. "Okay, you're going to find your dog. But guess what? I'm going to help you."

"What?" Her eyes widened. "I don't need your help. I'm perfectly capable of handlin' my own problems myself. You're just like the whole lot of them, thinkin' I can't even take care of li'l ol' me. Well, I'm goin' to show you all what I can and can't do."

Plopping her vast tote on the table, she scoot-scoot-scooted her way to the edge of the booth. As she stood, however, she found her way blocked by Myrna Stafford.

Stephen stifled an "Oh, great."

Cammie, true to her normally sweet nature, did much better than that. "Hello, Mrs. Stafford," she said. "Are you goin' to have a nice meal?"

Myrna surveyed her surroundings with her turquoise-smeared eyes. "No, an' I ain't come hightailin' it over here to eat any of Ellamae's overdone, overpriced food, neither. I came huntin' for you."

"Oh? What can I do for you?" Cammie asked, a question Stephen was beginning to think flew involuntarily out of her mouth anytime she parted her lips.

"No, no, no. Now you listen to me real good, girl," answered Myrna, waggling a scrawny finger under Cammie's pert nose. Myrna's bracelet of half dollar–sized coins jangled raucously. "I'm the one's gonna be helpin' you here. I came to tell you I know who stole your dog. An' your sisters' too."

Hope sprang into Cammie's eyes. "Really? Tell me, please do."

"Why, it's plain as the nose on your face, girl. You know right well nobody in Bellamy'd do a thing to hurt you or your sisters—no matter how much trouble y'are—so you know it couldn't'a been no one from here. Plain as day, I tell you. It was a fahrriner."

"Foreigner?" Cammie asked.

"Indeedy, so. An' you're the one what's harborin' him, too."

"Me?"

A nod of the orange-hatted head set her purple curls a-joggling. "Right in your own home, I tell you. If my bosom friend EdnaLou Sprague knew what you've gone an' done with the house her son provided you with . . ." Myrna grew misty eyed and patted her chest. After a bit of that, she turned her attention back on Cammie. "Missy, the one what's responsible for takin' them dogs of yours is none other than that geezer what calls himself Willie Johnson. Sure as sure. You look into it, an' you'll see I'm right."

Cammie sat back down on the edge of the bench. "Why would you say that? What do you know about Willie that makes you accuse him? He's never done anythin' that would lead me to think he'd be capable of anythin' so mean."

Myrna smacked her open palm on the table, clacking her coins again. She leaned closer to Cammie. "Why, girl, that's just the point I'm makin' here. You don't know nothin' about that man. He ain't from nowhere round hereabouts, now is he? How do you know what he's capable of or not?"

Shaking her head, Cammie leaned sideways against the back of the booth. "I'll have to give this some thought. I can't accuse someone just on your say-so."

"Mark my words, missy," Myrna said, shaking a finger. "He's the one." With that, she straightened and marched off, her coin bracelet catching on the strap of Cammie's sack. Before Stephen could move to retrieve it, the bag fell.

Glass broke.

Cammie looked at him.

He looked at Cammie.

Of one accord they stood and rushed to the door.

It was too late.

The stench of Marvelous Me had overtaken Ellamae's pride and joy thanks to Marvelous Myrna.

ELEVEN

CAMMIE COULD HAVE JUST DIED WHEN SHE HEARD THE bottle of perfume break. Her first instinct, of course, was to flee. To her amusement, it was her companion's, too. Her conscience, however, applied the brakes to her feet.

"We can't," she said to Stephen, who'd pulled up short behind her.

He sighed. "Of course not. Besides, we've got to get all these poor people out of here."

Nodding, Cammie headed for the nearest window. "Would you please see to that while I get some fresh air in here—"

"Camellia!" bellowed Ellamae as she charged out of the kitchen. "What have you gone an' done to my restaurant, girl? I thought you said you were taking yourself an' your stink home oncet you'd drunk your tea."

Cammie's cheeks burned with embarrassment as she hurried to the next window. "I'm so very, very sorry, Ellamae. We had an accident out here. But don't you worry. I'm taking care of things for you."

"We are taking care of it for you, Ellamae," Stephen said,

helping Shelley Tyler usher her five- and two-year-olds out the door. He followed his words with a look that chastened Cammie. "Why don't you go on home before you get a headache from the fumes? *We'll* call you as soon as *we're* done."

Ellamae raised her arms in defeat. "Don't bother callin'. I cain't be servin' this food up, anyways. Not with that smell what's gonna taint it. I'll come in extra early tomorrow and chuck it all."

"Oh, Ellamae," Cammie said, feeling worse by the minute. "I'm afraid I've made real trouble for you. Let me take care of the spoiled food so you don't have to, and I'll tell you what else. Send me the bill for the waste. I can cover it. There's no need for you to suffer that kind of loss on my account."

"Ahem!" Stephen uttered. "*We* will split the cost, Mrs. Sprague."

"But it was *my* perfume—"

"But *we* were talking to Myrna—"

Ellamae's white apron flapped between their faces. "I won't be takin' a red cent from neither of you, but I will take the both of you up on your offer to clean out the place. I cain't believe you just called that stuff perfume, Cammie. What's it for? Attractin' buzzards?"

Cammie smiled sheepishly, then made the mistake of glancing at Stephen, whose puffed-out red cheeks and pursed mustache made it only too clear he was trying to keep from laughing.

She lost it.

Collapsing into a booth, Cammie laughed herself silly, tears of mirth—and chemical irritation, too—pouring down her cheeks. In laughter-induced weakness, Stephen stumbled back onto one of the counter stools, his cheeks shiny with tears.

Ellamae rolled her eyes. "I'm takin' this ol' body on home. You two crazies go on ahead an' stay here with the stink. Laugh yourselves just plain nutty. Honest to Pete—" She fiddled with the cash register. "A body cain't count on a woman she's known since diaper days to act like herself these days—" She tossed a large bundle of keys on the counter, then headed for the door. "Wait'll I tell my Hobey 'bout this one. Man's gonna bust himself a gut laughin' but good. . . ."

Cammie grabbed a fistful of napkins and passed half of them to Stephen. She tried to mop up her nonstop tears, but before long called it quits. "You know we aren't about to be shut of crying until we clean up that stuff, don't you?"

He wrinkled up his face. "I know. But are you ready to do the deed?"

She wrinkled her nose right back at him. "No, are you?"

"Are you kidding? I'm the one who nearly bashed into you while trying to escape. If you hadn't been in my way, I'd be close to Anchorage by now."

Cammie studied him. "Are you sure about that?"

He shrugged. "Nah. I wouldn't walk out on anyone who had this mess to clean. And that's why I'm going to ask you, in all sincerity and genuine concern, to go home. I don't know what the ingredients of this stuff might do to you or the baby—"

"Stop. They're only perfume oils, Stephen." At his skeptical look, she chuckled. Again. "I won't argue—the combination's awful, but I can't imagine it'd be too harmful. It's purely my fault for buying the stuff, so I'm staying to clean. If you'd like, you can join me."

He raised his hands in surrender. "Since it doesn't look like I'm going to win this argument, I guess I'll just have to join you. Any idea where she keeps her cleaning supplies?"

"Somewhere in the back, I reckon. Do you want to go look? I'll dispose of the . . . well, the only nice way to put it is stink bomb, don't you think?"

Grinning, they took off in separate directions. Cammie gulped in a huge breath, held it, and picked up her sack.

Although it was toast, there were things in it she needed. Her wallet, for one.

"Terrific," she muttered.

"What's wrong?" asked Stephen, rolling an industrial bucket-on-wheels toward her.

"I just realized I'm going to have to get myself a new wallet. And they're hard to shop for."

He dunked a huge string mop into the steaming water. "They are? I've never had any trouble. You go to the store, grab one, and take it to the cashier."

"Hah!" Cammie said, rummaging through the ruined stuff in her sack. "Easy for you to say. Haven't you ever noticed how many different kinds and styles of wallets they have in stores?"

He squeezed the excess water from the mop with the levered press. "Sure. Black leather and brown leather. Easy."

At the far right corner of the bag, Cammie felt something soft with a hard metallic clasp. "There it is. I wouldn't want to throw it out." As she pulled out one of her most important possessions, she glanced up at Stephen.

He interrupted his floor-swabbing operation to pat the rear pocket of his pants, clearly reminding her of their discussion.

Cammie pointed at him. "I tell you, life's unfair. You men have it much too easy, if you ask me. There's a lot more than the black leather kind of wallet and the brown leather kind. You see, Stephen, there's the kind with a calculator, a coin purse, slots for credit cards and ID, checkbook, and dollar bills. Then there's the kind without the calculator, but with a mirror, comb, nail clippers, and a strap for lipstick. There's also the kind that pretends it's a wallet but is actually one of those daily organizer things with an address book, a weekly calendar, slots for credit cards, ID, dollar bills, a calculator, and the coin purse. Of course, you have to decide between the kind that folds into a small rectangle or the kind that stays its original length, and I must mention those that fit inside your pocketbook versus the kind that hangs over your shoulder on a strap like a purse—"

Stephen's gaping mouth cut off her explanation. He shook his head. "Okay. You win. Buying a wallet's more perilous than big game hunting in the wilds of the African continent."

As she wiped down the items in her bag, she grinned. "Toldja—"

"What's that?" he asked, cutting her off again.

"This?" She held up a small round object.

"Yeah, that. What else would I be asking about?"

"Now, Stephen," Cammie answered with a touch of amusement. "You know they don't license dumb doctors—or maybe they do, but you're not one of them. I'm sure you've seen one of these before."

"Of course I have," he said in obvious exasperation. "But what are you doing with a magnifying glass?"

"I can't believe I have to explain every last little thing to you." She set the glass object on the table and reached inside the sack again. "It's for examining evidence. Every detective knows that."

"Examining *what* evidence?"

The soggy mass in the other corner of her tote bag turned out to be her notebook. "When a detective comes across fingerprints, she wants to be able to study them right up close. Then she can compare them with any further evidence I . . . er . . . *she* finds during her investigation of the dognappings."

She remembered something she'd learned that day. "Do you have any idea how filthy that snack machine down at the gas station is? I was so disgusted by all the mess of stuff I saw through my magnifying glass. I tell you, I'm never buying another thing from one of those contraptions, and I'll be telling everyone I know about it, too. Wouldn't want them to go touching those things."

Stephen inexplicably again roared with laughter. Gasping, he managed to say, "So that's what did it."

"Did what?"

"Made you cry out, 'How disgustin'!"

Cammie gave him a reproving look. "Were you spying on me since way back then?"

"Guilty as charged."

"Oh, dear."

"Well, it's nice to have *that* little mystery solved."

She dropped her perfume-soaked notebook on the table. "But I made no progress on the big one."

Stephen looked up from his janitorial efforts, sympathy in his dark eyes. "I do think you should leave it to the experts—hey! Is that Aunt Sophie's little pad? Because if it is, I'm going to have to know where she bought it to replace it. She puts a lot of stock in that thing."

"So did I," Cammie responded, eyeing her charming booklet with dismay. "I liked hers so much I went and bought myself one just like it. Don't fret; this one's all mine to ruin all by myself."

He snapped his fingers. "See, there? You just solved another mystery for me. Don't get discouraged. I'm sure the PD will get the dogs back for you and your sisters."

Cammie smiled sadly. "I appreciate what you're trying to do. That's so sweet of you to say. But, you know, Maggie's and Lark's dogs are very valuable. They have outstanding pedigrees and all. I heard Maggie mention once that each of those two pampered pooches is worth over a thousand dollars. I'm sure whoever took them took advantage of that."

Stephen resumed his vigorous mopping. "You're sure someone stole them."

She noticed he didn't ask—or look at her as he did so.

"Oh, Stephen, please. Let's not kid anyone here. One dog running away, anyone can buy. But three of them? Belonging to three sisters? I don't think so."

He sighed, folded both hands over the end of the mop handle, and perched his chin on top. "I have to admit, even though I don't want to, that there's no chance of this being a random thing. Someone took those dogs."

He stood upright and swiped down his mustache with the back of his hand. "But if they stole them for their value, then why would they take Muttley? No offense, Cammie, but Muttley's . . . well, a mutt."

She blew her bangs off her forehead in frustration. "That's why this is so befuddling. It makes no sense."

Going back to his energetic scrubbing, Stephen muttered under his breath, "There's got to be a rational, logical explanation for this." He snapped his fingers again. "I know! Maybe we can meditate about it. After all, meditation lets emotions fall away so they don't cloud the thinking process. I bet then we'll come up with something."

Cammie bit her tongue before blurting out *her* opinion. She'd been about to suggest seeking God together, asking his help in finding the dogs, or at the very least, to help them understand why it had happened. Stephen's words came as a cold-water-bucket reminder.

Disappointment ran through her. Just when she was getting to like this man who so readily pitched in to help, who seemed so intent on protecting her baby—even before he set eyes on him or her—who cared so much for his great-aunt that he'd go out of his way to replace her unimportant but much loved notepad. . . .

She sighed in resignation. Then she shook herself. It was just as well. She'd been enjoying their banter so much that she'd forgotten about Stephen's lack of faith. The one thing she and David had had in common was their Christian beliefs. If she ever lost her wits enough to get interested in another man, she'd want one who loved the Lord as she did. As attractive and nice as Stephen was, she couldn't let anything grow between them. Not anything beyond a simple friendship based on their love for Miss Sophie.

Again she wondered why God had sent Stephen to Bellamy at this particularly vulnerable time in her life. What kind of lesson was God trying to teach her?

And then it hit her.

Ohdear, ohdear, ohdear!

Sneaking a peek at Stephen, she nearly kicked herself for her blindness. At the rate she was going, Myrna would likely have had to smack her over the head with the proverbial two-by-four before she put two and two together to come up with a measly four.

Willie wasn't the only newcomer to town.

Stephen had been around for only a few weeks. Not especially long before the first dognapping. And although Miss Sophie doted on him, how well could she really know him? He'd only visited her sporadically during his late teens and, as far as Cammie knew, never as an adult. His practice had kept him too busy.

Cammie's heart picked up its pace.

Could it be possible? Could a doctor be guilty of dognapping? And if so, why? If one could suspect sweet and suave Willie, then why not suspect Stephen as well? She could see the well-built doctor hauling around a hundred-pounds-plus of Buford and who-knew-how-much of Mycroft without too much trouble. Willie would have needed help.

Thieving cohorts? The two of them? They *had* taken up fairly quickly after meeting each other. Was it possible they'd known each other previously? That they'd hatched this plot together before coming to Bellamy? Myrna had been so certain of Willie's guilt. Maybe she was on to something.

Cammie shook her head. Too many thoughts were milling about, and none of them set too well with her. She didn't like to think that anybody she knew would be capable of hurting her, her sisters, or three innocent dogs.

Tomorrow morning she'd have to call Myrna and thank her for the tip. Perhaps the unhappy and unpleasant woman had at last done Bellamy's Blossoms a good turn. But how could it be true? It would go against everything Cammie had come to believe of Willie and Stephen.

Thanks to Stephen's stubborn insistence on helping her with her investigation, she'd have every opportunity to keep an eye on him now. If he was guilty, she wasn't going to let that too smart, too attractive, too . . . too newcomer of a doctor get away with dognapping.

If he was guilty.

Gathering up the last of the debris from the fragrance debacle, Cammie headed for the door. "I'm taking this to the Dumpster out back. It just won't do to leave it in one of the inside trash cans."

Stephen grinned. "Great thinking, pardner."

Partner.

Nuh-uh.

No way. No matter how much she had begun to like Stephen Hardesty, she wouldn't be hooking up with him for any more than this cleanup operation. And the detecting, of course.

"I'll take care of the food for Ellamae," she added. "You can go on home now. You've done plenty." *Who knew just how much?*

"Forget it," he argued. "I'm in this all the way."

"Fine," she said over her shoulder as she stepped outside. *And that's what I'm afraid of.*

As she trudged to the Dumpster, she prayed for guidance,

for clear thinking, for God's wisdom to show her how best to deal with the very disturbing Dr. Hardesty.

Back inside, she went to work tossing Ellamae's delicious cooking. Although the work kept her hands busy, her mind continued to mull over the situation. Since the possibility that Willie was guilty now existed, Cammie couldn't just let Miss Louella and the other potential crook conspire to hook up her dearest friend with a dognapper. She had to make sure the budding romance between that dapper, aged Casanova and Miss Sophie got itself nipped right in the bud.

Who was best for that job?

"Why, me, of course," she said, scrubbing a mammoth square pan used to keep food warm over boiling water.

"You what?" Stephen asked.

Only then did she notice that he'd sneaked into the kitchen and dried all the equipment she'd washed. "Why, I'm the best equipped to protect your Aunt Sophie from Willie Johnson. We can't let her grow any more infatuated with him—especially if he is the dognapper."

Stephen gave her another of those long, silent scrutinies.

Cammie lost her patience. "Go on," she hissed, "tell me what's roiling around in that mind of yours. Don't just stare at me with your beady glare."

"It just seems strange that in the course of less than an hour, you've gone from rejecting Myrna's ridiculous accusation right to accusing Willie yourself. That's a very rapid and, to me, incomprehensible about-face."

Cammie wiped the deep stainless steel sink with a wrung-out washcloth. "I've had time to think, and it's very simple, Stephen. Willie had opportunity—no one would ever question his coming and going in and out of my house."

"But not your sisters' houses."

"He didn't go into their houses. Their dogs were nabbed in their yards."

"Okay. I'll grant you that point."

"The motive's easy, too. Two thousand dollars' worth of dog."

"How about Muttley?"

She grinned triumphantly. "I figured that one out, too. That was to confuse the issue. You know, a red herring kind of thing."

"I'm not so sure I buy that one. It's stretching it."

"It's obvious you don't read mysteries or watch *Columbo* reruns, do you?"

"Is that what you're basing your suspicions on?"

Cammie sighed. "No. But I have to admit there is some merit to Myrna's theory. I like Willie Johnson and don't want her to be right. But I can't just discount her theory outright. I need to take action."

"I can see where you would feel that way, but tell me this: what about the means to do all this dog stealing? How would Willie actually go about it?"

Cammie began ticking off fingers. "McDonald's, Twinkies, and Butterfinger. Need I say more?"

"Okay. He could entice the dogs with the treats, but how would he get them to follow him once they were finished? Once they'd eaten the stuff, they'd want more in order to run off with the guy who gave it to them. And I can't quite see skinny, elderly Willie wrestling a bloodhound, much less a bullmastiff, into his car."

She took a deep breath. This was where the going got sticky. "He had help."

"Who?"

She swallowed hard. "I don't know, but I intend to find out. The first thing I'm going to do is stick to Willie like batter to a mixing bowl. And I'm going to make sure he makes no more moves on your aunt."

"What? Are you going to turn into the local professional romance buster?"

Stiffening her back, she remembered her decision to stand up for whatever she felt strongly about. "Laugh if you want, but I love Miss Sophie. Her welfare is important to me. So I can't let something awful happen to her without my doing whatever I can about it."

"I think you're making a mistake."

I'll just bet the farm you do. "Well, I don't."

"Has it occurred to you that you're sticking your nose into someone else's business? Into something that's none of yours? How would you feel if someone did it to you?"

Cammie gasped. Stephen was beginning to sound like Hobey. Could there be some truth to those questions? Would God use Stephen to make a point? The same one Hobey had made?

She shook her head. "That's not it at all. A friend is a friend through good and bad. And this looks pretty bad to me."

Stephen closed his eyes. When he opened them again, he waved toward her. "In your new role as investigator, are you planning to dress like that until you figure out that Willie hasn't done a single thing wrong?"

She glanced at her gaping coat. "I'll have you know, a trench coat is a very versatile garment. A detective can't know ahead of time when she's going to get rained on or when she's going to have to blend in with a crowd."

"Trust me. You're not about to blend in with anything if you wear that." He grinned mischievously. "Is there any chance the hat got the raw end of the perfume deal?"

Cammie wrinkled her nose. "Pretty bad, huh? It used to be David's fishing hat when he was a kid. I kept it, not knowing if I'm having a girl or a boy."

"In that case, keep it—just don't *wear* it."

"I'd already come to that conclusion." She dug in her coat pocket. "See? I took it off."

"Let's get serious, Cammie. What you wear isn't going to matter. I just don't think you should interfere between Aunt Sophie and Willie."

"I'm perfectly serious. I don't think you ought to help Miss Louella and the Garden Club—minus Myrna—push them any closer together."

They stared at each other—both stubborn, neither willing to give an inch. Finally Stephen threw down the towel he'd used to dry the kitchenware. "We're at an impasse."

"A Mexican standoff, I think they call it."

"So what are we going to do?"

"We? I don't know about we, but I'm going home. I left a kettle of chili and a pan of corn bread for everyone to help themselves, but I need to get back and clean up. You can go on home."

"Not without a promise on your part to leave Aunt Sophie and Willie alone."

"I can't do that, Stephen. I can't let her head into danger without trying to stop her before she gets hurt. And I have to make every effort to learn whether Willie stole our dogs or not."

Taking Ellamae's keys from her pocket, Cammie locked up the rear door. She headed for the front of the restaurant and closed all the windows. At the front door, she waited until Stephen exited, then turned the key to the dead bolt. She'd drop them off at the Hobeys' so Ellamae could get in to work in the morning.

Both headed south on Main Street, consumed by their thoughts. At the corner of Main and Hillside, where they had to part ways, Stephen faced Cammie, his eyes dark and intent. "I can't let you run straight into who knows what kind of danger. I have to remember my oath to protect life. I have two of them to protect with you. If you insist on sticking to Willie, then I have to insist on sticking to you."

Something in his gaze reached deep, making Cammie question her earlier decision to stay close to Stephen—for investigative purposes only, of course. This man had an uncanny ability to affect her, as the charge presently running up her spine proved.

Maybe it was safer if she went it alone. After all, she couldn't really risk any more trouble, and especially not in the form of this man. Romantic tingles weren't her thing anymore, for they'd proven her wrong in her marriage to David. "No, you don't," she said, shaking off the disturbing awareness of his body close to hers. "I'm perfectly capable of taking care of my baby and myself. I don't need a baby-sitter."

"I'm no one's idea of a baby-sitter, and you no longer have a choice. I'm in this to the end."

Oh, dear. He was stubborn. But was she in trouble, too?

"Fine," she said, recognizing she couldn't keep him from doing what he wanted any more than he could her. "Do whatever you feel you must. But I'm going to find those dogs."

"Fine. You do that. But I'm going to be there at your side every step of the way."

Those eyes did their thing again. A niggle of fear struck Cammie. "What exactly do you plan to do?"

A grin tipped Stephen's thick black mustache. "Why, my dear Widow Sprague, you and I will have the pleasure of double-dating with Willie and Aunt Sophie from now on."

TWELVE

By the time Cammie arrived home, someone had already cleaned her kitchen. How thankful she was for that unknown person, especially since she desperately needed a bath. By now she feared she'd lose her mind if she had to take another whiff of Marvelous Myrna—*Me.*

Once she'd donned a clean and fragrance-free outfit and was blow-drying her hair, Cammie felt like herself again. Then the reality of what she'd agreed to do after the diner de-scenting operation sank in.

She'd agreed to date.

Worse, she'd agreed to date Stephen Hardesty. Bellamy's one and only experimenting Buddhist.

True, it was for a good cause. Anything done to take care of and protect Miss Sophie had to be viewed as having merit. And of course, Cammie was honor-bound to investigate Myrna's theory about Willie and the missing dogs. The double-dating ploy made sense—in a way.

If Willie ever got around to actually asking Miss Sophie for a date, a minor detail Cammie considered to be in her favor.

Since he hadn't yet and he might not ever, she could try and keep Miss Sophie from going anywhere during the investigation. Maybe.

And maybe not.

But, dating?

Stephen?

Her?

The whole concept made her uneasy. Especially since she found her date-to-be much too attractive with his dark eyes and that thick, masculine mustache. And he was nice, too.

Too bad for her.

Especially since she knew what she could lose if she paid too much attention to Stephen and his positive traits—the predictable comfort of her life.

Heading downstairs, she decided a hot cup of tea and one of her apple spice bars would hit the spot. She wasn't hungry enough for a meal; the Marvelous Myrna—

"Oh, dear. I really have a problem with that name now, don't I?" Shaking her head, she filled the teakettle to the brim and turned on the rear right burner.

"Camellia, dear," Willie said, scant steps behind her. "What kind of quandary do you face? With what name? And when did you take up chatting with yourself? I've never known you to do that before."

Cammie gasped. She sat at the kitchen table and clasped her head in her hands. What was happening to her? Willie was right. She'd never talked to herself. That was one of Maggie's odder quirks. Not Cammie's.

It had gotten so that she hardly recognized herself anymore. And now that she thought about it, her investigative sally was more a Lark thing than it was hers. She remembered Miss Sophie saying how much she was becoming like her sisters. But she wasn't. She couldn't be. Could she?

"Willie," she said from behind her hands, "I just don't

know *what's* wrong with me. I find myself saying things I'd never say, doing things I'd never do, and I can hardly believe it's me."

"Do you perhaps mean things such as garbing yourself in the most abominable wardrobe this afternoon? Patronizing a tobacconist, of all places? You, the woman whose newspaper advertisement states that smokers need not apply as potential boarders?"

Cammie groaned, then peeked through parted fingers. "You too?"

"What do you mean, me too?"

"You saw me?"

"Ooooh, yes." He chuckled. "Too, eh? Who else saw you?"

"You mean besides the people I talked to?"

"Of course."

The teakettle shrieked, and Cammie hurried to turn off the burner. She poured boiling water into her favorite Blue Willow teapot, swirled it around to warm the porcelain, then dumped it into the sink. She measured a healthy dose of chamomile leaves and flowers, filled the pot with the steaming water, and brought it to the table to steep.

"Would you care for a cup?" she asked Willie.

"Please don't betray me to my beloved Sophie, but I can't stomach her chamomile brew. Give me a cup of Earl Gray any day—or night."

"Earl Gray it is." She reached into her tea cupboard, withdrew the appropriate tin, took her steeping ball from a nearby drawer, filled it, and placed it in a large mug. She covered the ball with the freshly boiled water and handed Willie his drink.

"Thank you, dear girl," he said. "Now let's return to what you left off with, shall we?"

"You're not going to let me off easy, are you?"

Willie winked. "Not when I suspect the tale's a humorous one."

"Okay, okay. A girl knows when she's beat." She proceeded to regale him with every aspect of her fruitless afternoon of detecting. But she patted herself on the back for judiciously withholding those details regarding Myrna's suspicions of Willie, not to mention her own concerns about Stephen.

It struck her as strange how she felt so comfortable with Willie in spite of the suspicions Myrna's words had brought her. Insanity seemed to lurk too close for comfort. But the truth was, Willie listened and really seemed to care.

By the time she drew her tale to a close, Willie was clutching his middle, evidently sore from laughing so hard. "You were right, Camellia dearest; you are not acting at all like your normal, sweet, calm self. And although I can appreciate the humor and excitement in your adventures as a pregnant P.I.—I, too, have a certain fondness for Columbo—my concern on your behalf is growing by the day."

"Not you, too!" she cried in dismay.

"I presume I'm in good company, then." Willie covered her hand in a fatherly gesture. She turned her fingers over and laced them through her friend's. She really didn't want him to be guilty of anything but being who he said he was: a retiree without roots.

"I'd never want to overstep my bounds," he started, "but I want to make sure you understand one thing. Stress is destructive, evil stuff. It can ruin a person's health, destroy relationships, make one lose all sense of perspective. And you, dearest girl—remember, please, that I see you as the daughter I was never fortunate enough to have—are living for two right now. You need not put yourself under such pressure."

"What would you have me do? Forget that someone stole the dog I love? That my sisters were robbed of their pets, too? I can't do that, Willie. And I can't understand why anyone would expect me to."

"No one does, I'm sure. What everyone does think, if I'm

not mistaken, is that at this point in your life, it's for the best if you leave it to the authorities to find the dogs."

"But they haven't learned a thing, and he's been gone—"

"Less than a week. And your child's due in . . . ?"

"About five weeks."

Willie took a sip of his now-cooled tea. "Need I say more?"

She shrugged, wondering if he was deliberately trying to scare her off his trail. Oh, how she wished that that absolutely, positively was not the case. She'd grown tremendously fond of the dapper old gentleman who'd showed up at her door.

"I have it!" he exclaimed. "I know just what you need."

"You do? I sure don't."

"Ah . . . but I have the advantage of age over you, my dear. You need a distraction. Something fresh and new, exciting, interesting, and fun. I have just the ticket."

Cammie looked at her boarder with skepticism. "What would that be?"

"No, no, no, no. I can't tell you what it is, Cammie. That would ruin my surprise. You know how splendid surprises are."

"Not all," she murmured, remembering the surprise call in the middle of the night that had changed her marital status forever.

"Well, darling girl, this one is. Tell you what. You meet my beloved Sophie and me in your garage at five o'clock tomorrow evening. You can join us on our delightful adventure."

Here she'd been thinking herself somewhat safe since she hadn't thought him ready to get up the gumption to ask her friend for a date. "Adventure, huh?"

He slapped the tabletop. "Just what the doctor ordered."

When he donned a speculative look, Cammie cringed. Her heart took up a litany of no's, which obviously wasn't heard. She shook her head for good measure.

"Say," Willie went on, seemingly oblivious to her chagrin, "I should think the doc would love to come with us. That's what I'll do. I'll give him a ring, and we'll make a foursome of it. We're sure to have a grand time tomorrow." And before she could offer a word of response, Willie left the kitchen, whistling a snappy tune.

Cammie took her pounding head in her hands again. She couldn't believe she'd walked right into that one. So it was going to happen, no matter how unsettling the notion of dating handsome, interesting, kind, generous, and experimenting Buddhist—you hear that, Cammie? *Buddhist*—Stephen Hardesty was.

Resigned to her fate, Cammie stood, took the teapot, cups, and her uneaten apple spice bar to the sink. She ground up in the disposal the treat she could no longer imagine swallowing, then rinsed the other things. She'd wash them properly in the morning.

Right then she needed to seek the Lord.

Because she'd wanted to stick to Willie so she could investigate the possibility of his being the dognapper, unlikely as it was, and because she'd wanted to stick to Miss Sophie to protect her from a potential thief—of dogs and hearts—Cammie had gotten what she'd wanted. But she was no longer sure it would be all that great. The old chestnut about being careful what you asked for had proven itself valid again.

On top of that, she was going on a date with Stephen Hardesty.

"Heavenly Father," she said, as she closed her bedroom door behind her, "what are you trying to tell me here?"

He didn't respond in any spectacular way—not that she'd really expected him to, just kind of hoped for a minor epiphany—so she took her Bible and her Wedding Ring quilt and curled up in her favorite armchair.

All the answers anyone could ever need the Lord had

already provided in this precious book of his Word. With humility and thanksgiving for God's farseeing provision, Cammie slipped into direct communion with him.

The next evening, Cammie met the trio by her garage. To her surprise, she didn't have to try and finagle a seat next to Miss Sophie.

"You girls go ahead and sit in back," Willie said. "Stephen and I can keep each other company up here. Besides, Cammie, if you feel so led, take a nap. We've a bit of a drive ahead of us. Take advantage of it."

Nap?

Nuh-uh.

Was this his latest effort to disarm her alertness? Cammie didn't know; she just knew the two wily males in front needed much watching. *Not much hardship in watching Stephen,* her impish mind piped in.

That was true enough, and she certainly didn't need reminding. As she'd thought when they'd first met, Stephen bore a strong resemblance to Tom Selleck in his old Magnum, P.I. role, with his thick dark hair, intelligent eyes, lush mustache, and tall, powerful build.

But Stephen wasn't the detective on this case; *she* was. Until she proved that he and his new best buddy, Willie, had nothing to do with her dog's—and her sisters' dogs'—disappearance, they were her prime suspects.

But, oh, Stephen was an appealing man.

On the other hand, he wasn't a Christian.

She was. And as the Bible said, never the twain should, could, or would come to a meeting of the minds—spiritually speaking.

Besides, she'd already proved herself a poor candidate for a romantic relationship. She'd fallen deeply in love with David, only to suffer the pain of his abandonment and neglect, the tragedy of abrupt widowhood, and the sadness of expecting a child who would never know his or her father.

Cammie couldn't put herself through that again, and she couldn't put her child through it either. It had taken a long time for her to accept her role and mission in life—to serve others for Jesus' sake. That was sufficient for her, she kept telling herself.

That, and keeping Miss Sophie from tying herself to another man, one who would likely die not long after the wedding bells rang—if they got that far. Willie was no spring chicken, and statistics showed that men lived shorter lives than women did.

Miss Sophie had already been widowed once. Could she stand to be abandoned again? Especially by a man who carried with him the taint of suspicion, however faint it might be?

"Oho!" that man crowed. "We're here."

Cammie drew up her five-foot-seven frame to its full height and blinked. "You've brought us underground?"

Stephen chuckled. "It would seem so, but we're just in a parking garage."

Cammie looked around for a clue to their location. She found none. "A parking garage where?"

"At the Baltimore Convention Center," answered Willie, a sense of pride rounding out each word.

Miss Sophie laid a hand on her date's shoulder. "Willie, dear, don't you think it's time to tell us what you've brought us to see?"

"On the contrary, my love," he answered, intent on finding a spot for his car in the crowded building. "I wouldn't dream of spoiling the surprise at this point. I want to see the expression on your faces when you catch your first glimpse of the magnificent beauty and power—"

He cut off his words. "Oh, no you don't, Sophie my girl. You're not going to trip me up. Just wait—splendid! There's one."

He parked in an empty slot, and Stephen helped Cammie and his aunt out of the car.

"Do you know what we're going to see?" Cammie asked.

"I haven't a clue." He nodded in Willie's direction. The elderly man attached a theft-prevention bar to the steering wheel, set the lock on the driver's side front door, and closed it. He walked to Miss Sophie's side, whistling a bright tune. "He's having such a good time that I'm willing to go along with him," Stephen said, chuckling.

Cammie studied her boarder. She had to admit that the hint of sadness his eyes occasionally wore was gone. Tonight he had a spring in his step, and his natural ebullience seemed to spill over and catch Miss Sophie in its sparkle. She offered a brief prayer for Willie's innocence.

"Shall we follow them?" asked Stephen, humor in his voice.

Cammie realized that Willie and Miss Sophie were holding the elevator door open for them, and she hadn't yet taken a step in their direction. "Lead on," she said, letting Stephen take her elbow.

Big mistake. His touch was sure, yet gentle, warm, and solicitous. It reminded her how easy it was to like him, how much he seemed to care for her safety and well-being, as well as that of her child.

At the elevator, she severed the contact and, contrariwise, felt momentarily lost, alone, cold. She gave herself a mental shake. *You're here to keep an eye on him and Willie, Camellia, and protect Miss Sophie, too. Stop this schoolgirl foolishness right now.*

Cammie felt a bump at her back, heard a sincere "I'm sorry, miss," and turned to acknowledge the apology. Instead she shrieked, bringing the elevator to sudden silence.

All eyes were on her as she pointed and babbled. "Th-that . . ."

The man who'd jostled her stepped closer. "Are you hurt?"

Cammie backed up into Stephen, who grasped her shoulders and steadied her. "D-don't come any closer with *that*—"

"Oh, Willie, Camellia," cooed Miss Sophie, "isn't that just the cutest thing you've ever seen?" To the stranger, she said, "May I?"

Beaming like a proud papa, the stranger answered, "Why, sure. She's very mellow and loves being loved."

And with that invitation, Miss Sophie began petting the greenest, biggest, most revolting dinosaurian beast Cammie had ever clapped eyes on.

"Miss Sophie," Cammie cried, "don't do it. That thing's likely to eat your whole hand for a snack and come back for supper still. Don't touch it!"

Miss Sophie gave Cammie a look of incredulity. "Why, Cammie, sugar, she's just the sweetest thing. Besides, Willie has a love for things of nature. He's told me all about iguanas and his lifelong fascination with them. Iguanas are vegetarians, just like your sister Lark, and she's yet to take a nip out of me." Turning back to the six-foot monster, she added, "This sweetheart isn't going to do me a thing wrong now, are you?"

Every muscle in Cammie's body trembled in revulsion when the animal—the reptile—slithered out its skinny black tongue in apparent enjoyment of Miss Sophie's tender ministrations.

Nothing would ever get Cammie to touch one of those things.

"Would you like to sit down?" asked Stephen, ever solicitous, when the elevator door opened.

"Yes. In the car, as it's facing west and heading home."

He nodded toward Willie and Miss Sophie. "And spoil their fun?"

Cammie glanced at their companions, only to note their total fascination with the monster the guy held close to his ribs. The iguana's well-rounded body told Cammie it had eaten quite well all its life. No amount of Miss Sophie's comparing its diet to Lark's would persuade her the thing wasn't about to chomp on the nearest human.

The iguana's long, gradually thinning tail hung down its owner's leg for at least three droopy feet. Marked in even areas of darker and lighter green, the appendage looked scaly, supple, muscular, and as dangerous as that of an alligator.

All the way down the living fossil's spine ranged spikes of a most disturbing sort. "What kind of crazy would cart one of those around . . . ?"

Cammie let her words die off as she realized that everyone around her—excepting Stephen, Willie, and Miss Sophie—sported his or her own iguana.

"Dear Jesus," she whispered, seeking help for her fear. To Stephen, she said, "Where are we? Some kind of gathering of lunatics?"

He chuckled and pointed to a banner over the ticket booths just ahead of them. "I don't think they think so. Look."

"'North American Annual Iguana Lovers Convention,'" she read. "There is such a group?"

"Evidently, and we're here with them." He stared at a woman who wore at least six infant reptiles on her jungle-printed shirt.

"How long do we have to stay?"

"I'm not the driver or the enthusiast. Willie's the one to ask."

Cammie peered at her elderly boarder, who'd struck up a conversation with a woman and her only slightly smaller iguana. The animation on his face and Miss Sophie's matching enthusiasm suggested that their return to Bellamy—and refuge from rampant reptiles—would not be imminent.

"I suppose," she said, "we'll just have to make the best of it."

"Of course."

Then it hit her. "Oh, dear. I haven't offended you, have I? I mean, you're not crazy about these prehistoric beings now, are you? Because if you are, then please accept my apology. Although I can assure you, I'll never *like* iguanas, much less become an actual enthusiast."

Stephen laughed. "At least you're running true to form. No, you haven't offended me. Iguanas are fine, but they don't do anything special for me. Watching you flip out over one, though, is another story."

The twinkle in his eye was a dead giveaway. "You tease. You remind me of my sisters when we were little. Since I was the youngest, they tormented me mercilessly."

"But it's all in good fun, Cammie, at least on my part."

A glance at his dark eyes assured her he meant it. "That's nice of you to say. I'd be in trouble tonight if you were as passionate about leftover dinosaurs as those two are."

"Come on, you two," called Willie. "We have thousands and thousands of these beauties to see. We don't want to miss any of them."

Cammie shuddered. "A fate worse than death, if you ask me."

Stephen just laughed, took her elbow again, and led her to the ticket booth. Seconds later, hands stamped with a cartoon iguana, they entered the main exhibition area.

"Oh my," she said faintly. "Willie wasn't kidding, was he?"

Stephen stared all around, obviously struck by the sheer number of reptiles in one location. "'Fraid not."

Resigned to her fate, Cammie followed her elderly friends, making sure she kept to the very center of the crowded aisles.

She didn't want to come any closer to the featured creatures than she had to. True, she had to dodge the owners, who for some unfathomable reason insisted on wearing their pets, but she figured as long as she kept her eyes wide open, she could avoid an undesired close encounter of the reptilian kind.

After walking a while, that bane of late pregnancy returned with a vengeance. "I need to excuse myself for a moment," she said to Stephen.

He looked at her belly, checked his watch, and smiled. "I'll help you find the ladies' room."

She blushed. "Just because you're a doctor doesn't mean you're always right."

"You're right about that. And I'm right about your needing rest-room facilities. Come on. This place must have plenty."

They excused themselves from Willie and Miss Sophie, agreed to meet in an hour at an appointed spot, and took off. As Stephen had said, they soon found relief for a pregnant woman.

When they resumed their stroll down the vendor-lined aisles, Stephen said, "I've seen plenty of iguanas, and I know your first, going-down-in-history glimpse was more than enough for you."

Cammie sputtered an objection, but he laughed and continued. "I'm hungry. Let's go find a snack bar or something."

"And get out of this craziness?" she asked, hopeful.

"As much as one can in these halls."

They found a place that served such culinary delights as hot dogs, hamburgers, pizza slices, and sodas of all flavors, the food colored and shaped—whenever possible—like, of course, iguanas.

Cammie munched on a lizard-head-shaped hamburger, while Stephen opted for pizza topped with enough veggies to form a remarkable likeness of an iguana. The food brought their humor out of hiding, and from there on, the show became one source of laughter after another. They roared over lizard-shaped fudge, lizard key chains, pillows with iguanas needlepointed on them, and every garment known to humankind embellished with the image of the featured animal.

That didn't even touch the more unusual. "Would you just look at that?" Cammie asked in awe.

Stephen followed her pointing finger and howled with laughter. "It's perfect for your home. The only thing you're lacking."

"Um-hmm," she answered, giddy at the absurdity. "My boarders would love an iguana-shaped toilet-seat cover."

Minutes later, they spotted another modern marvel. Behind the vendor hawking fifty-pound sacks of—could one fathom such a thing?—iguana kibble, Cammie spotted the next object of hilarity. "Why, Stephen, it's just the thing for you—for your office, that is."

"Oh, really?" he asked, his voice droll.

With a flourish, she sang out, "Dr. Iggy, I presume?" and indicated a tapestry wall hanging that depicted an iguana dolled up as a doctor. On the reptilian physician's examining table lay one of his brethren, its viperous tongue extended so the doc could look at its throat.

Cammie laughed at Stephen's pained expression. "I hope my patients don't see me like that."

"Oh, I doubt you have a problem with the female ones."

He dragged his gaze from the funny picture and scrutinized her. "What do you mean by that?"

Cammie gestured blandly. "Oh, nothing, nothing. Look. There are Willie and Sophie. Let's go see what they're up to."

"Having fun?" Willie asked, his smile spanning from ear to ear.

Cammie had to admit, "Why, *yes*. I'm having a wonderful time."

"So my darlings have won you over," he chortled. "I knew they would. There's not a soul who doesn't fall in love with an iguana the moment he sees one face-to-face."

Cammie struggled to keep from laughing out loud, but Stephen lost his battle right up front. He shook his head. "I don't think you've made an enthusiast out of Cammie yet, Willie."

"Ah, but I will," the older man said with a secretive smile.

"I'm not a bettin' woman," Miss Sophie said, "so I'm goin' to suggest you don't bet the bank on it, Willie. Camellia has a stubborn streak—of the most genteel kind, you understand."

"It's well hidden," Stephen said, grinning, "but I've caught its appearance from time to time."

"Well," Cammie said in a mock huff, "if you all are just going to stand there and poke fun at me, I'm going to take another look around. I'm sure there are countless iguana items I have yet to discover."

They decided to meet at the exit and leave for Bellamy in another hour. The two couples split up again, and Cammie and Stephen resumed their stroll down vendor heaven.

Before they'd gone too far, Stephen exclaimed, "Wow! It's just the thing."

"What? What is it?"

"Oh no. Willie's not the only one who gets to plan a surprise. Wait right here. Don't follow me, okay?"

Somewhat leery, Cammie nodded. "Okay, but if you're not back in five minutes, I'm heading to the exit to wait for everyone there."

"You've got yourself a deal. Just don't follow me."

As seconds ticked by, Cammie realized the reason she was having so much fun wasn't the convention itself—much less the animal it extolled. It was Stephen's company—his good humor, his solicitude, his willingness to make the best of a weird experience—that had made this outing great.

That scared her. *Lord, I don't want to like him any more than I already do. Please do something. Show me his warts and all.*

Her baby kicked and she smiled, covering the swell of her belly with her hands. As she rubbed, she thought of the day she would see her child kick and move and breathe on its own, in her arms. For her little one's sake, she had to stay strong.

"You make the loveliest picture of expectant motherhood," Stephen said, startling her.

"Why, thank you. What a nice thing to say."

"A very true one, Cammie." Holding up a sack, he again gave her that gorgeous mischievous grin that tipped his mustache in such an intriguing way. "Want to see your surprise?"

"*My* surprise?"

"Who else's?"

"Well . . ."

"Too bad. You're going to see it. Close your eyes."

"But I can't see it then."

"Close them anyway."

"Okay."

Her heart kicked up its beat when the warmth of Stephen's large, powerful frame drew near. For an instant Cammie fought the strongest urge to lay her head on that broad, strong chest. To take a brief respite when she could feel another person up close, someone she could count on, someone who cared for her.

The scent of Stephen—clean, spicy, and somehow uniquely him—teased her nostrils, inviting her to burrow into him to draw more of it in. She leaned toward him, then . . .

. . . something slapped down on her head.

She jerked back, realizing how close she'd come to making a grave mistake. Flustered—and embarrassed by the feelings she'd just experienced—she opened her eyes and spoke more sharply than she intended. "What are you up to?"

He gave her another of his penetrating scrutinies. Evidently he'd caught the change in her tone of voice. "Taking care of something we've discussed in the past. Remember that horrible green hat you wore for detecting purposes?"

"Of course." She reached for her head, but Stephen caught her hand.

"Now, wait. If you'll turn around, there's a mirror right there. That way you can capture the full effect."

With trepidation, Cammie did as asked. "Stephen! How could you?"

But he couldn't respond; he was laughing too hard.

On her head he'd set a hat. Not an ordinary hat, but a substitute for her other one, a substitute in the same vein. Sort of.

She stared at the monstrosity he'd bought her. "An iguana beanie, you fiend. Why, it's even got spines on its back, an awful, beady-eyed face, and a long scaly tail."

"It does indeed. But you haven't seen the best part yet."

Raising his hand to the back of her head, she felt him tug, and to her horror, her very own iguana-on-a-hat opened its mouth and slithered its snaky tongue out.

THIRTEEN

"WHERE'S WILLIE?" CAMMIE ASKED MISS SOPHIE WHEN SHE and Stephen found her alone by the exit at the agreed-upon time.

Miss Sophie shook her head and smiled. "I don't rightly know. He brought me here, made sure I was comfortable on this bench—now, Camellia, you sit yourself right next to me, hear?—then took off, sayin' he had to fetch his surprise."

Cammie sat. "I'm not sure I like the sound of yet another surprise. The first one was more than enough."

"Aww," Stephen said, "now don't tell me you didn't love coming tonight. Why, you even wound up with a brand-new Easter bonnet."

"Not hardly."

"You bought yourself a hat?" Miss Sophie asked. "Why, show me, dear; you know I just love pretty things."

Cammie and Stephen laughed.

Miss Sophie looked puzzled.

They laughed harder, and Stephen, unable to stop, reached into the bag with the beanie and plopped it back on top of Cammie's hair.

Miss Sophie *ooohed*. "Why, it's darlin', Camellia. I just knew you'd end up likin' these sweet babies."

"Wait, Aunt Sophie," Stephen managed to say between peals. "You haven't seen everything yet."

Cammie again felt the gentle tug and resigned herself to looking ridiculous under the iguana with the wiggling tongue.

"It's just too cute," Miss Sophie crooned, touching the spikes on Cammie's hat, caressing the tail, and tapping the bulging cheeks. "How could I have missed it? Why, I thought for sure we'd stopped at every booth here. I'd love to have one."

Cammie took off her topper. "You can have mine—"

"Why, Camellia!" Stephen said theatrically. "You wound me." He clutched his chest. "And here my only wish was to give my fair lady a token of my great respect and admiration."

Since Miss Sophie made no attempt to take the abomination, Cammie swatted Stephen with his "token." "Just you wait," she said. "I can see that reptilian physician wall hanging in your office waiting room, Dr. Iggy."

He gave her a crooked grin. "I asked for that one, didn't I?"

"Mm-hmm—"

"Cammie girl!" Willie cried. "Where did you find that perfect hat?"

Cammie turned to her boarder and froze.

Stephen said, "You didn't. Did you?"

Miss Sophie clapped. "Oh, Willie, you darlin', wonderful man. Please tell me you did."

"No," Cammie said on a moan. "Please tell me you didn't."

Miss Sophie ran to her beau's side and patted his lean cheek. "You did. You really and truly did."

"I decided it was time to fulfill a lifelong dream. And here she is."

With pride, Willie held out a massive iguana, bedecked with breathtaking spikes along its spine, and measuring a mammoth seven feet or so. "Meet Lana the iguana—after Lana Turner, glamour gal."

Cammie shuddered. "I'd really rather not." Then his words made full impact. She narrowed her eyes. "You *bought* that thing?"

He nodded, smiling and rubbing his monster.

Miss Sophie cheered and patted another spot on the beast.

Dread becoming a live thing in her middle, Cammie went on. "And you intend to take it back to Bellamy?"

Miss Sophie gave her a questioning look. "Do you feel all right, Camellia? You're sayin' the silliest things."

Cammie waved aside Miss Sophie's concern. "Willie? Do you intend to take that creature back to Bellamy?"

"Of course."

"In your car?"

"Yes."

"With us?"

"How else would I get him home?"

"Home?" she yelled. "What do you mean, 'home'?"

Stephen stepped up behind her and placed his strong, warm hands on her shoulders. They didn't help.

Especially not when Willie said, "I mean home. Upstairs in your house in the third bedroom from the front. Home."

"B-but—"

"You did say you had no trouble with pets," he reminded her, jutting his chin.

"B-but I meant *normal* pets. You know—cats, dogs, birds, bunnies, guinea pigs. It never occurred to me someone might bring home a *dinosaur.*"

Miss Sophie placed her soft hand on Cammie's forehead. "Honey, we've kept you out far too long. You're not makin' a lick of sense."

Cammie untangled herself from the two well-meaning but unhelpful Hardestys. "I'm making perfectly good sense. I never said he could bring a prehistoric monster into my home. Besides, where's he going to keep it? Not in his bathtub."

"Well, no," Willie answered. "Not permanently. I'm having a tank delivered and set up tomorrow. But for tonight . . ."

"No. No, no, no, no, no. This can't be happening to me." She turned to Stephen and jabbed a finger at his chest. "You're a doctor. Is there some genetic or physical cause for a woman's entire life to fall apart on her when she's pregnant? Any reason at all why it should careen from the miserable to the tragic to the ridiculous?"

When Stephen shrugged, Cammie began ticking off fingers. "First I connive and engineer a second honeymoon all by myself. It fails, and not long afterwards my husband dies. Then I find out I'm pregnant but minus the dad. My sister Lark comes home. Maggie's fired, then lands in jail. Lark runs afoul of a mobster. The two of them decide to take over my life. Doc Calloway retires. Our dogs get stolen. I discover Marvelous Myrna—*Me.* Now this. You tell me."

"Stephen, I'm afraid your dear aunt is correct," Willie said, moving quickly toward Cammie. "We must get our sweet girl home. Why, she's begun to rant and rave. Is this normal in pregnancy?"

Stephen, concern on his face, wrapped an arm around Cammie's shoulders. "Let's say it's not unusual in some odd cases. But it *is* time to head home. Come on, Cammie. I'll help you."

She shook her head and stepped away. "I don't need any help. I just don't want that lizard in my house."

"Okay. I think we all know that. But tell me something," Stephen, ever rational, said. "Did you say Willie could keep a pet when he first rented a room at your place?"

She squinched her eyes shut. "Yes."

"Then you don't have a case. Let's go home. I'm sure Willie and Lana will be no trouble." He led her from the exhibition hall.

Glad to leave the place, Cammie relaxed, if only a fraction.

Stephen went on. "I'll tell you what. The books I've been reading teach a great way to look at something like this. According to Zen, you just need to remember that everything is mere illusion. Then when you separate your self from attachment to the tragic or absurd yet fleeting concerns of life, you can let your concerns fall away and find peace in unity with the universal."

Cammie pulled to a stop and graced him with a glare. "There is nothing you can say to persuade me that thing Willie's holding is any kind of illusion that will fall away in any way, shape, or form. I can't understand how you can buy that fool concept one bit."

As Stephen opened his mouth, the iguana puffed out a sack under its bottom jaw. It was huge.

"There!" Cammie cried. "Tell me that's not real. One second ago, that . . . that *beast* had a saggy little wattle. Now Dino-girl has this gargantuan balloon under her head. I can see it from here, and I'm sure Willie can touch it—if he feels so led."

With a sniff, Cammie marched off in the direction of the elevators, madder than she'd been in ages. But as she stalked, her bravado faded. What had she done? She'd let her fear get the best of her. She'd behaved terribly, nothing at all like her normal self.

More like . . . Maggie . . . or Lark.

Worse yet, in a very un-Christlike way.

What was wrong with her, anyway?

One thing was certain. She didn't recognize herself anymore.

Did God?

Mortification was awful. Especially when it came seasoned with embarrassment.

As Cammie went through her normal motions the next day, she asked God's forgiveness for her terrible witness to Stephen. She also called Miss Sophie and apologized for her behavior, unable to give her friend a decent explanation for it.

She didn't have one.

When Willie made his unusually late and tentative appearance in the kitchen for breakfast, Cammie prayed for God to open up the floor and let her disappear. He didn't answer that prayer, so she stuttered her way through yet another apology.

She hoped she never had to set eyes on Stephen Hardesty again.

Cammie didn't know how she'd face the man after what she'd said to him. True, all that stuff about reality and illusion didn't add up to a whole ounce of sense, especially when he tried to explain away a perfectly real, live, and repulsive iguana.

Instead of ranting at him as she'd done, though, she should have listened to what he said, perhaps to understand him a bit better. Then maybe she could have presented him with Christ's truth and eternal reality in a way he might have grasped. That would have been the mature, Christlike way to act.

God had given her an opportunity to talk with Stephen, and she'd failed. What's worse, she knew that Stephen had a great need to find out how he should live his life. After all, he was spending all that time seeking for meaning and God through all that illusion gobbledygook, so he must be serious about his search. And she'd blown her chance to be God's servant.

As the day went by, she realized it wouldn't do to hope and pray she never saw Miss Sophie's nephew again. For one thing, it was an unrealistic hope. Bellamy was a small town, and Stephen was in Bellamy to stay. At least for some time.

Then, too, Jesus hadn't called her to the coward's way of avoidance. He'd called her to follow him, and in doing so, to offer unbelievers a glimpse of the Savior's presence in her life. Somehow, despite her mortification, she would have to face Stephen Hardesty again.

And somehow, she would have to make sure her behavior more adequately represented the one who had given his all for her. She felt called to show Stephen the love that could fill his seeking heart, to let him see in her the someone who longed to come and be the reality in his life.

Cammie prayed that God would equip her and she'd prove herself equal to that calling.

Every time Stephen remembered the excursion of the night before, he grinned. At least, he did until the reverberation of Cammie's rejection of his latest step in his faith search rang again in his mind.

He'd tried to meditate after he'd returned home, but it hadn't been his best effort. Bits and pieces of the evening had intruded on his concentration, and although he'd acknowledged them and allowed them to drift off—as he'd read he should do—they'd returned again and again, hogging up his time. And his tranquillity.

On one hand, the memory of Cammie's laughter made his day brighter. On the other hand, he had to admit that the iguana was pretty real. For the first time since he'd begun reading about the Buddha's path, he found it impossible to believe that all things were really illusion.

Cammie was right—there *was* something all too real about Lana the iguana.

Had he again stumbled on yet another flawed philosophy in his search for enlightenment? his search for peace? Was he a Buddhist in the making? or still a hungry seeker, longing for meaning and purpose in his life?

He faced tonight with more than a bit of trepidation. Both Willie and Aunt Sophie planned to have supper at Cammie's. They'd invited him to join them. Stephen wasn't sure how he'd react when he saw his hostess.

Could he just see her as the pleasant companion with whom he'd enjoyed an unusual event? Or would her rejection of the practice that he'd thought would offer him answers to his life questions build a greater wall of awkwardness between them?

How could she be so sure of her faith?

Why couldn't he be sure of . . . anything?

Stephen couldn't remember when a woman had rattled him so much.

"Lord," Cammie whispered as she rinsed off the broccoli florets she was about to toss into the salad, "you sure do have a sense of humor."

Less than two minutes ago, she'd answered her ringing doorbell and found Stephen on her front porch. He'd grinned crookedly, then pointed toward the stairs behind her.

"Willie invited me to watch the operation," he'd said and vanished in the direction of the scuffing and huffing and occasional pounding to which she'd been treated since three o'clock. Lana's permanent home had arrived.

Not only was the dinosaur in Cammie's house, but the would-be Buddhist was as well. "What's my lesson, Father?" she asked.

"Oh, honey, we don't ever know until he wants us to," said Miss Sophie, startling Cammie.

"Oh! I didn't know you were here."

"I just got here. Was that my Stephen I saw comin' in here just a minute ago?"

"The one and only."

"Hmm . . . must have come to play with dear Lana."

Cammie wrinkled her nose. "He can have her, as far as I'm concerned."

"Now, Camellia, dear," Miss Sophie chided, "I've never known you to be so close-minded. You simply have to turn your fear to the Lord and get to know that lovely animal."

Cammie shuddered. "I'll grant you, I do have to pray about my fear—and I will. But I'll pass on getting to know the dinosaur, thank you."

Shaking her head and *tsk-tsk*ing, Miss Sophie left the kitchen. But as Sophie took the stairs, Cammie overheard her question: "Lord? What are we goin' to do with that girl?"

"Just keep the lizard out of the girl's way," Cammie called, breaking broccoli with satisfying verve. It was green. Like iguanas . . . like Lana.

The meal went by quickly, the younger boarders demanding to know every last detail about their new fellow resident. Aside from a few thank-yous to compliments she received on the food, Cammie kept her peace.

As she cleaned up after the meal, she tuned in to her favorite contemporary Christian music radio station and hummed along in the sudden and welcome silence. Everyone had darted back upstairs to visit the star of the day.

Still, Cammie felt at loose ends. She missed Muttley more each day. There was something inherently comforting about a dog's enthusiastic presence, its warm body, its need for affection and friendship.

Not like a lizard.

Once the kitchen gleamed again and the perennial coffeepot had produced fresh brew, she went to the parlor, stoked the fire, and sat at her quilting frame. To keep from thinking of more disturbing matters, she focused on the piece before her. The manager of the better linens department at a large store in Leesburg had called her—out of the blue—and said she'd just seen one of Cammie's quilts. Did she do consignment work?

The conversation had thrilled Cammie. If things went the way the manager thought they would, Cammie would have a steady stream of orders for quilts. It gave her enormous satisfaction to know that someone would lie under one of her creations, keep warm, and treasure the colors, patterns, intricate piecing, and stitches she'd made.

Extra money wouldn't hurt either. Not that she was in dire need, but she had no idea how much it would cost to raise a child. She had reason to believe that between the money from David's insurance and investments, plus the income from her boarders, she could do fine by their little one. Still, a cushion for the future would help her feel just that much better.

"What kind of deep thoughts are you entertaining?" Stephen asked, entering the room.

"I thought you'd be upstairs with Lana's other faithful fans."

"There's only so much iguana a guy can take."

"Phew!" she said, laughing. "Here I thought I was the only one not enamored with that critter."

Stephen looked toward the kitchen. "Coffee?"

"Of course. Help yourself. Plus there's fresh zucchini bread. Take some of that, too."

Several minutes later he returned with a steaming mug and

a thick slab of bread. He sat on the floor with his back against the sofa, placing his snack and drink on the table in front of him. Breaking off a piece of her latest baking success, he popped it into his mouth and sighed his pleasure. "Hey, this is great stuff. Zucchini, you said?"

"Right. That's the absolute best-ever recipe, and believe me, I've tried plenty."

"Just like that's the finest quilt I've ever seen," he answered, nodding in her direction.

"Why, thank you, Stephen. I take great pride in my work. I love turning bits and pieces of cloth into something really special."

Wrapping his hands around the coffee mug, he stared into the dark beverage. Then he turned those deep, expressive eyes on her. "I don't mean to embarrass you, Cammie, but I pride myself on my honesty, so I'm going to say it anyway. You're a very special woman."

Her cheeks grew warm. "Thank you, but I'm probably the most ordinary one in town."

"No, you're not."

Her face flared hotter. "Okay, okay. I'll admit the detecting got out of hand, and . . . well, I might as well get right to it. I apologize for my behavior last night. It was uncalled for and indefensible. Please forgive me."

"For what? Speaking your mind?"

"No. For acting like a maniac, for mouthing off at you about your beliefs, and especially for giving you such a poor example of what a Christian is truly like."

Stephen sent her a quizzical look. "I'll agree that you went ballistic over the iguanas, and your comments were lively, to say the least. But I see nothing about your actions that could affect anyone's opinion of Christianity."

Cammie stuck her needle into her quilt sandwich and

stood. "It's just that fear isn't the right response for a Christian. True love of Christ drives out fear."

The questions in his eyes told her to keep going. "If I'd taken time to think through my reaction to the iguanas, I would have turned to God instead of to hysterics. Prayer is usually my first line of action in uncomfortable or frightening situations. But for some reason, I didn't pray this time. I haven't been my usual self lately."

Although he didn't say a word, his arched eyebrow asked questions. It also suggested that he remembered some of her recent "moments."

"Let me put it this way," she said. "I took my eyes off the Lord and let fear take root. As I said, I didn't give you the best example of a believer."

"But fear is a natural human reaction."

"Of course, but my life is filled with a supernatural presence. God can and does overcome all those human things. With the way I talked to you . . . I'm amazed you came over today."

"Wouldn't have missed another of Widow Sprague's incredible meals," he said, grinning.

Cammie got up and walked over to the hearth, held her hands out to the blaze, and thrilled to its warmth. "I'm glad you enjoyed it. But you must have had a thought or two against facing the madwoman from last night."

"Nothing that strong, but I did wonder if you'd be angry at me."

"Me? Angry?" Cammie began, pacing the room. "Oh, Stephen. You didn't do anything to make me mad. You weren't the one to discount my beliefs with a mouthful of smart words."

"You didn't do that. In fact—" He patted a spot next to him on the carpet. "Why don't you come and join me? I'm getting jumpy just watching you pace back and forth."

For an instant Cammie debated the wisdom of such an action. But then she decided it was silly for her to behave like a caged lion in her own parlor. And Stephen had proved himself a perfectly respectable, pleasant companion. He wanted to talk, and if she opened herself to the Holy Spirit's guidance, perhaps something eternal and important would come out of their chat.

"Okay," she said, slipping in sideways to accommodate her belly, and settled at his side. "What were you going to say?"

He again looked into his mug. "Your comments didn't offend me as much as they made me think. I have to admit you had a valid point. Beyond the comic value, as you said, Lana is very real indeed."

Cammie smiled. "I sure hope you're not expecting an argument from me."

Stephen shook his head. "On the contrary. You were right. And after I thought about it, I couldn't convince myself that Lana is a mere illusion. I couldn't meditate away her existence."

Cammie noted the furrow between Stephen's eyebrows. She placed a hand on his forearm. "But, Stephen, there *is* an absolute reality. And you're part of it. I am, too. Lana, Willie, Miss Sophie, and even my baby are part of it. And no philosopher from Asia or anywhere can deny it. We're all part of God's creation. We're real, just as he is."

Beneath her fingers, she felt his muscles tense.

"I'll accept that you're a certain form of reality." He covered her hand with his. "I can feel you; I can feel myself. If I wanted to, I'm sure I could go upstairs and touch good old Lana. But I can't touch God. How can he be real if there's so much in this world that's horrible, ridiculous, and unacceptable? That's why I've struggled so to make sense of my life and the universe. Up until last night, it seemed to make more sense to view life as the Buddha did, as an illusory image that soon slips into the void of memory. The experience itself soon becomes nothing. The only thing that's real is this moment. The here and now . . . but now I'm not so sure."

Cammie remained silent. A loud clunk rang out from the second floor. Laughter echoed, then ebbed, and the house grew quiet again.

"Okay," she said, "I'll agree that, like that noise those guys made upstairs, the moment's action fades. But here—" she placed his hand on her belly—"this is as real as one can get. A momentary action has repercussions that last forever. Think about it. Those nuts might have dented the upstairs floor. That would be the permanent effect of a passing sound."

Her baby kicked, and Stephen smiled. "Energetic little one."

"It's the most amazing feeling on earth," she said. "And it tells me my baby's real. Just as I know God is real. I know he's real because of the great things he has done in my life, the changes he has made in me. He took the little tagalong Bellamy brat, a scared orphan, someone who was always in the shadow of her bright and beautiful sisters, and gave meaning to her life. He has a plan for me, and I'm living it. Every day he reveals a little more of it to me, and as long as I'm obedient to his leading, I do great. It's when I fall back on myself that I goof up. Like last night."

"I still don't think you goofed up."

"But—"

He cut off her argument with a finger to her lips. "You have no idea how beautiful you looked last night, laughing and talking to me. Your eyes sparkled and your voice sang out. You're a lovely woman, Camellia Sprague, and I was proud to escort you to that crazy convention. That can't possibly have been a goof-up."

Cammie shook her head, intent on achieving her purpose:

to apologize to Stephen, to share the true message of Christ with him.

And then the strangest thing happened.

Stephen's eyes opened wider. He pressed her lips more firmly with the finger that still covered them.

At first she felt the pressure like gentle warmth, and then it sparked, fizzing through her with the brightest awareness. The spot where they touched tingled, and her eyelids grew heavy. Longing sprang to life in her heart.

Stephen drew closer, his finger now outlining her mouth.

Cammie tried to draw breath, but every part of her was paralyzed by his touch, his tender caress, the reality of his nearness.

He whispered her name, sliding his hand across her jaw and into her hair. Closing the distance between them, he covered the spot his finger had touched with his lips.

Cammie melted into that kiss, Stephen's firm mouth molding itself to hers, telling her he cherished her. The soft roughness of his mustache added a unique pleasure to their caress, a certain new intimacy, a knowledge of him she hadn't had until now. Despite herself, she returned the kiss with the same care, cherishing the feel of him up close, glad of his presence at her side.

When he pulled marginally away, Cammie drew a shaky breath. Before she could formulate a thought, however, he returned to their kiss, this time less tentative, somehow familiar.

At their renewed contact, she felt herself soar, her breath catching in her throat, her heart beating, pounding a thrilling syncopation she hoped would never end—

"Oho, my boy!" cried Willie from the doorway. "So that's the way the waters run. Sophie, my love, did you see that?"

"Oh, Willie, dear . . . ," she cooed. "Cammie, honey. Stephen . . ."

Cammie folded herself over her child, wishing she could disappear. To her dismay—and, capriciously, to her delight—Stephen covered her protectively, his arms still around her.

"I'd never even imagined such a thing," Miss Sophie said, a hitch in her voice. "And here it must have been happenin' right under my nose. You know how much I love the two of you. . . . Willie, I guess we need to be headin' home, to give this matter some prayer."

"I'll see you there," Willie offered. "That way the two love-birds can have more time alone."

"Wait!" Cammie's voice came out muffled by Stephen's shoulder as he still embraced her. She wriggled out from his clasp and stood awkwardly. "It's not what you all think. Why, it's . . . well, ah . . ."

Stephen stood also, crossed his arms over his chest, and with a very male smile, said, "Yes, indeed, Widow Sprague. Please do tell us. Just exactly *what* was that?"

FOURTEEN

IT HADN'T BEEN HIS MOST CHIVALROUS MOMENT, BUT Stephen had wanted Cammie to acknowledge the attraction he'd sensed between them from the second they'd met.

Insane, of course, but there it was. He was more attracted to Aunt Sophie's very charming, pregnant, widowed friend than he'd been to a woman in . . .

Had he ever been this affected by a woman?

He unlocked the door to his apartment and stepped inside. He'd always felt his spare, clean décor, including a couple of recent Asian additions, suited his logical mind. Normally, he'd relax as he crossed the living room and entered his bedroom. But today . . . he realized the walls seemed bare. A quilt would do wonders for the expanse over the geometric, metal headboard.

Dropping onto the bed, he lay staring at the blank ceiling, Cammie's dazed and amazed reaction to their first kiss blazing in his mind. She'd mirrored everything he'd felt.

When she'd stood to catch Aunt Sophie and Willie before they frothed the town of Bellamy into a romance-induced uproar, he'd felt the raw need for her to acknowledge what he'd discovered in her response to his touch.

She'd disappointed him when she hadn't proclaimed—what? Her undying love for him? How absurd.

No. That wasn't what he'd wanted.

But still . . .

The gnawing sensation inside him felt too familiar, too much like the lack he'd experienced while growing up. His parents had gone through the clinical motions of caring for his basic needs, but the affectionate touches, the words of love, hadn't been there. To be more precise, they hadn't rung true.

He knew better than to expect anything more from anyone. Anyone, that is, besides Aunt Sophie, who'd always been on his side, supported him, trusted him, loved him.

But then he'd met Cammie, who had awakened a sharp longing inside him. When they'd kissed, that longing had become a flame. Her vague waffling hadn't satisfied the hunger in his heart; it had only fed the fire. He'd needed to take her back in his arms and keep on kissing her until she confessed her feelings.

Feelings . . .

Just what did *he* feel for *her?*

He rubbed down his mustache, then ran a hand through his hair. He sat up, swung his legs off the side of the bed, and clasped his hands between his knees. He couldn't quite put his finger on how he felt about Cammie Sprague. He just knew he was everything but indifferent to her.

Even when they disagreed, he enjoyed her; he'd rather disagree with her on any subject known to man than agree with anyone else. And they had the matter of her medical condition and her refusal to let him see her through it between them. He felt that refusal as sharply as his parents' rejection of his chosen career. Of him.

Why *had* she fled his practice? For crying out loud, she was only pregnant. He'd delivered dozens of babies. Surely Cammie thought him capable of taking care of her and her child.

Especially her and her child.

As honest as always, Stephen acknowledged that he couldn't remain logical and detached from her situation, as a doctor should. But deep in his heart, he also felt he would do better for her and her baby than any other physician ever could or would.

It hurt to know she didn't trust him to do so.

Why didn't she?

Could he ever truly care about a woman who didn't trust him? One who saw life as dependent on some vague God out somewhere in his heaven? A woman with whom he couldn't share his soul?

He had no answers, just questions, more of them than he'd contemplated in a very long time . . . questions that refused to leave him alone.

He'd come to Bellamy in pursuit of peace, not romance. And certainly not romance with a woman who'd complicated his life in a matter of minutes after they'd met and continued to do so with alarming regularity.

Could he ever love the woman who had shaken the faith foundation he'd begun to think he could build for himself on Buddha's teachings? The woman who had shattered all semblance of peace in his life?

Cammie stumbled to her room, dazed by what had happened tonight. The installation of the lizard's tank had been nerve-racking, if nothing else. The thumps, hammer cracks, shouts, and chuckles had reminded her of the creature each time she managed to forget it and her behavior.

Then that kiss . . .

My goodness, what a kiss—kisses, if a body had to be perfectly accurate. Stephen had rocked her world with his caresses. His touch had stunned her with its tenderness. At the same time, she'd sensed that his longing and need for a relationship was as deep as her own. Could he possibly hunger for someone to care for him as she did?

It was a longing she had thought she could never allow herself to have again. After all, she had the Lord Jesus and knew that only he would never disappoint her. And she had the child with whom God had blessed her. The child she knew represented her new beginning as a single woman, a single parent.

Then the power of Stephen's touch had rekindled something she'd thought long dead inside her, something she'd thought David's neglect had killed.

She chuckled with irony. Even David hadn't been that thorough with his kisses on their honeymoon. After all the years of a loveless relationship, she'd never dreamed she could still respond to a man who reached for her with tenderness, passion, and need.

A tear rolled down her cheek. "Why, Lord? Why him? Why now? It's just so complicated, Father God. I'm pregnant. David died such a short time ago. And Stephen's not a Christian. How could I be so attracted to him?"

Cammie sat on her bed and took a tissue from the box on her nightstand. Dabbing the tears on her face, she could almost feel the masculine roughness of Stephen's mustache on her skin. She craved to know that touch again.

Cammie dropped her face into her hands and groaned. "Oh, Lord," she cried out in despair, "I thought I was so content and satisfied with my life before he came to town.

It wasn't an exciting life, but it was calm. Now I'm a mess. Everything's spinning around me, and I can't catch my bearings anymore. What's worse, I find myself wanting again. You know I vowed I'd never want again, after spending all those years wanting David's love, his attention, and his company, only to wind up with nothing in the end. I can't do it again, Father. You know I can't live like that again."

The constant sense of failure she'd known during those years wasn't something to which she could ever return. Knowing she mattered less to her husband than a column of numbers or the money that kept his memories of an underprivileged youth at bay had left her defeated and miserable. She couldn't imagine risking that possibility again. Her marriage had devastated her sense of self.

Now she had a child to think of. What kind of mother would she make if she put herself through that loneliness and need another time? That hopeless need for a man who would set her aside as soon as the honeymoon ended?

David had been more in love with his career than with her, and he'd only been an accountant. Everyone with a lick of sense knew that medicine was the ultimate mistress of its practitioners.

Loving Stephen could lead only to disaster. A doctor, and a seeking Buddhist to boot. They didn't even share a faith on which to build a lasting relationship. Cammie could never allow herself to fall in love with a man like Stephen Hardesty. No matter how tempting the prospect might seem.

No matter how lonely and empty the alternative would be.

Smack, smack, smack, smack!

"I do love this little ol' hammer," Louella said to Sophie as they stood at the front of the library meeting room.

"I've noticed that myself, dear."

Louella frowned. "But it doesn't seem to have much effect on them, now, does it?"

Sophie shrugged. "Try again. That way you'll have another chance to whack the podium tonight."

"My sentiments exactly." Louella followed through.

The rapid-fire chatter turned down a couple of notches.

"Ladies!" Louella cried. "I'm wantin' to call this regular meetin' of the Bellamy Garden Club to order."

Shushing hissed through the crowd.

"Well, now, that's much better," Louella said. "And we've got a couple of extra special items on the table tonight, so let's get on with our business."

In short order, she had all the officers give their reports, cutting off those with a tendency to ramble. When she'd seen to that chore, Louella set down her notes and cleared her throat.

"Ladies, our dear Sophie here has a treat for us tonight. She and her beau, Willie Johnson, went on an adventure night before last. While they were . . . wherever, she was charmin' enough to buy all of us a token of her affection. And now she's wantin' to share her gifts with her sister gardeners."

The door to the room opened and in stalked Myrna, again arrayed in unique attire. She carried her gray-and-blue zebra coat over her arm but had left her orange knit hat on. She'd tucked a bile green, drawstring-necked blouse into a mud-tinted skirt, and covered her feet and legs in alligator boots that had seen better days. As usual, she'd daubed her eyes with turquoise shadow.

"What's your hurry, Louella Ashworth? Catch your house on fire again?" Myrna chuckled, bringing up one of Louella's less-than-fine moments.

"Myrna Stafford," chided Sophie, "why do you have to be so mean-spirited?"

"Just speakin' the truth, Sophie," Myrna countered, removing her hat to let her purple sausage curls jounce all over her head at her pseudo-sage nod.

Louella cleared her throat again. "Let's get back to tonight's program, shall we? As I was sayin' before bein' so rudely interrupted, Sophie has somethin' special for us all tonight. Go ahead, Sophie, dear. Tell us everythin' about your adventure."

Sophie took her place behind the microphone. "Girls, it was the most excitin' thing I've done in years. You'll never believe it. Why, I tell you, Willie Johnson is just the most dashin', fascinatin' man one could ever imagine. Dear ones, he took us to this year's Annual Iguana Lovers Convention in Baltimore. Can you imagine that?"

A few jaws dropped. A couple of *huhs?* hummed. A handful of bewildered looks crossed paths.

"You know," Sophie continued. "Iguanas. Those lovely animals from the jungles of the world. They're the most amazin' critters the Lord put on earth—well, aside from us folks, you understand."

"Hmph! Ain't they those ugly bug-eyed lizard things with 'em funny things on their backs?"

"Myrna," Sophie said with great forbearance, "there is no such thing as an ugly iguana. No, my dear, indeedy not. I can freely attest to that, since I saw thousands of them in the flesh close up and personal-like the other night, and not a one could even be called unappealin' at its worst moment."

"I ain't buyin'," Myrna said, crossing her arms over her chest.

Sophie shook her head. "Anyway, sister gardeners, I found us the cutest things at the convention. I brought one back for each of you all. Of course, not everyone will be gettin' the same item. No, I picked everyone's gift individually for her. Hope you like them as much as I do. And don't you be expectin' extravagance, just fun and a trinket for remembrance, you hear?"

Sophie made the rounds, handing each of her friends a gift. Some received iguana key chains, others tiny rubber iguana sculptures; yet others received iguana sun catchers for their windows, and a few—Louella among them—got iguana slippers.

Finally Sophie reached Myrna. "I have yours right here."

Myrna tried to cover her curiosity with her usual sour look. "Well, then, let's have us a look at it already."

Sophie beamed. "Here you are. I think you're just plain goin' to love 'em. Wear them in fun and good health, dear."

The gathered gardeners all turned to face their colorfully clad member, curious about her gift. Myrna didn't make them wait long for her reaction.

"Oh! I cain't rightly believe my eyes. You actually had the sense to get me somethin' nice. An' useful. Why, they're plumb dandy, Sophie Hardesty—an' I'm plumb amazed. Tickled pink, too. Thank you, dear."

Sophie gave an audible sigh of relief. "Put them on so the others can see them."

Knowing herself the object of everyone's attention, Myrna took her time removing her gift from its box. With much ado, she clipped on three-inch-long emerald-and-black iguana dangle earrings.

She was truly a sight to behold.

Swinging her decorated head from one side to the other, she displayed her new baubles with inordinate pride. "Well, ladies. What do you all think? Ain't they the most elegant things you ever did set your eyes on?"

At first a stunned silence swept the room. Then a couple of discreet coughs were heard. A muffled titter sounded in the far right corner. A few whispers rustled out.

"Well?" asked Myrna, commandeering the attention again.

"Why don't you all just admit it? Sophie brought me the most splendid gift of all. I have a marvelous piece of jewelry to wear to my most important affairs now."

Sarah Langhorn stood, scraping her chair in her haste. "If you all will excuse me," she said, her words muffled by the hand covering her mouth, "I do b'lieve I left my stove on back at the house."

A red-faced Mariah Desmond set down her pen on the secretary's log. "I need the ladies' room," she said and sprinted out.

Philadelphia Philpott, with a saucy sparkle in her eyes, began waving her hand at her flushed face, then actually removed her heavy wool sweater. "It's kinda warm in here tonight, isn't it, Louella?"

Myrna stood, as huffy as ever. "I get it. You all are just so jealous of Sophie's singlin' me out for the best gift that you all either have to leave or change the subject. But no matter. I know what's what. Sophie chose me to give these lovely earrings to. An' you all just have to live with that. An' without me. I cain't taint myself with people as envious an' snide as you all are. Sophie, sugar, you know where I live. My door's always open to true friends. Not the sort what goes around pretendin' like all these other catty ones. See you real soon, right, dear?"

She stalked to the door. "Oh, yes, well," she said, turning, "I reckon a good turn deserves another. Sophie, sugar, you've been right nice buyin' me these gorgeous earrings, an' my conscience won't let me leave without warnin' you. That there Willie of yourn ain't all he's makin' himself out to be. Why, there ain't no one in town what knows spit about 'im. Secrets like that hide trouble. In his case, they're likely hidin' a bunch of stolen dogs. You make sure you watch yourself round 'im. I'll be seein' you soon, dear."

In the shocked silence she stomped out.

Sophie collapsed, stunned by Myrna's outrageous behavior

and heinous accusation. Moments later she groaned and covered her face with her hands. "I never meant to make such trouble. I can't believe she took those earrings seriously. An' that awful stuff she said about poor Willie . . ."

"That's it!" Louella declared. "That's that woman's last straw. Pray tell, ladies, what can we do with Myrna Stafford?"

Mariah walked back into the meeting room, dabbing her laughter-dampened eyes with a paper towel. "I don't know, Lou, but something's got to be done for the poor soul."

Florinda Sumner stood. "What, though? We can't be givin' her a taste transplant. You all know she was born with atrocious taste and a nasty streak. Plus, we've been prayin' for her since pretty near on to forever now, and we haven't seen the first sign of change in her sour self."

"We've always included her," offered Philadelphia in her soft voice.

Louella nodded. "Even when it made no earthly sense to do so."

The room quieted, all the women wondering how to help miserable, misguided, mean-spirited Myrna.

"You know," said Reenie Desmond Ainsley, "maybe we've gone about this all wrong. You know, the whole group's been willin' to welcome her an' all, but has anyone ministered to her one-on-one?"

"Honey," Mariah said to her youngest daughter, "I do believe you make an excellent point. Myrna's always made me uncomfortable, what with all her complainin' an' her grim outlook, so I haven't sought her out. Which isn't particularly Christlike of me, now, is it?"

"Don't beat yourself up about it, Mariah," said Sophie. "I can't rightly say I've done any better than you by Myrna."

Louella shook her head. "Me neither."

One by one, the gardeners confessed their individual failings. Again the room quieted.

"So," Louella said after a long silence, "what are we all goin' to do about it? Who's willin' to be the one to reach out to Myrna?"

The lack of volunteers was embarrassing.

"Actually," Reenie said, "I have someone in mind, but she's not one of us. She should rightly be, but so far, she's not been of a mind to join."

As if they were a flock of owls, the gardeners hooted.

"If no one here objects," Reenie continued, "I propose we ask Cammie Sprague if she'd be willin' to try an' minister to Myrna. You all know how sweet an' calm she is. An' she's always had such a powerful Christian witness. She's a true saint."

"Lovely girl, Camellia . . ."

"An' such a strong faith . . ."

"She loves the Lord so much, she'd sure be able to love even Myrna . . ."

Sophie stood, a doubtful look on her face. "I don't know, ladies. Cammie isn't too fond of Lana."

"Who's Lana?" Louella asked.

"Why, it's Willie's darlin' new pet. She's a lovely iguana from the Amazon. Easiest thing to love, but Cammie just won't cotton to her."

"Sophie, dear," said Mariah in her business voice, "Myrna is no iguana. I'm right sure Cammie will have no trouble takin' her under her wing."

"I dunno," said Ellamae Hobey, standing for the first time. "You all know I keep to myself at meetings, an' I do my work an' all, but I just want to mention somethin' here. I ain't so sure mixin' Cammie Sprague with Myrna Stafford is such an all-fired good idea. You all remember what a mess they made of my diner the other day, now, don't you?"

"I was there," said Philadelphia. "My clothes still reek of that stink of theirs."

"Oh, nonsense," said Louella. "If I were a bettin' woman, which I'm not, as you all know, I'd bet that was an accident, Ellamae. You can't go blamin' a girl for such a thing."

Ellamae looked affronted. "You know I'd never blame a body for an accident, Lou. But I sure do blame Cammie for buyin' that awful stuff. D'you b'lieve she says it's perfume?"

"For skunks, maybe," Philadelphia said in her carrying whisper.

A piercing whistle cut through the chatter. Everyone turned to Reenie again. "That doesn't make any difference here. Accidents and perfumes don't have a thing to do with Myrna's disposition. An' if anyone's likely to touch her heart, it's goin' to be Cammie an' no one else. Now, who's willin' to talk to her about it?"

Everyone turned to Sophie. She raised a cautionary hand. "I'm perfectly willin' to talk to my dearest Camellia, but I can't promise you all anythin' will come out of our talk." She sighed. "I hate to have to agree on this, but Ellamae's right. Cammie . . . well, she hasn't been herself lately. Why, she reminds me more'n'more each day of those two older sisters of hers."

"And what's wrong with my precious Magnolia?" asked Louella, as protective as ever of her sort-of surrogate daughter.

"Don't you go castin' aspersions on my darlin' Lark, either," warned Mariah, Lark's soon-to-be mother-in-law.

Sophie sighed in exasperation. "Nothin's wrong with those girls. I just meant they aren't Cammie, and lately, Cammie's been actin' more like them than like herself. I can't begin to predict what she may say—or do—next."

"Besides," said Ellamae, a playful twinkle in her eyes, "Cammie might be too busy to go frettin' about Myrna these days. Seems she's bein' kept awful busy by a certain newcomer doctor these days."

Sophie's eyes widened. "Ellamae, I never said one little word about it. Not at all."

A number of interested stares beamed her way.

"Oh, dear," she wailed in distress. "Besides, we were talkin' about Cammie and her sisters, not Cammie and Stephen. And Louella, Mariah, I didn't mean no disrespect, as I'm sure you know perfectly well, toward Maggie or Lark. They're dear girls, too. I just don't know what Cammie's goin' to be sayin' or doin' from one moment to the next, and I don't want anybody to get her hopes up."

Somewhat appeased, Louella said, "Sophie, dear, you can always try. Like you said, there's no tellin' what Cammie will decide to do."

"Oh," said Mariah, "I suspect that, like always, all things will one way or another work out for the good of those who love the Lord. . . ."

Cammie listened to Miss Sophie's tale, sipping her chamomile tea. When her friend reached the end, she set down her cup, braced herself for the worst, and said, "Why are you telling me all this?"

"Well, honey. It's like this. The girls at the Garden Club all know what a prayer warrior you are, what a powerful witness you have, and how sweet-natured the dear Lord made you. We all feel if anyone can soften that crusty Myrna, it's you, and only by the grace of God."

"Just what is it you all want me to do about Myrna?"

"We'd like you to . . . well, minister to her. Maybe take her under your wing a mite. We're sure the Lord can use you in a powerful way to reach her hard heart."

Cammie weighed what her friend had just said. Lately she hadn't felt like much of a witness—in fact, she'd failed the Lord where Stephen was concerned. Now the Garden Club ladies wanted her to reach out to Myrna. Was this another one of their crazy notions? Or was almighty God planning to use her in a different, powerful way to touch a soul for him?

"I'll pray about this," she finally answered, "and unless the Lord closes that door on me, I'll do my best to serve him—and Myrna, of course. I always aim to do my best to help those around me."

Sophie's sigh of relief ruffled the silk flowers arranged in Cammie's antique washstand pitcher on the coffee table. "You'll have serious prayer coverin' for this endeavor, you know."

"Thank you, Sophie. That's all we can do—including me."

"That's all a body can ask for," Sophie said. "Although this ol' body's got a mighty itch of curiosity right now."

Cammie stood, hoping to forestall what she knew was heading her way. "Let's . . ." Frantically she tried to find something to derail Miss Sophie's train of thought. Again, she missed Muttley—not just for his presence, but for the real and practical diversion walking him would have provided.

"I know," she said, "let's go visit that new hardware store. I'm dying to see what garden tools they carry. Come on, Miss Sophie, grab your handbag, and let's go shopping."

Miss Sophie didn't budge. "Camellia Bellamy Sprague, I'm too old for you to try and bamboozle me at this stage of the game. You sit yourself right back down and run me by that fool explanation you tried to give me and Willie about that kiss we saw. And don't give me that 'It's not what it seems' nonsense, girl. I know a kiss when I see one. And you and my nephew weren't playin' checkers right then, you know. What exactly were you doin' kissin' him?"

To her own horror and dismay, Cammie burst into tears.

FIFTEEN

A FEW DAYS AFTER AUNT SOPHIE AND WILLIE FOUND HIM and Cammie kissing in her parlor, Stephen had yet another reason to question the wisdom of his move to Bellamy.

"Who's next?" he asked Laura, his office assistant.

"Miss Louella Ashworth in room B."

Stephen arched an eyebrow. "What's wrong with her? When I saw her downtown the other day, she looked great."

Laura checked her notebook. "She said she was having trouble walking, what with the pain in her—"

"Don't tell me. Her feet, right?"

"You don't think even she'd . . . ?"

"In a heartbeat. Let's go tackle the Garden Club's boss." And see what sort of evangelistic tool Bellamy's social maven had brought him.

Sure enough, Miss Louella was in rare form. She chatted, asked pointed questions about his childhood, his schooling, his marital status—all stuff she already knew—and, interestingly enough, the time he was spending with Cammie Sprague.

Only then did she get around to her feet. "I'm afraid," she said, "I've picked me up some of those loathsome—" she dropped her voice—"plantar wart things. Can you imagine? Me! I've prayed and prayed that you can help me, else I'll just die from mortification."

"I think we can handle it," Stephen answered, ready to bet his brand-new X-ray machine and stress-test treadmill he'd find nothing wrong with Miss Louella's feet.

Knowing the routine by now, he stepped outside. He leaned against the door and wondered whose idea this elderly invasion of his office had been. Then again, what did it matter? He felt on the receiving end of arrow after arrow of condemnation for something of a private and personal nature.

He had yet to read a word the women had given him.

"Yoo-hoo!" called Miss Louella from inside. Evidently, she was in a hurry to get to the real reason for the visit.

As expected, both her feet were fine. "You could use a richer moisturizer," he said when she glared at his diagnosis. "Your skin's a little dry. Other than that, you have healthy feet."

"Well, now, then," she said, as she stepped down from the exam table, "since you've solved my foot problem, I'd best be on my way. But before I leave, I have a little gift for you. From the Garden Club, you see. A sort of welcome-we're-glad-you're-here token of our appreciation."

"You shouldn't have—"

"Oh, yes, we should have, and so we did." From the chair where she'd laid her coat, she took a navy blue, wrapped parcel tied with a white satin ribbon. "Use it well, often, and in good health."

Stephen had no alternative but to take the offering. He gave Miss Louella a brief thank-you, said good-bye, and headed straight for his consultation office. There he tore off the paper and stared, speechless, at a black leather-bound Bible.

The pamphlet he'd understood—even the inexpensive paperback Gospel, but this represented an investment of the women's limited resources. His spiritual condition must really matter to them.

But why? Why did the Garden Club ladies care this much?

He opened the book, leafed through the fine, gold-edged pages, then let it fall open at random. A cluster of words jumped out at him:

"Don't worry about anything; instead, pray about everything. Tell God what you need, and thank him for all he has done. If you do this, you will experience God's peace, which is far more wonderful than the human mind can understand. His peace will guard your hearts and minds as you live in Christ Jesus."

Okay. It sounded pretty enough. But what did it *really* mean? And where was God? Stephen had never known God or his presence. He vaguely remembered hearing stories in Sunday school all those summers he'd visited Aunt Sophie. But what did it mean to live in Christ Jesus? Jesus had died a couple thousand years ago.

The part about peace? It would be great, if it existed. A peace more wonderful than the human mind could understand would suit Stephen just fine. But how did God dispense it? How did one achieve it?

Had Cammie achieved it?

With more questions than answers, he shook his head and placed the Bible on top of his bookshelf. The words had stirred back to life a years-old want inside him; he'd always hungered for inner peace. But those same words had also filled him with more questions.

They'd left him with less peace than he'd had before . . . before half the healthy elderly feet in Bellamy had paraded past his eyes in an effort to convert him.

Convert him to what?

That evening, Stephen found himself on Cammie's front porch again. He hadn't been able to persuade Willie to meet him downtown for their stroll to Langhorn Park. The old gent had insisted he wanted to stay close to home for Lana's sake.

Not that Lana would ever notice Willie's absence.

So Stephen had surrendered to the inevitable with as much grace as possible but without his normal equanimity.

What would he say to the woman he'd held in his arms? The woman who'd quivered at his touch, his kiss? The woman whose presence had taken residence in his thoughts and dreams and refused to budge?

"Hello there, Stephen," that very woman greeted him, her voice as soft as always, even if a bit surprised. She averted her eyes. "I didn't realize you were comin' here today. Will you be stayin' with us for supper?"

He shrugged. He hadn't thought that far ahead. "I guess Willie's calling the shots tonight. He wanted to play chess, but he didn't want to come to my place. Lana loomed too large on his mind."

"Lana would loom far too large in any normal person's mind," Cammie commented, letting him inside. "As far as I know, Willie's eatin' with us, so I'll just count on one more. How'll that do for you?"

"Fine, fine."

Yeah, right. Fine. He felt like a fool, exchanging inanities with Cammie. He had questions for her, about her. And above all else he had the greatest urge to take her in his arms and cradle her close for a long, long time.

He was afraid that long, long time looked a lot like forever.

Instead of behaving like a madman, though, he followed her into the kitchen, which to his surprise held a visitor. The last person he could have imagined sat at Cammie's table peeling potatoes.

"You remember Myrna, don't you?" Cammie asked, her mouth quirking at the corners.

"Who could forget her?" He extended a hand to the older woman. "I'm pleased to see you again. Although I didn't realize you were a frequent visitor here at the Widow Sprague's."

Myrna gave him one of her cold-fish looks. "You're too green around these here parts to know much about much. Camellia invited me to teach her a few of my recipes."

That was one of the weirdest things Stephen had ever heard. Cammie? Needing to be taught recipes? "I . . . see."

Myrna nodded her purple head. "I'm a right fair hand in a kitchen, I'll have you know. My son, Bernie, says there ain't a body on earth what can make grits to touch his mama's."

Grits. Mush. That was Myrna's specialty? What could *she* teach a kitchen virtuoso like Cammie?

Stephen figured it was in his best interest to fade into the background and ask Cammie for an explanation to this unusual event at a later time. "Well, ladies, I hope you have a great time swapping tips. I'd better find Willie before he thinks I've forgotten all about our chess game."

With every step away from Cammie, Stephen's curiosity grew by exponential proportions. What was she up to now?

After what he'd seen thus far, anything was possible.

After supper that evening, an odd meal consisting of myriad potato renditions, Stephen waited for the younger boarders to drift off to their individual pursuits. Myrna had eaten and run home to watch some show on TV. Aunt Sophie had begged off the evening, saying she had things to do at home with

Miss Louella and Mariah Desmond, and Willie had dashed up the stairs to spend more time with lumpy, green Lana.

That left Stephen with the perfect opportunity to grill Cammie—discreetly—about Myrna's visit and the reason for subjecting her diners to the potato-fest.

When he approached the kitchen door, however, he realized that someone else had reached Cammie before him. Suze McEntire, Cammie's high school senior, sat at the table, her eyes teary and swollen, her nose red from crying.

"But I'm crazy about him, Miss Cammie," the girl cried.

"I'm sure you are," answered Bellamy's favorite housemother. "But think on it a bit, Suze. You're headin' to college at the end of the year. So's he. And you're goin' out west near your folks, aren't you?"

"Um-hmm."

"Does it really make much sense to let your feelings grow any stronger with that in your future? Besides, if the Lord wants the two of you together, why, I believe there's no power on earth that'll keep you apart. No matter how many times he breaks up with you."

"But it hurts."

Cammie dried her hands and came to her charge's side. "I know it does, and I'm so sorry, sugar. You know, of course, you can take that—and all your other troubles—to the Father, and he's sure to heal them all."

Suze drew a hitching breath. "Pray with me?"

"Of course."

Cammie's respect for the teen impressed Stephen, as did her nonjudgmental attempt to help her look beyond the immediate. Her tenderness moved him, as it always did, and made him wonder what it would be like to feel it focused entirely on him.

". . . we ask this in your name, amen."

The ease with which she turned to prayer struck him again.

She relied on her God for everything. How? He knew he had only himself to count on. What did she know that encouraged her to trust an invisible God?

He suspected she'd be happy to tell him, but was he ready to hear it?

Suze hugged Cammie, then said something about homework. He darted out of the way before either female realized he'd witnessed their talk and waited for his opportunity.

When Cammie began singing along with the radio, he walked up behind her. "Can I help?"

"Stephen! I thought you'd be upstairs with the lizard." When he shook his head and pointed toward the sink, she smiled. "Well, I'm nearly done. All that's left to do is brew the coffee. Would you like to do that?"

Stephen eyed the large urn. "I've never made more than a Mr. Coffee pot's worth at one time. How about if I wait until you're done, and then I can help you any other way you need."

She nodded, keeping her back to him. Cammie worked smoothly, her gestures spare, economical, but efficient. She dried the kettle where the mountains of spuds had apparently been boiled before Myrna had done her thing on them, then stowed it under the counter next to the stove. Turning, she went to the table and, focusing on its already gleaming surface, scrubbed the top within an inch of its life.

Hmm . . . seemed Cammie was having trouble getting past the surprising intimacy of the kisses they'd shared too. Either that or she was hiding something. Considering the woman herself, both were quite possible.

"So," he said more jovially than he'd ever spoken before, "care to tell me all about tonight's cooking lesson?"

Cammie scrubbed harder. "Oh, I happened to mention that I was lookin' for some new recipes to broaden my repertoire, and Myrna offered to teach me some of her tried-and-trues. That's all."

The incessant scrubbing, the refusal to meet his gaze, and the overly rosy cheeks visible behind the wings of glossy brown hair left him no doubt of one thing: Cammie *was* hiding something. He'd be willing to bet the kisses had rocked her, too. But at the moment, it seemed something else was on her mind.

"And potato soup, creamed potatoes, baked potato balls, and a potato omelet were the intriguing new offerings you garnered for your efforts. Interesting. I would have thought an expert like you could make any of those concoctions in her sleep—*if* she should ever want to."

Cammie whirled toward the sink, rinsed the dishcloth, wrung it out, hung it on the hook in the backsplash, then went to the pantry closet at the far end of the room. Without a word, she withdrew an industrial-sized can of Colombia's best grind and carted it over to the urn.

Obviously, making coffee had become as difficult as boiling and mashing potatoes—the endeavor took all of Cammie's concentration.

"Look," Stephen finally said, "something's going on here, and your avoidance of me isn't winning you any points. I'm getting worried. The last time you and Myrna got together, you emptied out the Dinner Diner—not to mention every sinus cavity within miles. What are you up to?"

She sighed, her slender shoulders rising and falling. With a thud, she put down the coffee can, gripped the counter edge, then turned to face him. "I . . . ah . . . decided it was a good idea to cultivate Myrna's friendship. She's a lonely old woman who has made more enemies than friends. Even her son avoids her."

"You mean the Bernie who loves her grits?"

Cammie's lovely smile put in its first appearance of the evening, and warm pleasure washed over Stephen.

"The one and only Bernie Stafford."

"Is he like her?"

She turned back to the coffee urn. "I can't say. He's much older than I am. I've seen him a time or two when he's come to visit her, but I hear he could give her a run for her money when it comes to complainin'."

"Hey, you're doing that all by yourself," he objected when she measured grounds into the filter-lined basket and replaced the lid on the can. "What's my job?"

Cammie nodded at the urn. "Fill it to the marker with cold water."

"And then?"

"Then we put the basket back in and stick the plug into the wall."

"That's it?"

"Makin' coffee isn't rocket science," she said, a hint of teasing in her voice.

"The way yours tastes, it might as well be. Mine usually tastes of dredged-up pond bottom."

"Yuck! Thanks for the compliment, but I'm sure you're exaggeratin'." When he shook his head, she waved a dishcloth at him. "Don't go gettin' too silly, now. Let's see. Would you prefer fudge-topped brownies or sweet potato pie?"

"I didn't see either of those at supper."

Cammie laughed. "No. We had potato doughnut holes, remember?"

"Who can forget Myrna or her menu? Which brings me back to my original question. Why all this sudden interest in Myrna?"

She gave him an exasperated look. "You're not goin' to let this go, are you?"

"A man needs determination these days to finish med

school and build a thriving practice. I haven't made it this far without a solid dose. So, go ahead. Help me understand this new friendship. And I'll take a piece of pie chased down with a brownie. Anything to get the taste of spuds out of my mouth. Don't get me wrong. I like potatoes just as much as the next guy, but enough was enough."

Laughing, they headed for the parlor, each carrying a mug of coffee, and Stephen toting his plate of spud-free treats.

Tonight, to forestall any discomfort, he went straight to an armchair at right angles to the sofa. Cammie curled into the corner of the love seat, where she'd folded a russet, cream, and brown quilt. She hugged it close to her chest and took a deep breath.

"It's simple," she began, staring at the flames in the hearth. "A number of us recently realized we hadn't done right by Myrna—"

"From what I've seen, there's not a person alive who could do better by that sour woman than you and the rest of the women in town already do."

She caught her bottom lip between her teeth, a habit he'd noticed popped up each time she felt uncomfortable about the topic of discussion.

"You put it just right," she said. "No person alive could—maybe—but since those of us who noticed are Christians, we're called to do better than that. We're called to show compassion, strength, patience, and love. That's what God wants us to bring to all our relationships, since he's the source. We haven't tapped into that source when it comes to Myrna."

"I don't get it."

"I can tell." She sighed. "Let's see. Up until recently, we'd sort of tolerated Myrna, figurin' she was just the way she was. It occurred to us that no one had reached out, one-on-one, to really love her, as God would love her. Someone suggested I reach out to her. I prayed about it, realized I hadn't been the kind of Christian God wants me to be, and asked his forgiveness. Then I went about rightin' that wrong."

"Okay. Let me see if I have it straight. A bunch of women got tired of Myrna's antics, and they figured you were kind and nice enough to consider taking on the meanest grinch in town. Since I have yet to see you say no to anything asked of you, not to mention jumping up and trying to fix and solve everything that's going on, you of course took on the reforming of Myrna Stafford. Without once thinking that you might have more than enough on your plate already."

Cammie shook her head. "That's not it at all. We care. These ladies have grown up with Myrna; they've known her all her life—"

"Then why didn't they reach out to her before? Why did they wait to ask you?"

She shrugged. "I don't know. I think . . . well, maybe because she doesn't object too much to me. Besides, she did care enough to come and warn me about—" she lowered her voice and looked at the ceiling—"you know, Willie and the missin' dogs."

"Oh, come on. I was sure you'd figured out by now what a crazy theory that is. Willie couldn't have done anything like that. Besides, it's not going to do you any good. I'm not buying why you, the busiest woman I know, need to take on another project."

Instead of speaking, Cammie hummed a few notes. "Whatsoever you do . . ." she sang, "for the least of my brothers, that . . . you do unto me. . . ."

"I'm afraid I don't recognize that song."

"My grandmother used to sing it to me when I was a little girl. They're actually Jesus' words. And I try to live by them, even if I do fail sometimes. They mean that when I'm reachin' out to others—even Myrna—I'm lovin' Jesus too.

After all, God made us all—you, me, Miss Sophie, Willie—in his own image."

Stephen shook his head. "I don't get it. Jesus was a man who lived a long time ago. True, he taught good things. But I don't see why you would call him the source of strength, patience, compassion, and now love. Besides, I don't see much godliness in Myrna."

Cammie smiled. "Jesus was—*is*—much more than a wise rabbi. Jesus is the Son of God. He died on the cross for our sins, and God brought him back to life even though he was dead. Now he lives forever through his resurrection. Because of this, those who come to God through faith and love in Jesus, God adopts into his family. We become Jesus' brothers and sisters."

"Okay. Let's say that there is a God. So why would we need to come to him through anything like the resurrection?"

"Because none of us is perfect, nor are we ever capable of his perfection. We all fall short. I certainly know about that," Cammie said, laughing. Then she added, more seriously, "Before Jesus was born, God required his people, the Israelites, to offer a sacrifice to atone for their sins—they killed a lamb each year. Then God in his mercy gave us his own Son, who became the Lamb of God once and for all time. After his sacrifice on the cross, God's people no longer had to sacrifice their sheep year after year to be forgiven. Through acceptin' Jesus' sacrifice for us, we have the Father. Without him, we're left to our own sinful ways."

"But the resurrection couldn't have happened. Someone rolled over the stone. I've read the history books. Who knows who bribed the soldiers at the tomb? And if Jesus died so that everyone could have a connection to God, then why is the world such a mess? Why doesn't everyone hook up to God?"

"Because God asks one and only one sacrifice of us, and it's not an easy one. We must have faith. You already asked for proof about the stone. God says we must *believe* that he moved that stone and resurrected his Son. With faith, we can do what he asks of us—*before* he tells us why, even when obedience is difficult and painful."

"Then why obey him at all? He seems pretty tough."

Cammie's smile turned enigmatic. "Because he knows that sometimes we only learn the hard way, through tough lessons. Then too, the prize for obedience is peace, the peace that comes only from doin' God's will."

Stephen stood, disturbed by the things Cammie had said. "I can't just say, 'Hey, God, what do you think your will is for me today?' He's just not here. How do you find out his will? How do you know what he wants? Other than obedience and blind faith."

"You have to come to know him, and the way to do that is to welcome and accept Jesus' sacrifice as your own. It was, you know. For you, just as much as for me."

"That's it? I say okay and I get to know him?"

"Well, not automatically. But you seek him in the Bible, you talk to him in prayer. And when you accept Jesus, God fills you with his Holy Spirit, who'll guide you, teach you—even change you—if you listen."

He shook his head. "So then you're one of those people who go around saying they hear voices—and talk with God? I'm sorry, Cammie. It just doesn't make sense."

"It does," she answered, "when you open your heart to—"

"So this is where you've been hiding," Willie said, strolling into the parlor, Lana in hand. "I don't blame you, boy. Cammie's one lovely lady."

Stephen glanced at the lovely lady in question and noticed how rapidly she'd blanched. Her eyes were glued on Lana's reptilian features.

"Tell you what, Willie. If you're interested in that chess game, I'll play once you put your pet back in her home.

Otherwise, I'd just as soon call it a night. Lana still makes Cammie nervous, and I'm not about to chase a woman from her own home."

Willie sighed. "I'm trying to train Lana to me, you know. Get her used to me, to my voice, my smell. All the books say I need to spend hours and hours with her. I'm afraid I'm going to have to pass on our game." He turned to Cammie. "Honestly, Cammie girl, Lana won't hurt you. You just have to make friends with her. She's a very sweet iguana."

"I'll take your word for it," she answered in a faint voice. "Just don't ask me to share the evenin' with her. I'll go to my room. You two—*three*—can have the parlor for the game. Good night."

Stephen watched Cammie leave. Behind her, she left words of faith, a faith he couldn't grasp. Would he ever understand her?

Did he first need to understand the God she loved?

Cammie looked out her window at the clear autumn night sky. She'd done it again. She'd failed God. The God of second chances had given her that second chance to reach Stephen for eternity's sake, and she'd failed to do so.

"Oh, Father, you know I'm not particularly eloquent—that's Lark. And I've never been pert and pretty and vivacious—that's Maggie. I'm just homebody Cammie, and I'm afraid that doesn't make for a powerful witness. I tried to share you with Stephen tonight, but my efforts were pretty puny, I'd say.

"Please forgive me, Lord. Especially since I'm coming to care for him. I care what happens to Stephen Hardesty here, in Bellamy, but even more, for eternity.

"I guess Maggie and Lark are right. I *am* pitiful Cammie,

who can't do things right. I can't even share my faith successfully. Father, please do your mighty work in me, so I can be the woman you want me to be. . . ."

An idea popped into her head. She'd once heard a very powerful song whose words had long remained with her. Cammie smiled. Now she knew what she wanted to ask God.

"Father, please fill me with your Son's strength, power, patience, and courage, so that those around me will see Christ in me. I want to be the Jesus they see."

SIXTEEN

SINCE STEPHEN HADN'T SEEMED RECEPTIVE TO MYRNA'S suspicions of Willie, and since Cammie continued to harbor a few suspicions about Stephen all her own, she was glad she hadn't revealed much of what she and Myrna had discussed during their "potato-fest," as he'd called their visit.

"That there little old man has chummied up with you an' Sophie Hardesty right quick," Myrna had said for starters. "Why, just think on it a while, girl. He comes to town, and not much after that, dogs start disappearin' left an' right. An' it ain't just any ol' dogs, neither. You're pretty tight with that dear, darlin' Sophie. Plus them sisters of yourn are tighter'n ticks with Louella Ashworth and Mariah Desmond. 'Sides, the man's livin' right here under your roof, Camellia. Knows where you're at all the time, an' he can pretty much figger out from what you say what your sisters are up to."

"Oh, I'm not so sure about that, Miss Myrna," Cammie answered. "My sisters and I don't get on too well. We've all promised to make a better effort, but I guess longtime habits are hard to break. I don't think anyone's likely to learn much about them from me."

"But Willie can from sniffin' round that Sophie, you know. I bet she knows from her housemates what Maggie an' Lark are up to. An' I bet he learns it without Sophie knowin' what's hittin' her."

"That still doesn't answer the big question: Why? Why would he steal our dogs?"

Myrna gave a long-suffering huff. "Why? That there's the easiest part to figger out. Everyone knows we ol' folks ain't got much change to spare. An' he keeps that ol' gas-guzzlin' Caddy of his runnin' all over the place. Plus he bought himself that there iguana. He needs money, Camellia. Ain't them dogs of yourn pretty pricey ones?"

"Maybe Maggie's and Lark's are, but my puppy's a mutt. He's valuable only to me. Still, I do miss him something fierce, you know."

Myrna frowned, then shook her purple curls. "Well, it ain't gonna be too long 'fore your little one comes. You won't have yourself no time to waste on no dog."

"Oh, please don't say that. I'm sure Wiggon's got the investigation under control. He'll find our dogs, and I'll get my Muttley back. Soon, too."

Although Cammie spoke the words, her faith in Wiggon's abilities—not strong in the first place—had already faded to almost nothing.

Myrna echoed Cammie's reservations. "Pah! That Wiggon's got no more'n spuds like these here mashed ones in his head. What's he done about them dogs? What's he told you about his all-fired investigation?"

"They're waiting for the results from the state police lab tests."

Myrna's eyes widened. She leaned over the pile of potato peels. "Do tell. What'd they be lookin' for, d'you reckon?"

"I'm not quite sure about that. Maybe evidence of—" she had trouble voicing her greatest fear—"poison."

"Poison? Who'd want to poison them dogs? They're sure worth a lot more alive than dead." Myrna waved her vegetable peeler. "Nah. Don't go frettin' about it, Camellia. An' don't you go frettin' 'bout no dog, neither. You're goin' to be havin' yourself a baby in a few weeks, now. Why, I recollect when my Bernie was born. My, my, he was the homeliest little bundle ever! Sure purtied up right quick, though, with them black eyes an' hair."

Having seen Bernie a couple of times, Cammie smiled at the evidence of maternal love.

She let her guest ramble, focusing on Myrna's comments about Wiggon's abilities. The thought of this particular cop's talents and her fear of poison shot Cammie's anxiety straight to the fore.

"Tell you what I'm going to do," she said, rising. "I'm going to call the PD right now. See if I can find Wiggon. I have a few questions for him, and I'm going to get some answers. Now, too."

With Myrna's amazed gaze on her, Cammie dialed the number and waited while the dispatcher put her through to Wiggon's extension.

Thankfully, he answered right away. "What can I do for you?" he asked when she identified herself.

"You can tell me what's going on with the investigation into my dog's theft is what you can do."

"Cammie? Cammie Sprague? Izzat really you? You sure it ain't Lark talkin'?"

"It's me, Wiggon. Camellia Bellamy Sprague. Now, are you going to talk to me, or am I going to have to go to the chief?"

"No, no, there ain't no need for that. Oh, say, Jill says she likes the idea of settin' up a time with you so's you can play with the twins so's she can get her hair colored up an' curled.

Why she'd want to go an' do a fool thing like that, I sure don't know, but that's where it is. An' you did say you'd like to help her out, an' all—"

"Stop wiggling, Wiggon." Cammie knew that wasn't nice. But she also knew the police officer always waffled and squirmed when conversations and situations became uncomfortable or unpleasant. It was obvious he knew something he didn't want to share.

"Well, Cammie, it ain't all that great a news. On the other hand, it ain't all *that* bad, neither—"

"Wiggon, please. Spit it out. You've got me so nervous, the baby's kicking the stuffing out of my ribs."

"Sorry, Cammie. I didn't mean you no harm. It's just . . . well, like I said, it's not that great a news. You see, we don't have nothin' to go on but them wrappers. And . . ."

"And . . . ?"

"Well, there *was* somethin' funny 'bout them. They had Sleepitol all over 'em."

"Sleepitol? What's that?"

"That's that stuff on Tee-Vee commercials folks buy when they cain't get to sleep nights. Now who would have themselves a hard time sleepin', I cain't figger. Me, I'm out before my head hits that pillow, you know."

Cammie didn't feel led to share with Wiggon her bedtime woes, much less how well she'd come to know the ins and outs of insomnia. "You mean, someone put sleeping pills in the stuff the dogs ate? Pills to put the dogs to sleep?"

"Yep."

A worse scenario occurred to her. "How badly would it hurt them? I mean, could it . . . could it kill them?"

"'Pends on how much of it they used, you know. The state police doc wasn't right sure of quantity, but he said they'd have had to use a whole bunch of it to do much to big pooches like Buford or Mycroft."

Fear knotted her muscles. "But how about Muttley? He's only a little puppy."

Silence rang out over the line.

"Please tell me, Wiggon."

"Well, that's just it, Cammie. Without knowin' how much Sleepitol they put in, the doc cain't rightly say whether it would do Muttley harm or not. Now, don't go frettin', you hear? We ain't found us no dead puppy, you know."

Around the lump in her throat, Cammie said, "Yet."

"Aw, Cammie, he ain't gonna die. We're gonna find your dog. I promise. I'll go over the file again, straightaway. You'll see. You go rest your feet, now. You're carryin' that big baby inside you an' all."

"Thanks, Wiggon," Cammie said.

"So?" Myrna asked the instant the receiver hit the cradle. "What does he know?"

"Not much, besides traces of Sleepitol being on the wrappers we found."

Satisfaction beamed from Myrna's face. "So . . . not much. Toldja, didn't I? That there boy don't know nothin'. I tell you, Camellia, it's that fahrriner livin' here what did it."

Cammie sighed. She had no other clues. "I might as well look into that. Seriously, I mean. And I do appreciate your telling me all this. Not that I like any of it, but still—"

That conversation with Myrna was the reason Cammie hadn't been willing to give Stephen any answers. Had she shared what was troubling her, he would have had more questions about her latest alliance than he'd had before.

She wouldn't have known how to answer him, since she still had some niggling questions about Stephen's possible part in the felonious dognapping scheme.

Cammie sighed, wondering how long it would take her to fall asleep tonight. If the past few nights were anything to go by, she might as well settle in with a good book instead.

As for her thoughts making sense, well, they pretty much matched all that had happened recently. What would come of it all?

On Sunday afternoon, the day after the potato-fest, Cammie and Stephen wound up double-dating with Willie and Sophie again. Staying true to form, Willie had insisted on keeping their destination a secret. Cammie had wondered if the man had once worked for the FBI, the CIA, or some other governmental alphabet soup. He loved the cloak-and-dagger stuff.

She thought about asking him, but as she entertained that notion, it occurred to her that if he had been in some secret office, experience in covert activities made Willie an even better suspect in the dognappings.

She sighed, staring at the back of the elderly man's head. Today he'd insisted on sharing the front seat with Sophie. Stephen sat on the other side of the wide rear seat opposite Cammie, evidently consumed by his own thoughts.

She closed her eyes, remembering the church service earlier. She'd prayed for guidance, seeking God's wisdom instead of relying on her own. And she'd again asked God to reveal his will to her, to show her what to do in this situation.

But today, no matter what, she meant to stick to Willie like gum did to a sneaker in August. *Groan.* There she went again. This time, she'd been thinking in Maggie-like form—a very scary thing, to be sure. Mismatched and garbled clichés were her sister's stock-in-trade. *Not* Cammie's.

"Are you all right?" Stephen asked.

"Of course, I am. Why do you ask?"

"You moaned."

Cammie closed her eyes again. Things had gotten so bad, she couldn't even think in peace anymore. "You know,

Stephen, if one more person asks me if I'm all right, why, I might have to answer no—just to see what they'd do. That's about the size of my conversations these days."

"Not all," he said, his voice serious, his eyes more so.

In an instant those two evenings they'd shared returned to her thoughts. Forcing herself to set aside the feelings the memory of their kisses brought, she focused instead on their conversations. It appeared they'd made an impact on Stephen.

Or so she hoped. She'd hate to think that all he remembered were the kisses. Not that she could forget them, but she hoped she'd left on him her mark for the Lord's sake.

The burden of Stephen's lack of faith in God weighed heavily on her. Especially since she'd tried to witness to him, and the results had been so pitiful.

Surely she could do better.

About to pick up again where they'd left off, she prayed for guidance and waited for the words to come.

They didn't.

She remained silent, feeling silly, since Stephen still looked at her in his quiet, penetrating way. She wondered if that was a trait he'd acquired from meditating. But even though curiosity filled her, her mouth seemed reluctant to form any words.

Lord, are you telling me this is the wrong time? Is that why I can't come up with a simple comment?

The silence continued, and Cammie sank right into it, resting her head on the back of the seat. Willie had warned that the drive would be fairly long.

By the time she woke up, Cammie realized it was midafternoon. "Where are you taking us this time, Willie?"

"We're here. I'm just parking."

"Parking where?"

"Take a look. I'm sure you'll recognize the place."

Cammie wrestled her every-day-more-awkward body upright and peered out the front. "The Capitol! We're in D.C. What are we doing here?"

Willie chuckled. "See? Those civics lessons required in high school do indeed pay off. You recognized your whereabouts right away."

"But that doesn't tell me why we're here."

Stephen reached over and placed a hand on Cammie's shoulder. "Willie says he has another surprise for us."

"Oh, please," she begged, "not another dinosaurian one."

"No," Willie answered, his voice taking on a note of concern. "But I did struggle with leaving poor Lana at home. You should have seen those sad little eyes when I put her back in her tank. I know she's terribly lonely by now."

Miss Sophie shook her head. "Oh, dear."

"I don't know, Willie," Cammie said, considering. "I saw an awful lot of those critters at that show, and not one lizard had an expression any different from the next. They all looked . . . reptilian. The whole time I was there."

"See? That's why you must get to know Lana. The dear girl has the most expressive eyes."

Cammie darted a look at Stephen and caught him smoothing his mustache with thumb and forefinger in an effort to keep a straight face. She rolled her eyes. "Whatever you say, Willie. She's your baby."

"Isn't she, though?" the old man said with pride in his voice. "And you're about to be privileged enough to meet yet another one of my babies—of sorts."

Cammie looked warily at the face reflected in the rearview mirror. "This one's not reptilian, right?"

"It's not even alive—in the normal sense, that is. But you'll see." With that, he turned off the Caddy's engine. "Come on. You're going to learn how much fun you've been missing all this time."

Cammie let Stephen help her out of the car, grateful for his lovely manners and undeniable strength. "Thanks," she said. "I dread to see what he's got up his sleeve this time."

"Never fear," Stephen answered, his shoulders shaking with quiet laughter. "I'm here, and you can count on me. I'll protect you."

His words stole Cammie's breath away. If only they were true. If only she could trust him, lean on him. In spite of trying, she'd never lost her wish for a partner in life.

And Stephen had so many good qualities. He had a great sense of humor, a strong dose of responsibility. He was intelligent, respectful of those around him, and had sufficient perseverance to have made it through medical school, as he had pointed out. From what his patients said, he was also a fine doctor—gentle, devoted to them, and thorough in their care.

And yet, the very characteristics that made him a fine physician and greatly appealed to her were the ones that frightened Cammie the most.

She took in a shuddering breath and studied the man at her side. His strength showed in his every movement, athletic and powerful. He'd obviously worked to maintain his well-developed body in excellent physical condition. His square jaw and direct gaze spoke of confidence, self-knowledge, of certainty of his place in life.

Still, she remembered some of his earlier statements. Stephen believed in . . . well, nothing, really. He seemed to have found a measure of peace in his practice of Zen. But Cammie knew that peace wasn't the mere lack of something troubling or difficult.

From their conversation on faith, she knew that he was still seeking. That made getting personally involved with him even more dangerous. And that's why she couldn't lean on Stephen, no matter how wonderful the prospect might seem. She had to lean on God the Rock, a foundation that would never crumble.

Besides, how could she trust another man with her life again? David had shown her how fleeting love was for the male of the species. To her, "until death do you part" meant just that: forever, not until the job got more interesting or more demanding.

Sighing, she withdrew her arm from Stephen's clasp and wandered over to the rear of the car, where Willie was rummaging in the trunk. "What are you looking for?" she asked.

"My surprise," Willie answered, chuckling. "And here it is."

With great fanfare he displayed a strange object that consisted of metal tubing, a black saucerlike thing at one end, and a handle with controls of some sort on the other.

Stephen came up behind her. Cammie turned. "Don't tell me," she murmured. "We're going to contact a gaggle of political aliens in D.C."

Stephen laughed. "Not quite. Just watch."

Willie slammed the trunk shut and, with a chattering Miss Sophie clinging to his free arm, headed to the Mall that extended straight out from the reflecting pool in front of the Capitol Building. As he walked, he kept his gaze on the ground, all the while smiling to his animated companion.

"Here," he said several minutes later.

Miss Sophie released his arm, and the three tagalongs watched him go into action.

After a fair amount of button-pushing, Willie's contraption began to hum. With a satisfied nod he lowered the round, dark platter to the ground, and began waving it over what fall-brown grass the millions of visitors had left in place. He took short steps, intent on the surface . . .

"What's he doing?" Cammie asked.

"That's a metal detector," Stephen answered. "But your guess is as good as mine as to what he's looking for."

"Treasure, son!" cried Willie when the machine beeped. "You have no idea how much great stuff people lose that you can find with one of these. Hand me my tool, Sophie dear, if you please."

From the small canvas bag she carried over her arm, Miss Sophie withdrew what to Cammie looked like a very ordinary garden spade. Willie took it from her and bent to the ground where the metal detector beeped the loudest and separated the sad clumps of dying grass.

Seconds later he groaned. "Not this time, I'm afraid." He held up a soda-can pull tab. "But the day is still young, and I shall carry on."

After about twenty minutes, Cammie looked around for a bench. At this point in her pregnancy, too much walking wore her out; she wanted to spare her legs. "Do you mind if I go sit somewhere?" she asked Stephen.

"Absolutely not. I'm not crazy about collecting soft-drink debris. I see an empty bench over there. How's that look to you?"

"Perfect."

They sat, and Stephen told her about D.C. He'd visited the capital of the United States a number of times, and he was happy to describe some of its more famous and interesting attractions. The monuments she'd seen pictured, but he told her interesting details about the Smithsonian Institution, the various art museums, the Museum of Natural History, and the Capitol Building itself.

"We'll have to bring you back once the baby's born," he said. "You can do a lot of sightseeing with the baby in a stroller."

"Hmm . . . I was planning on using one of those kangaroo-type pouches. I like the idea of keeping my little one close."

He nodded. "They're wonderful. They free your arms, and the baby stays close to your heartbeat, like when it was inside your womb, which is great. But you'll want a stroller, too. Don't forget how fast babies grow."

Just then Cammie became aware of a commotion not too far from where they were sitting. "Stephen, look!" She rose and began running—well, a modest waddle was more her pace—toward her friends. "The police. It looks as if they're arresting Willie and Miss Sophie. We have to hurry."

As they approached the scene of the disaster, Cammie noticed myriad mounds of dirt in the vicinity of the dynamic duo. She groaned.

Stephen glanced at her as he measured his steps to hers. "What is it?"

She waved toward the destruction. "Just look at what those two did. It looks as though someone set loose a pack of demented groundhogs."

Stephen's groan put hers to shame. "You follow at your pace. I've got to hurry. Defacing federal property and vandalizing a national monument is a serious offense."

Cammie pulled up short. "Oh, my goodness."

They'd done it again. As a result of Willie's ludicrous idea of entertainment, the two men had managed to split up Cammie and Miss Sophie, thereby keeping Cammie's suspicious eye away from Willie. Who knew what he'd been up to?

For all she could tell, he might have buried evidence in his prairie-dog hills all over the Mall surface. And there were enough folks wandering around, enjoying the lovely fall weather, that an accomplice could easily have made off with . . . whatever.

Had Stephen known what Willie was up to?

She studied the man, now pleading on behalf of his older

friends. Stephen's expression was serious, but neither strain nor stress showed on his features. His demeanor toward the police officers was respectful, his tone of voice controlled and well modulated, even though she couldn't make out his words.

She remembered the gentle way he'd helped her ease out of Willie's car, the caring way he'd taken her to a bench in search of comfort, how he'd spoken of the benefit of closeness between mother and infant. And she couldn't help but take note of his real concern for Willie and his great-aunt.

How could he be part of whatever had happened to the Blossoms' dogs?

Somewhere along the line, Cammie had either heard or read something about Buddhists adhering to strict vegetarian tenets out of compassion for living things. Although she'd seen Stephen wolf down her stew, meat loaf, and various other meat entrées, something told her his feelings toward animals would probably rival Lark's. And Maggie's. Not to mention Cammie's.

Could a physician trying Buddhism on for size harm a dog for the sake of a few thousand dollars? A man whose career—even in a small town—surely provided him with a comfortable living?

Could Stephen, the man she'd begun to care for, steal a dog? *Her* dog?

Her heart said no. What did her head say?

It said to wait on the Lord. He would reveal Stephen's innocence or guilt.

"I still can't believe you were able to talk the cops into letting these two go," Cammie told Stephen for the third time as they walked back to Willie's car.

Stephen shrugged. "I figured my best bet was to appeal to their sense of, first, the ridiculous. Can you imagine the headlines? 'Elderly Couple Arrested for Unearthing Pull Tabs on Federal Lawn.' "

"Unfortunately, I *can* imagine it. Now that you've lived in Bellamy for a while, can't *you* imagine the scandal?"

"Willie would love the attention."

"But your aunt would die of mortification."

"Well, no need to worry. They avoided arrest."

"What else did you appeal to? You did say their sense of the ridiculous was only the first thing you appealed to."

"Logic. I suggested that restitution might make Willie and Aunt Sophie think twice before digging up federal property in the future. Since she's a master gardener, she is a natural for fixing the mess."

Cammie chuckled. "They did look kind of odd patting back the clumps of dirt they'd dug up. I noticed all sorts of folks staring at them, what with Miss Sophie's flowered wool dress and heels and Willie's pin-striped suit and gray fedora."

"They are a pair."

Then Cammie realized that she now knew. This was *not* a dognapper. Stephen was too caring to hurt a dog or its owner. She still had doubts about Willie's innocence, especially since he'd thought nothing of tearing up the Mall in search of hidden treasure. But her questions about Stephen's character seemed to fade with the afternoon sun.

As soon as they'd buckled their seat belts, Willie pulled away from the scene of his crime. Miss Sophie, in charge of the entertainment, chose a big-band-music radio station and turned the volume up to LOUD.

Cammie came to a decision. Under cover of the blaring brass, she leaned closer to Stephen. "I have something to tell you," she whispered so the two in the front would not overhear.

"Go ahead. I've been told I'm a good listener."

"Well, it's about Willie. And Myrna—sort of."

At Stephen's quizzical look, Cammie said, "I'm wondering even more now about Willie's guilt."

Stephen chuckled. "I was sure that potato-fest would lead to nothing but trouble. Look at him. Willie's a harmless old gent. He's out to charm my aunt, nothing more. Have you noticed how he dotes on that dumb iguana? You really think a man like that would harm a dog?"

Although he'd made a possibly valid point, his laughter rubbed her the wrong way. "Well, so much for being a good listener, Dr. Hardesty. The least you could do is take me seriously. But you're just like everyone else. Silly little Cammie. She can't do anything right on her own."

"I never said that—"

"You didn't have to. You laughed at me and my theories. You laughed at my fear for my dog. So much for your helpful attitude. For all I know, you're in cahoots with Willie."

"What? Are you crazy?"

Stiffening her spine, Cammie scooted farther to the opposite side of the car. "Not at all, Dr. Hardesty. I'm as sane as they come, probably saner than you, and I'm going to prove it to you and to everyone else. I'm going to find out who stole our dogs. And on top of that, I'm going to find the dogs, too. You just sit back, laugh all you want, and watch me do it."

As soon as he spoke, Stephen knew he'd stuck his foot in his mouth—big time. Cammie's expression in the soft light of dusk revealed hurt and anger. Then she moved as far from his side as she could.

But he was right. Willie didn't have a felonious hair on his silver head—no matter how much Cammie wanted to prove herself capable of unearthing the culprit. Who knew why she even felt that need?

He regretted hurting her and regretted his laughter. But he didn't regret pointing out her mistaken suspicion. He simply should have done so differently, in a gentler, more Cammie-like way. Now he'd have to find another way to get closer to her again.

Something about this woman fascinated him. Her smile did wonderful things to him, and talking with her challenged him in a way no one had challenged him before. Her faith was such an integral part of who she was, yet he struggled to grasp the basis of it. That elusive element in her prodded him to get to know her better, to understand her love for God and Jesus.

Then, too, her warmth and generous hospitality reached out to a lonely part of him in a way that nothing else ever had. He felt at home in her house, something he'd never experienced before.

The car made a sharp turn, and the sleeping Cammie slid across the slick leather seat. Although the seat belt still held her in place, her shoulders and head slumped over toward him. Noticing how uncomfortable her position looked and knowing how much sleep a pregnant woman needed, he undid his own safety harness and scooted closer to her. He slid an arm around her back, drawing her against his body for cushioning, and cradled her head on his shoulder.

The warmth of her next to him felt just right. He experienced a sudden certainty that she belonged right where she was—at his side. The soft herbal, feminine scent of her hair wafted up, and Stephen realized he was very close to nirvana.

He realized he would die a happy man if he could fall asleep with Cammie's head next to his for the rest of his life.

SEVENTEEN

THE DAY AFTER THE MALL FIASCO, CAMMIE WOKE UP READY to tackle the dognapping investigation herself. Wiggon had as much as admitted he hadn't done a thing—other than send a bunch of junk-food wrappers to the state police for testing.

That was good. But now that he knew someone had put the dogs to sleep, obviously to steal them, what was he doing about it?

Instead of calling the cop himself, this time Cammie made use of the ladies' network. She called Jill Wiggon.

"What do you know about the investigation into my dog's theft?" she asked her friend without much preamble.

"Only that Cecil's worried sick about it. An' that they don't seem to know much about what happened to those critters of yours, seein' as they don't have much to go on."

Just as Cammie suspected. "Do you know what they're planning to do about that sorry state of affairs?"

"You cut that out right this minute, Curtis Cecil Wiggon!" Jill yelled at one of her darlings. "Sorry 'bout that, Cammie. The boys are all the time into somethin', you know?"

The sound of a moving chair screeched across the wires. "What were we talkin' 'bout? Oh, yes, you'd asked if I knew somethin' about the investigation. Goodness, girl, I don't know nothin' what goes on down to that police department. Cecil don't talk shop when he comes home, you know. He wants to eat, play with the boys, an' watch himself some Tee-Vee."

Cammie sighed. At least she now knew her suspicions were on target. "Thanks, Jill. I appreciate you taking the time to talk to me. Oh, and about that promise I made, when would you like to go for your hair appointment?"

"How's next Thursday morning at ten? That'll give me two hours for Gladys to do me up right. Then I can come get my rascals, feed 'em lunch, and stick 'em in bed for their naps."

Obviously, the harried mom of twin terrible twos had given her upcoming excursion much thought. Cammie wondered if someday down the line she, too, would hope someone would offer relief from her parenting duties, even if for a couple of hours.

"Sounds fine to me," Cammie said and soon hung up. Then she telephoned Maggie.

"Good mornin', Marlowe Historical Restorations," her sister chirped.

"Morning, Maggie. I was wondering if you knew anything more about the dogs' disappearances than I do—or than the police."

"Not hardly, sissy. This all looks as clear to me as it would to a mole come up in the midday sun. An' I've been so blue, Elvis an' his old suede shoes haven't got a thing on me."

Cammie sent a brief prayer heavenward and took a deep breath. "Well, then, what are you doing tonight after supper?"

"Tonight? Let me check our calendar here. Hmm . . . I don't see anythin' down for tonight. What's wrong? Are you feelin' poorly? I told you you shouldn't be workin' so hard, cleanin' house for all those people, and all—"

"Maggie, listen to me, please. I'm fine. I was just wondering if you and Lark would mind coming over. Maybe the three of us can make some sense of this mess. You know, look and see if we can find any kind of pattern here—besides the junk food, of course. Something. I just can't stand the sitting and waiting for nothing."

"Why, Cammie, dear, that's the nicest thing you've ever done! You've turned to me for advice. Now don't you fret, honey. I'll be there right as rain this evenin', and I'll set all your worries to rights. Now if the police would only do as much . . ."

Cammie shook her head. Maggie was off and running, the idea of sisterly wisdom shining bright in her headlights. At least she'd agreed to come over. Maybe, just maybe, and by God's grace, the Blossoms could set their differences aside long enough to figure out what had happened to their dogs.

She bid Maggie farewell as soon as she shoehorned a word in edgewise. Then she really had to gather up her courage. Bracing herself, she phoned Lark.

After about thirteen rings, Lark picked up the phone. She must have dropped the receiver, considering the amount of clattering and muttering that followed. Finally in her froggiest, sleepiest morning voice, the eldest Blossom said, "'Lo?"

"Morning, Lark, it's Cammie."

"Cammie!" The phone again rattled and banged, Lark muttered some more, and after a bit of what Cammie assumed must have been rummaging to find the elusive cordless, Lark cried out, "Are you all right? The baby's not comin' yet, is it? It can't. It's too soon. Call the fire department. Call Wiggon. Call the hospital. I'll be right—"

"Settle down, Lark. I'm fine, and the baby is, too. I haven't gone into labor." Remembering what she'd said to Stephen, Cammie now knew she could never worry someone needlessly, no matter how tired she grew of hearing the same question over and over again.

Lark yawned prodigiously.

"Goodness," Cammie commented, "are you only now waking up, Lark? Why, it's already a quarter to nine. Oh! Don't tell me. You just finished putting together another issue of your magazine."

"A quarter to nine is not *that* late, Cam. Not everyone rises before the chickens like you, you know. And, yeah, not only did I finish the next issue of *Critic's Choice,* but I also did the one to follow. I wanted to have the end-of-the-year copy at the printer's early so I don't have to think about it the last few weeks before my weddin', seeing as how Rich and I scheduled it so close to Christmas and all."

"Oh, dear. I'm so sorry I woke you. Why don't you go back to sleep, and I'll call you again later this afternoon—"

"Back up there, Squirt—"

"Now, Lark, how many times did Granny Iris warn you about calling me that? Goodness knows, I'm no squirt anymore, especially now that I'm about to become someone's mama."

"Well, you are about to become someone's mama, but I'm reservin' judgment about you being grown up. Just look at that house full of strangers you have there. I've even heard rumors that one of them is the prime suspect in the dognappin' case. Now that I've finished editin' my magazines, I'm going to focus on findin' our dogs. You can be sure Scoop Bellamy's goin' to figure out what happened and why."

Not certain she liked the tone of her oldest sister's voice or her takeover attitude, Cammie nevertheless decided to go for broke. "I'm glad you feel that determined to learn what happened, Lark. I'm as intent on that goal as you are, and from what Maggie told me, she is too. We're planning to meet at my place tonight after supper to pool ideas and plans.

We hope to get further than either one of us has on our own. Would you like to join—"

"Don't go doing anythin' crazy before I get there. Remember, Maggie landed in jail once already. I'm the only one of us with investigative experience. What time do you want me over? Can we speak without the likelihood of eavesdroppers? Do you have any idea where those boarders of yours go when they're not at your place nights? It'd be interesting to see what they're up to. After all, the only strangers in town live at your place."

It looked like Cammie wasn't the only Blossom whose ear Myrna had bent of late. "If you're going to be accusing my renters, Lark, why don't you be thorough and accuse Stephen Hardesty as well? He's the very latest to arrive in Bellamy."

"A doctor?" Lark asked. "I don't think so. They're generally kind to animals—of the canine as well as human sort."

"But if he's unlikely to be a thief on the basis of potential kindness or his lofty profession, why would you suspect anyone under my roof? I'm renting to a high school senior, two community college students, and a retiree. They were kind enough to take pity on a widowed, pregnant lady looking for company and a little extra income, too."

"Give it up, Cam. I'm too sleepy to discuss anythin' this important right now. Let me catch me some rest so we can talk to your heart's content tonight. Now, you listen to me. Don't go runnin' straight into any kind of trouble on account of that dog of yours. Remember, Maggie's and my pets are missin', too. Neither one of us has run off half-cocked—and neither one of us is even pregnant, meanin' we don't have as much at stake if we did chase off after a dognapper."

"Lark, I only called to invite you for a brainstorming session. I didn't need the lecture. No one in her right mind would equate serving my sisters a cup of after-supper tea the same as running off half-cocked after anyone."

Lark's silence was satisfying. "Fine," she finally said. "You made your point. Just don't do anythin'—strange, you understand—until we get there, you hear?"

Cammie sighed. "I hear. Can I expect you around seven?"

"Of course."

After replacing the receiver, Cammie collapsed on one of the kitchen chairs. All she'd done was phone her sisters, but she felt as though she'd run the Kentucky Derby. She really wasn't looking forward to this evening. If she was this exhausted after just talking to those two on the phone, how would she feel when done wrangling with them in person?

"Wait, wait!" Cammie cried.

Although Lark and Maggie had arrived less than a half hour ago, the three-way discussion had quickly escalated to a difference of opinion that now threatened to become an out-and-out argument. This was not what Cammie had envisioned.

"Please listen to me," she begged. "This is wrong. We're not getting anywhere. Where's our faith in all this? Where's our focus?"

Maggie and Lark fell silent. They looked down at their partly filled cups of tea. Cammie studied first one woman and then the other, wondering what was going through their minds. She knew what she wanted to say, but for so many years they'd disdained her reliance on prayer that she didn't know how they would react to her suggestion despite their avowed rededication to Christ.

Still, a strong urge in her heart prompted her. "I think we started off on the wrong foot tonight. We've been talking and thinking all on our own strength instead of calling on God's wisdom and guidance. Would you all mind praying before we say anything else?"

Lark's green eyes met Cammie's. "Only if I can start out by askin' the Lord's forgiveness, and yours and Maggie's, too."

"I'm the cart before your horse, there, Lark," added Maggie, a sheepish expression on her delicate, beautiful face.

Cammie reached a hand to each of her sisters. "Would you like to start us off in prayer, then, Lark?" she said joyfully.

"I meant it, Cam," said the redhead, bowing her head. "Father God, I ask forgiveness right up front tonight. I got so wound up in this mess with our dogs that I took my focus off you. I was busier focusin' on the problem and my own way of solvin' it than on seekin' you for the solution. Please forgive my blindness, Lord, and bless us now with your presence. I'll trust your Holy Spirit to guide our conversation so we can make wise and fruitful plans."

"Wait, wait!" cried Maggie. "I've got my own mess to clean up with God. Father, you know me and my fear of bein' seen as some fancy gewgaw instead of a capable woman. So when Cammie called me this mornin', why, my pride took off faster'n a hound after the hare that beat the tortoise flat. I know that's wrong, Father. Please forgive me. Help me be the sister Cammie needs, the sister you want me to be. And I'm goin' to thank you for the answer I know you've already worked out in your wisdom."

"Hold on!" Cammie said. "I've got my own straightening out to do, too. Lord God, I let my fear of Lark and Maggie seeing me as nothing but a silly baby sidetrack me, and I focused on being tough rather than on being open to you. I'm sorry, Father. I know better than that. I'm going to trust you to soften my heart to receive my sisters' counsel, accepting it as though coming straight from you. In Jesus' name, amen."

They sat in silence, aware that something magnificent had happened. Although none of them spoke, the atmosphere wasn't strained or uncomfortable—for the first time in their lives.

"You know," Maggie said after a while, "it occurs to me that I might be able to learn somethin' without doin' anything risky or crazy."

Lark covered Maggie's hand again. "I'm sorry, Mags. I shouldn't have said that to you. You're not crazy, and you did solve the vandalism case over at the Ashworth Mansion. Please forgive me."

Maggie smiled. "Of course I forgive you. Don't think on it a moment longer. Now, as I was sayin', I can probably ask questions of my ladies down to the county jail. You all know I go down once a week to minister to them, don't you?"

Cammie and Lark stared at each other, dumbfounded. "I had no idea," Cammie said. "How long have you been doing this?"

Maggie shrugged. "Ever since my Clay and I came home from our honeymoon."

Lark ran a hand through her curls. "Whatever led you to do it?"

Maggie blushed. "Don't tell me you've forgotten I spent a night there not that long ago? I'll never forget the despair I saw around me, the fear I shared with the other women. I couldn't just leave and not go back to help them. I can't do a thing about their crimes or their sentences. I mean, if they broke the law, why, then it's only right for them to pay the consequences. But I can always share with them what got me through that night."

"You mean . . . ?"

"That was the night I truly understood who God is and what it means to be his child."

Cammie reached out to her sister. "He is a redeeming God, isn't he? Only he could work something so good from the disaster of your arrest."

Their words ceased again. This time, however, not for long.

"Anyway," Maggie said, "I think I can ask my ladies if they know anything about dog stealin' in these parts. Some of them were locked up pretty long ago, and the stories they tell, why, they'd like to curdle a cow's milk practically before she chews her cud. If there's anythin' professional-like goin' on here, I'll find out."

"You know, Mags," Lark said, "you've just given me an idea. I'm going to propose a feature on petnappin'. That'll give me enough of an in to look at records and ask all kinds of nosy questions."

Cammie blushed. "I'm sorry, Lark. I know I've called you nosy many times, and it's not right. Please forgive me. You're just so capable and good at finding out stuff. I'm afraid my one and only effort proved me less than talented in the investigative field."

Lark gave her a knowing look. "You mean the afternoon you ran around town wearin' that coat in seventy-five-degree weather, those sunglasses as the sun was going down, and that plug-ugly hat of your dead husband's? The day you nearly conked yourself out on cigar fumes, then wiped out Ellamae's diner clientele with your newfound perfume?"

Laughing and wailing, Cammie hid her face in the space created by the arms she crossed on the table. "Stop! Have mercy on me. I've already heard a few times over how silly I looked. Besides, I'm never going to forget the stench of Marvelous Myrna—er . . . Me!"

"Marvelous Myrna?" Maggie asked between peals of laughter.

"Well, it is kind of hard to separate the event from the woman who actually caused it."

Lark pointed at Cammie. "Now don't go tryin' to shift blame, sis. You bought the stuff."

Cammie nodded. "True, I did, but only in an effort to help

Lucille. You know how they need every cent now that her baby sister's on that expensive chemo for leukemia. Myrna's the one who caught her gaudy, fake, half-dollar bracelet on the handle of my tote bag. That's how she dragged the thing off the table."

Maggie sobered up first. "Well, did you learn anythin' we can use for all that trouble?"

"Nothing other than whoever bought the junk food did so knowing no one would be able to track him down. Why, you'd never believe how much of that stuff people in Bellamy consume. And cooking's no great hardship, you know."

Lark's expression grew thoughtful. "You know, maybe you did learn somethin' valuable after all. You learned that whoever did the stealing was either very smart or had experience in this kind of thing. Someone knew how to cover tracks well."

Cammie nodded slowly. "And they didn't leave any other evidence behind. At least, none that has been found so far."

"That means," Maggie said, twirling a blond curl around a finger, "that even though it's more'n likely the thief is a stranger to town, 'cause I can't see our friends takin' our dogs, he could also be from here. Anyone could have bought Twinkies, a burger, or the candy bar."

"That's what I've thought all along," Cammie said, relieved. "Just because we don't think anyone we know stole our dogs doesn't necessarily mean that it's someone who's new to town. It could be a neighbor, and then again, it could be some stranger who drove through and just . . . oh, I don't know . . . goes around taking other people's dogs."

"But why?" Lark asked.

"Yes," Maggie echoed. "Why would someone do such a thing?"

Making the sentiment unanimous, Cammie added, "Why, indeed?"

Five days later, late on a Saturday afternoon, Cammie made another quick decision. This one came easier than the one where she'd foolishly decided to trust Stephen Hardesty. Willie and Miss Sophie wanted to take a walk in the woods by Langhorn Park.

Since Stephen and Willie had so far thwarted Cammie's every effort to pump the older man for personal details, she jumped at the opportunity to tag along and perhaps mine for informational gold.

By the time she met up with the elderly duo, however, Cammie had reason to question their sanity—if not her own as well. They were loaded down with a bucket, a paint scraper, and a brown paper bag with handles. She didn't dare ask what they'd stowed in the sack.

"Wait up!" she heard Stephen call as they took off down the street.

"Is he coming along, too?" she asked Willie, unable to keep the dismay out of her voice.

"Why, of course," answered Willie. "He's my dearest friend."

Miss Sophie reached over and patted Cammie's shoulder. "Just as you're mine, dearie. It's so much more pleasant to share with friends these delightful adventures Willie takes us on."

"'Delightful,' Aunt Sophie?" Stephen asked, catching up with them. "Are you sure your encounter with the D.C. police was a delightful experience?"

Miss Sophie shuddered delicately, her white knot of hair quivering. "Not exactly, Stephen. But it did work out in the end, as my dear Mariah always says." Turning to Cammie, Miss Sophie added, "You know, honey, 'God causes everything to work together for the good—'"

"'Of those who love God and are called according to his purpose for them.'" Cammie smiled. "If I've heard Mrs. Desmond quote that verse once, why, then, I've heard her quote it a million times."

Miss Sophie nodded. "And you know, dear, she's right. God's Word is right. All things do work out for those who love and trust the Lord."

Cammie glanced at their male companions. A sickly twinge in her middle led her to say, "I hope so, Miss Sophie. I sure do hope so."

The foursome said nothing more, underscoring the awkwardness that had grown between Cammie and Stephen after he had laughed at her suspicions. Unfortunately, as was the usual case, Willie and Miss Sophie took off at a brisk pace that Cammie, with her now greatly bulging belly, couldn't match. Stephen, with his overblown sense of responsibility, measured his steps to hers.

Cammie wished he wouldn't. She preferred to walk alone, to watch him and Willie, to stay alert for any telling action or chance comment.

But with Stephen always at her side, she couldn't think of much but him. He snagged such a great portion of her attention. She couldn't stop thinking of the times they'd shared, the laughter, the conversations, and especially those tender, passionate kisses.

"What are they up to?" Stephen finally asked.

"I wouldn't know. I thought Willie might have told you."

"He called me and said he and Aunt Sophie were going for a walk in the woods. Would I like to join them? He didn't even mention you."

"I had a similar call from Miss Sophie. No mention of you, either."

"Um . . . Cammie?"

"Yes?"

"I'm sorry I laughed at you the other evening. I know I offended you, and that wasn't my intention. That may be the reason they didn't mention to us that the other was coming along. This is probably their way to get us to make things better."

"I accept your apology," Cammie said. "And you may be right. They're having such a grand old time on these 'adventures,' and they've grown so accustomed to our company, that it's likely they'd give us the opportunity to patch things up. Like with children, you know?"

He shrugged. "What I did was pretty childish."

"Let's just forget it, okay?"

He gave a grin. "Forget what?"

Chuckling, Cammie relaxed. Until they entered the woods. Although she'd worn sturdy walking shoes, she was leery of the ground littered with fallen branches and of the mosses and lichens that covered the forest floor. She didn't want to get careless and risk a fall.

Stephen, always attentive, remained at her elbow at every step. "Are they crazy?" he asked. "I thought they'd use a trail, not scramble over forest garbage. Did they forget they dragged you along?"

"Oh, hush," Cammie cautioned. "Look at them. They're having a blast. I can crawl along as well as a couple of senior citizens. I'm not an invalid; I'm only pregnant."

"Yeah, well, I still think this is going too far—"

"Now what?" Cammie asked, noting that Willie had stopped, crouched, and was inspecting the ground. "Don't tell me he's about to repeat his groundhog routine?"

"No metal detector," Stephen pointed out.

"True, but look at the bag your aunt's carrying. Who knows what they have in there?"

"Only one way to find out what they're doing. Let's go ask."

They didn't get a chance, since Willie launched into a serious and erudite discourse. "Notice, my darling Sophie, that here, where the canopy above has grown to shade the ground, we find excellent specimens of *Hylocomium splendens* and *Pleurozium schreberi*—"

"Why, Willie Johnson," Miss Sophie crooned, "if you aren't just the sharpest man. Look at that perfectly lovely Hyli . . . hylo—hyplutonium—" she ran a hand over her mouth—"mrhmssmumt."

Willie nodded absently, still studying his find.

Stephen leaned toward Cammie. "I knew I'd seen that stuff before. *Hypleucozmium splendeschberibum,* of course. I'd know it anywhere."

Cammie chuckled and shook her head at the two Hardestys' antics.

Willie continued pattering. "If you look closely, you'll see how the *Pleurozium* is following its typical pattern. It's everywhere. In a relatively short time, why, I'd say it'll have choked out all other competition and overrun the entire area. But only where the shade abounds, you understand. These would be excellent choices for one of our projects."

Looking determinedly interested but a tad dizzy from the incomprehensible lecture, Miss Sophie nodded. "Whatever you think is best, Willie. I trust you."

Everything in Cammie ached to yell, *No, don't! He could be the one who stole my dog. And he may steal your heart, only to break it to bits.* But she bit down on her tongue, knowing she couldn't say a word. She had no proof.

Oblivious to her turmoil, Willie used his paint scraper on a rock. *Scritch, scritch, scritch.* Cammie's curiosity urged her forward, and she watched the man lift a bunch of what looked like moss from the ground.

To her amazement, Miss Sophie smiled beatifically, opened

a clean, empty margarine tub, helped Willie stash the stuff inside, then returned the container to her bag.

Cammie turned to Stephen. "Why would he want a wad of moss?"

Miss Sophie's grandnephew shook his head, obviously mystified too. "Beats me, but let's just let them continue. So far, they haven't broken any laws or collected any more reptiles."

Cammie grimaced. "Praise God."

Stephen shot her a glance but said nothing. Cammie felt somewhat disappointed. Another lost opportunity, it would seem. But she couldn't really bring up the subject of faith under these rather ludicrous circumstances.

"Oh, Sophie, dearest!" cried Willie as he stepped into a small clearing. "Look at this magnificent *Ceratodon purpureus.* It's nearly as ravishing as you. I say we take it. Look how well it's grown on these sunny rocks. It should do as well for another of our projects."

A dazed Miss Sophie nodded. "Here I'd always heard say the *Craterodontus* had become extinct with its brother dinosaurs. It's nice we have one of them left us these days. But it doesn't look like it moves much anymore. Still, it sure does have a nice color to it."

"Indeed, and if it runs true to form, we're likely to locate a patch of nice *Cetraria islandica,* too."

Willie bent to more scraping. Miss Sophie opened up another recycled plastic tub and added it to the earlier one when it was full.

"Shall we?" asked Willie, crooking his elbow at his date with a suave grace to rival Fred Astaire at his best. Miss Sophie took hold with her free hand, and they resumed their walk.

"Watch out!" Willie cried out.

"Wha—" Miss Sophie stumbled. "Oh no!"

A hideous stench struck Cammie's nostrils. "Oh, my. That does smell awful, doesn't it?"

Stephen wrinkled his face and shuddered. "Oh, yeah."

Miss Sophie limped to a dense patch of moss and began scraping the sole of her shoe against the brownish-green growth.

Staring at what had caused his outburst and soiled Miss Sophie's shoe, Willie said, "I'd never have thought to find *Splachnaceae* out here—it's too far for people's pets but not far enough for wild animals. Still, as surely as the splendiferous Sophie Hardesty has stolen my heart, there it is."

Stephen stepped toward the source of the smell.

Willie scowled. "Stay back," he barked.

Cammie didn't think she'd ever smelled anything this strong, this ripe. She had no interest in getting closer.

"What's so strange about another kind of moss?" Stephen asked, evidently not finding anything noteworthy—except the fumes that kept his face twisted. "You've been scraping and picking the stuff at every rotten log or rock you've found. There's nothing strange about another species."

"If it were just any old species," Willie answered, removing his surgical glove and scratching his nose, "I wouldn't either. But this kind of bryophyte only grows on one kind of host."

"What kind's that?"

"Can't you smell it?"

"Yeah, it smells like—"

"I know what it is!" cried Miss Sophie. "It's—"

"Dog's—"

"Yes, Willie," cut in Miss Sophie, her expression none too happy.

Her date, however, wore a formidable frown. The shadow from a nearby tree conspired to turn that scowl into a menacing glare.

Cammie studied her companions. Was there a conspiracy?

Willie continued, oblivious to her thoughts. "I doubt any of Bellamy's best is likely to run out here to do its thing, so to speak."

Cammie gasped. There it was. Her first real clue, and Willie seemed suitably perturbed that someone had seen it.

Her heart began to pound. She had to get back to Bellamy to tell her sisters what she'd found and notify Wiggon of the first break in the case. If she wasn't much mistaken, either Buford, Mycroft, or Muttley had gone this way and left his unmistakable mark.

Why couldn't she have found something simple like one of the dog's collars or a tuft of hair? What could she say to make anyone believe her? She knew she was onto something, but she faced a monumental problem. She was thankful for this first real clue, but she needed help, and she needed it fast. *Please, Lord, help me to know how to handle this situation.*

Ellie continued [illegible] of her thoughts. [illegible] of [illegible] herself to [illegible]
[illegible]

[illegible] there was [illegible] her [illegible] Rather [illegible]
[illegible] [illegible] to [illegible]
[illegible] when [illegible]
[illegible]
[illegible] that [illegible]
[illegible]

[illegible] and
she [illegible] What could [illegible]
[illegible] She knew she was [illegible]
[illegible]
[illegible] and [illegible] the
[illegible]

EIGHTEEN

MOMENTS AFTER HER PRAYER, CAMMIE KNEW WHAT SHE had to do. "Excuse me, you all. I have to say it's been fascinating, but I must hurry home. I just remembered—"

What? What kind of excuse could she offer to make a quick and innocent-seeming getaway? She didn't want to alert Willie—or Stephen—to what she'd just discovered.

"Oh, yes. I just remembered I left my pumpkin butter cooking. I have to get back and turn it off, else it might be a patch of leather on the bottom of the pot by the time we finish here. See you all back home."

Cammie took off, unwilling to wait and see how her words struck the others. She had to get to Wiggon and her sisters right away. They in turn had to get back out here before the evidence vanished or was destroyed—

"Oh, dear. There I go again, leaping in like Lark would," she said to herself, coming to a complete halt. "What shall I do, Father? I need help, but I also need to stay here and see that no one tampers with that clue."

As she waited for divine guidance, heavy running pounded

up behind her. "Cammie!" Stephen yelled. "Are you nuts? What are you doing, running off by yourself like that? It's getting dark. You might fall and hurt yourself."

Squeezing her eyes shut, Cammie pursed her lips to keep from uttering a sharp comment. How could a woman get mad at a man who seemed to always have her well-being and that of her child in mind?

If that was what it truly was. Doubt had entered her mind again. And therein lay her problem. How did she shake Stephen off without coming across like a shrew?

"I'm only going home. I recollect which way we came, and it only took us a half hour's steady walk through the trees to reach Willie's first collection site. I'm in no danger here."

"Accidents," Stephen countered in an infuriating, overly patient voice, "are called *accidents* because they're unpredictable. You can't be certain one won't happen to you. I want to—no, I *need* to—make sure you're okay. Chalk it up to a professional quirk, all right? There's not a patient in Bellamy who would come to me for medical care if I was negligent and you suffered an injury. No matter how stubbornly you fought me to have your own way."

She sighed. "Fine. But it's silly for you to leave when you were having so much fun with Willie and your aunt."

"Fun? Watching her step in a pile of dog doo?"

"Yes, well, I meant earlier."

Stephen stopped and stared at her, his eyes dark. "Something about those dog droppings sent you running, not a pot of pumpkin or anything like that."

Cammie looked away and resumed walking. "No. Really. I have to get back home to the pumpkin butter. I did leave it cooking."

True enough. What she failed to mention, however, was that she made that recipe in her Crock-Pot, therefore risking no burn. But Stephen didn't need to know that. Just as he didn't need to make the same connection she had. Who knew if Willie had sent him to . . . what was it they said in movies? Oh, that's right. To do damage control.

Catching up to her, Stephen shrugged. "Fine. But I'll still walk back with you."

"Don't you think it might be wisest if you stayed with Willie and Miss Sophie? They're older and could hurt themselves out here. They're more likely to need your medical attention than I am."

"Yes, but there are two of them. I believe in the buddy system. I repeat that in my practice who knows how many times a day."

Cammie gave him a brilliant smile—or at least she hoped it positively sparkled. "Why, then, you're in luck, Stephen. I'm not alone. My baby's with me so there *are* two of us to begin with, plus Jesus goes with me wherever I go. Don't you fret another minute. Just get on back to your Aunt Sophie, and I'll see you all once you get back. In fact, come over for some honey bread and pumpkin butter after the moss collecting's over."

Again, Stephen regaled her with his silent, piercing scrutiny. Finally, when she reached the conclusion that he wasn't going to say anything further, she picked up her pace. Maybe back in Bellamy she could shake loose of him and do what she had to do.

Under no possible circumstances was Camellia Bellamy Sprague going to shake Stephen off that easily. The minute she turned tail at the odoriferous clearing in the woods, Stephen knew something was up. He'd taken only long enough to ask Aunt Sophie and Willie to meet him back at Cammie's once they were done hunting down mosses to their hearts' content.

Now her evasive comments confirmed his gut feeling. The lady protested way too much. And her pace had picked up to a near run. Why was she in such a hurry? Where was she going? Was she meeting someone?

That possibility bothered Stephen more than he wanted it to. He didn't want a woman to mean so much to him. But there it was. Cammie mattered. He didn't want to think of her running back to town to meet another man.

Nothing in her actions or demeanor had ever given him that impression. In fact, from her reaction to their kisses, he knew he was the first man to come so close to her since her husband's death. Still, a lovely woman like Cammie would soon have numerous men seeking her company. That image stole Stephen's peace.

He wanted to claim her for himself.

He didn't know what to do about that feeling, especially since he and Cammie didn't have much in common. He'd always heard that for a relationship to succeed, the partners had to share attitudes and interests.

Aside from a great sense of humor and love for one Sophie Hardesty, Stephen couldn't think of much else he and Cammie shared. Well, she did love to cook and he did love to eat. But he didn't think that counted as much of a starting point for a relationship. Oh, and they both loved that goofy dog someone had stolen from her. There again, though, that didn't make for a very solid base for sharing their lives.

The things that really mattered . . . well, it was there that they had their differences.

Especially in view of Cammie's sincere, strong Christianity. Stephen couldn't imagine depending on a God he couldn't see—or on anything other than himself. During his years of spiritual searching, he'd found nothing supernatural anywhere he looked. Then he'd tried Zen. It was the only path that had seemed to make sense—for a while, anyway. After all, it taught that a man had to bear his own responsibility toward humankind, the earth, and its other inhabitants—the universe. Because everything was connected, the concept of the self was, at best, an illusion . . . yet that was the part that hung him up these days, that illusion thing.

Cammie had made her point with the undeniable reality of Lana the iguana.

But Stephen knew reality wasn't all it was cracked it up to be. He'd experienced the reality of relationships that had left him empty, lonely, frustrated, and hungry . . . for something. In reaching out unsuccessfully to his family, Stephen had learned he couldn't look to anyone else to satisfy his emotional longing. After all, emotions weren't tangible. In that regard, Zen's detachment made sense to him.

In contrast, Cammie's Christian faith taught the ultimate in attachment. She relied on God for everything. And she reached out to everyone with whom she came into contact—"being a good witness," she called it. Yet, in his opinion, Cammie's lifestyle of attachment to God and serving others couldn't possibly lead to peace. Need prompted both. And need led to busyness rather than peace.

He couldn't let himself need Cammie, for eventually, she'd let him down, too. Everyone eventually did.

Except for Aunt Sophie. She was different, special.

That was why it mattered so much to him to make available the best possible medical care to everyone in Bellamy. He had to keep his great-aunt alive as long as possible. He didn't want to think what he would do when the one person who had always loved him—unconditionally, at that—died. Who would love him then?

He didn't want to look to Cammie for that kind of fulfillment. And since they diverged so radically in their philosophical views, it was best for him to avoid caring any more than he already did.

There's your problem, pal, a mischievous part of his mind taunted. *You* do *care for her. You want her, and you want her to care for you.*

"Well, we're home," Cammie said brightly—too brightly—bringing him out of his thoughts. "I'll see you later, once Willie and Miss Sophie return for that bread and butter I promised, won't I?"

Stephen frowned. "You're kicking me out only to ask me to come back later?"

She blushed. "Well, no. At least, that wasn't my intention. I would never send anyone away from my home. I just reckon a busy man like you has to have somethin' to do evenings other than follow a pair of senior citizens on odd outings or baby-sit a perfectly capable pregnant lady."

"This is my night off. My backup is on duty. Even doctors get a break, you know. I've left my patients in good hands, and I need a break to return fresh to the office in the morning. It's not healthy for a man to do nothing but work."

Cammie gasped and stared at him as if dumbstruck. Her hazel eyes studied him.

Had he sprouted feathers or an elephantine trunk? What had he said to cause such a strong reaction? Had he offended her? Said something stupid? He didn't think so. He'd only voiced very simple and sensible concepts.

"That's wonderful," she finally said, "and I'm sure you must have somethin' else relaxing to do."

"Well, I was looking forward to a cup of your coffee."

She closed her eyes, and Stephen knew without a shadow of a doubt that Cammie wanted nothing more than to get rid of him. That made him more determined not to go anywhere.

"Come on in, then," she said climbing the porch steps reluctantly. "I'll make a fresh pot of coffee."

Both went straight to the kitchen, he to the coffee urn, and she to, of all things, a crockery cooker in the corner of the counter. Even Stephen knew those things could stay on practically forever and the contents would have to work hard to burn.

After she peered through the glass top, she said, "If you'll excuse me—"

"Cammie, please stop. I know you're doing everything you can politely do to get rid of me, but I'm not moving. Just tell me what you're up to. It'll be much easier on both of us. That way I won't have to imagine all kinds of crazy things, and you won't have to work so hard to find excuses."

He watched her struggle, then come to a decision. "Fine," she said, taking a chair at the table. "Join me and I'll tell you. But you have to promise not to laugh at me again, okay? No matter how silly you think what I'm goin' to tell you is."

Stephen couldn't keep his eyebrows from rising. "It's about Willie and the dogs, isn't it?"

"Yes."

He thought back over everything he knew of her suspicions. Then it hit him. His lips curved up. He fought the grin, but his mustache tickled his upper lip. He wriggled his nose, hoping to ease the itch, but it didn't help.

She scowled. "I told you not to laugh at me, Stephen Hardesty."

"I'm—" The word squawked out with a renegade chuckle. "I'm not laughing. I'm ah . . . coughing."

"And I'm a circus sword swallower."

That did it. He roared. He howled. Tears ran down his cheeks, not only at the image of the pregnant woman swallowing a trick sword for the crowd under the big top, but at the nutty conclusion to which she'd jumped.

She stood, her pert, small nose tipped way up. "Very well, Dr. Hardesty. I believe it's a fine time for you to take yourself on home and let me mind my own business."

"You can't be serious."

"I've rarely been more serious in my life."

"You really think Aunt Sophie stepped into a pile of fresh evidence?"

"Not at all. That wasn't fresh one bit—remember the stench!"

Stephen dug himself into deeper trouble by laughing harder still. "Moss on manure . . . clues to a dognapping . . . and you, of course, have busted the case wide open."

Cammie's shoulders stiffened even more. "That remains for the police to determine. I just need to do my civic duty as a good citizen and report my findings."

They were going to have a field day down at the PD. "Well, at least you've given up on that wild idea of Willie's guilt."

"How do you figure?"

Oh, great. She hadn't. "Think about it, Cammie. Please. Would a dognapper take his date, her nephew, and her snoopy friend right to the doggy toilet he'd set up? I don't think Willie's that stupid—I don't think he's stupid at all."

Satisfaction gleamed in her eyes. "I don't either. And that's why it all fits just so. He has an accomplice somewhere who isn't half as bright as he. That's who took the dog—or dogs—to that spot to relieve themselves. Didn't you notice how fiercely he frowned when Aunt Sophie stepped into it?"

Somehow Stephen couldn't quite make her two plus two come out to four. "I think he just scowled at the smell—oh, and at finding his something-or-other moss where he hadn't expected to."

"Very well, Dr. Hardesty, you're certainly entitled to your own opinion. I, on the other hand, have to do what I believe is right. You may choose to accompany me or just head on home."

With that, she turned and picked up the phone. From what

Stephen overheard, she asked her older sisters to meet her down at the PD. Both agreed.

As soon as she hung up she let herself out the front door, leaving him no alternative but to follow, dreading what he suspected was to come.

She was a hit at the PD.

Stephen knew the old brick walls hadn't rung so loudly with laughter in years—if ever. At first even the sisters looked at Cammie as if she'd flipped. Slowly, however, the two other women came to her way of seeing things.

None of the officers did.

Neither did Stephen.

In spite of that, the chief enjoyed every moment, especially when he sent Wiggon to the woods to collect the evidence, since Cammie refused to leave the premises until something was done about her dog's situation. Wiggon's fellow officers hooted him out the door. The tall, skinny cop left, muttering under his breath about Jill and her crazy friends.

By then the three sisters had huddled near the front door, and from the amount of whispering going on, Stephen feared further trouble. But the Blossoms, as he'd heard everyone in town call them collectively, shared a group hug and went their separate ways. He hurried to catch up to Cammie.

"What do you expect them to do with . . . well, with what Willie and Aunt Sophie found?" he asked.

Cammie shrugged. "It's not so much that they have to do somethin' with the evidence; they just need to recognize it as evidence, you know?"

"And you're satisfied?"

She didn't answer.

"Well?" he prodded.

"I will be soon enough."

With that cryptic comment, she pressed her lips shut. The autumn night had a nip to it, the welcome warmth of Indian summer a thing of the past. The sliver of moon overhead seemed more sharply etched against the jet-black sky than usual. Spurts of wind kicked up dead leaves from where they'd fallen.

Stephen felt invigorated despite his insane evening. Of course, it didn't hurt having Cammie at his side, even when she'd made it perfectly clear she didn't want to talk. They didn't have to. He was content just to be with her.

Nutty though she was, Stephen admired the way she'd gone against the grain and insisted on what she believed was right. She hadn't backed down. It took courage and strength to do that, and Cammie had demonstrated an abundance of both, even before an unsympathetic crowd.

She'd never lost her temper. True, she'd grown a tad icy toward him because of his laughter, but she hadn't said anything rude or argumentative. She'd just stated her position and carried out her intentions. He wished he knew as clearly what to do in moments of decision. He wished—

"Stephen!" she whispered loudly.

"Huh?" he responded, startled.

"Hush, and just look over there. Do you see what I see?"

He looked in the direction she indicated, but he saw nothing of note: a small bungalow-style house, a street sign, a van pulling away.

"How about you tell me what you see, and I'll tell you if I see it too?"

She sighed. "Well, you can't see it anymore," she said in her normal voice. "He's gone."

"Who's gone?"

"Why, Bernie Stafford, Myrna's son."

Somehow he'd missed something in the conversation.

"What's so strange about Bernie Stafford—other than his mother?"

"'Oh, shush!'" she admonished, chuckling. "What's strange is that I saw him at all. I mean, he never comes to town much, and what's more, he was skulkin' out of her house and into that van."

"'Skulking?'" he asked, grinning at Cammie's word choice.

"What would you call him pressin' up against the side of the house, slinkin' around the shrubs, then dashin' into the van and not turnin' on the headlights as he drove away?"

"If you put it that way, then I guess I'd have to call it skulking, too. But are you sure that's what he was doing? Are you sure you're not letting your imagination continue down the road it's traveled this evening?"

"Are you sayin' I'm makin' this up?"

"Not at all. What I'm suggesting is that you've had such an exciting evening that the earlier events may be coloring your perception of what you're seeing now."

"Terrific. Now I'm seein' things that aren't there, right?" She walked faster. "I think it's a fine time to say good night, don't you, Dr. Hardesty?"

"Not at all, Widow Sprague. You promised me fresh honey bread and pumpkin butter. I plan to claim it—*after* I've seen you safely home."

She sniffed and kept up her brisk pace, not deigning to answer. At this point, though, Stephen didn't care. He'd gotten what he wanted. He'd found out what had sent Cammie running from the clearing. He'd made sure she didn't wind up in more trouble—or worse, arrested for her wacky tale. He'd tamped down her impulse to accuse the unfortunate Bernie Stafford of who-knew-what crime and had left her no choice but to tolerate his presence at her side all the way home.

The bread and butter would be icing on his proverbial cake.

They walked into absolute chaos in Cammie's kitchen.

"Wha—what happened?" she asked, blanching.

Stephen couldn't help echoing her sentiment. "What's going on?"

In front of the counter, Willie and Aunt Sophie stood paralyzed, much like a pair of jewel thieves caught in the act. Their clothing was filthy.

That was the least of what Cammie and Stephen observed.

On the old and well-loved oak table sat a mountain of large rocks, while additional small boulders littered the kitchen counters. Globs of dirt spotted the floor in a random pattern of organic polka dots. Stephen soon identified the whirring noise at the scene of this current crime as that of the working blender.

The daring duo had something spinning in the appliance, something he fervently hoped would not be part of his bread-and-butter snack. It looked a sickly gray-green, and whooshed up the glass sides of the blender jar, licking dangerously at the black lid. As messy as the kitchen already was, unless someone turned off the machine, it could soon become even more so.

"Stop that thing!" he yelled in order to be heard by the elderly statues.

Aunt Sophie reacted first. "Of course, dear, whatever you say."

She turned to the blender as Willie blinked and leapt into action. Both reached the knob at the same time, causing the contraption to bobble. The lid flipped off, and spurts of dingy muck flew everywhere, several slapping Stephen in the face.

"My kitchen!" Cammie wailed as another flying effluvium struck her hair. "What have you done to it?"

Stephen didn't care; his only thought was ending the maniacal spewing of gloppy gunk. He flew across the room, shoved the culprits aside, and yanked the plug from the outlet.

Blessed silence filled the room.

"Now," he said, his voice controlled, "explain what this—" he wiped goop from his mustache—"all means."

As soon as he saw Willie's perky grin, he realized they were in for yet another "adventure" tale. He wasn't disappointed.

"Why, son, this is why we went moss gathering in the first place. True, it's a lovely pastime in and of itself, but neither your aunt nor I have the facilities to display the beauties we found."

"The rocks," Cammie said in a weak voice. "Why are they here? What other national monument did you two dig up to get them?"

Aunt Sophie waved. "Oh, sugar, there's no need to lather yourself like that. Why, these are my very own rocks. Well, actually, they're the rocks from our house, the one I share with Lou and Mariah, you know. So I didn't do nothin' troublesome."

Stephen debated whether to hold Cammie upright or to shake an explanation out of Willie and his equally dotty date. Since Cammie had found her way into a reasonably clean chair, he approached the perpetrators.

"Cammie has a valid question. Why did you two bring a small quarry into her kitchen? And what *is* this slop?"

"Well, son," Willie said, his voice the epitome of reason, "we needed to apply the formula to the rocks right away. We're still planning to take them back to the girls' house tonight. Care to give us a hand?"

Cammie stood. "Don't you dare, Stephen. Not until they tell me what they've smeared all over my kitchen. And me."

Stephen smiled grimly. "Good point." He crossed his arms over his chest and said to Willie, "You heard the lady. Now tell her what this is."

"It's very simple. We put twelve ounces of buttermilk and one-half teaspoon of sugar into the blender, added the moss—"

"Moss!" Cammie's revulsion echoed Stephen's.

Willie didn't seem to notice the interruption. ". . . and processed it only long enough to break down the moss and mix the ingredients. Well, all but this last batch."

He gave Cammie and Stephen a baleful glare. "You distracted us and it blended a bit too long, I'm afraid."

"Oh, dear," Aunt Sophie said. "Is it spoiled now?"

Willie patted his ladylove's arm. "Don't you trouble your pretty little head, Sophie, my darling. If it is spoiled, why, we'll just go gather more specimens."

"You still haven't explained the reason for the rocks," Cammie said, patting an especially large and dirty one on the table.

Willie picked up a spatula, scooped a bunch of the blended moss, and smeared it on the nearest boulder. "We need to spread the mix on the rocks, of course. We couldn't do that outside in the dark, could we?"

Cammie turned to Stephen, a beseeching look in her eyes. She faced Willie again and asked the question Stephen was dying to have answered. "Why would you want to smear rocks with sour milk and moss?"

As though speaking to a pair of not-too-bright children, Willie enunciated very clearly. "So that Sophie—"

"Are you trying to blame my aunt?" Stephen asked.

Willie gasped. "I would never do such a thing."

Cammie sighed. "About the stuff on the rocks . . . ?"

"Indeed," Willie answered. "You do know that Sophie is a splendid master gardener, don't you?"

"Well, yes."

"And you realize she's absolutely brilliant, right?"

"Mm-hmm."

"And her garden's sheer perfection, isn't it?"

"Of course, but—"

"Well, then, surely you realize it took me no more than a minute's appraisal to notice it lacked only one thing."

Cammie leaned closer. "What's that?"

Willie beamed. "Homegrown moss!"

NINETEEN

THE NEXT DAY CAMMIE SET THE OLD, DELICATE ROYAL Worcester porcelain teapot in the middle of her again-spotless kitchen table and smiled at her sisters. "I can't thank you both enough for coming over on such short notice."

Lark shook her dark red curls. "No need. When you said you had additional information for us, I began calling in more favors, and I think I'm onto something, too."

"About the dogs?" Cammie asked.

"Yep."

"Well, I'm no slouch in this lily pond either," Maggie said triumphantly. "I have plenty to report from my ladies down to the jail."

"Have a cup of tea," Cammie urged her sisters, pouring one for herself. "Then let's pray and start our meeting."

Smiling, the three held hands and asked the Lord's blessing on their discussion. In a private prayer, Cammie thanked God for the new spirit of collaboration between the three Blossoms.

Then Lark said, "I'll start, if you'd like."

"Go ahead," said Cammie. "With all your contacts, you're likely to have come up with the location of the dogs, not to mention the name and address of the culprit by now."

"Don't I wish," Lark answered. "But I do think I have something. When I called my old editor at the *Baltimore Sun,* he said there's a rash of unlicensed labs doing animal testing in the mid-Atlantic region."

"Does that mean what I think it means?" asked Maggie.

"If you're thinkin' they don't go through the sanctioned, government-regulated channels to obtain their subjects, you're absolutely right."

Maggie winked. "Typical Lark. Usin' five-dollar words when penny ones would do. But of course you've hit the nail right smack on its risin' ugly head, and that shoe fits what I learned so well it's singin' and marchin' in with the saints in New Orleans."

Lark hooted with laughter. "And that string of clichés isn't just like you, now, is it, Mags?"

"Clichés?" Maggie asked, clearly affronted. "Why, I'll have you know, Lark Bellamy, I would never stoop to usin' clichés in my conversation. I just have a way with a fine turn of phrase."

Cammie shook her head. "Would you two please stop? Maggie said—I think—that she'd learned something that added to what you'd learned, Lark. Why don't we hear her out?"

"Oh, but she's such fun to tease." Lark sobered. "You're right, sissy. What *did* you find out from your prison ladies, Mags?"

"Well, Halvernia Pouterbell said she knew a man who sold dogs for a livin'. So I asked her what kind he bred. She said he didn't breed 'em at all. He just found 'em and sold 'em to people developin' medicines and such. So I asked her where he found these dogs he sold. She said he found 'em everywhere he looked. Then I wanted to know just where he looked. From what he told Halvernia, it seems he has some fool notion about backyards bein' open spaces. It appears he's never heard about trespassin'—or likes to forget he has."

Lark and Cammie leaned closer to Maggie. Cammie's mind spun with the information, adding and subtracting from her theories faster than she thought possible. "Did Halvernia tell you where this man is from? I mean, where he lives—and steals, you understand."

Maggie's smile dripped satisfaction. "Indeed I did. He lives over to Leesburg, my dears. Right in our backyard, so to speak."

Leesburg. Anyone could drive in and out of Bellamy from Leesburg without any trouble at all. And if it was someone familiar with the area, someone the residents of Bellamy knew, even if only at a distance, they could carry out just about any awful kind of deed.

Cammie leaned back in her chair, nibbling on her bottom lip. If that was the case, then Willie could be as innocent as Stephen insisted he was.

Or not.

After all, Willie could be the mastermind, and the person in Leesburg could be the brainless muscle.

She nodded. That could work. Myrna had been so certain of Willie's guilt that perhaps she'd discerned something Cammie had missed. But then Myrna was known to be wrong and mean-spirited, too.

"Oh, dear," Cammie said. On the other hand, the Leesburg connection didn't get Stephen off the suspicion hook either. He could be the mastermind—or co-mastermind with Willie—and the hulking help be the one dashing in and out, risking detection.

"Well?" asked Lark, obviously not for the first time.

"Well, what?" countered Cammie.

"When did you take up talkin' to yourself like Maggie?" the eldest Blossom asked.

Maggie spluttered like a boiling teakettle. "I don't talk to myself—"

"I haven't taken up Maggie's bad habits," Cammie said in self-defense; then she blushed. "Well, I have been told I've been sort of muttering under my breath of late. But I don't talk to myself like Maggie does."

Maggie stood and slapped the table. "I'm only goin' to repeat myself once. I don't talk to myself."

"You probably do it so often you don't even notice when you do," Cammie said with a soft smile. She reached out for her sister's hand. "Sit, please. Besides, it's the most charming thing to hear you make some of those funny comments of yours. Nothing wrong with that. But *I* don't talk to myself."

Somewhat mollified, Maggie sat. "Anyway," she said, "you're still shilly-shallyin', like Granny Iris used to say. What was it you learned, Cammie? And does it have anythin' to do with what Lark and I learned?"

Cammie nodded again. "Yes, it does. It has plenty to do with what you and Lark just said. Myrna Stafford—"

"Aw, Cammie, not another of Myrna's stories. I thought you had enough sense not to listen to that gossipy woman."

Maggie stood. "Oh, well, at least we now know there's a dog thief in Leesburg, and that there are unlawful labs operatin' on the eastern seaboard."

"Wait a minute," Cammie said, her voice as stern as she could manage in the company of her two older sisters. "I do have plenty to share with you two, and it would be a shame if you missed out on important information because you let old prejudices color your listening."

Sheepishly, Maggie nodded and took her chair again. Lark remained silent but retained her skeptical expression. "What did Myrna tell you?"

"Now listen . . ." Cammie revealed Myrna's and her suspicions based on Willie's foreigner status, his possible efforts to divert her attention with iguanas, defaced federal property, the introduction to dung moss, homegrown bryophytes, and his courting of naïve Miss Sophie. She especially emphasized the smelly discovery in the forest and Willie's strong reaction in its wake.

When she finished, Maggie and Lark kept their peace. After a bit, Maggie spoke, shaking her long blond curls. "I don't rightly know, Camellia, honey. That's a passel of night crawlers you've tried to weave into whole cloth there for us. They're not stayin' together too well, you know?"

"I have to agree with both of you," Lark said. "The theory that an outsider would steal the dogs is sound, but I can't see Mr. Johnson carting dogs to places where people would do unspeakable things to them on account of his being a newcomer to town."

Cammie gave Lark a pointed look. "Aren't you the one who accused him of taking advantage of me?"

"Well, getting you to do him special favors like baking his favorite pastries and keeping his room nice and clean is one thing. It's quite another thing altogether to encourage the abuse of dogs—you do know what all happens in those unlicensed labs, don't you?"

Cammie nodded. "Of course, Lark. It's bad enough when they use animals to prove the safety of medicines that will save millions of human lives. I can accept that. But the other . . ." She shuddered. "No, I've watched too many news programs showing the horrors."

Lark's green eyes blazed. "That's what I mean. I don't think your boarder has it in him to physically hurt another living thing."

Cammie again thought of Lana. "You may have a point

there." She told her sisters about her unwelcome green guest. They laughed.

Laughed and laughed and laughed.

Much too much, in Cammie's opinion.

"Getting back to our original subject," Cammie said when she'd had enough of their hilarity, "we can't be sure he's innocent, though. I don't want to believe he did it, but for all we know, he could be a former actor, skilled at fooling folks."

"True," Maggie said, "but somethin' in my heart tells me he's not the one. He just doesn't look the sort, you know."

Again Lark hooted at her sister's comment. "Remember how nice and normal serial killers look."

"Now, ladies," Cammie cautioned, hoping to restore sanity to the conversation, "we have no bodies here. We're only dealing with a thief."

"That we know of," Lark conceded grimly.

"You know," Maggie began, "we do have us another stranger in town. And of everyone around, you likely know somethin' about him, Cammie. There's those who've wagered on the weddin' date already."

Cammie blushed. "Hogwash. I'm not a candidate for another marriage. Especially with Stephen Hardesty."

Lark waggled her eyebrows. "Methinks you stumbled right into that one, sissy. Mags never mentioned a man's name."

"But he *is* a stranger," Maggie repeated.

"Nobody knows much about him," added Lark, growing serious.

"He's a doctor, for goodness' sake," Cammie countered.

"That's not a point in his favor," argued Lark, standing. Her eyes sparkled. "Some of history's most vicious, cold-blooded killers have been doctors. And rumor says that you've been spending too much time with him as it is."

Cammie stood and stared her sister eye to eye. "Last time

you said he couldn't have done it on account of his being a doctor. Which is it, Lark?"

Lark just shrugged.

"Fine. If you suspect him, then I have an advantage. If Stephen's the one, which I doubt, why then, I'm in the perfect position to investigate him. You can do your research into illegal labs, Lark." Cammie turned to the other Blossom. "And you, Maggie, can track down other victims of Leesburg's dognapper. I'm going to keep right on doing what I've been doing. I'm going to stick to Stephen Hardesty like that dung and its moss did to poor Miss Sophie's shoe."

"Ooooh, Cammie," Maggie said in admiration, "you've been pickin' up some vivid phrases lately."

With brief good-byes, her older sisters left. Cammie dropped back into her chair and laid her forehead on her palms. So that was what her life had come down to. She always sought to find the image of God in everyone she met; now she had to look with suspicion on the two men she had come to care for.

"Oh, be honest with yourself, Camellia," she muttered. She didn't just care for Stephen Hardesty. In spite of her better judgment, she was falling in love with him. Even though she saw only heartbreak in her future.

Yet she'd agreed to spy on him.

What kind of craziness had overtaken her life?

That evening Cammie's call took Stephen by surprise. Especially her pretty apology. "I'm so sorry, Stephen. I did get a bit snippy with you the other night. That really isn't like me at all, and I'd like to ask your forgiveness."

"You didn't do anything to need forgiveness—"

"Oh, but I did. I again responded in a very un-Christian way."

"Consider yourself forgiven then," Stephen said, still not getting the whole Christian thing. Would he ever understand this woman and her faith?

"I'd like to ask a favor of you," she then said.

"If it's something I can do, it's yours, of course."

"Well, I think it's goin' to be very easy for you. I'd like you to keep a close eye on Willie come evenings—those you're not on call, you understand."

Tucking the receiver between his ear and shoulder, Stephen leaned back in his leather office chair and twiddled a pencil. "Are you still on that kick?"

"It's not a kick. And if you're so sure Willie's innocent, why then, this'll be a cinch now, won't it? All you have to do is spend time with your friend, maybe play some chess, that kind of thing. Besides, won't it feel good to prove me wrong?"

Stephen frowned. What was Cammie up to now?

"Are you saying," he began, "that you have changed your mind? That you think Willie's innocent and want me to prove it?"

"Not exactly, but I do need you to prove his innocence or guilt."

"And you want me to spend time with him."

"Yes."

"Without my aunt or you."

"Mm-hmm."

This was too easy. Not the kind of thing he'd come to expect from Cammie. She was hiding something. "And what are you planning to do?"

"Me?"

"No, the cheese guy on the moon. Of course I mean you. What are you going to do while I'm snooping around Willie?"

"Why, nothin', Stephen," she answered in the softest, silkiest, most Southern voice he'd ever heard. "I'm goin' to stay home, finish my quilt, make my baby's layette, and, you know . . . grow my baby, I guess."

Yes, she was heading for trouble. Only problem was, he had no idea what kind of trouble she'd cooked up this time. "Okay, Cammie. You've got it. I'll become Willie's shadow while you grow your baby. I'll let you know if I learn anything out of the ordinary."

"Oh, Stephen, thank you. You don't know the load you've taken off my mind."

No, but I sure know the load you've dumped on mine. "Ahh-haaaa . . . anything to help a pregnant mom."

After they hung up, Stephen found satisfaction in only one thing. If Cammie hared off on another detecting sortie, he'd have no trouble finding her. Not only was Bellamy a very small town, but the woman he'd realized he was coming to love—as nonsensible as it was—was unmistakable in her Columbo getup.

Especially if she wore the great iguana hat he'd bought her.

Following his instincts, Stephen laid out his plan before Willie, who jumped on the bandwagon immediately. Of course, Stephen didn't mention Cammie's suspicions, just the fact that she'd taken it upon herself to solve the case of the missing dogs.

"Well, son," the elderly suitor expanded, "spending every free waking minute with the love of my life is hardly a hardship. Especially if it frees you to keep our darling little Camellia from any harm."

"You're a man after my own heart, Willie Johnson."

"Ah, but am I a man after your great-aunt's heart as well?"

Stephen laughed. "Not my business, friend. That's up to her to know and you to ask her about."

Willie made a sound of disgust. "How did I know you'd say something to that effect?"

"Because you know it's right, and besides, you're coming to know me by now."

"A privilege it is, my boy. A true privilege."

"I feel the same way about you, Willie, and I wish you luck with Aunt Sophie. She's a great lady who deserves a true gentleman like you."

"Thanks for the heads up. I'll try to live up to your trust."

"Just keep her away from Cammie for a while. And me."

"Will do."

Later that evening, Stephen lay in wait for Cammie in the shadow of the fall-bare forsythia bushes at the edge of the Sprague property. He hoped this didn't turn out to be a waste of his time, but something deep in his heart told him it wouldn't be. Somehow a strange and never-before-experienced prompting fed his determination to look out for that very special woman and the child he couldn't wait to meet.

Any child of Cammie's had to be a very special person indeed.

As he wondered how he'd respond to meeting that baby face-to-face, the back door to the boardinghouse creaked open, then shut. Faint thuds followed, and Stephen assumed they were the footsteps of one very pregnant if adventurous woman.

Before long, he spotted her unmistakable shape, shrouded as expected in the straining trench coat. In keeping with the late hour and the lack of light, she'd opted out of the huge sunglasses and, to his great disappointment, wore no iguana on her head. Instead she'd tied a nondescript scarf babushka-style around her head. Inconspicuous Cammie Bellamy Sprague was not.

Hoping to remain undetected, and in deference to his large

bulk, he gave her ample lead time, hoping to reach any corner she turned before she went around the next bend. But to his frustration and disgust, she'd vanished by the time he made it to the end of her street. "Now what?"

She couldn't have followed Willie, since he now sat at the home of that terrifying trio, Miss Louella, Miss Mariah, and Aunt Sophie. Stephen was sure the older gent's three attentive hostesses were indulging him in grand Southern style. Willie had assured him that Cammie would know his whereabouts for the evening.

She wouldn't go back out to the forest to check on her "evidence" at night, would she?

Not by following the direction she'd taken. To go to Langhorn Park and the woods, she would have had to take a right-hand turn on her street. Instead she'd veered to the left. That could only mean one thing: she was headed downtown.

Why?

He knew whatever had sent her out this late had something to do with her missing Muttley—

Wait!

"I bet that's it," he said under his breath and began jogging. Cammie had probably never forgotten the cops' laughter at her evidence. What would keep her from following Wiggon around in the hopes of checking out whatever further evidence he found that related to her case? Nothing, now that she figured she'd made sure he and Willie were busy together.

He headed for the PD. But two blocks before he got there, he noticed the van they'd spotted the other night, driving in the direction from which he'd come. If it did in fact belong to Bernie Stafford, the guy wasn't paying Mama Myrna a visit. He'd gone right past her bungalow.

Maybe Cammie *had* seen something strange. Maybe it had nothing to do with the Staffords. Still, it begged investigating, if for no other reason than he'd lost Cammie's trail and his curiosity had been piqued.

The van traveled slowly, respecting the twenty-five-mile-per-hour speed limit. Either the driver was admirably law-abiding, or he didn't want to risk a ticket for speeding.

Whichever one proved right, Stephen stayed close enough to the vehicle to see where it went. Another reason to keep up his physical fitness. He had good reason to commend his instincts, too, when he turned down the lane that led to Langhorn Park and spotted his quarry by a cluster of trees at the edge of the woods.

At first, the area appeared deserted. He heard nothing. But then the most disturbing whimpering, muffled cries, gagging noises, and a strange dragging sound reached his ears. Then the most impossible sight materialized before his eyes.

The very pregnant woman who held his heart in the palm of her hands was scurrying out of the woods, arms wrapped around the very green, very large Lana the iguana. The iguana she'd vowed never to touch.

Neither female appeared happy with the situation.

Then things turned ugly. The man from the van ran up to Cammie, snatched the reptile from her hands, flung it down, and twisted one of her arms behind her back. Stephen ran toward her before her first cry of pain hit his ears.

Rage blinded him for the first time in his life. "Let go of her!"

"No, Stephen, run!" Cammie yelled. "Get the police. Don't let him hurt you."

Was the woman crazy? Stephen ran faster.

The man holding Cammie glanced up, then dragged her to the van. When he opened the side door, the overhead light went on, and Stephen caught the gleam of something metallic in his hand.

"Git out of here," the guy snarled, reaching into the van and withdrawing a length of rope.

Stephen stopped. He wanted nothing to jeopardize Cammie.

"Do what Bernie says, Stephen. Please. Go."

The man slapped Cammie. She cried out.

"Shut up," Bernie said as he tied her hands at her back, then pushed her toward the van door. Cammie resisted until her captor did something that made her moan. She lurched forward.

The sound of something running roughshod through the detritus-covered forest floor startled everyone.

"How was Mama to know you didn't want nothin' but dogs," Myrna whined. "Why didn't you tell me, Bernie? I woulda found more dogs for you, but I figgered that there green thing would be more interestin' to work on. 'Sides, son, it was the hardest one of all to take. It wouldn't eat none of that there Whopper I bought it, so I couldn't get it to sleep. An' here I crushed up my last two Sleepitols. Now how'm I s'posed to fall asleep? You know I ain't got no money to be wastin' for nothin'."

"Quit your whinin', Mama. Help me get her in the van. I gotta get rid of her before she turns me in to the cops."

"Get rid of her?" Myna's voice grew shriller. "Bernard August Stafford, just what are you talkin' 'bout? You're not gonna do a thing to that little girl. Why she's expectin'. All's she did was see me luggin' the lizard here an' follow me. If you had a brain in your head, you'd take that right big beast of that silly Willie Johnson's an' sell it. I bet you it'd bring you a right nice piece o' change."

Bernie didn't listen to his mama. Instead he forced the sobbing Cammie into the front seat.

Stephen watched, heart in his throat. At least Myrna was on Cammie's side. What was he going to do? How could he rescue Cammie?

Just then Bernie picked up the reptile and started to shove it into the van. Then to Stephen's amazement, Bernie screamed and fell to the ground. He colorfully cursed Lana and her claws.

With silent thanks to the reptile, Stephen grabbed his chance. He leaped on the writhing man and worked to pin him down. But Bernie, despite the pain that twisted his Myrna-like features, fought back. A few of his punches went wide, but others hit their mark.

Stephen, repelled by the thought of harming another being, sought to dodge rather than to hit. He wrestled the wiry Bernie, using every ounce of his strength to stay in place.

Myrna ran off into the woods, howling and sniveling.

"Get offa me," growled her pride and joy. When Stephen didn't comply, Bernie followed his demand with a bucketful of profanity.

Stephen made a quick move, straddled Bernie, and tightened his knees on either side of flailing legs. He yanked the man's right arm straight over his head and covered the foul mouth with his own forearm, putting an end to the offensive tripe.

Just then Willie ran up. "Lana, darling," he crooned. "Just what are you doing here? It's so cold. You poor baby. Come with Papa now, and I'll take you back to your lovely tank."

"Forget the iguana," Stephen said, still holding Bernie down. "Go help Cammie."

Willie refused to leave either lady in distress. Cradling his iguana close to his chest, he hurried toward Stephen and the bucking Bernie. "Where *is* Camellia?"

"In here," Cammie cried, her voice rough.

Stephen bent back to his task now that help had arrived.

But Bernie wasn't done yet. With a twist of his head, he dislodged Stephen's arm off his bottom jaw enough to open his mouth and sink his teeth into flesh. Stephen gasped but pushed down harder despite the pain, the memory of Bernie slapping Cammie providing temporary analgesia.

As Willie stepped by them on his way to Cammie, the petty crook managed to yank Lana's long tail. The sudden movement startled Willie, who staggered and dropped his pet. As Willie fought to regain his balance, Lana took matters into her own hands—or something. Stephen saw it coming, but the reptile moved too fast for him to do more than rear up out of her way.

With a violent, powerful whip of her tail, Lana whumped Bernie Stafford in the head. A strange *whoof* puffed from the man, and his muscles went lax under Stephen.

Relieved, Stephen scrambled to his feet, Cammie's and the baby's safety his only thought.

The sudden sound of an invading army behind him made him spin around. Yet another incredible sight met his eyes. Aunt Sophie and Miss Louella, dressed in military dress whites, of all things, were dragging the screaming and howling Myrna between them, while Mariah Desmond, similarly garbed, marshaled a considerable contingent of elderly troops in her wake.

"Why are you all bein' so mean to me? Everybody's always mean to me," Myrna bawled. "I ain't done nothin' bad. An' you all know I'm all alone in the world, 'ceptin' Bernie. Let me go home now. It's late an' a body's gotta sleep, you all know."

"Myrna Stafford," Aunt Sophie said, "my Willie told me he had a very special mission to perform tonight, providin' backup for Stephen. Thinkin' on his words a mite, I wondered if it mightn't have somethin' to do with the Blossoms' missin' dogs. I talked it over with Lou and Mariah, an' we decided to call out our newly formed an' now official Garden Club Patrol Brigade."

Could that explain the navy uniforms?

"Indeed," concurred Miss Louella, standing tall. "We knew our fine town could use our diligence and experience in criminal matters. And no one could have been more surprised than we were when we found Myrna runnin' around like a chicken with her head cut off, moanin' and groanin' about her Bernie and Camellia, plus, of all things, Willie's iguana."

"I just knew, Louella," added Miss Mariah, "that uniformin' our force would encourage the most professional results. And besides, those military-surplus boys were such dears. Don't we all look just right for the job?"

Her gray-haired troops nodded.

"Then," the girdle queen continued, "when somethin' crooked our way came, why, we were all ready for action. And see? Didn't we all just perform like the well-trained company we are?"

Stephen rolled his eyes.

"What I still don't rightly understand," Miss Mariah continued, "is just exactly what is goin' on here?"

"Would someone *please* untie my hands?" Cammie cried from inside the van.

Stephen flushed. "I'm coming."

But Bernie had begun to recover. He wrapped his hand around Stephen's ankle and pulled. Stephen landed on the man, pinning him back down with his full weight.

"We're comin', Cammie," cried Maggie Marlowe. "The Garden Club ladies were right to call on our help."

"Hang on there, sissy," yelled Lark.

As one Blossom untied the knots, the other hugged and comforted the third.

That's when Wiggon arrived in a flurry of siren, flashing lights, and whistle blowing. He leaped from the patrol car, weapon drawn. "Don't nobody make a move now. Everythin's goin' to be just fine. I've come to save the day."

TWENTY

AS USUAL, STEPHEN INSISTED ON WALKING CAMMIE HOME, once Bernie, Myrna, and the naval Garden Club had been dealt with. Now that Bernie had talked and she knew what had happened to the dogs, she wanted nothing more than to take off and find the illegal lab. But she knew she'd never get away from Stephen if he got a whiff of her intentions.

She *had* to find the dogs—before the kingpin of the organization learned what had gone down in Bellamy. And, oh, she was relieved to know that neither Willie nor Stephen were in any way involved.

Although she should have been happy to have the perpetrators of the thefts behind bars, Cammie couldn't help a certain sense of grief. "Poor Myrna," she said.

"Poor Myrna?" Stephen asked, obviously stunned by her words.

"Why, yes. Didn't you hear her?"

"Every whiny last word."

"Then I'm sure you realize how desperate she was."

"That didn't give her the right to break the law and take

your dog. And don't forget how she lied to you, blaming Willie just to throw suspicion away from her and her son."

"Think on it a moment, Stephen. She's all alone in the world—no one could call Bernie much of a son, now, could they?"

Stephen snorted, rubbing the ribs the younger Stafford had abused.

She went on. "Myrna's husband died years ago and left little money behind. She had to retire from her custodial job at the school last year when she turned sixty-five, and her Social Security benefits barely cover food and heat for her home. I never knew she was diabetic, but I do know that insulin, syringes, and testing materials cost plenty. In her mind, her life was worth more than a couple of pampered pets."

They stopped, and by the glow of a streetlamp, Cammie saw Stephen shake his head. "Lack of money didn't give her the right to steal," he argued. "She could have asked for help. I'm sure Medicaid—"

"Doesn't cover all—as you, of all people, well know. Besides, I didn't say lack of money gave her the right to steal. She sinned, but I feel compassion for her. Pride kept her from telling anyone about her situation, and that's the saddest thing of all. The Bellamy Community Church has a benevolence fund. She would have qualified. Besides, any number of us would have helped her with her medical costs. I would have. I don't have a lot, but I have enough to help someone stay alive."

"I knew you'd say something like that," Stephen said in outrage. "Why can't you accept that you're not responsible for everyone else?"

"I don't think that at all," Cammie said, shocked by his outburst. "But God does call me to feed the hungry and clothe the naked in his Son's name."

"You really would give the shirt off your back, wouldn't you?"

Cammie smiled. "Well, maybe not my maternity top, but if I had an extra coat, I'd give it. An extra loaf of bread, too. And money? If it would show Christ's love in sharing it, of course I'd give it away. Myrna's soul matters more than the dollars in my bank account. I look to God for provision, Stephen. He supplies my every need—physical, emotional, and spiritual. He has never let me down, and he never will."

"You mean that. Even though your husband's dead."

"Mm-hmm." Should she tell him? Perhaps not all. "God didn't kill David, or anything like that. David's choices had consequences. He had a habit of working very late in Baltimore. Driving home one of those nights, he crashed. God didn't make him work that late; David chose to do so. He drove himself so hard that he worked until his reflexes were affected."

Stephen's gaze turned speculative, but he said nothing.

Cammie smiled, remembering Stephen's many kindnesses. "I suspect you'd show as much compassion as I do, no matter how little you liked the recipient."

When Stephen remained silent, she resumed walking. They continued like that for another block. Then he said softly, "I don't know if I could be that generous to someone who'd done nothing but irritate everyone around."

"Wouldn't you be generous if you knew that sharing the love that had first been given to you would make a difference in a miserable and needy person's life?"

They reached Cammie's front porch. Stephen stood by the steps as Cammie went up, his expression thoughtful in the glow of the light fixture by the door.

Cammie tried again. "It's simple, Stephen. God loved me so much that he gave his Son for my sake. Jesus loved me so much that he went to the cross at Calvary so that God could forgive my sins and I'd have eternal life with him in heaven. The presence of his Holy Spirit in my life is even more evidence of his love for me. He has never left me nor forsaken me, no matter how tough things have been. And that's what I feel I must share with a soul who hasn't yet realized it can all be hers for the taking. Just for saying yes. "

"You make it sound so simple," he said, shaking his head. "But I can't see how it works."

"You don't have to. You just have to accept and receive. That's it. God's done the hard part already. All we have to do is say, 'Yes, God, I accept your loving gift of salvation. Teach me your ways.' "

"But what about all that stuff about everyone being a rotten sinner since before birth because of Adam and Eve's original sin?"

"It goes beyond that. We aren't perfect due to our natural tendency toward pride and selfishness. God wants us to acknowledge that, confess it to him, and ask his forgiveness. He's always ready to forgive. Then through his grace, he showers us with love, joy, and peace."

Stephen gave her another of his piercing looks. This time, however, a question came with it. "Explain something to me, then. If God grants you peace through his grace, as you just said, then why are you always running everywhere, wearing yourself out, doing for everyone? You're mothering Suze, baby-sitting Aunt Sophie and Willie, working at the church with the baby something-or-other, investigating the dog thefts, and trying to rehabilitate Myrna. Don't forget all the cooking and cleaning and quilting you do, too. I see you rushing around in a hectic blur much more than I see you at peace."

Cammie drew in a sharp breath. "I don't do that. I just feel the need to help wherever I can. The Lord calls us to serve others in his name, and that's what I do."

"Okay, I have another question for you. How do you know God's called you to wear yourself out doing all that? Too much can't be what he wants from you, not if he loves you as much as you say he does. Don't you think he wants you to rest for your baby's sake? Besides, I've seen Aunt Sophie spend hours with her Bible. She says that's when she really does business with God. When do you do that?"

Something shifted inside Cammie. It hurt. "I read my Bible every day."

"I'm sure you do. It's one more thing you do 'in service,' as you put it. If God is a God of peace, I don't see the evidence of his peace in you. I feel more peace when I try to meditate than you seem to have in your busy life. And even though I'm a doctor, I don't spend every breathing moment fighting disease. I pace myself, knowing I can do more good that way than by wearing myself to the bone. What good would I do my patients if I never took time to recharge my engine, so to speak?"

Cammie shook her head weakly. "I don't do that."

"Sure looks like it to me."

Both considered what the other had said. Then Stephen landed a punishing blow. "Are you trying to follow in your husband's footsteps?"

The blood drained from Cammie's head. She reached for the banister and clung to it, needing its solid bulk to stay standing. "I think it's time you went home, Stephen."

"And not return, right?"

"That's up to you. First you'll have to recognize how wrong you are about me; then maybe you'll want to come back to visit."

"I'm not sure a visit's all I want, as crazy as that is. And until some things change, I can't stand to watch you destroy yourself for no logical reason."

Cammie's head began to spin. He cared. He'd just said he

wanted more than to just visit. But he had a very ugly image of her. A very flawed concept of who she was. That view of her reflected the greatest barrier between them.

He lacked faith in Christ.

"I understand, Stephen," she said. "Some things do have to change before we can ever consider anything more than visits. I wish you well, and I'll continue praying for you."

He pursed his lips and gave a curt nod. Then, spinning on his heel, he left, his footsteps measured and unhurried.

Cammie waited until he was out of sight before sagging against the railing. *Dear God . . . what just happened here tonight? Oh, Father, should I have pressed him with your plan for salvation?*

She knew the answer even as she asked God the question. *Not if you'd done it for your own sake.*

With a sobbing breath, Cammie stood tall again. She went into the house, knowing she had a lot of business to do with God. Not that Stephen was right about her. No one had ever called her a Martha. She wasn't like that at all.

But, oh, how wonderful life could be if Stephen were a different kind of man.

An hour later the doorbell rang, shocking Cammie. No one ever came in the wee hours of the night.

When she answered, her surprise grew greater. Hobey stood on her porch, a large steaming tureen in his hands. "My Ellamae wouldn't let me steal a wink o' sleep until I brought you this," he said, handing her the container. "Careful, now. It's hot."

Cammie gave him a puzzled look. "What is it?"

"Breakfast for your boarders. She made sausage gravy, so's

you wouldn't hafta in the mornin'. We heard what you done 'bout 'em dogs an' Myrna an' her boy."

Blushing, Cammie stood aside. "Come on in while I put this away."

Hobey followed her into the kitchen.

"Ellamae was sweet doing this, but she didn't have to. I'm fine. Besides, I had a lot of help."

"So I hear say. But it all came *after* you hauled one of 'em fat iguanas around, wrestled a crook, an' landed tied up in that van. That there's a lot for a lil' pregnant gal, now."

Cammie shook her head. "Not you, too."

Hobey took off his cap and stared at her. "You know, Miss Cammie, your Granny Iris was a dear friend, an' I know she's likely spinnin' in that grave o' hers, watchin' what you're doin' to yourself these days."

"And just what do you think I'm doing to myself?"

Rubbing his nearly bald head, Hobey looked at her intently. "Sometimes a man's gotta say what God's laid on his heart, no matter how little the person he's sayin' it to wants to hear it."

Cammie frowned but waited for the wise and caring giant to continue.

"You been to Sunday school since you was born, right? An' you read your Bible regular-like, don't you?"

"Of course. You know that."

"An' you go to church of a Sunday, too."

She nodded.

"Well, then, girl, you hafta know all 'bout Martha an' Mary."

"No! I'm not—"

"Hush, now, child. I ain't finished yet. From where ol' Hobey stands, it sure looks like you're so busy tryin' to show everyone you've done gone an' grown up an' all, that you've turned yourself into one great Martha. How long's it been since you just sat at the Lord's feet and rejoiced in his presence? in his peace? in his love? and remembered he's your Father, in control, your almighty and all-powerful God?"

"But he's called me to serve his children in love—"

"Sure, he did. He called all of us to do that. But which one of Lazarus's sisters did he say was doin' the best thing? The one what was too busy fixin' up her house an' doin' for everyone else—or the one who gave her all to listen and love him?"

Cammie's breath left her body. In the short span of an hour, she'd been accused of the same thing twice. Was the Lord using Stephen, a nonbeliever, and dear, godly Hobey to speak to her? *Was* she trying too hard to prove herself? Had she lost her way? Had she strayed from Jesus' side in her efforts to do for him?

"I don't think I'm doing that at all," she said, her voice lacking strength. "But I will think on it, Hobey. And pray a lot, too."

"'S all I can ask, Cammie, girl. I'll be gettin' on back to my warm bed now. You call us if you need anythin', hear?"

"I hear."

She closed the door after her visitor and went back up to her room. She'd heard Hobey . . . and Stephen. But was it really God who'd spoken?

Much later in his own apartment, Stephen still struggled to fall asleep. Every inch of his body ached from the tussle with Bernie Stafford. Even though Bernie was much smaller, anger and fear had lent him strength he otherwise would have lacked.

The pain in Stephen's body, however, was nothing compared to the frustration and confusion Cammie had left behind in his heart. The woman had a way about her. . . . She single-handedly, in that gentle, Southern way of hers, worked on a man's protective instincts, then thwarted him at every turn.

She couldn't see what she was doing to herself, so Stephen wanted no part of her crusade to make the world a better place for everyone around her. That meant he had to stay away from her—even if it was the hardest thing he'd ever had to do.

Well, that, and figuring out her faith.

She'd talked about God's love. Stephen had never known love of the sort she'd described. He couldn't deny his wish to know it.

Still, as he tried to look at all these issues logically, one at a time, a small voice in the back of his mind kept warning him that Cammie was again heading for trouble. He ignored it.

Sort of.

But when it refused to be quiet, he surrendered to what he'd begun to think of as the inevitable. He rose, dressed, and headed back to Cammie's.

When he got there, he found the place dark. He felt foolish for humoring his fears, but then it occurred to him he might be too late. She might have already taken off for parts unknown to do who knew what.

He suspected what she might be up to—if indeed she was up to anything tonight. They still hadn't found the dogs. And he knew she was determined to find them.

At the time of her arrest, Myrna had been unable to unburden her guilty soul fast enough. She hadn't known all the details of her son's activities, but she had known enough to give Wiggon sufficient reasons to book mother and son. She'd revealed that although the dognapping operation was centered in Leesburg, she'd insisted—she and Maggie Marlowe, of all people—that the unlicensed lab Bernie supplied with dogs was located in Baltimore.

If Cammie was crazy enough to go after the missing pets, she'd need her vehicle. Stephen would make the supreme sacrifice for the woman he loved and sleep cramped and kinked in the backseat of her van. He wasn't about to let her drive alone to Baltimore at this time of night.

There. He accepted that reality. He loved Cammie, even though his past experience warned him that loving her would lead to nothing more than disappointment.

And pain. He'd already known pain in his parents' benign neglect, their eventual rejection. He'd learned that loving hurt.

Cammie's voice rang in his memory. *"God loved me so much."*

Could that apply to him too? After all, Aunt Sophie had spent a lifetime loving that same God Cammie did. And loving him, Stephen. Cammie was the most caring person he'd ever met—aside from his great-aunt. Both claimed to love because God first loved them. It was something to ponder. But not necessarily right now. He had a pregnant woman to protect. As a doctor and, especially, as a man.

To his relief, Cammie's sky blue chariot was where it belonged. Again Stephen marveled at how crazy she made him. No matter how hard he sought detachment from relationships, she'd found her way into his heart. And he wasn't going to relinquish his feelings for her with any kind of ease.

He found the door to the vehicle unlocked. He climbed in, and with kind thoughts for his bed in his condo, lay down on the rear seat. Now to wait and see how stupid his bright idea turned out to be.

No more than ten minutes later he had his answer. Cammie, dressed in black head to toe, slipped into the driver's seat, clicked the garage-door opener, and backed out of the garage.

It was all Stephen could do to keep from crowing in

victory. How well he was coming to know the lovely Widow Sprague.

"You can climb out of the backseat now," she said, pulling out of the driveway. "You'll be more comfortable ridin' beside me."

Sheepishly, Stephen came out of hiding. Before he could ask her how she'd known where he was, she spoke again.

"I did wonder what was takin' you so long."

Stephen turned to her in shock. "What did you say?"

Without taking her gaze from the road, Cammie waved. "You know what I mean. I can't go anywhere without you shadowin' me, so I figured it was only a matter of time before you showed up tonight. What took you so long?"

So he wasn't the only one who'd become acquainted with the other's quirks. "I had a second, different kind of battle to fight."

She glanced his way. He was pleased to note in the glare of streetlights the concern on her pretty face. Although his feelings may have been unwise, it seemed that at least they were not one-sided.

"Are you hurt?" she asked.

"No. I won."

"Who'd you fight?"

"My common sense."

"What did you fight about?"

"You."

That surprised her.

He went on. "Common sense told me it was stupid to feel the way I do about you, and that it wouldn't do me any good to lose sleep over a woman so stubborn she refuses to listen to reason. I won when I told my common sense I'd lose sleep over you whether I stayed in bed or not. So I came. You proved me right."

She sighed. "I'm not stubborn. I just know what I have to

do. All my life I've been the baby Blossom. Everyone's insisted on lookin' out for me, takin' care of me, never lettin' me find out what I can and can't do for myself. That's no way to live."

"You're looking at it all wrong. Everyone cares for you and wants to help you."

"I'm not so sure of that. It feels as though everyone knows I can't do anything right, so they tell me how to do it—their way, of course."

"Sometimes another person can see things from a better perspective."

"Sometimes they can't."

"Still, ever since I met you, you've been running off in all directions doing crazy things. I'm worried about you, not to mention that baby I'd like to see born in great shape."

"I appreciate your concern, but I can make my own decisions. I have to find those dogs. I have to prove I'm as capable as everyone else, as capable as my sisters, as capable as God created me to be. No one needs to manage my life for me. The Lord and I can handle it just fine."

"So it's a matter of pride after all."

She gasped. "Pride? No. Of course not. It's a matter of self-respect. I need to know I can achieve a goal, that I don't need my sisters tellin' me how to live my life. That I can sometimes tell them a thing or two."

"I see I'm not going to make a dent in your obstinacy."

"I'm not obstinate. Lark's the obstinate one. . . . Well, and Maggie's pretty bad, too."

"You know what? You three Bellamy women are all alike. You're stunning to look at, and you are smart, sassy, stubborn fireballs. From what Aunt Sophie has told me, you were all cut from the same mold, and the mold was shattered after you were born."

"Hah! Shows how little you know. Maggie's stunnin', yes.

And Lark is smart. They're both pretty sassy, too. But I'm not any of those things, so I guess in your mind that leaves me as the stubborn one. Well, I guess I'll take stubborn, especially since the other side of stubborn is determined. I'm determined to do what's right."

"I suppose that means finding the dogs."

"Yes."

"Might I ask where we're going? Even though I think I know and wish I didn't."

"To the lab."

"Where else?" He sighed. "You know where it is?"

"Mm-hmm."

"How'd you learn the location?"

"Maggie has a friend down to the jail who knows the boss of the operation."

"Maggie gave you the address to this place? It's hard to believe she didn't come charging to find her Buford the moment she knew where he was. I thought she had more sense than to set you off on another wild-goose chase."

"You're askin' for trouble, Dr. Hardesty."

"Did she or didn't she give you the address?"

"Didn't."

"So how do you know where to go?"

"I have my ways of learnin' things, too."

"I'm afraid to ask."

"I'll tell you anyway. Jill Wiggon knows the wife of one of the guards down to the county jail, the one who helped Maggie start her women's prison ministry. Jill's friend talked to Maggie's friend and got back to me with an address."

"So that's where we're headed."

She turned, parked, turned off the ignition, and grabbed a flashlight. "That's where we are."

"This isn't Baltimore, Cammie."

"The lab we're lookin' for isn't the one in Baltimore," she

said with a smug smile. "There's another one, a smaller one, here in Leesburg. That's where our dogs are."

"How would you know that? No, don't answer. I know. Jill found out from Wiggon what Bernie had to say, right?"

"Well, Mr. Smarty, if you're goin' to be of help tonight, you'd best be gettin' out of the van. We can't retrieve any dogs while you're sittin' there playin' twenty questions."

"And you just finished telling me only your sisters are sassy? Woman, you don't know yourself at all."

The operation was indeed small. The brick building consisted of only one floor, running long and narrow down half the length of a small city block. A naked lightbulb barely illuminated the entrance. Cammie stunned Stephen when she picked open the door with a hairpin.

"Talented, aren't you?"

"A woman does what she has to do."

"Even when it means rushing into danger? This is crazy, you know."

Cammie nibbled her bottom lip. Stephen reached out and tugged gently. "Don't do that . . ."

The touch caught them both by surprise, reminding Stephen, and perhaps Cammie, too, of their kisses. If her dazed expression and the longing in her eyes were anything to go by, she hadn't forgotten either.

"Cammie—"

"No," she said softly, trembling. "Please. Not now."

Despite all he'd said and thought earlier that evening, he knew he'd speak from his heart. Sooner or later. "Okay. Some other time. But we *will* talk, you understand."

She nodded. Before he knew he was going to do so, he kissed her. Brief though the touch was, it brought back the hunger and need he'd felt for her before. It strengthened his desire to keep her close at all times, showed him that his feelings for her were true, deep, and powerful.

They amounted to only one thing.

Love.

No matter how he dreaded it. No matter how hard he'd fought against it.

And she wanted her dog back. Regardless of how ridiculous her whims might be, he realized that putting her needs in a prominent position and doing all in his power to meet them was something he wanted to do for a very long time. For the rest of his life.

Stephen sighed. "Okay, let's go get the dogs."

Since no alarm had sounded, they crept in as silently as a pregnant woman and her escort could. They found the guard at the front desk, leaning back in a leather chair, ankles crossed on the desktop, gaping jaw releasing stentorian snores.

"No wonder he can't hear us," Cammie whispered.

Stephen chuckled. "Maybe that's how he muffles out the barking."

"What barking?"

"You're right. I don't hear a thing. Are we in the right place?"

"I'm as sure as I can be." Cammie pointed to two doors. "That one's kind of fancy," she said of the wooden one. "I doubt they keep dogs behind it, but the other one's steel. Let's try it."

A metal medallion on the wall opened the door, releasing the stench of unclean kennel and the din of desperate dogs. Stephen and Cammie closed the door behind them and beamed the flashlight around them in circles. What they saw horrified them.

Wire cages ranged from floor to ceiling, the dogs stacked four high. Some of the animals were near emaciation, too depleted even to complain. Others fought their constraints, hitting the cage doors with their heads, batting with their paws, gnawing with their teeth. Stephen saw a couple of small bags of poor quality dog food, and water levels were low in those cages equipped with dispensers.

"This is a sin," Cammie said, rage in her voice. "I want to take them all home."

"Why doesn't that surprise me?"

"Oh, I know I can't, so let's find ours and call someone who can do something about these other poor beasts."

"Let's go."

They went up and down the crowded aisles, their hearts breaking at the plight of the animals. Then Cammie cried, "Look! There's my Muttley."

She ran to the cage and released the catch. The pup flew into her arms, yipping with joy. She hugged him close, feeling that his ribs were more prominent than they'd been, and tears flooded her face. A big pink tongue dried every one.

"Two more to go," Stephen said, growing grim. "I'm going to do something about this the minute we're gone. I have to. This place isn't about advancing medicine; it's all about greed."

"You're a good man, Stephen," Cammie said.

"And sometimes a bright one. Isn't that a bloodhound?"

"Mycroft!" Cammie exclaimed. "And look, there's Buford right beside him. They look thin, don't they?"

"Yes, but they probably haven't been in here long enough for any real harm to have occurred. I'm no vet, but I think they'll be fine once we get them home."

They sprang the dogs and hurried back to the metal door. When Stephen opened it, however, a high-powered flashlight blinded him from the other side. "Hold it right there," barked a voice. "You have the right to remain silent—"

"Wait!" cried Stephen. "We're not the bad guys. We're the owners of these dogs!"

"That may be," answered the official, "but you're about to remove evidence from the scene of a crime."

"Oh, Harvey," said Lark from behind the man, "that's my baby sister, Cammie, and Bellamy's new doctor. They're okay, just a little misguided when it comes to police procedure. They mean no harm. My sister Maggie told me where I'd find them—and she was right."

To Stephen's relief the light went out. Plunged back into what felt like total darkness, he wondered if any other man had ever done such a stupid thing for the woman he loved.

Amid the cacophony of barks, howls, yips, and growls, the Animal Protective Agency's people rounded up the caged animals and let the Blossoms take their dogs. Buford danced at Maggie and Clay Marlowe's side, surprisingly light on his feet for a bullmastiff his size. Mycroft alternated his nuzzling between Lark and her fiancé, Rich Desmond, while Cammie refused to set Muttley back on his feet.

"Would you like me to drive?" Stephen asked once the authorities gave them the okay to leave. They'd found out that Lark had called the police. But by the time they arrived, the guard had escaped. None of the other dognappers could be found, either.

"I'd appreciate that," she said, sounding tired. Stephen noticed the smudgy circles under her eyes. "Take a nap. I'll have you home soon."

"It's okay now, Stephen. We got the dogs back. We're all okay."

"I'll be the judge of that after the baby's born."

When he didn't get a smart retort, he glanced at her. She'd already fallen asleep. Calm descended upon him, and the drive felt short and smooth. Everything was right with his world.

Cammie hugged Muttley to her heart, glad to feel his solid, warm little body next to hers. But she had been awakened by sharp discomfort. The tightening began at her back and wound its way around her belly. It was three weeks early for her baby to come, and she hoped and prayed the cramps were only that—cramps or false labor contractions.

She wanted to crawl into bed. She was so tired. Thankfully, everything had worked out at the lab. Now all she needed was a good night's sleep.

But when they arrived at her house, things changed fast and for the worst. "Stephen," she cried as she reached the porch. "My water . . . the baby."

He ran up the steps behind her and stood transfixed, mindful of the liquid pooling at her feet. She followed his gaze.

The stuff was dark, wine-colored. Blood.

Something was wrong—terribly wrong.

Cammie couldn't hold back a panicked cry. "My baby!"

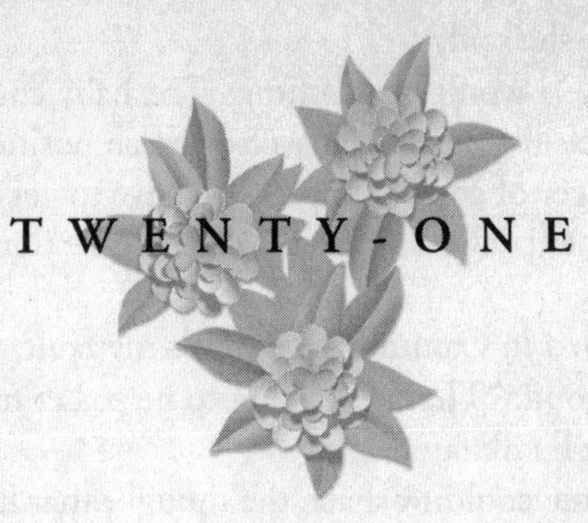

TWENTY-ONE

FEAR CLOSED CAMMIE'S THROAT. SHE COULDN'T SWALLOW. All she knew was the pain that built, crested, then blessedly ebbed, only to repeat itself and build to still higher peaks.

A glance at Stephen's face confirmed her fears. Her baby was in trouble. "Am I going to lose my baby?" she asked, her voice a terrified whisper.

"Not if I can help it." He helped her into the house and to the parlor. "I'm glad you have so many quilts around, even though I'm afraid the one I use right now will probably have to be thrown out."

"It doesn't matter. I can make another one. My baby's what counts."

He took the gold-and-brown, Split Rail Fence–patterned quilt from the love seat and spread it on the floor. "Please lie down. I'm going to call for help."

Cammie nodded and allowed him to help her, gasping when the next contraction hit.

Stephen placed a hand on her tight abdomen and palpated the mound of her child. His face grew grimmer.

"Tell me," she said.

He sighed. "I won't lie, Cammie. The baby could be in danger. It feels like it's in transverse breech position, and there's a danger of cord prolapse. We have to get you to a hospital immediately. You need a cesarean section right away."

Tears pooled in Cammie's eyes. "It's my fault, isn't it?"

Stephen stood. "That isn't going to help. Let me call for a chopper. We'll talk later."

But Cammie couldn't shake the thought that her child could die because of her stubborn insistence on finding the missing dogs. She loved Muttley, and she'd had something to prove—to herself just as much as to everyone else—but her child. "Dear God, don't let my baby die," she cried, sobs racking her.

Another contraction struck and stole her breath.

Had she been a Martha? Up until a few minutes ago, she would have vehemently argued anyone who'd suggested that, as she had done with Hobey and Stephen. But now, with the consequences of her actions vividly real, she had to face facts.

She'd deceived herself. Instead of focusing on what God had given her, she had looked at what she felt she lacked, what she wanted from everyone around her. She'd wanted respect, admiration, perhaps even a little pity.

Worthless things when compared to her child's life.

She hadn't had to find the dogs herself. Because of Lark's quick action, it had taken the authorities only a few minutes longer than it took her to arrive at the lab.

She *had* been too busy doing things—good things, true—to sit at God's feet, as Hobey had said. She hadn't given God full control and trusted him to work things out for her. She'd gone ahead and bustled around fixing and fussing to the point where she'd risked the gift he'd given her, this precious baby who represented her fresh start.

Again her body travailed to give birth.

What hope did her baby have now? After what she'd done?

Perhaps she didn't deserve this child. A woman who endangered such a vulnerable little one probably didn't deserve to be a mother. But, oh, how Cammie longed to have her child, to know she hadn't done her baby irreparable harm.

"Dear God, forgive me . . ."

From somewhere deep inside, a Scripture emerged: *"Be silent, and know that I am God!"*

"They're on their way," Stephen said then, reaching her side and looking anxious.

Cammie drew a deep breath. It was time to put her faith on the line. "I'm going to trust God with the outcome, with my child. I'm leaving all control to him—not to you, not to the chopper, much less to me. All, Stephen, all."

He shook his head. "I wish I could understand more about your devotion to God."

Cammie winced. "All I can tell you is that you'll never understand God or faith until you yield control of your thoughts, your mind, your feelings to him. Until you accept his never-ending love."

The next pain caught her by surprise. Cammie moaned. Stephen wiped her forehead.

She savored his cool touch. "Did you understand what I said?" she asked.

"Hush. You said it earlier. This isn't the time."

She shook her head. "I need you to understand. God is in complete and total control. In our Creator you'll find your being, your meaning, your future, and that peace you've talked about so much."

"I find peace when I meditate—"

"Maybe, but that's just a temporary kind of false peace. It's that emptiness you talked about, right? When you stop meditating, the problems and needs you wiped out come back.

True peace is falling back into God's arms, trusting his wisdom, knowing yourself cared for, loved infinitely. His peace is full of love, of him—" Cammie's keening wail cut off her words.

Stephen glanced at his watch.

When the contraction eased, Cammie reached out and clasped Stephen's arm. "You'll never find God's peace . . ." She stopped, out of breath. ". . . until you turn your back on the emptiness and open your heart to Christ's love."

Cammie's words struck Stephen hard. He'd known how she would feel from years of hearing Aunt Sophie speak the like. But coming from Cammie, the sentiment carried more urgency, especially when she felt it important enough to share at a time when she could scarcely breathe.

The tall grandfather clock in the foyer ticked away the time, making him aware of every second that flew by, making him aware of the reality of Cammie's situation.

Without monitoring equipment, he didn't dare perform an impromptu C-section. Especially when he lacked all that the newborn might need. Cammie's best hope was for the Life-Link chopper to arrive in time.

Anxiety rocked Stephen. What could he do? The woman he loved might not only lose her child, but also lose her life. Right now, all his medical training couldn't do a thing away from a hospital.

Desperation clawed up his throat, and Stephen teetered on the brink of madness. This was the fear, the lack of control, he'd always hated. This was precisely what he'd sought to leave behind with the detachment Zen cultivated. As the Asian philosophy taught, he tried to quiet his thoughts, empty his mind. He began counting his breaths. One, in . . . out; two, in . . . out—

Cammie cried out. Stephen winced. He smoothed her bangs off her forehead, held his breath when her hand convulsed around his. She gave him a weak smile when the contraction ended.

He'd never felt this helpless. "I wish I could help you more—"

"Hush," she whispered. "You're here, and God's with us. Think on that."

Instead of doing as she asked, he again tried to meditate. But each time he sought to relinquish the troubling thoughts of the moment, reality intruded.

Defeated, he finally faced facts. He wasn't in control—not of the situation, not of his thoughts, not of his feelings. He wasn't part of some amorphous nothingness, nor was he part of some cosmic oneness either, as Zen said. He was a man, an individual, very much in love with one particular woman, and utterly helpless in the face of her greatest need.

Buddhism had failed him. Where could he turn?

He stood, went to the front of the house, hoping to see the arriving medics. But nothing.

As he stood there, Cammie's sweet voice rang in his mind. *"God is in control,"* she'd said. *"In our Creator you'll find your being, your meaning, your future, and that peace you've talked about."*

As the clock continued its merciless ticking, Stephen came to a decision. All the religions and philosophies he'd checked out in his quest for spiritual enlightenment had failed him; he had nothing else to lose, and according to Cammie, everything to gain.

"Oh, God," he cried out, "I don't know how to do this, but please help me. Help me; help Cammie. If you're really out there, help me see you. Show me that you're in control.

Show me how real you are so that I can never deny you again. I have nothing—no one else—to turn to, so I'm going to trust you as Cammie said I should. If you love me enough to sacrifice your Son for me, as she and Aunt Sophie say, then I accept that—I accept him. I want to know that kind of love and your peace. And, oh, please help us. Don't let Cammie's baby die."

He returned to Cammie's side, took her hand in his, and comforted her through her next contraction. Then the one after that.

The sweetest music Stephen ever heard was the shriek of a siren approaching the house. Wiggon ran in, followed by two medics. "How is she, Doc?" he asked.

"I'm not sure, but better, now that you brought us help. Thanks."

Wiggon blushed and patted Stephen's shoulder. "Save the thanks. I got us a chopper to get Cammie to the hospital."

The medics soon stabilized Cammie. In no time, she was airborne, headed for the hospital in Leesburg, Stephen at her side.

Once there, he scrubbed for the C-section surgery, although he opted to sit by her side rather than assist. Cammie was sedated, but before she closed her eyes, she whispered, "Thanks."

Stephen's heart nearly broke at that faint voice. He stumbled through the words of yet another prayer, this one a plea for heavenly guidance for the medical team.

To his great joy and relief, the delivery went well. Both mother and child did fine, although the big observer with a mustache under his surgical mask was seen drying a tear or two. That siren Stephen had thought so musical and wonderful couldn't hold a candle to the cry of Cammie's newborn child.

He left the recovery room nearly giddy with joy. He

hurried to the bank of phones to share the news with all their friends back in Bellamy.

Once everyone had been duly notified, he found his way back to Cammie's room and collapsed in the green vinyl armchair by her bed. Stephen watched her sleep, a mantle of peace on her sweet features. A miracle had happened, and he felt honored to have witnessed it. God had spared Cammie's and her child's lives in answer to prayer. He sat at her side, humbled by the God who'd cared enough to listen to a man who for so long had denied him.

"Forgive me, God, for my blindness," Stephen whispered awkwardly. "You already forgave my disbelief and listened to my prayer. How can I thank you? There's not enough in me to do that. I do need help, though. Cammie spoke of so many things I know nothing about, but she said you'd teach me. Please forgive my sins, help me learn, help me live, as Cammie said, for you, in service to you, the God who helps even a man who doesn't know you well. I want what she has in you."

Leaning back in the chair, Stephen sighed. What a night. They'd put a pair of woeful dognappers in jail, they'd retrieved the Bellamys' stolen dogs, Cammie's child was born, and he'd experienced God's mercy firsthand.

Slowly, he felt himself relax. His breathing grew deep and comfortable. The tightness in his neck eased. He stretched out his legs, crossed his ankles, and smiled. Cammie looked beautiful even after labor and delivery.

And he felt great. A comfort, deep and rich, suffused him, warming every corner of his heart and mind. He'd never felt anything like this before, not even after his best crack at meditating. Could this be . . . ?

"Oh, God, is this your peace?"

Still smiling, Stephen edged forward in his chair. He

reached out and touched Cammie's soft cheek, slipping a lock of silky brown hair behind her ear.

"Sweet dreams, Camellia," he said tenderly. "I love you."

As Cammie awoke from the sedative the doctors had administered, she noticed Stephen asleep in the chair at her bedside. Joy flooded her, and she finally recognized how much she'd come to love this man.

She loved him, even though she feared that love could never be—at least, not until a time when their spiritual differences could be resolved. She'd strayed far enough from God in her Martha efforts; she wouldn't consider building a relationship without the Lord at its base.

"Father, I pray that you will find the right person to touch Stephen's heart. He wants peace, Lord, and only you can give lasting peace. He needs you, Lord Jesus, and if there's anything I can do as your witness, show me—"

"Still trying to fix things for everyone, are you?" Stephen asked, his voice rumbly from sleep.

Cammie blushed. "Not exactly. I was just praying for you. . . . I hope you don't mind."

He shook his head. "Don't ever stop. I have a lot of learning to do."

"What do you mean?" she asked, startled.

He stood and carefully sat on the edge of her bed. He took her hand in his and, as always, his warmth rushed through her.

"I mean," he said, "that I followed your advice when I found myself with a laboring woman, a baby in breech presentation in a hurry to be born, and nowhere to turn. You were right. What I learned in Zen left me high and dry. I was . . . looking for God down all the wrong paths."

Cammie blinked. "Stephen, am I hallucinating?"

"No." He chuckled. "And I'm the one who's just waking up. To reality—God's reality."

"Are you serious?"

This time he laughed out loud. "I've never been more serious in my life. I cried out to God while I waited for the Life-Link chopper to arrive. I couldn't leave you to get something from my office to ease your pain. I didn't dare perform a C-section away from the hospital. I had nowhere to turn but to God. And he came through, just as you said he would."

Her heart swelled with joy for the truth he had found. "Oh, Stephen, I'm so happy for you."

"Me, too. And I have you to thank. You showed me the way. You had the courage to speak your faith, even when I didn't understand. You went ahead and showed me how you lived it, and when you faltered, you pointed that out too. You've given me so much. You led me to God's love!"

The knot in her throat kept her from speaking. Tears poured down her cheeks, but she smiled, the brightest smile she could remember smiling in years.

"While I'm being so serious," he said, cupping her chin in his other hand, "I need you to know that I love you. You've come to mean more to me than anyone else. I know this is probably the worst time for me to say it, after all you've gone through. But I can't hold it inside any longer. I want to marry you, Cammie—no rush, you understand—"

"Here's your precious little bundle," chimed a nurse, walking into the room and carrying a tiny, pink-wrapped infant. "Time to get acquainted."

Cammie dragged her gaze from Stephen's and down to her child as the nurse gently handed her to Cammie. She caught her breath. "Isn't she beautiful, Stephen?"

Turning, he leaned against the headboard and wrapped an arm around Cammie's shoulders. Cammie felt cherished, special. And now she knew, beyond the shadow of a doubt, that she loved Stephen. Had he really meant that interrupted proposal? Oh, how she loved him!

"She's an angel, just like her mama," he murmured, running a large finger down the soft, pink cheek.

A couple hours later, after the baby had been taken back to the nursery, Stephen and Cammie were talking quietly when the other Blossoms arrived. "How could you, Camellia Bellamy Sprague?" asked Lark.

"And here we warned you and warned you," Maggie added.

Cammie glanced from one sister to her other, puzzled by their latest attack. "What are you two talking about?"

Lark plopped her backpack on the armchair Stephen had just vacated. She gave him a pointed look. "Dr. Hardesty, I'm so glad you're here. We brought Cammie's bag with us but forgot it in the car. Could you please fetch it for us? It's in the red Escort in the maternity parkin' area. Here's my key."

Stephen caught the key and gave Cammie a puzzled look, but she shrugged, having no idea what her sisters were up to. "I would like to have my things," she said. "I'm glad they brought them."

He walked to the door. "I'll be right back."

The minute he left the room, Maggie turned on her. "I swear, sissy, you're battier'n a cave in daylight. Why're you lettin' that man romance you so soon after David's death?"

Lark shook her head. "Don't you know better than to let pregnancy hormones push you into an estrogen-induced romance?"

Although Maggie's accusation had initially stunned her, Cammie regained her voice in no time. "Please. Would you two listen to yourselves? What are you doing?"

"We're tryin' to keep you from makin' a big mistake, Cammie; that's what we're doin'."

Cammie shook her head. "No, you're not. You're butting your noses in where they don't belong."

"But we're your sisters—"

"Mm-hmm," she said, cutting off further argument. "My sisters, but not my conscience. And certainly not God."

That shut them up. Cammie drew a deep breath. "Please remember how well things worked when we came together. You know, when we each investigated on our own, then pooled the information?"

She waited for a response before going on, but all she got were reluctant nods. "Well, I think that's the way the Lord wants us to live. Each one of us has her own life, individually, and we can come together to share and support each other, but with respect. We need to learn to be sisters, in the flesh, and especially in Christ. Not like this. This hurts."

"Oh, dear." Maggie's blue eyes pooled with tears. "You're makin' good sense, Cammie, and I'm real sorry. I just don't want you to wind up hurt again."

"I understand that, Maggie. But neither you nor I can decide if I will or won't get hurt. All we can do is trust in God."

Lark put a hand on Cammie's shoulder. "Seems to me the youngest Blossom's turned out the wisest one."

Cammie shook her head. "Age isn't important, Lark. That's just something superficial. We need to let that go and focus on what really matters. We need to share our faith and our love. God will take care of the rest." And as she talked, Cammie knew that she'd have to apologize to Miss Sophie for behaving just like her two meddlesome sisters did toward her. She couldn't protect Miss Sophie; only God was in control.

Maggie frowned. "But what about that doctor . . ."

"Please don't spoil this special moment for me. Put away that unnecessary urge to protect me. Stephen is a wonderful man. I have to believe God brought us together. Do you know he accepted Christ last night?"

Maggie's jaw gaped.

Lark blinked. "He did? But I heard he was a Buddhist."

"Although he was reading some Buddhist books, he was more a seeker of God—just winding down the wrong path," Cammie answered with a smile. "I want you both to remember how tough things were for me while I was married to David. I never saw him, and he liked that just fine. Stephen isn't like David. He believes in pacing himself, in living a peaceful life. Yes, he's a doctor, but he doesn't spend every minute doctoring folks."

As her sisters considered Cammie's words, the room grew still. Although she'd known her feelings for Stephen ran strong, she hadn't known just how strong until she'd had to defend him to Maggie and Lark. She loved Stephen, and if the Lord willed it, she would someday become his wife. If only he'd ask . . .

Just then the nurse appeared, baby in her arms. "It's time for the little one to eat again," she said, smiling as she placed the child in Cammie's arms.

The baby whimpered, and Cammie glanced down at her daughter. The tiny fists waved and delicate features crumpled. She raised her gift from God to her shoulder, crooning softly.

Then she noticed Maggie's face. Tears washed her cheeks, sliding past a gentle smile. And tough Lark didn't look so tough now as she stared in awe at her brand-new niece.

"Isn't she sweet?" Cammie asked.

Lark shook her head. "She's so much more than sweet. She's the miracle of life. Just like the life Jesus gave each of us in him. I'm so sorry we marched in here, tryin' to tell you how to live. We have to put behind us our old notions of sisterhood and let Jesus teach us all over again. It won't be easy, but I think we're finally on the right track."

Maggie nodded. "Long's we look to God for guidance, I'd say we can keep our trains from derailin' on that trip."

The baby made a soft sound, and Lark stepped closer. She reached out and touched a little hand. "So what are you goin' to name her?"

"I think Daisy is sweet," Maggie offered.

"Too borin'," said Lark. "How about Pansy?" Closing her green eyes, she considered the name, then shook her head. "Nah, too wimpy. Oh, I know. Lobelia's a cool flower."

Cammie's eyes widened with horror.

"Petunia's cute," tried Maggie. "There was that singer from England in the sixties—"

"That was Petula," Lark cut in. "And I've never heard of a flower by that name."

"Would you two stop?" Cammie begged. "I was thinking of Lily."

"The perfect name," Stephen said, stepping into the room. As he did, a massive flower arrangement took his place in the doorway—or so it seemed, since the blossoms completely hid the poor deliveryman. "And look whom I found wandering the halls."

Willie and Sophie entered the room. "Do you like the flowers?" Willie asked. "I even made sure that the florist included camellias, magnolias, and larkspurs. If I'd known, I'd have had them throw in lilies, too."

"They're beautiful," Cammie murmured, enjoying the colorful array.

Miss Sophie bustled up, leaned over, kissed Cammie's cheek, and cooed over the baby. "Are you still goin' to let me be her granny?"

"Of course I am. Want to hold her?"

Sophie reached out curving arms and took the baby, then gave Willie an adoring smile. "Only if you let me tell you somethin'."

"What's that?"

"Well, honey girl, if I'm goin' to be this little darlin's granny, why, then, she's got herself a grampa too!"

Beaming, the elderly couple displayed their matching wedding rings. "We'd been planning the surprise for days," Willie said. "And then Myrna stole our thunder, so to speak. So we went ahead and got married anyway. At our age, we don't want to waste even a single day together."

"But, Miss Sophie," Cammie said, a twinge of fear hitting her middle, "this is so sudden. Are you sure you're doing the right thing?"

Miss Sophie let Lily wrap dainty fingers around one of her own. "Yes, sugar, I am. God brought me my dear Willie at a time when I'd started to feel my life was practically over. But since then, why, this wonderful man has made me see I'm as young as I want to be, and I sure don't want to be ancient right now."

Willie nodded. "I know all about feeling ancient, and it's absolutely dreadful. I took my retirement after forty years with the same Fortune 500 company. But all I had to show for that career was a boxy and boring apartment and a suitcase full of clothes. Since I had nothing better to do with myself, I started traveling. I went from town to town, visiting this big country of ours. It was purely by God's mercy that I stumbled onto Cammie's house. It's the first home I've had since my first wife died. And you know what? It won't be my last."

Sophie nodded, softly rocking Lily from side to side. "Do tell them, Willie, dear."

"We'll be buying ourselves a little house when we get back from our honeymoon. But first, Sophie and I are going away for a truly grand adventure."

Stunned by the news, Cammie gave her boarder a wary look. "What are you up to now, Willie Johnson?"

"I'm whisking my lady-wife on a safari for the young-at-heart. Neither Sophie nor I can wait. We leave next Thursday."

"But—"

A knock came at the door, cutting off Cammie's next comment.

"C'n I come in?" Hobey asked.

The group made room for the friendly mason. "I hear say you had yourself a baby girl, Camellia."

Cammie gazed at her daughter. She still couldn't believe the child had been born healthy and strong. "That's right, Hobey. Want to take a peek at her? Her name's Lily."

Hobey leaned over Sophie, and a grin split his homely face. "Purty little thing, with a purty little name. How'd you all like our newlyweds' news?"

With a quick prayer for a long and happy marriage for the Johnsons, Cammie swallowed the last of her objections. "It was a surprise."

Hobey blushed. "Well, folks, I have me another surprise for you all. I've just got me my official ministry certificate, an' you all are lookin' at the new pastor over to the Bellamy Community Church—oncet the reverend retires next month, that is. That's why I've been so busy in Leesburg."

A chorus of congratulations rang out.

Lark hugged the masonry contractor. "Is that why you asked me to help you with your grammar and such?"

"Yes, ma'am. I needed to take me some tough tests. We did right good, you know."

Maggie followed her redheaded sister's lead, only her hug caught the gentle giant around his middle. "And that's why you quit the men's Bible study. My Clay couldn't figure that one out. So now you'll be the boss down to the BCC instead of at Hobey's Masonry."

"Yep. My oldest boy's called, says he's ready to come home

an' make his mama happy. He's gettin' married an' wants to raise hisself a family right here in Bellamy."

"Oh, Camellia, honey. You'd better take your baby back," Sophie said, handing Lily over. "I have to call Ellamae. Fancy that. The two of us celebratin' families and babies all at the same time. What a blessin' the Lord's given us."

Stephen resumed his former spot at Cammie's side. "I guess I have an announcement to make, myself. I already told Cammie some of this, but I'm going to make no secret of my intentions."

Cammie blushed. "Stephen! Not now—"

"Yes, Cammie. Now." Everyone was riveted. "This beautiful woman," he said for starters, "has shown me what was missing in my life. She led me to God, and is teaching me all about love—real love. I told her that earlier, and I let her know I intend to marry her the day she's ready to become Mrs. Stephen Hardesty. No matter how long it takes her to decide."

Sophie dropped the phone. "You've really left that Zenny—"

"Boodhy," Stephen cut in, "stuff behind. You know I've been searching for years. I've found what I was looking for in God and his love. I'm with you now, Aunt Sophie, and with Cammie, too."

Tears shone in the old woman's eyes. "Praise be to our Lord and God. He really is good to us."

Hobey clapped a hand on Stephen's shoulder. "I'd be right honored if you'd allow me to baptize you in Jesus' name."

Stephen chuckled. "I'll be needing more than that. I know I have a lot to learn. I'm as new at this as our little girl—" He stopped, then looked at Cammie. "I want you to know that as far as I'm concerned, she's part mine, too. Unless you want it otherwise."

Cammie's tears began to flow. Tears of immeasurable joy. She shook her head in helpless wonder.

He wrapped an arm around her shoulders. "I want you both forever. And the day you're ready to walk down an aisle to me, I'll be there ready to say 'I do.' "

Cammie nodded slowly, a soft smile dawning from behind the tears.

Before everyone in the room, Stephen sealed his promise with a gentle kiss.

"Well, ain't this a fine way to drum me up some bidness," Hobey said, his eyes suspiciously damp. "I do my first weddin' ever—that'd be Sophie's an' Willie's, here—get me a new convert, a baptism, an' maybe 'nother weddin' for the future all at oncet. I'm ready to marry up the two of you when you and Jesus decide it's right. It's a fine day for Bellamy, I'd say."

Maggie and Lark looked from Cammie to Stephen to Lily. They shrugged and smiled. "Looks like another Bellamy weddin's hoverin' somewhere over the horizon," Lark said.

"And another feather in my matchmakin' cap," said Miss Louella as she entered the room. "Seems your Granny Iris put the right woman in charge of her girls—her Blossoms, as she used to call you all. Bellamy's Blossoms."

A Note from the Author

Dear Reader,

What a visit we've had in Bellamy! I hope you've enjoyed it as much as I have.

As is always the case, the Lord has used my work to refine me further. "Be silent, and know that I am God!" What an awesome concept! One admittedly as difficult for me to understand, absorb, and appropriate as it was for Cammie.

Before this Bellamy's Blossoms series, I never thought I put much of myself into my writing, especially into my heroines. But I know now that God used Camellia, the youngest Blossom, to teach me many lessons, the least of which was that one. As the mother of four, I'm well known among friends as a mama bear—a preshrunk one, at that. At four-foot-eleven, I don't look like I'm ready to tackle any threat to my cubs, three of whom hover above the six-foot line. But don't test me!

During the process of bringing Cammie and Stephen to life, I had to deal with a number of situations that were out of my control. Such situations are tough on anyone, but even more so on a world-class worrier like me. You see, I couldn't hover over my cubs when I was injured and had to spend time in bed. I couldn't fret them out of their troubles when I had a story to write, one that consumed my creative juices.

Yet day by day, the heavenly Father was there, encouraging me through his mercies, his perfect Word, and the Christian sisters and brothers he sent to help me. He taught me how to be still, literally and spiritually, and rest in the knowledge that he is indeed God. Once I took my hands out of his way, he took better care of my children, my work, and me than I ever could have. And by not trying to do everything, which is my natural bent, I've finally realized I actually allowed those who stepped up and took over to be blessed too.

God is good. And he loves us with an everlasting love.

In that love,
Ginny

About the Author

A former newspaper reporter, Ginny Aiken lives in south-central Pennsylvania with her husband and four sons. Born in Havana, Cuba, and raised in Valencia and Caracas, Venezuela, she discovered books early on and wrote her first novel at age fifteen. (She burned it when she turned a "mature" sixteen!) That first effort was followed several years later by her winning entry in the Mid-America Romance Authors' Fiction from the Heartland contest for unpublished authors.

Ginny has certificates in French literature and culture from the University of Nancy, France, and a B.A. in Spanish and French literature from Allegheny College in Pennsylvania. Her first novel was published in 1993, and since then she has published numerous novels and novellas. One of her novels was a finalist for *Affaire de Coeur's* Readers' Choice Award for Best American Historical of 1997, and her work has appeared on various best-seller lists. Ginny's novellas appear in the anthologies *With This Ring, A Victorian Christmas Quilt, A Bouquet of Love,* and *Dream Vacation.* If you missed *Magnolia* and *Lark*, the first two novels in the delightful Bellamy's Blossoms series, be sure to pick them up soon.

When she isn't busy with the duties of being a soccer mom, Ginny can be found reading, writing, enjoying classical music while indulging her passion for needlework, and preparing for her next Bible study.

Ginny welcomes letters written to her in care of Tyndale House Author Relations, P.O. Box 80, Wheaton, IL 60189-0080, or by E-mail at GinnyAiken@aol.com.

CURRENT HEARTQUEST RELEASES

- *Magnolia*, Ginny Aiken
- *Lark*, Ginny Aiken
- *Camellia*, Ginny Aiken
- *Sweet Delights,* Terri Blackstock, Ranee McCollum, and Elizabeth White
- *Awakening Mercy,* Angela Benson
- *Abiding Hope,* Angela Benson
- *Faith*, Lori Copeland
- *Hope*, Lori Copeland
- *June*, Lori Copeland
- *Glory*, Lori Copeland
- *Freedom's Promise,* Dianna Crawford
- *Freedom's Hope,* Dianna Crawford
- *Freedom's Belle,* Dianna Crawford
- *Prairie Rose,* Catherine Palmer
- *Prairie Fire,* Catherine Palmer
- *Prairie Storm,* Catherine Palmer
- *Prairie Christmas,* Catherine Palmer, Elizabeth White, and Peggy Stoks
- *Finders Keepers,* Catherine Palmer
- *Hide and Seek*, Catherine Palmer
- *A Kiss of Adventure,* Catherine Palmer (original title: *The Treasure of Timbuktu*)
- *A Whisper of Danger,* Catherine Palmer (original title: *The Treasure of Zanzibar*)
- *A Touch of Betrayal,* Catherine Palmer
- *A Victorian Christmas Cottage,* Catherine Palmer, Debra White Smith, Jeri Odell, and Peggy Stoks
- *A Victorian Christmas Quilt,* Catherine Palmer, Debra White Smith, Ginny Aiken, and Peggy Stoks
- *A Victorian Christmas Tea,* Catherine Palmer, Dianna Crawford, Peggy Stoks, and Katherine Chute
- *Olivia's Touch,* Peggy Stoks
- *Romy's Walk,* Peggy Stoks

COMING SOON (Fall 2001)

- *A Victorian Christmas Keepsake,* Catherine Palmer, Kristin Billerbeck, Ginny Aiken

HEARTQUEST BOOKS BY GINNY AIKEN

Magnolia—Magnolia Bellamy can't believe she's just hired a carpetbagger to restore the fabulous Ashworth Mansion. Against her better judgment, Maggie hires Yankee contractor Clay Marlowe, whose credentials are impeccable. Clay loves a challenge. But he hadn't reckoned on the delicately beautiful Magnolia Bellamy, the project's self-appointed overseer—nor on the meddlesome but lovable ladies of the Bellamy Garden Club! A rollicking, delightful novel from award-winning author Ginny Aiken. *Book 1 in the Bellamy's Blossoms series.*

Lark—After the highly successful launch of her literary magazine, Lark Bellamy has come home. Rich Desmond's discovery that tempestuous, redheaded beauty Lark Bellamy is back in town shatters his peace of mind. The last thing Rich needs is a supersleuth like Lark searching for answers to his mysterious behavior. When Lark turns her investigative skills onto the mystery Rich is determined to keep cloaked in silence, she uncovers a startling revelation. Can their budding romance survive as Lark reveals more and more of the truth? *Book 2 in the Bellamy's Blossoms series.*

Log Cabin Patch—In a logging camp in turn-of-the century Washington State, a Log Cabin patchwork quilt symbolizes the new hope awaiting a lonely young woman. This novella by Ginny Aiken appears in the anthology *A Victorian Christmas Quilt.*

OTHER GREAT TYNDALE HOUSE FICTION

- *Jenny's Story,* Judy Baer
- *Libby's Story,* Judy Baer
- *Out of the Shadows,* Sigmund Brouwer
- *Ashes and Lace,* B. J. Hoff
- *Cloth of Heaven,* B. J. Hoff
- *The Price,* Jim and Terri Kraus
- *The Treasure,* Jim and Terri Kraus
- *The Promise,* Jim and Terri Kraus
- *Winter Passing,* Cindy McCormick Martinusen
- *Rift in Time,* Michael Phillips
- *Hidden in Time,* Michael Phillips
- *Unveiled*, Francine Rivers
- *Unashamed*, Francine Rivers
- *Unshaken*, Francine Rivers
- *A Voice in the Wind,* Francine Rivers
- *An Echo in the Darkness,* Francine Rivers
- *As Sure As the Dawn,* Francine Rivers
- *The Last Sin Eater,* Francine Rivers
- *Leota's Garden,* Francine Rivers
- *The Scarlet Thread,* Francine Rivers
- *The Atonement Child,* FrancineRivers
- *The Promise Remains,* Travis Thrasher